The Dragon's Crown

BOOK TWO of the SPIRIT SWORD SAGA

Jonathan W. Thurston

A THURSTON HOWL PUBLICATIONS BOOK

ISBN 978-1-945247-04-0

THE DRAGON'S CROWN

Copyright © 2016 by Jonathan W. Thurston

First Edition, 2016. All rights reserved.

A Thurston Howl Publications Book
Published by Thurston Howl Publications
Knoxville, TN

jonathan.thurstonhowlpub@gmail.com

Cover design by Scott Lewis Ford

Printed in the United States of America

10 9 8 7 6 5 4 3 2 1

To Temerita, ever-faithful.
To Sherayah and Travis: we three, together, unstoppable.

Gevás

Northern Continent

Obsidian Plains

Astra

Libris

Ruvion

Hurale

Western

Continent

Pureau

Saldir

Rulia

Temple
of the
Spirits

Arvon

The
Pyramid

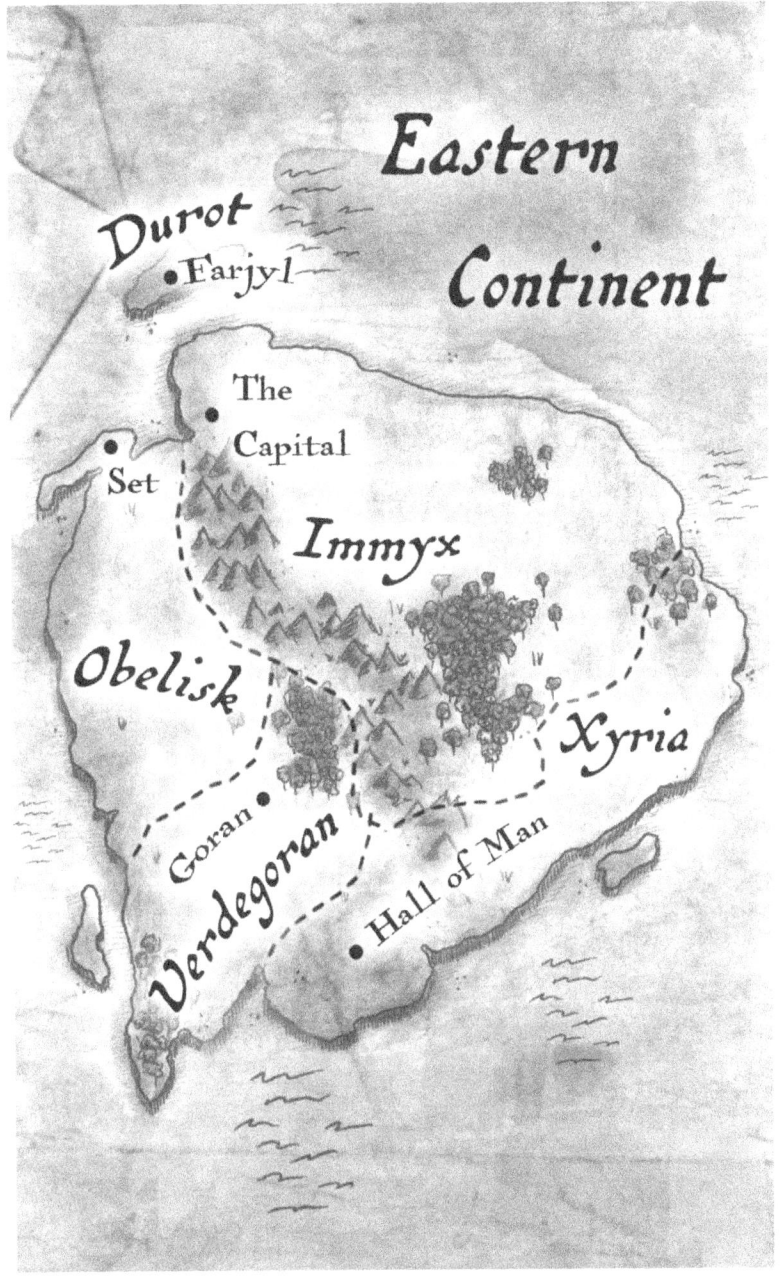

Southern
Continent

Macela

Heaven's Isle

Dream
City

Mashan
Telis

Helio

Varyx

Alerris

Terin

Apolis

Gryphos

Norlante

Leik

Contents

1,000 Years Ago – 1
The Second Obsidian War

O ut of the silent darkness came a fiery explosion that illuminated the night and cast jagged shadows over the battlements and across the advancing militia. The young soldier cursed his luck and followed his captain closer to the immense steel fortress. Another explosion struck the militia of Helian swordsmen and gunners, and the red light of the *mysteria*-induced flames revealed the humanoid Shadows that lined the tops of the fortress walls. Amongst the black creatures were a few ember mages, sorcerers who focused on the Element of Fire; these sorcerers continued to cast explosions upon the militia.

The soldier could remember when Lord Ferro of the East had turned to the Darkness. Many ember mages who had been in Lord Ferro's service joined Dagan and even now protected his ash-colored palace. He swallowed nervously: he had never fought at one of Dagan's fortresses. The Great Lord Lux had given the order for this army to penetrate Dagan's defenses and set up a command post here.

The soldier's captain called out, "Come on! We need a hole in this wall now!"

One of Lux's sorcerers released a spell of Force that blasted a gap into the wall of stone. Instantly, a wave of Shadow swordsmen poured from the hole and attacked the soldiers. This particular soldier despised *mysteria*. The business of mages was no business of his, and he wanted nothing to do with the strange ability. Fighting with the sword was something he could do, however. Though he had become more capable with the blade over the years, the Shadows seemed to have gained strength, as well. They were no longer the usual amateur swordsmen he had fought so long ago; they had become masters of swordplay.

His thin blade slashed through the misty images with ease as each one became mere wisps, and even their swords evaporated before his eyes. In the rage of battle, he forgot his comrades, his objective, and his own desire for self-preservation. He was one with the blade, and in the eyes of his captain, comrades, and even enemies, he was a blur on the battlefield; he was a berserker, wild and furious with every sweep of the blade.

Together, the group eliminated most of the opposing Shadows. The men cheered with patriotic pride and held their swords high as they charged into the fortress that had served as Dagan's Palace.

This soldier had not heard the specifics of the matter, but from what he understood, Dagan had been seen elsewhere in the underwater world of Gevás: he would be away from his Palace for a while. Because of this news, the Great Lord Lux had decided to send this small group of soldiers to the Palace to try to uncover information about Dagan's plans, particularly in regards to rumors about a weapon of his. Perhaps, the group would even be able to capture the fortress.

Once they were past the walls, they were in the barren courtyards that made up most of the inside of the fortress. In the center were several buildings. His captain spoke excitedly, "Careful, men. Forward!" The soldier reflected on what they all knew probably lurked inside, the Y'mordi. *I know they destroyed the Academy years ago...two of them...by themselves.* The Captain gestured toward a building, and, as they approached the tower, the soldier considered the technology that had made this Palace.

His father had been one of the pioneers of this world. This soldier was one of the first-generation children of Gevás. Before the Great Lord Lux's discovery of it, everyone had lived on Earth, the world that lacked the miracles of advanced technology. By a stroke of luck, the people of Gevás had developed innovative machines that would rival Earth for centuries.

The band of soldiers ran swiftly toward the tower, but their progress was halted by a figure in a black robe. The figure stood there with her hood lying across her back. Her blonde hair was in a ponytail that this soldier almost found to be attractive. Her deep green eyes stared coldly at the group of soldiers.

Her lips curled into a sadistic smile as she spoke softly to the men, "None of you are supposed to be here. Die."

Without so much as lifting a finger, several circular ripples of air, discs of the *mysteria*-based Force, appeared in the water around her. Their rapidly spinning edges seemed to be razor-sharp and produced currents of their own in the warm water of the Eastern Continent. The figure blinked, and before any of the soldiers could react, the Wind-comprised discs tore through the small army multiple times, sending blood and body parts flying into the sea.

The soldier was knocked to the ground by the falling torso of one of his comrades. The stench of the blood filled his nostrils, and he tried not to breathe. His eyes darted around the area in terror as he saw that no one was left standing. His eyes would recognize a face and bring to mind a name, now a tombstone engraving in his mind. He knew these men. No, he *had known* these men, but their stories were over. His captain was dead. The man he had shared stories with earlier in the day was dead. His friend from training was dead. The stench of blood was not just the general smell of war to him. It was the overpowering sensual remnant of his comrades. He was the last soldier.

As he pondered his next action, a voice entered his thoughts. *Do not move, soldier. Do not even breathe if you do not want the Y'mordi to notice you.*

The soldier's chest froze in its position as he tried to hold his breath. His mind replied to the demanding, feminine voice, *Who are you? What's going on?*

I am one of Lord Dagan's prisoners here in this fortress.

Suddenly, the female Y'mordi turned and left the mass of bodies. She faced a nearby Shadow, "Dispose of the garbage." The Shadow returned a prompt salute and gestured for its fellows to help it.

The voice returned. *Listen very closely to what I have to say, soldier. It could save your life and mine.*

Alright, I'm listening.

The Shadows began dragging bodies across the courtyard. The soldier almost sighed in relief when the torso that was still hiding him had not been chosen yet.

Good. In a few seconds, that Y'mordi will be back at her post, and you will be free to sneak around the fortress. As soon as she disappears, I will guide you to my prison. Though I am skilled at mysteria, *my prison is warded from any spells, so I cannot free myself. Only a sword can release me. When I give you the signal, you can start heading deeper into the fortress. If you encounter any Shadows, kill them.*

Got it, he replied in thought.

After several minutes had passed, the Shadows returned, ready to move more of the bodies. They came closer and closer to where the soldier was.

The voice echoed in his mind, *Are you ready, soldier?*

Now?

Now.

He leaped up from his hidden position and began slashing at the humanoid mists that surrounded him. Thought and feeling left him as he combatted the black beings. He fought as if he could sense every move of the Shadows before it ever happened: his body naturally dodged each movement of the Shadows' blades, and his own sword flowed through the water. Within seconds, each had faded into thin tendrils of black smoke.

Suddenly, the soldier felt strangely compelled to move to a nearby doorway. He approached it, almost in a daze. He did not want to look back: the bloody mass that was once his closest companions and fellow soldiers still lingered behind him. As he opened the steel portal, a metallic hallway appeared before him. Though he could not explain it, he felt as if he knew his way around the place.

He asked the voice in his mind, *Is this weird familiarity your doing?*

Yes, it is. I am merely leading you to my prison. Keep going. You are almost there now, soldier.

He continued walking through the labyrinth of tunnels with growing curiosity and fear. The voice in his mind could be an Y'mordi as easily as an ally. The only reason to trust the voice was that he was still alive, and the rest of the militia were not.

Finally, he entered a silver, spacious passage that had eight massive pillars lining its length. The white lights that hung from the ceiling along the hall emitted an eerily dim glow, casting shadows across the walls. He suspected that he was now underground. As he stepped further into it, voices came from another connecting hallway. The voice in his head echoed, *Hide!*

He immediately leaped behind one of the decorated pillars. He could hear a voice.

"Watch over the room carefully. The Dark Lord Dagan wishes to have it occupied soon." This voice was high and girlish. Because of the human-like nature of the voice, the soldier suspected it was probably one of the Y'mordi. A response never came, though.

The soldier stayed frozen in place, listening carefully for more sounds, but the hall remained silent. The voice returned to the soldier's mind. *Alright, the Y'mordi is gone now. All that's left are two Shadows guarding the door. Once you open it, you will find me on the other side. Wait—someone else is coming.*

The soldier could also hear the approaching footsteps.

The voice spoke softly in his mind. *It's more of those filthy Shadows. They are becoming increasingly annoying. Very well. It is time to divert their attention.*

Suddenly, a booming roar filled the columned hall as a part of the far wall exploded, leaving a gaping hole. Thinking it to be an attack, the Shadows ran to the hole and entered one of the hallways in an attempt to chase whoever had cast the spell, but the guards at the door remained at their posts.

Now, soldier. Get rid of the guards.

The soldier retorted sarcastically, *You couldn't take care of them, too?*

The voice snorted in annoyance. *I want to see if you are the one who will truly free me.*

No response came to the soldier however. He analyzed his situation in the hall based on his location. He was still several yards from the mysterious, guarded door. It would not take much for these Shadows to sound an alarm. His blade would have to be swift in order to kill them.

As his head turned, an idea struck him. His hand reached out to grab one of the dim lights that hung from the ceiling. Luckily, the next pillar hid his wandering hand and allowed him to silently slice the cord from which the light was suspended, and its glow remained.

He wheeled around and slung the electric lantern at the two guards and observed them hissing in panic from the explosion of light. By the time they recovered from the shock, the soldier flew to their position and struck with his shining blade. The Shadows dissipated.

The soldier heard a sigh of relief from the feminine voice in his head. When it spoke, its voice was rushed but not without some excitement. *Quickly!*

He kicked open the door, but there were no lights in this room. Not even the dim light of the hallway lit its interior. The soldier kicked the still flaring electric light into the room and beheld a sight he had not expected.

A long, serpentine shape was curled up on the steel floor, its wings long and flattened against its back. The Dragon rose onto all four legs, and the chains that held its body to the floor stretched taut. The white scales on her body shimmered in the light. "Quickly, cut these chains if you can!" said the White Dragon with a mouth filled with several rows of razor-sharp fangs.

Before the soldier could react, he and the Dragon heard a voice approach from one of the farther hallways.

The soldier glanced hesitantly at the thick chains and hissed, "There is no way that I can cut through those with this sword! It would be impossible!"

The Dragon shook her head, and her snakelike tail whipped back and forth impatiently. "No, I can't use *mysteria* on the chains, but I can give your sword power. It can break through them, I assure you."

Hearing the voices coming closer, the soldier hacked at the chains, and with every slash, the iron links shattered. A voice called from the hallway, "Someone's freeing the Dragon! Kill them!"

The soldier turned to see a red-robed ember mage standing at the entrance to the cell, ordering the group of Shadows to attack. The soldier braced himself for the attack, killing each one that came too close to him. When the ember mage was the last one standing, the mage said cockily, "You will not escape this fortress alive. I have already alerted the Y'mordi."

Without hesitation, the White Dragon summoned a cloud of Ice that blasted through the corridor, freezing everything inside it. The spell had frozen the ember mage solid. Not even its heart beat any longer. The spell had hit the soldier's arm, and it stung with a throbbing agony.

The Dragon spoke softly, "We need to leave, soldier. Can you get on my back?"

The soldier regarded the Dragon in awe and terror, but when he heard footsteps running toward them, he complied and approached the Dragon's side. Using his good arm, he leaped onto the White Dragon's back and then noticed her pale wings. As they stretched outward, filling the cell, he beheld the Dragon's full size, easily forty feet from head to tail.

Hold on, she said to the soldier with her mind.

Another powerful spell of Ice demolished the ceiling above them, turning it into shattered sheets of ice, and the Dragon flew upward through the storm of frozen shards that now fell upon them. The soldier squeezed his legs tightly against the creature's sides and tried desperately not to fall. He kept his head low to the Dragon's white scales and felt the ice nick his skin and smash into his black head of hair.

Finally, the ice no longer hit him, and he cautiously raised his head. They were high in the water above the fortress. Before either of them could enjoy their freedom, the single Y'mordi appeared in front them and hovered in the water by that strange force *mysteria*. The soldier frowned at the blatant witchcraft.

The Y'mordi's blonde hair swayed in the current as she spoke. "Dragon, return to your prison. The Dark Lord Dagan would not be happy about this."

The Dragon's voice resounded throughout the soldier's mind. *Besides a few parlor tricks, I am not the greatest with* mysteria. *I am not sure I can defeat her…*The voice sounded miserable and discouraged.

The soldier responded, *No, you have gotten me this far alive, and I am not going to give up now! Charge into her, and I will handle the rest!* He knew that it would be a risky attack, but if his plan worked, both he and the Dragon could achieve their freedom and find safety.

After a moment of hesitation, the White Dragon obeyed and rushed at the Y'mordi. In surprise, the Y'mordi summoned a chain made solely of Wind—each link was made of swirling wind energy. She knew that if the Dark Lord Dagan could not have this Dragon, then he would want it killed rather than be free. A spell of Force lifted her higher to avoid the head of the Dragon, and she allowed herself to fall in order to strike its back, but her attack was blocked by the soldier on the Dragon's back.

The soldier used his sword to break straight through the chain as he had done in the Dragon's cell. The blade continued its path and cut through the Y'mordi's body. She screamed, and, like the Shadows, she faded into black tendrils of smoke that trailed into the sea.

Exhausted, the Dragon and its rider flew away, neither saying a word through thought or voice.

The pale full moon with its black starlit background illuminated the sea. Below the Dragon and soldier was the frozen wasteland of the Southern Continent. To anyone they may have passed, the two were a blur of white across the horizon. The cool current washed over them, pushing against them in time with the beat of the Dragon's wings. The soldier looked down, admiring the dragon's shadowed silhouette on the ground far beneath them. Even in the middle of the chaos of the world, at this moment, all he felt was peace.

The soldier broke the silence. "Are you getting tired yet?"

The Dragon nodded her head in confirmation. "Yes, and I am sure you need to stretch your legs, human."

The soldier nodded his head, content with stopping for a while. "Yes." Though the view had been absolutely spectacular when they were so high, riding on the ridged back of a Dragon was still a difficult thing to become accustomed to. All the same, he felt an amazing sense of freedom with the cool current brushing against his face.

Now, tens of miles away from the Palace, they descended to land on the frosted wasteland. Though the frigid weather seemed comfortable to the Dragon, the soldier was beginning to freeze, and his blackening arm was intensifying in pain. He used his good arm and sword to strike the ground, and it lit up to create an azure flame.

The Dragon's eyes widened in surprise at the act. "How did you do that?" she asked with curiosity.

The soldier replied with his teeth chattering, "It's just a fire. Surely, it is not that strange of a sight, is it?"

The Dragon lowered her head in embarrassment. "Actually…I have never seen a fire before. Once I was hatched, Dagan imprisoned me through the power of Darkness. He wanted me to grow enough so that I would be a powerful weapon against a man named Lux. Until I was ready for training though, he chained me and cast a spell so that I could not use *mysteria* on the cell."

"But, didn't you use *mysteria*?" inquired the soldier.

The Dragon nodded. "I found a loophole, a small crack in the spell. I could use spells that reached outside the cell. I began feeling my way around the castle by sensing everything with *mysteria*. That was how I was able to lead you around the place. Yet, even with me guiding you, I could not have escaped without your help."

The soldier came closer to the fire. "Just so you know, I did not go there to help you. I am one of the Great Lord Lux's soldiers. My comrades and I were sent to take over the fortress or at least gain some information. Then, the Y'mordi attacked us." Remembering his fallen, massacred comrades was hard, and it brought tears to his eyes.

The Dragon sighed and replied, "Yes, I know, but I thank you nonetheless. In reality, I do owe you. Though we saved each other, a life for a life, I damaged your arm."

"Don't worry about it. Once I get back to the Palace, a mage will help me." He grimaced at the thought of *mysteria* being used on him once more. However, he wanted to be able to use his arm again.

"The moon…it is beautiful," muttered the Dragon in awe.

The soldier turned to her. "You have never seen it before?" he inquired.

She shook her head sorrowfully. "No, but I have caught glimpses of it in the minds of those who came to the fortress. Even then, I never truly perceived its magnificence."

Together, they looked up at the celestial orb.

The soldier finally asked the question he had been meaning to ask the Dragon for a while. "What's your name?"

The White Dragon turned to face the soldier with her soft green eyes. For the first time, the soldier was really taking in her elegant appearance. Her long, serpentine body glittered in the moonlight, and she had two long whiskers coming from her snout. Her wings were narrow and almost thirty feet long. The green eyes were what captivated him the most, however. He knew the legends about Dragons. They said that a Dragon's soul dwells just beyond their eyes. "My name is Kohana. What is your name, soldier?"

The soldier smiled. "My name is Tatsu."

Sensing something suddenly shift in the current, Kohana whipped her head to the side to see a man in a black robe standing there. She growled softly, "Who are you?"

Tatsu reached for his sword. It was a simple enough blade, though the hilt was made of an extremely light iron. He pointed it at the man. "What do you want?"

The man pulled back his hood to reveal a scarred face with red spiked hair. "I am called Y'ran, General of the Shadow Armies, second of the Y'mordi. The Dark Lord Dagan has been requesting your return, Dragon."

Tatsu could hear Kohana's voice scream in his mind. *No! We just escaped from there!*

Kohana growled again, more angrily this time. "You can tell him that I will not be meeting his demands. I am free, now."

Y'ran roared back at the White Dragon, "Free? No one is free from the Great Lord of the Darkness! His Shadows will take over this world, and you choose to side with the losing team? You are a fool, Dragon!" In fury, the Y'mordi summoned a lengthy hammer. The weapon was taller than Tatsu but easily carried in one hand. He charged at the Dragon and soldier.

Tatsu ran at the Y'mordi, and sword met hammer. The two metals struck again in a quick jab, and then they clashed a third time as an overhead swing. Kohana watched this struggle in exasperation. She did not want to hurt Tatsu, so she decided instead to take advantage of their mental connection.

Tatsu, duck!

As soon as Tatsu bent low, a wave of Ice shot right over him, freezing the Y'mordi. The Y'mordi retaliated with a Heat spell right on time, and the Ice spell was weakened before it had hit him. Though he was not dead, most of his body was frozen solid.

Tatsu rose to strike the final blow to the Y'mordi when Y'ran loosed one of his arms by melting the ice around it. The strong arm grabbed Tatsu's blade and, turning the metal white-hot in his grasp, bent it back at Tatsu.

The sword pierced straight through Tatsu's chest, causing Tatsu to howl in pain. Y'ran melted the rest of the ice and kicked the soldier to the ground. Kohana released another wave of Ice, and Y'ran leaped out of its path. His eyes almost revealed sympathy. He did not smile when he spoke with a solemn tone. "I will not kill you, Dragon…because I know what it is like to have someone close die. I want you to know that pain yourself. Return to the Dark Lord Dagan, and perhaps he will bestow mercy on you." Without another word, the man summoned an ovular and fire-rimmed tear in the water, a Gate, and disappeared into the night.

Kohana approached the body of her fallen comrade with tears streaking down her snout.

She put a shaking claw on her friend's shoulder and tried to cast a spell that would heal him, but nothing happened. His chest still moved up and down roughly against the blade, but she could not bring herself to pull the blade out of him. Her head lowered to his chest, and she perceived a faint heartbeat that was slowing gradually.

From the sky, an orb of light descended. It came closer and closer to the two. Then, at lightning speed, it struck the sword that still protruded from Tatsu's chest. The blinding light sent violent convulsions through both Tatsu's and Kohana's bodies. In their minds, the two saw brilliant displays of color, and the world seemed to spin around them.

Finally, the Dragon fell to the ground beside Tatsu, both unconscious. The sword was now lying several feet away from them. Kohana's breath was sharper, and her chest was heaving rapidly, though her heartbeat was steadily reverting to its normal pace.

Tatsu, on the other hand, was more still. Though, he looked almost dead now, the wound in his chest was gone, and the pulse of his heart was returning to life.

The Wandering Sorcerer

The sun was rising at last. Though Dragenopn had had no sleep the previous night, he was ready for today. It was going to be a great day, and he knew that to be true.

He climbed off his bed to stand on the chair below it: the bed was five feet off the ground to accommodate a desk beneath it. He had always hated the beds in college dormitories because of their absurd height. It was not difficult to lower the bed, but that meant moving the desk beneath it, and that meant that he would have less space in the room. His chair had become the stepping stool to get in and out of bed. The room itself was small but large enough to accommodate two of these bed-desk sets as well as a keyboard near the window. It easily could have fit another couple of desks in the room, but Drage was hardly ever there anyway.

Because his roommate was still asleep, Drage tried his hardest to make as little noise as possible as he rushed to put on some decent and comfortable clothes. He dressed in an airy t-shirt, embracing the laid-back atmosphere of Saturday morning.

He went to his computer and searched for the tournament schedule. Today was the day he was going to win the state fencing tournament.

As his noisy printer hummed to life, Drage could hear his roommate groaning in the other bed. However, the schedule printed without waking him, and Drage prepared for the tournament. For years, he had been in fencing clubs and had finally passed the tryout to get into the college fencing team. It had been one of the greatest days in his life: he had spent months preparing for it, and it had been incredibly rewarding seeing that hard work paid off.

Most of his life, he had practiced the finesse of a true fencer. Since he had been young, he had used a wooden sword with his half-brother Matthew. Then, in high school, he had inherited from his father a powerful Sword, the Sword of Destiny.

The memory of the blade compelled Drage to go to his closet where the silver Sword was hidden. The double-edged longsword was made entirely of metal: even the hilt held the same reflective luster of the blade. As he looked at the Sword now, he marked its eerie blue glow. For the past few weeks, it had been emanating that light, but he did not understand why. He could remember one other time when it had glowed in this manner. When he had been trapped in an underground cell beneath the Y'mordi's spire in Gevás, this Sword had saved his life, and when it did, it had glowed blue.

He could not help but wonder if the Sword was feeling more alive at this moment. He knew that the Sword of Destiny was possessed by some spirit, and, often, it had a mind of its own, especially when it had protected him against Maris. As he closed the door to the hall with a noisy creak, his roommate rolled over once more.

The dormitory itself was soundless as Drage had expected. Everyone had probably been partying the night before and had not woken up on this amazing Saturday morning. Surprisingly, since he had begun his college life, he had become accustomed to waking up just as early on the weekends as he did on the weekdays. It was not as if he had that much to do: He simply wanted to watch the sunrise. It was not a far walk to the beach, and he reveled in the vivid colors that painted the sky in shades of pink, orange, and even purple. The crimson sun was breathtaking for the college junior, and he often found himself staring deeply into its depths and feeling an all too familiar sensation: the desire for something greater.

As he walked, he recalled what had happened five years ago. He had traveled to a world that rested at the bottom of a truly endless ocean and had found that it was possible to survive there. During his time in Gevás, he had discovered his father, the truth about his half-brother's past, and his own abilities in the magical force known as *mysteria*. Though the experience had been thrilling—and more than sated his thirst for adventure—it had ended in sadness.

He had had to leave his half-brother Matthew, his beautiful girlfriend Aria, and his other new friends Draconis, Marqest, and Lilian. He had also just lost his father to a terrifying battle with a half-horse, half-human sorcerer named Maris.

Thinking of that black name reminded Drage of the most horrifying instance during his time at Gevás: when he had been imprisoned in the Obsidian Plains. The Y'mordi, a group of seven beings who served the Darkness, had placed him in an underground cell, and it had been truly miserable place. There had been no food, no people, no light, and no warmth. To make matters worse, Drage had been suffering from a terrible curse that Maris had placed on his heart.

Even now, five years later, Drage could feel a remnant of that curse deep within his heart. Though the curse no longer controlled his thoughts and actions as it once had, it sometimes drove him to dark and depressing thoughts. The curse had also given him two black irises. Though they had once been brown, they were now completely black.

When he finished his descent of the stairs, he straightened his cotton jacket and opened the door to feel the cold breeze hit his face, stinging his skin. He pulled the jacket tighter against his body and began strolling through the autumn leaf-covered campus.

Cameron Kane approached the tall white house by the beach. His black leather jacket clung to his skin, and his reddish-brown hair reached to both the left and right sides of his head at eye level. His blue jeans had several holes in them, and his sneakers padded up the stairs to the entrance. His fist knocked the white, wooden door loudly, though he was in no particular hurry. He waited two years to finally arrive here, and he could wait a few more seconds.

However, he did not have to wait long. A woman appeared at the door. She had brown hair and was dressed rather formally, as if she was preparing to go to work herself. "Can I help you?" asked the sweet voice.

Cameron smiled eagerly at the woman. "Yes, does his Majesty Lord Helius reside here?"

The woman's eyes widened in shock as she held out an open palm that sent a powerful sphere of Force that knocked Cameron several feet backward and into the air, so he landed hard on the ground. He leaped to his feet quickly in surprise.

The woman replied, "Why do you seek Drage?"

Cameron clenched his teeth and felt in his heart for the flowing strength that mysteria brought him. "Drage? Is that his first name then? I have been looking for him for a while now. Can you tell me where his Majesty can be found?"

The woman grimaced unhappily, "Yes, I know where he is, but I would rather know your intentions first, stranger. Why are you looking for my son?"

Drage had finally made it to the fencing tournament. Of course, he was rather early, but that did not bother him in the slightest. At least, it gave him some time to practice, though many of the members in the fencing club would laugh at the idea of Drage practicing: He had managed to defeat every one of them without having received a single hit himself. His years of training both with Matthew and in Gevás had definitely paid off with the club.

He went to the bathroom to change into his fencing attire. He had never felt too comfortable in the tight and usually unbearably hot suit, but it was part of the rules. He grabbed his sabre and went to one of the practice areas. To his surprise, there were already several fencers already practicing. He made careful observations of their form as he watched for a few seconds. Then, he began his own warm-ups.

For the most part, his own fighting style was a combination of his own training mixed with elements of the Way of the Dragon acquired from Draconis, the Golden Dragon. He held his sword low and sideways in front of him as if to protect his feet. Though the form actually required a lot of moving around the field, professional fencing used much less space. To compensate, Drage frequently had to focus more on swordwork than footwork. Manipulating the sabre fluidly, he struck at an imaginary opponent.

Though no one in the room could feel it, Drage was utilizing the powers of *mysteria*. Through the Element of Light, he could perceive everything around him without having to look in that direction, giving him the ability to see all attacks and respond accordingly. When he closed his eyes, it was as if he could sense where objects were all around him. In his mind, he could see behind him and through walls. He felt it was cheating when he was fencing, but he saw need of it for the day when he returned to Gevás. He was the heir to the Crown of Light, and he was spending his time on Earth to prepare himself mentally and emotionally for that challenge. Also, he wanted to become much more masterful in spells of Light. This feat would require much practice, which Drage had been doing since he had returned to Earth, constantly connecting to that aura of perception.

Within a few hours, the rest of his club had arrived along with most of the other competitors from other schools. Then, the order was posted. The schedule had each round organized along with where they would be taking place. Drage went to his first area eagerly. Based on the schedule, it seemed that each competitor would face around fifteen rounds, which was a high number in fencing.

Drage was now in full attire, and he felt himself start to sweat immediately under the thick layers. After all the preparations were finished, Drage finally fought his first opponent. He saw the fighter bounce lightly on his feet, eager for blood, so he decided to wait for the enemy to make the first mistake, and the other fencer obliged him.

With a powerful lunge, the opponent attacked, and Drage knocked the point away from his own body and counterattacked with his own strike. The round ended with Drage victorious.

Each round occurred the same way: Drage would predict through *mysteria* his enemies' moves and retaliate with almost catlike reflexes. Having not been tapped once by an enemy sabre, Drage began feeling more and more confident as the tournament continued. After winning the semifinal round, he went to observe the other semifinal round to see how strong his next competitor would be. The two fencers, at first, seemed almost equal in skill, but, then, one fencer's sabre was thrown from his hand and found the enemy sabre at his chest. The move had happened so suddenly that Drage had almost not seen it. For that split second, he felt a disturbing wave of unease wash across his heart.

Puzzled by the obviously experienced nature of his soon to be opponent, he approached the gym where the final fight was to be held. The president of his fencing club came closer to him and stood beside him. "Good job, Drage. I'm sure you can beat this guy," he began. Drage could sense a hint of fear in the president's voice, however. "Just do what you always do, and our club will carry the trophy, okay?"

Drage nodded quietly and stepped up to begin the final round. As soon as he opened his heart to *mysteria*, he felt it: His opponent was using it as well.

He brought his sabre to its starting stance, and moments later, the battle began.

Drage ignored his regular caution and focused entirely on aggression. He was confident that the people watching him had never seen a fencer fight as intently as he was now. Focus and determination ruled him, not letting any emotions get in the way. However, the mysterious opponent was matching every strike with an appropriate block, though Drage could sense that this quick shielding was caused by *mysteria*. The enemy was casting spells to make his blade move of its own accord.

Suddenly, he felt the metal tap his body, and he knew that he had been hit. Seconds later, the attack repeated, and Drage was losing.

Drage decided it was time to quit going easy on his opponent. He summoned more energy from the Light and increased the speed of his attacks. This time, the enemy was hard-pressed, and finally, his sword was knocked from his hand. When Drage attempted to make his own strike, the enemy held out an open hand, and a wave of Force, in the semblance of a ripple in the air, knocked Drage backward. Drage stood swiftly and noticed that all time had been frozen. Some people were frozen in mid-cheer; others were pre-occupied with their phones, still in the middle of some text. The fans at the roof of the gymnasium were stopped, and Drage sensed a lack of movement throughout the building.

However, the enemy fencer still flourished his sword at the end of the fencing strip.

Drage spoke softly, "Who are you?"

"Are you the one whom I have sought for years? Are you his Majesty Emperor of Light Helius?"

Drage clenched his teeth at the question. He had technically not received the title yet, but this person seemed to know who he was nevertheless. "I am not Emperor of Light yet. I'll repeat myself, though: Who are you?"

The fencer responded with a sigh of relief. "I am Cameron Kane, your Majesty. Like you, I was born on Earth, but I am a mage, a sorcerer, to be exact. When I heard that Gevás was under war, I came to join the terra, but the leader of your Majesty's Council intervened and told me that I could not join the terra. He said that only a mage with a degree from the Academy at Gryphos can become a mage in the terra, so I have been seeking you for an appeal."

Drage gaped. "You came this far for this long just to get an appeal?! I am not even Emperor yet."

Cameron shuffled his feet guiltily. "Well…not exactly, your Majesty. It was my original intention, but when I heard about your feats on the battlefield against the sorcerer Maris, I thought…that perhaps you would make me your apprentice, if I proved myself to you."

Yelling, Drage tightened the grip on his sabre. "I am not even technically a mage! I can't teach you about *mysteria*. I'm still learning it myself. Besides, you look older than me. You are probably a master of it without my help." He could not believe what he was hearing. Then, the other words the man said hit him. Gevás was still under war. He could not help but wonder what had happened in his absence. At the same time, he wondered how much he could help this traveling mage. Perhaps, he could teach him what little he did know. Having an apprentice sounded like an interesting idea. Drage was flattered but knew it simply could not work.

Cameron, however, would not be disappointed. "I am quite confident that you are greater than you say you are, your Majesty. All that I ask is that you teach me what you do know."

At Cameron's words, Drage experienced a sharp pain in his heart: the curse of Maris. It brought him into the reality of his weakness quickly, and he felt whatever interest he had felt in training an apprentice vanish."I am not fit to train anyone, yourself included. Go find someone else."

That dark sensation always made Drage feel sick to his stomach and brought a horrid taste to his mouth. It came rarely, usually only once or twice a month, but it was here strongly now.

Cameron glared sadly at the heir to the Crown of Light. He had spent so much time trying to find the man, and then, it was all for nothing. In a fury, he reached out for the powers of Fire and unleashed a fireball at Drage.

Drage reacted rapidly, evading the flaming sphere just barely. "Are you trying to kill me?!" he roared. The fireball exploded against a wall, leaving no damage due to the frozen time.

Cameron growled, almost at the point of tears, "Show me how strong you are. Defend yourself, and if you cannot, then I shall believe that you are as weak as you claim. Fight me." The two of them were still in their fencing outfits, and Drage had yet to see his opponent's true form.

Drage was well aware that he had extreme potential in the arts of *mysteria* if he tried to use it, but he did not want to prove the mage right. He wanted Cameron Kane to leave as soon as possible. Too forcibly had the worlds of Gevás and Earth been mixed here, and Drage was not comfortable with someone on Earth knowing who he was and *what* he was.

Before Drage could react, he was completely engulfed in solid earth. Though his lungs cried out for air, he knew what to do. He focused on the one thing that could get him out of this mess.

Within seconds, the Sword of Destiny materialized into his hand, and the dirt became like sand to its magical blade. The Sword of Destiny was enchanted by a spirit to reduce friction and slice through almost any surface with ease. A second slash freed Drage from the ball of earth, and he leaped out of it with a third and concentrated strike releasing a wave of blue energy from the Sword that was aimed at Cameron.

A white shield of Light appeared in front of Cameron, but it was not powerful enough, and Cameron went flying several feet into the air from the strength of the blast, screaming out as he did. When he landed hard on the ground, more shocked than incapacitated, Drage broke through Cameron's Time spell and created his own spell of illusion to make everyone think he was simply wielding his sabre. As far as everyone in the room could see, Cameron had fallen to the ground, unable to fight. Although they were perplexed as medical personnel rushed to check on the fencer, the crowd cheered Drage's success as a voice rang out, "And Dragenopn Helius is the winner of this year's tournament! Congratulations!"

As the crowd surrounded Drage in celebration, he could make out the fencer that turned to leave the area with his now un-masked head lowered in sorrow, disappointment, and confusion. Drage saw he was a red-haired man young enough to be his older brother. A part of Drage felt sorry for Cameron, but he knew that it was for the best. Drage was not fit to help anyone yet.

His walk took him to the beach, and he gazed deeply into the horizon, trying to capture its magnificence in his heart, but he only found nervousness and fear overwhelm him. He simply did not have time to worry about Gevás now. Until he got rid of the remnants of Maris's curse, he was not suitable to rule Helio. Yet, he felt so guilty for how he had treated Cameron Kane in the tournament. His head lowered to look at the still blue-hued Sword in his hand. To anyone else on the beach, it would appear to be a simple fencing sabre, but that was merely Drage's spell of illusion.

He had learned how to bend light in this manner a couple of years ago and had truly enjoyed practicing that particular spell. It allowed him to train his skills in *mysteria* at a new level.

As he sighed deeply, a voice rose over the crash of the waves against the shore. "Hey Drage!" He turned to see his roommate walking briskly to where he was standing.

"Yeah?"

"How did your tournament go?" inquired the young adult.

Drage ran a hand through his still sweat-drenched, brown hair as Matthew had done so often and replied, "Well, we got first place!"

The roommate grinned contentedly. "Awesome! I'll be sure to tell everyone else I see. I actually came over here to tell you that you have company waiting for you at the dorm. I had been leaving to go check out that new restaurant. I'm supposed to be meeting Ryan there. Anyways, it was a guy and a girl. They said they were old friends of yours, and to be honest, they looked pretty trustworthy, so I let them in the building. I told them to just wait in the lobby. Was that okay?"

Drage nodded in bewilderment. Who would be coming to see him? He had not really kept in touch with the people who had been his high school friends, so what old friends would be waiting for him at the dorm? "Yeah, that's fine. Did they say their names?"

Drage's roommate looked to the sky, trying to remember the names. "Uh…yeah. The guy's name was Matthew, and the girl was Aria…I think…"

His heart leaped at the mention of the two names. He immediately straightened his slumped shoulders and felt his energy return. "Oh, ok. Well, thanks for letting me know!"

"No problem!" replied the roommate as he continued his walk.

Drage ran in the opposite direction toward the dorm, but once he was sure that no one could see him, he summoned a golden, glowing Gate. Stepping through, his view shifted from the windy beach to the cramped and stuffy dorm room. He was not alone.

Aria and Matthew tackled Drage in a strong embrace, and he could not help but laugh in surprise and joy at reuniting with his two best friends. "Aria! Matthew! How's it going?"

The two stepped backward, and Aria was the first one to catch Drage's eyes. A smile lit her face as she rushed to hug him, her arms enfolding him in her embrace. She was still beautiful with her sapphire blue eyes and soft brown hair. Her body was warm, and she seemed to have matured physically— she seemed stronger. Drage smiled back and held her tight, his heart racing at seeing her again.

As he looked up, he realized that Matthew, on the other hand, looked almost exactly the same. He was standing there with arms crossed and a smirk spreading across his face. The only noticeable difference was the drastic change in height. Though Matthew had always been taller than both Drage and Aria, it had only been by a few inches. Now, he was taller by almost a foot and a half.

"Wow, you're a lot taller than I remember, Matt!"

Matthew ran a hand through his black hair and grinned. "You've grown too, Drage." He leaned back against Drage's chair.

It was then that Drage realized that his two guests were sopping wet: They had not dried off since returning to Earth. "You two are drenched!" he exclaimed.

Aria gasped in slight embarrassment and stepped away from Drage, closer to Matthew. "Oops, I guess I forgot. Heh, I'm so used to being wet that dry is a relatively new concept for me now." She pulled a wand from her sopping green robe and swished it in the air, creating a circular motion. Gradually, the water that was dripping from the duo's clothes collected into an aquatic sphere in midair. As she moved her wand, the sphere moved as well. She released it once it left the open window.

With an impressed laugh, Drage glanced over at the door to make sure it was locked. Turning back to his friends who seemed to be examining his room with interest, he asked, "What are you guys doing here?" He could not believe that they were actually here, standing in the middle of his dorm room. It had been five years since he had last seen either of them.

Losing his smile and glancing at Aria once before facing Drage again, Matthew began with a noticeably deeper voice than Drage had remembered. "Well, Drage, Gevás is under some serious trouble right now, and Marqest actually decided that it was time to see if you would come and help. When you left, the real war began."

Aria nodded and continued, "They call it the Third Obsidian War, and it has been a very bloody battle so far. Everything has become more dangerous, and nowhere is safe anymore. Marqest thinks that you could be what saves us now."

Though a part of Drage truly did want to go with his two friends, he felt the tug of Maris's curse inside him. He thought back to when he almost killed both of his friends because of that dark possession. He had not felt it that strongly since he defeated Maris, but he still felt it. That left him hesitant. "Guys,

I am not strong enough to help. I'm sure Marqest thinks I must be really strong by now, but I am not that different."

A frown came to Aria's face in confusion. "What is it, Drage? What's wrong?"

Drage swallowed in slight fear. He had not wanted to say it. Nevertheless, he reluctantly explained. "The reason I haven't tried to come back is…I still have Maris's curse inside me. It never left."

Matthew and Aria gasped. Matthew began in shock, "Are you sure? That's nearly impossible though. That Y'mordi killed him years ago. How could it affect you?"

Drage shook his head. "I don't know. It's nowhere near as powerful as it used to be, but sometimes, I feel its dark pull, its toxic gravity. If it gets worse, there's no telling what I might do. I can't go back with it still there. I can't lead Helio, and I can't fight as the Prince of Light should."

Matthew put a comforting hand on his half-brother's shoulder. "Drage, if you haven't gotten rid of it by now, then maybe you really do need the help of a mage. You're not doing anyone any good by staying here. Gevás needs you."

Aria smiled. "He's right, Drage. We need you."

Drage thought for a moment, considering what his two friends were saying. He sighed as he replied, "Well, I guess it couldn't hurt to see how Draconis is doing, huh?"

Before Aria could happily summon a Gate, Drage interrupted, "Hey, not in here. My roommate will freak out if the whole room becomes more soaked than it already is." He turned to the window and released a Gate that glowed brightly with the light of the sun. It hovered a few inches from the window, pouring freezing water from its spiral form. With a running leap, he entered the Gate and stepped into the aquatic world Gevás. The memories of Earth quickly fled to the crevices of his mind, replaced by the frightening yet exciting adventures he had experienced on Gevás.

He was back.

Fire and Light

Randir's bare chest glistened with a mixture of salty sweat and blood, while his black pants had several rips and tears that revealed more gashes. He had short crimson hair that spiked and a large burn mark that went down the right side of his face. The man hung by his arms by a chain attached to the ceiling. All was still in the circular stone room, until a deep breath finally emerged from his cracked and bloody lips. His heart beat for the first time in five years, and to him, nothing had happened. Being under Stasis was not comparable to sleep or unconsciousness. It was loss of all feeling and perception. His red eyes moved to the other man in the room. "Is it done?"

The man in front of him wore a white robe. He had a white ponytail and golden eyes. He swallowed nervously. If he was caught doing this, his leader Y'tal would torture him mercilessly. "It has been five years, Y'ran."

Randir replied, "Y'tal?"

"He is elsewhere here in the Palace of Shadows. He's too focused to be aware of what's happening here." Five years ago, Mali had taught Randir how to put himself into a state of complete immobility that only Randir or Mali could release. It was an interesting variation of Stasis that Mali had learned from Lord Lux when he had served him almost a thousand years ago.

"And the Great Servants of the Darkness?" The seven Y'mordi had been spending their lives in search of the seven mythical beings.

Mali responded hesitantly, "Y'tal has heard from the Voice of the Shadows once more. He claims that this time the Great Servant is in the dragon world Sharl Vran. His name is Kusvor Cairon. He is actually the King of the world now…That's how I knew it was time awaken you again."

Randir winced, the cuts on his body reminding him of the torture Y'tal had put him through. He looked around the room, not surprised that it was still the cold stone from five years ago. Glancing back at Mali, he repeated, "Five years, huh?" The white-robed Lord of the Shadows nodded. "How much has changed?"

Mali growled. "Not too much. What do you want to know specifically?"

He squinted and attempted to remember a mission he had undertaken at Sharl Vran. Each of the five worlds corresponded to one of the five main Elements. Sharl Vran's was Wind. "Yes, Sharl Vran is the only world that has a king ruling its entirety, is it not? The last time I was there, I was reporting on the government. I remember the Golden Dragons ruling the world, and they segregated the Black Dragons from their society."

Mali nodded. ""That is right. However, things have changed there. They changed around Mentiris's time 150 years ago. Their ruler was overthrown by the Black Dragon Kusvor Cairon, and now the segregation has reversed. The Golden Dragons are outcasts in Sharl Vran. One of the most interesting things however is that the world's name remained the same."

"Oh?"

"Vran was the last name of the ruler before Cairon. Typically, the world is named after whoever is ruling it. So, logically, it would be called Sharl Cairon, but Kusvor insisted on keeping it Sharl Vran. Despite being a dictator, Kusvor apparently believed he was not worthy of the full inheritance of the throne…some dragon code of honor or the like." Mali turned to the door. "Anyways, we must hurry. Y'tal will not stay busy forever." He stretched out a hand, and a glowing bar of light appeared in it, transforming suddenly into a silver katana. He leaped above Randir. His blades slashed through the chains, and Randir fell to the hard floor.

He rubbed his wrists painfully as Mali landed behind him. He stood slowly and then turned to face his rescuer. "You know what I must do, do you not?"

Mali grimaced but nodded. This would be the only way that Y'tal would not suspect that Mali had been the one that had freed Randir.

Randir raised a hand as he whispered, "I'll make it quick." He concentrated on a powerful spell, and a fireball left his hand, causing Mali to explode into a cloud of ashes. "Sorry, Hector," he muttered, remembering his friend's older name.

Another spell created a Gate comprised entirely of Fire. As soon as he was about to exit the Realm of Darkness in Gevás, a voice spoke from the still open door. "You escaped."

He did not have to turn to recognize the voice to be that of the Y'mordi leader Y'tal. "Y'tal…my spell was a timed variation. I learned how to make the Stasis last for a set time period." He hoped that his lie would fool Y'tal. He did not want Mali to be blamed for his escape.

Y'tal smirked. "Perhaps, and what do you intend to do now? I see you already disposed of Mali, though I do not know what he was doing down here."

"I am going to Earth," explained Randir without turning to face the short, boy-like Y'mordi. When they had turned into the eternal Lords of the Shadows, they had all been mystified of the shadowed boy Y'tal, whose face they had never seen. "I shall seek the legendary Black Joker. Maybe, he can interpret the Voice of the Shadows better than you. He might be able to find these Great Servants quicker." He knew Mali had intended him to go to Sharl Vran, possibly to get to Cairon before Y'tal, but he knew he had to try this first.

"Are you saying that I am incompetent, Y'ran?" questioned Y'tal challengingly.

Randir sighed. "Y'tal...during the first two Obsidian Wars, you were the Dark Lord Dagan's greatest pet. He taught you how to interpret the Voice of the Shadows. Despite that training, it took you a thousand years to find the first Great Servant of the Darkness. You may have gotten better as the years went on, but you remain a slow worker. We do not have time for this. If the Black Joker can help, then I shall enlist his aid."

Y'tal did not address Randir's desire to seek the Black Joker. He merely returned the sigh and said, "You truly are brave, Y'ran, albeit stupid. Your strength and craving for power were the reasons for the Great Lord of the Dark Dagan to choose you to become one of the Y'mordi. Loyalty was always an issue for you, however, unlike Y'lam. When the Great Lord of the Dark saw your deepest fears in the final Trial, he knew that in order to permanently ensure your loyalty, he would have to make your fears come alive. That was your real trial all along, Y'ran: He made you burn your city. He made you kill your wife."

A wave of anger and hatred flooded through Randir's heart. He tried his hardest to not think about her face, to not hear her voice, and especially to not think about what he did to her. His fists clenched as he struggled not to try to wring Y'tal's neck. He managed to tighten his jaw and growl, "What do you want?"

Y'tal grinned beneath his hood that hid his face entirely. He had never revealed his face to any of the Y'mordi. "Go to Earth, and seek out this Black Joker. I know of the legends well, and if they speak truly, then he could at least aid us in taking over the worlds. Do not go with the impression that he will have the ability to interpret the Voice of the Shadows, however. Interpreting the will of the Darkness is far more complex than you could imagine, Y'ran.

"We have found one of the Great Servants, and he is in Sharl Vran. As with Maris, we shall use him to our advantage. With some time, we could possess the entire dragon world. The Voice has told me that Kusvor Cairon will be the only Great Servant that is on Sharl Vran."

"And the other worlds?"

"The Voice of the Shadows was able to tell me that the worlds Waldann and Menx are devoid of any Great Servants."

Randir considered this information for a moment. "That means that the other Great Servants of the Darkness will be on either Gevás or Earth."

Y'tal stepped forward deliberately. "Yes. That is another good reason for you to go to Earth. If we can take that world over, we will be one step closer to finding the Great Servants. Perhaps, the Black Joker can hand the world to us, if the legends are to be believed, that is."

Randir growled viciously, "Why are you trusting me all of a sudden? It reeks of one of your plans, Y'tal."

The Y'mordi leader laughed maliciously. "Regardless of my absolute hatred toward you, you were trusted by the Great Lord of the Dark Dagan to second me in every movement I make. I trust each of the Y'mordi in different ways, Y'ran. I shall trust Y'dax to advise me when I need it, and I shall trust Y'lam to serve me regardless of my orders. Likewise, I shall trust you to get the job done. You are the one who killed Maris and brought me his blood. That was your doing alone."

"I'm just your puppet then?" inquired Randir.

"Perhaps…Loyalty is an interesting thing, Y'ran. At times, you are serving whom you want to serve, but then at other—"

"You do not know the first thing about loyalty, Y'tal." He said this even as he realized he was betraying his loyalty to Y'tal. Still, he was loyal to his true master, the Darkness. "Tell me: Who are you? There's no way the Dark Lord Dagan accepted you purely because of your skills in the Trials. Your identity intrigued him. Who are you?"

Y'tal did not respond however. "Now, I am Pullatus, though the Great Lord of the Dark Dagan gave me the name

Y'tal. I did have a name before then, but I shall not grant you that particular information. My identity will be known by you one day, Y'ran, I assure you. Go to Earth, and seek out the Black Joker. Do not stray from my orders this time, Y'ran, or you will find yourself facing a harsher punishment than you did last time, and I am confident that the previous torture is considerably fresh on your mind."

Randir did not respond. In fact, the blood was still dripping from his bare chest, and he thought back to Y'tal using the Darkness to force Randir's skin to slowly pull itself apart, inch by inch. He remembered his own screams echoing through the room. He stepped into the fiery Gate with displeasure. The water faded into air, and Randir realized that he was on Earth, the strange earthen world.

He found himself standing on an enormous snow-capped mountain, one among many. His head tilted backward to face the cloudy sky, and long and deep roar emitted from his lungs. The snow around him melted to a small river that went downward to the base of the mountain. The image of his hammer colliding with Ophelia's skull was blazing in his mind, as was his fierce desire to kill Y'tal.

However, the reason he was seeking the Black Joker had nothing to do with Y'tal, the Great Servants, or control of Earth. The reason he sought the mythical being was simple: He wanted to be free of the bonds that connected him to the Darkness. He no longer wanted to be one of the Y'mordi. Perhaps, the Black Joker could sever that bond.

The only real question was where to start. The greatest knowledge source would probably be the Ring of Elders, the secret council of mages that governed the *mysteria*-wielding community on Earth. That meant that the next question was how to find them. He grinned as an idea came to his mind. If the Ring of Elders regulated control of spells, then they would definitely investigate if some bizarre event occurred.

Without a moment's hesitation, he concentrated on his heart's true Element and unleashed an immense wave of Fire that spread down the mountain and throughout the valley beneath it. Gradually, the flames intensified, creating a heat that turned the mountain rocks white-hot. The fire spread through the woods, setting each tree alight, and the crackling sound brought pleasure to Randir's ears. The miles of mountains around him were ablaze.

As he stared into the embers, a memory came to him. They reminded him of a starlit night. He could almost see that soldier's face in his eyes, that soft beautiful face. Her name had been Stehl, though she had been under the alias Terrell. Disguised as a male, Captain Terrell had led the brigades of the Emperor Regin's terra for years and had met Randir while he had been seeking the seven Guardians of Light five years ago. After he had saved her from a member of the Emperor of Light's Enigma Brigade, she had vowed to spend her life hunting down the elusive Enigma Brigade. He could not help but wonder how she was doing now.

He shook his head. For some reason, she kept appearing in his thoughts, though he could not explain it. He thought the only woman who could enchant him was Ophelia. He felt almost disloyal even thinking about Stehl.

Suddenly, several Gates appeared around the scorching mountain, and people emerged from them, extinguishing the Fire with spells of Water, spouts that stemmed from their wands and engulfed the flames.

Finally, one of the newcomers glanced at Randir and pointed a silver wand threateningly at him. Randir prepared to shield himself from any spells that would come at him.

However, a voice called out from another person, "No, not yet." It was a woman's voice, and she called with a tired yet demanding voice. She turned, with her long brown hair and blue eyes, to face Randir. "Who are you, sorcerer? I can tell that you are not from this world."

The Y'mordi grinned then. The Ring of Elders had answered his call. He knew only they would respond to such a great use of *mysteria* on their world. "My name is Randir, and I seek information about the one known as the Black Joker. Can you tell me anything about him?" He did not care for formalities. He wanted the answers now.

The woman was taken aback by the request. "Mr. Randir, I am the head of the Ring of Elders, and I demand to know why you have set half of these mountains alight. I don't know where you come from, but there are rules for *mysteria* here."

"Damn your rules," Randir sneered. "You want me out of here? Answer my question, witch."

The woman smirked. "Then, you should know the Black Joker is nothing but a myth."

Randir could sense her lies, could sense the Darkness ripple in her heart. "You are lying to me, Elder. Tell me what you know of the Black Joker, and I won't rip this world apart."

The other Elders stepped back in shock. The leader responded calmly, "Well then, if you know that the Black Joker is real, then you must know why I cannot give you the information you seek. He was a leviathan that I would rather not reawaken. The destruction that you threaten Earth with would be nothing compared to the chaos that the Black Joker could summon. I know of you, Randir, and I have heard of your unusual exploits. Why do you seek such a monster?"

Randir, for a moment, did not reply. How did this woman know him, and who did she think she was, asking him all the questions? "Elder, I require the Black Joker to perform a feat for me that I believe that no average mortal could perform. It is my understanding that the Black Joker could possess such power. Am I wrong in that assumption?"

She was silent. Finally, she raised a hand, and all of the other Elders disappeared into their own Gates. She had ordered their retreat. Her feet, however, stood planted on the mountainside. "You are not wrong in that assumption, Randir, but you are foolish if you think that he would ever bow to your wishes. I know what games you take pleasure in playing. I assure you now that he supersedes such trickery. When he awakens, he shall have one goal in mind: destruction, even for he who awakens him."

"So, you know nothing of how I could find him?" inquired Randir eagerly.

"No, I know nothing. The Ring are the ones who imprisoned him centuries ago, but I was not around then, and the information was never passed down. It was meant to remain a secret."

Randir replied curtly, "Why didn't you attack me? The Ring of Elders could easily have done something to me, so why didn't you?"

The woman gave a final glance to the man with the bare chest and red hair. "There was once a day when you saved my son…twice, I might add." With that being said, she vanished into a Gate of her own. Randir was still as confused as when he had asked the question. He had never been the type of individual who saved others. Her words remained a mystery to him.

Suddenly, another Gate appeared. From its watery depths, Mali emerged. "For the top of a mountain, it's pretty warm out here," he commented somewhat humorously.

Randir nodded to him in greeting. "You respawned fairly quickly."

Mali returned the nod and replied, "Yes, being in the Dark Realm gives that advantage."

"And did Y'tal or Pullatus or whatever you want to call him suspect anything?"

The blonde-haired Y'mordi shook his head. "I do not think so. When I came back, he asked me about what had happened, and I told him that I had sensed something strange. When I opened the door, you attacked me. That's all I said. He seemed to believe it, and he asked me to assist you in finding the Black Joker. You can't seriously be looking for him, can you? What happened to Sharl Vran?"

Randir nodded gravely. "He might be the only one who can separate the bond between me and the Darkness."

Mali gaped then. "Now, I know you're joking. You can't stand against the Darkness like this! If Y'tal suspects even the slightest hint of what you are trying to do, he will make you suffer worse than you could possibly imagine. Doesn't that scare you at all?"

"No, Hector, it doesn't. I have to try. Look: I signed up for this job under the impression that I would gain immense power from it. I wanted a piece of the world, but when he made me…you know…I lost everything. I had nothing left, not my name, my kingdom, or even my love." Randir found himself shaking despite himself.

"Victor, he did that to all of us," commented Mali, using Randir's first name. He considered placing a hand on Randir's shoulder but stopped himself. "We all had our old lives taken away from us. The twins lost the Academy, Ixion lost his master, and I lost my whole life. It's true that some of us may have lost more than others, but I don't think that any of us felt the hurt greater than anyone else."

"Would you…" began Randir hesitantly as he turned to face Mali. "Would you take it back if you had the chance to do it over again?"

Mali thought about it for several minutes, and the two stood there in silence. At last, Mali responded, "No, Victor. I would not change anything. My allegiance is to the Darkness, and that will not change. Unlike the Light, the Darkness is rewarding and just. Being an Y'mordi allows me to serve the Darkness to the maximum of my abilities. Maybe one day, the Darkness will no longer have need of me."

Randir smirked in pity of Mali. "That was how you always were, wasn't it? You found the greatest joy in life to be appreciation. All you ever wanted was to be recognized for your work. You never thought of a life of freedom, only a life of servitude. To my knowledge, you have only changed sides twice: when you left Lux to serve the Dark Lord Dagan and when you decided to help me against Y'tal."

The man in the white robe shifted uncomfortably. Changing the subject, he said, "Have you found out anything yet?"

Randir sighed deeply in frustration at the situation. "Yes and no. The Black Joker is not a myth. The Ring of Elders just verified that for me, but as to the whereabouts of the being, I have no idea."

"Are you sure that no one in the Ring knows of his whereabouts?"

"No…" said Randir hesitantly. He was not confident yet of the knowledge of the Ring of Elders, especially their head. "I might be able to use the Ring to my advantage yet, but that will require a great deal of work. We will need to start by gaining some background research on the Elders. We need a way to get to their head."

Mali looked out into the horizon in slight fear. "You know that I cannot go against Y'tal's orders as freely as you can, right, Victor? You may be seen as a rebel, but I am seen as the loyal one here. If I am to help you undercover, then I need to have my loyalty appear strong."

The other man felt the cold begin to drown out the warmth of the flames he had created. The hairs on his bare back began to rise. He shivered and summoned a black robe, dark wisps trailing from its fabric. "I know, Hector. Claim you are just…watching over me. Report to Y'tal if you must." He found himself remembering Y'tal's words about him being a mere puppet of the Darkness. Could it be true? Was that really all he was? A pawn for a black-robed kid? "The Black Joker…he might be my only hope…"

Of Honor

"Well, after you left," Aria explained, "the Emperor's Council decided that the Crown of Light would have to wait for you, which meant that they would be in charge of managing Helio's affairs until you returned. So, you remember how a long time ago the anima were exiled, right?"

"Yeah," Drage responded.

"Well, when Maris started making the anima of the West and North rebel, that started what's already being called the Third Obsidian War. Emperor Regin from the East has joined forces with the Emperor's Council to try to quell the West."

"What about the North?"

Matthew replied, "They're in a civil war. Half the continent wants to stay under the rule and protection of Helio, while the other half is fighting for independence."

Drage asked, "Have you guys been fighting in this?"

Aria tightened her fists as she cursed through her teeth. "When the Council took over, they passed a new decree that only Academy-trained sorcerers could serve in the terra."

"That meant that Aria could no longer be a wand master despite her having passed the Prophet's test," continued Matthew. "She decided to enroll in the Academy."

Drage was puzzled by the term. "The Academy? What's that?"

"The Academy is the largest school in Gevás. There are several small ones throughout each kingdom, but the Academy is the most influential, most expensive, and most prestigious school there is. It's in the city Gryphos of the kingdom Norlante. It's the kingdom to the east of Helio," Aria said with an almost lecturing tone.

"What have you been doing there?" Drage inquired, bewildered by the idea. Though he had thought about Gevás constantly during his time on Earth, he had never thought about there being schools.

"I have been training in the Elements discipline. That means that I've been studying how to use *mysteria* and its effects. It will take me a few years to be a qualified sorcerer, unfortunately." She lowered her head in sadness. When she had succeeded in the duel against Master Valdridge five years ago, she had achieved a wonderful position in the terra only to have it taken away after the first battle. Now that the country was deep within the war, she was stuck in school, learning about spells she had already mastered.

"That's absurd. Years ago, you proved you were better than most of the mages in the terra."

Aria shook her head. "It doesn't matter how good I am. The Council wants strict control over the sorcerers in the terra. They want as few independent thinkers as possible."

The three were silent for a while. Unsure what to say to comfort Aria, Drage turned to Matthew. "And what about you, Matt?"

Matthew sat down on Drage's old bed and sighed. "Well, after the battle, I went to stay with my dad, the Prophet of Wind, you remember." For most of his life, Matthew had been labeled as adopted by their mother Elizabeth, but when the trio had come to Gevás, they had discovered that Elizabeth was

Matthew and Helen's real mother, but the Emperor of Light John was not their father. For some reason still unknown to all of them, Elizabeth had marked Matthew differently from his sister Helen. Though Drage had asked his mother numerous times over the past five years, she would not relent to his questioning. "I spent a lot of the time just learning about the form Time. In case you couldn't tell, time has been frozen here for a while now."

Drage looked around in shock. He had not noticed anything different. They were in a meeting room in the Palace of Light. A long conference table filled the room, and Drage sat on the corner of it while Aria sat at a chair and Matthew stood by the window. Granted, there was nothing besides them that would have been moving here. "I hadn't noticed…"

Matthew smiled and gave a short laugh. "That is because I have really developed the spells. I cast the spell on every bit of the world except this room. To be honest, I haven't done all that much since you left. As my father instructed me, it has been more beneficial for me to just stand back and let the world do what it wills. However, this past year I have been trying to involve myself with Helio again. That was when Marqest found me. He told me what Aria has been doing and suggested that we try looking for you, which brings us to where we are now. So, what about you?"

In the forests of the Western Continent, a Silver Dragon broke through the naval vehicles and charged at the Golden Dragon. The Silver Dragon's fierce claws reached out toward Draconis, but the mighty Golden Dragon's massive sword blocked the attack and made its own powerful counterattack that slashed through the silver scales and brought the Dragon to the ground. Draconis landed beside the silver, flailing body and held his sword to the creature's neck, which caused the Dragon to stop its violent movements.

The Silver Dragon spoke, "You are a disgrace, Draconis of Helio. Your own kind is dying everywhere. Before long, the

Golden Dragons shall cease to exist, and you will be to thank for it. Even Sharl Vran is losing its Golden Dragons."

This information was complete news to Rexam Draconis. His claws flexed as he growled, "What?! What are you talking about?"

A sad smile appeared on the injured Dragon's face. "I came from Sharl Vran not too long ago. The world is so much different than it used to be. The remaining Golden Dragons are all in the prisons of King Cairon."

Draconis did not know where to start: His questions seemed infinite. "But…why are you fighting with the rebels? The Dragon's Clause exempted you." Around 150 years ago, the Emperor of Light Seth Mentiris had banished all non-humans into exile, but the next Emperor Bral Helius had created a caveat that allowed Dragons that came to Gevás after the exile to be free. Draconis had always despised the exile but had never protested it because of his loyalty to both the Helius family and the Emperors of Light. It was not his place to question the laws of this world.

The silver-scaled Dragon responded meekly between his shaking breaths, "I still fought because I knew that someone had to. The way that Dragons are treated here is filthy. I would not allow those humans to treat us that way."

Draconis was simply appalled by what the Dragon was saying. This idea of pride over logic and responsibility to Helio seemed so new, revolutionary, and considerably extreme, yet a part of Draconis found the slightest truth in it.

As the amber-rimmed eyes watched Draconis cautiously, the Silver Dragon's muscles finally relaxed, and with it, that amber light faded from his eyes. Draconis's tried to swallow the lump in his throat as his thoughts reeled with what the Silver Dragon said.

Another explosion illuminated the water in a flash of extraordinary light. Draconis ducked to the ground as shrapnel from a naval vehicle fell down on him. None of it hit him, and he allowed his thin but strong wings to stretch and raise him high into the water.

To him, the most shocking piece of information had been the events that had been occurring on Sharl Vran. It had been a century and a half since he had been back at his home. His home had been in one of the major cities in the dragon world. Like most Golden Dragons, he had lived in luxury. With servants aiding his daily actions and an energetic environment providing him with a lively childhood, Rexam Draconis had experienced a comfortable life in Sharl Vran.

Remembering his servants, friends, and family only reminded him of the grief as well. The grief was marked by the memory of a blazing fire. Fire. It was an Element of great power, warm passion, and tragic demise. He could clearly remember that night as if it had occurred last night.

His mother had prepared a wonderful meal, and afterward, his father had sparred with him. It had always been Draconis's fondest wish to join the King's army. As he had become ready to go to bed, an explosion of flames lit up the city. The raid had been completely unexpected, and no one stood a chance against the Black Dragons that slaughtered the draconian citizens.

A fiery blast had ripped Draconis's house to burning shreds. As the young Draconis had looked around calling for help anxiously, one Black Dragon landed right beside Rexam and stared maliciously at the young Dragon. Draconis had fallen back into the rubble of his house and gaped up at the black behemoth. Its fearsome red eyes seemed to glare deep within Draconis's soul. The Black Dragon had wielded an ancient weapon of the Dragons called the twofold, a unique sword that possessed two parallel blades protruding from the hilt, giving it the appearance of a dangerously long eagle's claw. Perhaps, it was an instant of pity that had flashed through the Dragon's eyes when he had kicked Draconis harder into the ground instead of beheading him on the spot. Then, he had merely flown away.

Regardless of the intention, Rexam had been the only survivor of the city in the massacre. Only later had he discovered that the Dragon that had spared him was none other than Kusvor Cairon, the leader of several rebel Black Dragons. Cairon had attacked every Imperial City in this manner and had eventually assassinated the King Vran himself, which had given Cairon the Dragon's crown. Draconis had known some of this, but not the extent of tyranny the Silver Dragon had claimed.

Shifting his thoughts to the remainder of the battle around him, he became aware that much of the enemy army was failing. Helio's navy was winning.

Matthew unfroze the flow of time. He had frozen it in order to give the three of them as much time as they needed to catch back up since they had been separated. "Alright, I guess the next thing we need to do is get you to Marqest. He should know what to do about your curse, Drage," said Matthew.

Drage nodded nervously. He was not eager to confront Marqest, because he knew that Marqest would likely try to convince him to accept the Throne of Light finally.

"Would you rather use a Gate or walk?" inquired Aria.

Drage responded, "I would like to just walk, please. I want to see how much everything has changed."

As they traversed the tile floor through the main hallway and observed the silver walls of the Palace of Light, Drage became aware of the effects of age on the structure. Rust was beginning to show, and cobwebs were scattered into most of the corners that he could see. "What happened to the servants who lived here?"

Matthew replied with a tone of sorrow, "Unfortunately, without the Emperor here any longer, they all left almost immediately when you did. The Emperor's Council still meets here, of course, though."

"The Emperor's Council…Who is in that?" Drage knew the Council was acting as the ruling body in place of him, governing all of Helio's affairs as both a political kingdom and a warring faction.

Aria answered this question, "Well, the only ones you know would be Mistress Leona, Master Valdridge, Marqest, and Draconis. There are two or three others, though."

The rest of their walk was in silence. Drage was completely taken aback by how the walls of the Palace had rusted and cracked. It felt spooky to him.

When they opened the door to the Throne Room, Drage was even more surprised. The golden chandeliers that had filled this room with vim and vigor were dark and lifeless now. He stopped his spectating walk and focused on those once gorgeous chandeliers. As he cleared his mind, they gradually brightened to create their usual, brilliant display of light across the room.

Aria was thoroughly impressed by the spell. "Wow, Drage, it seems you have developed your ability, as well. You didn't need a wand, an orb, or even words. How did you learn control without a focusing element, much less without instruction?" Drage knew *mysteria* was based on one's emotions. Casting the right spell required knowledge of the Element but also the right emotional focus. For most, this involved an incantation, an orb, a wand, or a staff usually. Not having the luxury of formal training, he had had to learn it himself over the past five years.

Drage's mind was still distant, however. "I just sort of…did it, I guess. I never thought much about it. After fighting Maris, I didn't really see the need of using words. Come to think of it, I never had to use words, unless I was using Maris's Darkness."

A voice came from the door to the entrance foyer. "Oh? And what brings such a welcome guest as the Prince of Light to the Palace of Light?"

The trio turned to see Marqest standing there along with the rest of the Emperor's Council.

Matthew addressed the Council politely. "Excuse me, Master Marqest. Lord Helius has returned, sir." Though Marqest had almost become a friend five years ago, his new position in the Emperor's Council had been one with which he demanded the utmost respect even from Matthew and Aria.

A nod from Marqest signaled for Matthew to be at ease. "Very well, Matthew. May we have a moment alone with Lord Helius, Matthew and Aria?"

As Drage's two best friends left the room, Aria noticed the glare that Mistress Leona was giving her. Although Mistress Leona was her frequent mentor, she was also an instructor at the Academy. Aria was technically supposed to be at the Academy right now, not chatting with Dragenopn Helius in another kingdom.

Once Drage was alone with the Emperor's Council, Master Valdridge began, "Prince Helius, have you returned with the intention of taking your rightful place as Emperor of Light?"

"No," said Drage sternly. No matter how nervous he was deep down, he knew that he would not relent. "I have to come to help with this war, if I am needed, that is." He could not believe he was saying it, but he decided that it would be both the best negotiation and an excuse to see Matthew and Aria for a while longer.

One of the Council members that Drage did not know spoke, "Hello, Lord Helius, my name is Viso Tharlam." The man was in a white robe and had a weathered face with thinning hair. "I served your father for several years. I hope you'll understand me when I say that the greatest aid you could do this kingdom would be to accept the crown. People are talking in the streets, and trust in the Light is fading slowly."

"What do you mean 'trust in the Light is fading?'" Drage growled.

Tharlam responded, "People are starting to question...your Majesty...that the Emperor of Light knows what is best for Gevás."

The first emotion that Drage felt was anger. He leaned forward with fists clenched as he half-snarled, "Then, that was your fault. If the Council was taking care of the kingdom, then no one else is to blame, not me, not my dad, and not even the war."

Instantly, Tharlam backed down and did not say another word. Marqest commented calmly, "Dragenopn, I am not going to force you to accept the crown now, so do not worry about that. Rather, I am satisfied with the proposal you have made." He spoke to Valdridge then. "May I speak to you for a moment?"

He pulled Valdridge aside, which left Drage to face the rest of the Council, though he was still quite upset with the news of the people's distrust. "Where is Draconis?" he asked forcefully.

Mistress Leona responded, "Master Draconis is actually on the battlefield against the rebels now. He has been with one of the naval fleets on the Western Continent."

Drage only became more frustrated with the state of things. "Why didn't you get rid of the law that exiled the anima anyways? We shouldn't be fighting this war. It's no surprise that everyone is upset about it."

"It would have been senseless to change the laws," countered Mistress Leona. "Before the exile, the Eastern Continent had always despised nonhumans. It was because Emperor Mentiris exiled the nonhumans that we obtained the support of the East. If we give alliance to the exiles, the Eastern Continent headed by the Emperor Regin would turn on us. Fighting the exiles is a long and arduous war, but not an impossible one. If we were to fight the Emperor Regin of Immyx, the war would never end. That would be an exercise in futility."

Tharlam added, "Hundreds if not thousands more of your people would die, your Majesty. Disbanding the exile law would be the ruin of Helio."

Although he understood what he was being told, Drage felt a moral complication.

Finally, Marqest and Valdridge rejoined the group. Valdridge began, "Lord Helius, we would like you to serve as a general in the terra."

Most of the Council was as surprised by the request as Drage was. However, after a few moments, many of the Council members nodded in assent.

Matthew grumbled to Aria, "He needs a higher position than that. They just want to keep a close eye on him."

Drage was at a loss for words. "I-I-I can't lead even that many people. I'm still learning."

Marqest waved away Drage's protest. "It shall be fine. You shall train at the Capital in Immyx. The Emperor Regin has some of the finest military facilities in Gevás. You will learn the ways of war there."

The final excuse came to Drage's lips. "Marqest, I still have the curse. Maris's Heartbind never left me."

The Prophet of Water tried not to reveal his shock. "Well, then, we shall have to fix that. You have borne that blight for long enough." The Prophet eyed Drage's chest with concern. "If Maris has survived in your heart, then he has likely survived in other ways, as well." Before Drage could react to what Marqest was suggesting, the Prophet gestured for Drage to follow. "Come with me, Dragenopn. We are going back to Heaven's Isle."

As he prepared to summon a Gate, the doors burst open, and Matthew and Aria rushed into the Throne Room. Aria exclaimed, "We want to come, too!"

Mistress Leona interrupted her there, though. "Aria, you are to return to the Academy at once! Once you have achieved a mastery in the discipline of Elements, you can participate in this war."

Aria was not pleased with this response, but before she could argue, Matthew implored, "Master Marqest, I would really like to come with the two of you. I have been training under the instruction of one of the Prophets for five years. I can manipulate the form Time almost as well as my father, and I think that I could also become a general if you willed it."

Growling, Marqest responded, "Being a general is more than about fighting. It requires leadership, boy."

Drage responded coldly, "Marqest, do it."

Marqest seemed to consider the request, and he turned to Valdridge. "Master Valdridge, what would you say?"

The Prophet of Light nodded approvingly, and Matthew smiled.

Realizing that Aria was upset, Drage turned to her and gave her a comforting hug. He did not want to be separated from her so soon, but he could see that he clearly had no choice in the matter. "I'll be back soon, I promise."

Aria stared at him with cold, blue eyes. "I'm not sure how well I can regard your promises anymore, Drage." His eyes widened in surprise. She moved her hand and put something into one of his pockets. "In case you need me..." A Gate appeared behind her, and she stepped into it to enter the Academy at Gryphos.

Staring after her, he wondered what that was all about. "Alright, Dragenopn, Matthew, this way please," commanded Marqest softly. His own Gate appeared, and the three of them left the chilling Southern Continent to reappear on the waste land known as Heaven's Isle.

As the navy parked their vehicles to rest for a few hours, Draconis began feeling considerably restless. The dying words of the Silver Dragon on the battlefield had shaken him. How chaotic were things back at Sharl Vran? He felt as if he had to know, yet his responsibilities here were holding him back. He had a duty to serve and protect the Emperor.

He started a campfire on the ground by focusing on anger, a simple enough emotion to summon. The Western Continent was warm enough, but it was a small way to vent his frustration, and the glistening flames seemed so hypnotic.

The Emperor's Council had sent the navy here with Draconis as a general to try to suppress most of the exiles and to regain much of the Western Continent. With most of the enemy's government officials assassinated, a new government would need to be erected, and the Eastern and Southern Continents would require a secure Continent in order to reestablish the government.

Suddenly, a soldier approached Draconis in the camp. Draconis regarded the soldier with a nod as the man offered a salute.

The soldier said, "Eh, don' min' me, General Draconis, sir. Or do it be Master Draconis? Anyway, I was jus' stoppin' by ta see if ya needed any help or anythin'. General Silverpike's da name, but you c'n call me Mirah. Spelled em-eye-ar-ei-eich, but said like mee-rah."

Draconis was surprised by the man's overall demeanor. He was dressed like a naval officer, but he walked and talked like a foreigner. "Excuse me, General...Mirah. You are not from Helio, are you?"

"No, sir. I come from Verdegoran in da East. But, I spen' da past decade or so in Port City o' Mashan Telis. I was jus' a simple merchant den."

The general's story intrigued Draconis. "Oh, really? That is very interesting. How did a merchant from Verdegoran became a general in the Emperor of Light's navy?"

"Heh, dat is a good ques'ion, Master Draconis. Seems like i' was jus' a 'righ' place, righ' time, y'know? Been flyin' ships me whole life."

"Well, we are glad to have you. I would like to talk more, but now I am somewhat preoccupied." Draconis stared into the fire.

However, General Silverpike did not take Draconis's hint and only sat beside the Dragon. "O'? An' what's da great Golden Dragon 'ave on his mind? Mirah promises 'e won' tell a soul."

With a charmed smile, Draconis decided to divulge a little. The whole time, he stared into the fire, speaking as much to himself as he was to Mirah. "Several years ago, my family was killed by a Dragon named Cairon. While I ran away, he spent his time taking over the land and gained a lot of power. I am just now finding out that he has been ruling in a way that mistreats most of my kind. A part of me wants to go there and fight him, but I have responsibilities here."

Mirah patted Draconis's scaly back quite forcefully as he commented, "Y'know, I've always been one to 'ppreciate a man of duty. Can' stand a man who only looks out for 'imself. But y'know what? Sometime, a man gotta remember what he's fightin' fer. Dere is no worthy cause dat needs constant 'elp. Dere is no debt dat needs eternal payment. Dere is no war dat is wort' fightin' forever. Mebbe, you could take a leave an' take back what's yers. Den, you can come back an' help out here."

Draconis felt an uncontrollable compulsion to do as Mirah Silverpike suggested. Somehow, he trusted the man. Perhaps, it would be fine if he just went back to Sharl Vran for a little while and assessed what was going on there. The Golden Dragons might need his help if Cairon was terrorizing them.

He stood and prepared to leave. "Mirah, could you do me a favor?"

"Why, o' course! Anythin' for da great Golden Dragon!"

"Send a messenger to the Emperor's Council. I'm going away on leave for an emergency. I will accept any punishment they see fitting upon my return."

Mirah responded with a prompt salute, "Yessir!"

Draconis held out a hand, and a Gate that leaked several bubbles of air into the sea appeared. He flew into it, and it gave Mirah the image of a sea serpent slithering into a cavern. Finally, the Gate closed behind his golden tail.

As Draconis flew through the warm air, clouds brushing past him, memories swarmed through his mind: memories of home, family, friends, and the red eyes of Kusvor Cairon.

The Hall of Murals

The castle had retained its golden structure despite Kusvor's followers' many protests. He did not want to change too much from the previous era. Despite his obvious rule over the world, he felt as if he had cheated. The crown was meant to be inherited, yet he had taken it by force. He knew he should not be considered a true king.

Kusvor Cairon allowed his eyes to scan over the once magnificent city. From this elegant tower, he could observe the daily lives of his people. The castle was just as King Vran had left it in his passing, but the city was in nearly total ruin. His people, the Black Dragons, had viewed the golden buildings as a reminder of the past, when the Black Dragons had been considered outcasts, and when the Golden Dragons had ruled the world. Despite Kusvor's protests, the Dragons had torn the buildings apart, and Kusvor had not made any attempt to rebuild, leaving the ruins surrounding his castle as a reminder of what they had overcome.

For over a hundred and fifty years, he had been seeking the remnants of the aureate race in the high hopes of extinguishing them from the face of the planet, but a few still remained. Those who had surrendered to him had received the penalty of a lifetime in the dungeons, while all others were slaughtered. The Black Dragons had been considered as filthy mongrels for too long, he had decided all those years ago. Kusvor Cairon had signaled the dawn of a new era, one where the Black Dragons ruled this world of clouds, where the floating islands of this world were all connected under an obsidian banner.

He turned from the window and began descending the stone stairs at last. His figure was serpentine and slender, and he wore a chainmail suit. It was customary for a King to wear the battle uniform at all times, but a light green robe covered the chainmail. It was of the utmost importance to portray a dual image to the people who served him: an image of power and an image of wisdom.

Though politics had not been his main focus, he had been attempting to gain the support of the other Dragon races in the eradication of the Golden Dragons, but not many other races were interested in the project and instead wanted to fight King Cairon and his militaristic stealing of the throne. However, no Dragon had yet waged war against the Black Dragons.

When he finally reached the bottom of the stairs, his two newest servants were waiting for him.

The two women in black robes made hurried bows and commented in unison, "Good evening, King Cairon."

Kusvor grunted a small approval and walked past the two humans. He had always despised humans when they came to Sharl Vran: they were foreign and strange, and did not belong in the clouds. To many Dragons, humans were simply a myth, but Kusvor had seen them occasionally in the past. He had seen ambassadors come from Earth, Menx, and Gevás. He knew of the other worlds. However, he had never spoken with them personally. A few days ago, these two women had come to his castle, had been led in by his guards, and offered him a ludicrous proposition. They claimed Kusvor Cairon had been chosen to lead the legions of the Shadows to conquer Sharl Vran entirely. He had been skeptical at first, but gradually the two had softened him to the idea, and he almost felt proud. They had convinced the guards of their good nature, and he, too, was starting to believe they were only trying to help him gain power.

One of the women spoke as they followed Kusvor, "My Lord, might I ask you a question?"

Her twin gave her a stern look that warned the other not to go too far.

"You may," was Kusvor's response.

The woman swallowed somewhat fearfully before continuing. "We know that you have the intention of getting rid of the last Golden Dragons…Would you be interested in learning how to use the Darkness in order to find them?"

Kusvor stopped in his tracks. Without turning, he replied, "Is that possible?" The idea had never occurred to him, and it was a considerably enticing one now. It was an advantage he did not want to overlook.

The girl bowed her head. "Yes, my Lord. With the powers of the Darkness, you can do almost anything: topple nations, crumble your enemies, and track down the Golden Dragons."

"Sarn, Arnim," he said, addressing the two women. "Come with me."

Giving each other hesitant looks, the twin Y'mordi followed Kusvor Cairon through his castle.

The three of them stood in the massive throne room of the golden fortress. Like the rest of the castle, this particular room had maintained its fascinating splendor, and every inch of the area was shining with a gold light. Despite his utter hatred for the Golden Dragons, he held honor first and foremost. He respected the old ways.

"King Cairon," ventured Sarn. "What are we doing here?"

Kusvor turned to the two women and responded. "Teach me. Instruct me in the ways of the Darkness. If it will aid me in my search for the Golden Dragons, then we do not have a moment to lose. I want them dead." His red eyes glimmered ominously in the golden light of the room.

Arnim spoke for the first time, "Excuse me, King Cairon, but why do you want the Golden Dragons executed so much?

They are in no position to attack or even threaten you." He hissed, "My reasons are none of your business, human. I would not expect you to understand the affairs of a Dragon anyways."

Arnim bowed deeply in apology. She was never one to offend or to make a rash decision, but apparently, it was a sensitive subject. She could learn her place, though she wondered if her twin Arnim could do the same.

Kusvor commanded, "Teach me."

The twins looked at each other once more, and then they held their open palms out toward the Black Dragon and allowed their connections to the Darkness to take over their hearts. They became instantly aware of the vast concentration of Darkness that was already in Kusvor's heart. They focused their energy on that Darkness and observed it as it resonated with their focus. Their hearts connected their vast pool of Darkness with his heart. It was not the bond of the Y'mordi, but it was close.

Y'tal had taught them how to perform this spell. He had said that it would awaken the Great Servant's true nature and hence unlock the powerful Darkness that lay dormant in his heart. Supposedly, the Great Servant would be able to summon Darkness almost effortlessly. Y'tal had used the same spell on Maris five years ago.

Kusvor's black eyelids closed as he felt the intoxicating sensation of the eternal Darkness filling his mere existence. Even with his eyes shut, he felt the world around him differently: his senses of smell and hearing were more refined. The glow in the room began to dim as Kusvor embraced this new power.

"How is it…that I feel so alive now?" he asked softly.

Sarn responded, "That is the feel of *mysteria*. It is the unseen force that resides in all hearts. The Darkness is an Element without limits. With it as your weapon, you will be nearly invincible."

The red eyes opened, and he held out a black, scaly hand with sharp claws protruding from it. A black orb, surrounded in purple light, engulfed his hand. "How do I unleash this power? How do I use it?"

Instead of allowing Sarn to answer, Arnim replied calmly, "Merely will the power inside of you to become real. Make it leave your heart and materialize into the physical world."

Kusvor experimented with the idea for a few seconds, but nothing happened. Finally, the sphere around his hand began to grow as he concentrated. Then, it shot out toward the back wall. When it collided with the gold, a gaping hole was created, and all around it, the wall had been stained black.

Though they knew it had only been a simple spell, Sarn and Arnim could tell that Kusvor was significantly pleased by his newfound abilities. The wicked smile on his face was proof of that.

Kusvor was in the lower basements without the company of the two servants. As a way of practicing the powers of the Darkness, he tried to see this room without the use of light. By focusing on the Darkness, he could observe every detail in the room more vividly.

Across the walls, several ancient murals were painted. He had been to this place multiple times since he had become the king. They told the history of the world Sharl Vran.

He approached a particular section of the murals and beheld the dawn of the outcast of the Black Dragons. There were eight races of Dragons, and they had existed in tribes those several millennia ago. The tribes had fallen into a small scale war, and the ones who became the victors were the Black Dragons by means of a new technology, the weapons known as the twofolds. With two poison-laced, straight blades protruding straight from the hilt, they had been the most dangerous weapons in Sharl Vran at the time.

As Kusvor walked, the next mural revealed an image of a Golden Dragon fighting a Black Dragon. The legend was that a Dragon appeared from the heavens and attacked the leader of the Black Dragons. After disarming the leader, the Divine

Dragon of the Heavens banished the leader and all of his kind to the caves that existed in the south side of the world.

The twofold weapon had been labeled as too dangerous and banned for any civilized Dragon to use, and the Golden Dragons, the descendants of the Divine Dragon of the Heavens, began their rule of Sharl Vran.

The hall of murals continued for a long way, but Kusvor was not particularly interested in the rest of the world's history. When he had been a mere dragonet, he had heard the stories of the Divine Dragon of the Heavens, the Dragon tribes, and the twofold weapon. He became obsessed with the tales. He saw how all the Dragons around him suffered: little food, no government, no wealth, and no pride. He wanted to be like the Dragons of myth. He wanted to the chivalrous leader of the Golden Dragons, the honorable hero everyone looked up to. He started with a sketch in the sand: an outline of the twofold. By the time he was a young adult, he had begun the re-creation of the legendary weapon, and he practiced his skills with the fearsome twofold in battle with Black Dragons and other exiles. Realizing it was a superior blade and gave the Black Dragons a metaphorical edge, Cairon rallied all the exiles, creating a vast army he had trained to perfection. Once Cairon had crafted enough twofolds to arm his military, he knew he would lead the Black Dragons against King Vran. The tyrant must fall—if not to the law, then to the sword. Although Cairon had become a warlord, the Black Dragons demand he take the throne. Thus was his rule established from the blood of a fallen king. He knew this to be the future.

When he was ready, the Black Dragons left their caves and attacked every major city that had been protected by King Vran. The goal had been to kill every Golden Dragon in sight. Faced against superior weapons, an organized military, and ambush after ambush, the Golden Dragons were powerless. These Imperial cities were all burned to the ground, and many of the floating islands that made up Sharl Vran had been stripped bare of life.

Suddenly, he remembered one such raid. He had led an attack against a village that was particularly close to where the Imperial capital was, and it had begun a little after sundown. As the place had been roasting, Kusvor had stumbled into a house and had found a poor dragonet. Obviously, his family had been killed. He did not know if it had been pity, fear, cowardice, or mercy that had emerged in his heart on that night, but whatever the reason, Kusvor had only knocked the dragonet aside.

More than likely, that dragonet was either dead or imprisoned by now, but to this day, Kusvor could not figure out why he had not killed the dragonet. He had clearly been a Golden Dragon and therefore Kusvor's sworn enemy, but he had let him live nevertheless. This dilemma had been haunting him since that night.

Then, as he gazed at the mural with the Divine Dragon of the Heavens and the Black Dragon, he felt something unusual in his heart. It was as if the effect of *mysteria* was stronger within him. He grinned for a moment.

Even the essence of my heart despises that Divine Dragon. He is the cause of all of this chaos. The Black Dragons had won the war, yet they obtained no prizes. That one Dragon took all honor from us, then. We were left with nothing. Though Kusvor had certainly not been alive during that time, the consequences of that historical event had affected his entire life.

He turned from the mural and began his return to the upper floors.

Sarn leaned against the golden wall impatiently. "Why are we always stuck with the idiots, Arnie?"

Her sister responded as she pulled back her hood to reveal her blonde ponytail, "Because this is what Y'tal has ordered us to come here. Call them whatever you want." Her face remained completely blank, though Sarn's face showed how upset she was. "You are the fastest one of us, and Y'tal likes to use you as an extra guard for the Great Servant."

Sarn merely scowled. "Being a bodyguard was always your job, even when the Dark Lord Dagan was around. Back then, I was a messenger though. I was never the fighting type. Typically, I just had to wait around at his fortress for more orders."

"You are still so hasty, Sarn," replied Arnim. "You cannot expect Y'tal to give us different orders if you refuse to change your personality. If he sees that you are skilled at other things, then he will use your strengths well. You haven't really been practicing the way you used to do so."

For once, Sarn did not have a crude remark. She had admitted to herself long ago that she found no sense in training her fighting abilities any further. Sure, she was stronger than most on Gevás, but she was not half as strong as most of the other Y'mordi. Fighting was Randir's specialty, not hers. If Y'tal needed a fighter, he would be the one that would be chosen for the job.

Thinking of Randir made her feel a pang of worry however, and she brought this emotion to Arnim's attention. "Hey, when do you think Randir is getting out of Stasis?"

Arnim's face changed to an expression of clear disgust at that moment. "What does it matter? What do you see in that pig anyways?"

Randir had always flirted with the two of them, but Arnim had never been impressed and had in fact despised Randir from the start. He was always so rebellious and never followed the rules. He lived with his head in dreams and memories. These were qualities that Arnim did not by any means admire.

Sarn made a childish, pouting face as she exclaimed, "He's not a pig!" She calmed down and thought back to him hanging in the prison in the Palace of Shadows. "Besides, aren't you the least bit worried about what will happen to him when he does get out? Whatever weird Stasis he's in…it'll break somehow before the end. Right?"

Arnim considered the question for a few seconds before saying, "Who knows? We don't know who did it, if anyone. Y'tal claims that Randir put himself into Stasis, a very odd possibility indeed. The form of Stasis is another mystery as well. No one can seem to break the spell, not even Xarden."

Sarn pushed herself from the wall and began pacing. "This place makes me restless, Arnim. I can't take it anymore." The walls had lost their luster, and all was silent in the halls. "I love this world so much, but we are stuck in this miserable castle. All the windows block out the wind. I can't take it."

Arnim rushed to her sister's side and put two gloved hands firmly on her shoulders. "Sarn, get a grip. We still have a while to go yet. Summon a Wind if you need to, but do not become too restless. Relax. You're usually pretty good at that."

Gradually, a breeze filled the room though there were no open windows. The breeze strengthened to a level that created ripples in the robes of the two Y'mordi. Sarn sighed and relaxed her fists. "Okay, Arnie, I guess I can wait it out. I think I will be fine."

"Are you sure?"

Sarn responded with a quick nod.

Suddenly, a door opened, and Kusvor entered the room. He growled at them instantly, "What are the two of you still doing here?"

"What do you mean, King Cairon?" inquired Sarn in puzzlement.

As he looked at the two of them, he found his dislike of humans grow into burning hatred. He felt a sharp pain in his heart as he felt the Darkness tighten around it. Although it hurt, he felt stronger. "If your goal was to protect me, then your goal has been fulfilled already now that I have the powers of the Darkness. There is no further need to shield me. No Dragon could stand against me. Why are you here in this world still?"

Arnim took a hesitant step forward and faked an explanation, "We are well aware of your hatred for humans, King Cairon, but we wanted to behold your power nevertheless. That is the real reason for us coming here." She paused, considering how to elaborate.

Luckily, Sarn offered, "Now that you have reached your true potential, we only wish to serve you. It is a great honor to serve a king who can wield the Darkness. Before long, you will be a true master of its power."

The twins waited patiently, hoping that Kusvor would accept their lie. The truth was that they had to ensure that Kusvor did conquer this world and then fully possess him through the Darkness. Once that happened, the Y'mordi would more or less have total control over Sharl Vran.

Finally, Kusvor replied softly, "I shall allow you to serve me yet, but you should be prepared to fight if need demands it. If I fight, so shall you, understood?"

They responded with a deep bow and a "Yes, King Cairon."

Kusvor approached one of the windows and surveyed the city around the castle. He whispered to himself, "If they are tired of the gold, then so be it. It is indeed time for change. I have been frustrated for too long by these Golden Dragons. Now, they shall be eradicated once and for all. Let the blackness rain down across this world."

His heart opened to the Darkness and little by little, and he let the Darkness fill him and swarm around him. The twins watch as the golden shine faded into black mist on the walls. "Come," he called to the women servants. Without another word, he charged through the window and allowed his gray wings to spread out as he flew above the castle and city.

Sarn and Arnim also leaped through the window and followed in pursuit. They were not in the least bit surprised when they felt a sharp tugging at their backs. Long, white wings sprouted from their backs, extending to full length instantly. They could fly almost as well as the dark king of the Dragons could. When they had entered Sharl Vran, the heart of the world had granted them new strengths that allowed them to survive better, which included these wings. In this aerial world, flight was the only regular means of transportation across the floating islands. As the mode of flight for the Dragons was through wings, so would visitors to the world possess wings.

As they reached the peak of the castle, Kusvor roared to the Y'mordi twins, "Is it possible to block out the light of the sun?"

The twins were fully appalled by Kusvor's spontaneous aggression that had come with his new powers. Sarn replied, "Not at your level, but allow me, King Cairon."

Kusvor nodded in approval as Sarn held her hands up to the sky. Her hood fell to her back, and a forceful Wind surrounded the three of them. Above them, the clouds assembled in a way that covered the entire sky for miles. Adding a few spells of Darkness turned the clouds pitch-black and strengthened their density, and the light of the sun faded from their view. It was as if an eternal night had taken over the Imperial capital.

As several Shadows—in the forms of black, wispy Dragons in this world—began to appear in the sky, Kusvor grinned maliciously. Though he did not know it, his heart was gradually becoming consumed by the Darkness.

Master and Apprentice

Elizabeth was home from another day at work, and it had been a fairly easy one, as well. Though she had always told her children how much she loved being a lawyer, it had always been one of her greatest hates in life. She secretly craved the life as a mage back on Gevás.

However, she was the head of the Ring of Elders, so she still had practice in the ways of *mysteria*, but it was not the same to her. On Gevás, she had had a great amount of people respecting her for her power and abilities, but here, the Ring of Elders were the only ones who even knew of her abilities. Not even her daughter Helen knew of her capacity in *mysteria*.

Feeling rather depressed, she sat down in her kitchen with the blue and white tiles, and she considered how empty the house was. All the dishes were in their cabinets; the counters and table were clean. No kids ran through the house, and there were no messes to clean. She pensively stared out the window.

A new danger had surfaced on Earth: the Lord of the Shadows. Randir was seeking out the legendary Black Joker, an entity that had been sealed away by the Ring ages ago.

She had felt surprisingly inclined to give Randir the information he needed solely because he had helped her son

Drage on multiple occasions on Gevás. She had been quite concerned about the fact when Drage had recounted his adventures to her.

Now, however, she regretted giving the Lord of the Shadows so much information. If he located the whereabouts of the Black Joker, this whole world would be in extreme peril. It had taken the whole Ring back then in order to seal the Black Joker. From what Elizabeth had understood, the Black Joker had been a malevolent prankster that delighted in advising rulers into starting wars and causing chaos. When the Ring of Elders had finally found him, he had retaliated with a shocking amount of *mysteria* that swiftly overwhelmed the Ring. It had taken multiple battles for the Ring to be able to defeat the Black Joker and immediately imprison him afterward.

As to where the Black Joker was located now, Elizabeth had only the faintest idea.

Suddenly, she heard a knock at the door. She rose to open it, and when she did so, she found the youth with the reddish-brown hair and leather jacket standing before her.

"Mr. Kane…" she muttered. "Did you find Drage?"

He appeared to be exhausted and almost depressed. "I did, but he was not what I had expected him to be, by any means. He turned me down flat."

Elizabeth sighed. Though at first, she had been quite scared by the young mage, she had honestly hoped that he would find a friend in her son. "Surely, he was not that bad, was he?" She gestured for Cameron to come inside the house. She had no intention of holding the conversation at her doorstep. Their steps were the only noises throughout the house. Her home seemed so empty and quiet without her three children there.

"We argued for a while, but he made it quite clear that he wanted nothing to do with me. He refused to even use *mysteria* against me. When I pushed him to try, he merely summoned that Sword of his. He treated me like I was a joke." He sat down at the kitchen table, while Elizabeth began boiling some water for tea.

Elizabeth found herself feeling disappointment toward her son. Cameron was an innocent enough person and would not have done anything wrong to Drage. Of course, she had known from the moment that Cameron had introduced his request to her that Drage would not allow Cameron to be his apprentice. Her hope had been that her son would listen to this man and at least offer some useful advice.

Drage had changed so much since his adventures in Gevás. He had become more sullen...more reserved. He never attempted to make new friends and seemed to have lost his spark. She supposed that Aria and Matthew had experienced a much more pleasurable time there, but Drage's time in the Y'mordi's cell in the Obsidian Plains must have been an absolutely horrible occurrence. Naturally, she would have blamed her husband John for allowing that to happen to her son, but Drage had revealed to her that the sorcerer Maris had killed John. That news had saddened her deeply. Granted, she had not seen him since Drage was just a baby. She had left John, knowing that he had to remain to lead Helio. She had not expected that to be the last time she would see him.

She finished the tea and gave Cameron a cup of the hot liquid. "How much sugar?" she asked tenderly.

Cameron only shook his head dismissively and waved a hand over the cup, using *mysteria* to sweeten it and cool it to a more reasonable temperature. Before he took a sip, he said, "I have been looking for him for years, but it was all for nothing. I don't know what to do now."

Elizabeth shrugged. "He might come around eventually. Drage wasn't always so pessimistic actually. On the contrary, he used to be very friendly and talkative. I suppose he still is that way with some of his closer friends, but he was never the same since he returned from Gevás."

The mage in the leather jacket, however, did not care that much about Drage Helius anymore. He stared intently at his cup, struggling to look Elizabeth in the eye while he was so upset. "No, I am done with him. I will not beg for him to take me now."

"Then, what will you do?"

Cameron hesitated before saying, "I think that the only thing I can do is join the Emperor's terra and work my way up the ranks. With that military experience, they might make an exception and allow me to become a sorcerer."

Elizabeth nodded sadly. "You are probably right. If the Emperor's Council is being as strict as you say, then you will have to show them that you have what it takes in a battle before they will find credibility in your strengths."

"I just wish that the Council was more accepting of help. I could probably beat some of the sorcerers they already have there. I am older than that girl Aria who became a wand master after being a sorcerer for only a week. Why couldn't I have come a little sooner?"

She was well aware of what Aria's situation had been. Drage had filled Elizabeth in on most of the details, and she too had been surprised by Mistress Leona's decision to make Aria a wand master, 3rd class. Nevertheless, the exception had been made then. Gevás seemed to have changed a lot since Elizabeth had last been there.

She offered soothingly, "You will get there, Mr. Kane. I am sure of this fact. I have to ask though: Why did you come back here? If you were already set that you would not talk to Drage again, why did you come back?"

Cameron looked up at her through his long hair. "I don't know. Maybe I just needed to talk to some—"

Suddenly, Elizabeth felt something through *mysteria* and summoned a Gate as she grabbed Cameron. The two fell through the Gate that led to the small dock outside the house that stretched out across the lake. The sound of a massive explosion hit their ears as they fell onto the wood.

They stood rapidly and watched the house burst into flames. The roof had caved in, and the walls were splitting too as if the flames had intense weight to them. Waves of heat washed over them from the burning ruins.

Cameron exclaimed, "What just happened?!"

Tears filled Elizabeth's eyes as she watched her home burn to the ground. "Why did you do this?" she asked the figure she knew was standing behind them.

Randir spoke sternly, "I know you can fix it, Elder. I merely wanted to ask you if you were sure that you had no other information regarding the Black Joker. I—"

Before he could finish his explanation, Elizabeth manipulated the lake, creating a serpent consisted entirely of water that wrapped around Randir and dragged him under the water's surface.

Cameron was dumfounded, "Was he serious? Are you one of the Elders?"

Elizabeth's brown hair swayed fiercely in the smoking wind. The heat from Randir's Fire spell was already making her sweat. "Yes, Mr. Kane. I am the head of the Ring of Elders." Cameron's eyes went wide as he took a step back. "Do you know the legends of the Lords of the Shadows, Mr. Kane?"

He stumbled for the right words. "Well…I…Yes, I know the legends. There were seven of them in Gevás a thousand years ago. Along with being Servants of Dagan, they were powerful sorcerers and terrifying warriors, right?"

Finally, Randir shot out from the lake and landed on the beach, drenched. He grinned as he regarded Elizabeth. "That was a rather tough spell to get out of, Elder. I believe, however, that you did not answer my question. Do you have the information?" he repeated.

"I told you once, and I shall tell you again. Stay out of it, Randir. You will only get yourself into more trouble than you are asking for." She unleashed a blue wave of Stasis to trap Randir, but he sidestepped away from the spell. With a grunt of annoyance, she cast a spell on the beach itself. In an explosion, the sand whirled around Randir in a storm, and it started to create a mound around him, attempting to bury him alive. Before he could react, Elizabeth tightened the sand to become a solid stone block with Randir trapped inside it.

Cameron was in utter awe at Elizabeth's strength.

"Mr. Kane, they are real, and for some reason, they are here on Earth, or at least this one is. He is threatening whatever peace this world has. If he has his way, every living being here could die."

Gradually, the stone block began to glow red-hot. It was melting from the inside. Cameron replied, "What are we going to do? If the legends are true after all, the Lords of the Shadows should be almost impossible to defeat."

"Maybe, just maybe, he will take the hint." More sand joined the stone block and covered the parts that were melting. She focused her *mysteria* to strengthen the spells, making it harder to melt.

Randir had finally had enough. The whole stone block exploded in a flash of lightning. The stone pieces turned to sand as they left his body. "Are you done with your tricks, Elder?"

Elizabeth retorted, "Are you done with this Black Joker business?"

Randir's red eyes seemed ablaze at that moment. "Do you think that I would not burn other things of more importance, Elder? You told me that at one point I saved your son. I could go back on that and hurt him. I am not a man you wish to cross, Elder." He prepared a fireball. "Tell me how to find him."

Elizabeth prepared a defensive spell herself. "We can do this all day, and it will just leave you more frustrated than you already are. You will accomplish nothing."

Growling, he turned away. A Gate made of Fire appeared in front of him, and he stepped into it, embracing its heat.

Elizabeth drove away from the small community of Paradise Shores sadly. Her family's home had blown to destruction, and her own life had been threatened. Memories of Gevás came swarming back to her, and she began to realize that her time here on Earth, her time with her children, had only ever meant to be temporary—all an illusion in the end.

Meanwhile, Cameron Kane watched the scenery go by in confusion. "We could have fixed your house," he offered.

"No, too many people saw it on fire more than likely. I couldn't just fix it up and tell them that they were hallucinating. I also do not have the time to be worrying about maintaining my regular life at this point, either. Randir is threatening the whole world, and I cannot worry about keeping the house tidy."

"Well, why are you driving instead of summoning a Gate?"

Elizabeth sighed. "It's comforting…and I've charmed it with a barrier. It's small, but the Lords of the Shadows won't be able to track or find us."

Cameron turned to face Elizabeth. "Okay, you need to tell me what is going on here. What is this Lord of the Shadows wanting here? What could he do to endanger the whole world?"

"A long time ago, there was an entity, a mage, known as the Black Joker. No one knows where he came from or what he really was. As fuel for his sick humor, he manipulated kings, queens, leaders, and generals to start wars and spread his ideals of chaos throughout the world. He delighted in the pain of others and in their deaths, so the Ring of Elders at that time tried to get rid of him. However, he was a lot more adept with *mysteria* than they expected. Their spells could mark him, but nothing could kill him. Their only option was to try to imprison him."

Cameron was still perplexed. "What does this have to do with the Lord of the Shadows though?"

Elizabeth elaborated, "Randir believes that he can find where the Black Joker is imprisoned. He plans to use the entity for some kind of power, though I am quite confident that once the Black Joker is freed, he will merely wreak havoc across Earth and not do as Randir wants him to do."

Then, the two were silent for several minutes. Cameron was considering what they could do to stop Randir. He scratched his chin thoughtfully, scowling. "What if we just pestered him?"

"Excuse me?"

"What if we tried to slow his progress? If he is constantly coming across dead ends and has us to worry about fighting every step of the way, he might just give up."

Elizabeth frowned first. "I don't know, Mr. Kane. He has threatened to come after those I care for, namely my children. I am not sure he will just give up as you claim."

"Can't we go and find them and give them the same barrier you used on the car? It's a step in the right direction."

She considered this as she stared into the distance. "Perhaps, you are right. It's a start anyway, Mr. Kane."

"You know you can call me Cameron, right?"

"I'm going to assemble the Ring of Elders. Together, all of us can get rid of this problem. I suppose you will have to come as well, though." She summoned a massive Gate in front of the moving car that engulfed it instantly. They appeared in the desert.

Elizabeth exited the car as a brilliant light so bright it rivaled even the sun filled the sky. "That will signal the other Elders," she explained to Cameron who had just gotten out of the car as well.

Within a few seconds, several other Gates appeared, bringing the other Elders. Once all the plainly dressed and gray-haired Elders were standing in a ring-like formation, Elizabeth began their sudden meeting. "I have terrible news. The man we met with the other day was indeed a Lord of the Shadows, and he does indeed seek the Black Joker." This statement generated many gasps and quiet conversations along the Ring.

Cameron was feeling excitement, nervousness, and utter shock at what he was experiencing: He was sitting in at a meeting of the Ring of Elders.

Elizabeth continued, "However, I have a plan for stopping him."

An outburst came from another of the Elders, "Who is that boy with you?"

"This one?" Elizabeth gestured to Cameron. "He is a mage I have taken as my apprentice. Now, please, let us focus on the matter at hand."

Cameron could not tell if she was lying or telling the truth. Naturally, he would have suspected it to be a smart and impressive lie, but something in her voice said otherwise.

"We are going to attack him everywhere he goes. At every point, he must meet resistance."

An Elder replied, "How are we going to find him?"

"Leave that to me," Elizabeth said calmly. "Know that I am going to mark him so that any one of you could track him down, and we will take shifts at attacking him. Make sure to use all of your knowledge of *mysteria* and do not aim for a kill. Aim to annoy if anything. If he is pestered enough by us, he will surely leave over time."

The Elder that had asked about Cameron inquired, "How sure are you of this plan? One-on-one, he could kill any one of us."

Elizabeth snapped, "That's why we must always strike in threes. I am quite confident we can do this. Any other questions?"

The other Elders shook their heads. Their Gates reappeared as they left the meeting place.

Finally, Cameron and Elizabeth were left alone again.

Elizabeth went forward with her plan. "Now, we need to place a tracking device on Randir." She held up her hand to dispel the Light above them and replace it with a massive fireball that spread across the sky, giving the appearance of a burning sky: the fire roared and rippled from horizon to horizon like a cloud of flames.

Cameron interrupted her working mind, "That was a pretty clever lie you made back there."

However, Elizabeth kept focusing on the spell. At last, she replied, "It was no lie. If it is okay with you, I would like for you to be my apprentice."

In an instant, all of Cameron's worries about Drage, joining the army, and becoming a sorcerer in Gevás disappeared. He had been given the opportunity to be the apprentice of the head of the Ring of Elders. His heart seemed to stop. With eyes wide, he responded shakily. "I would like that very much."

Though Elizabeth was showing no reaction, Cameron could not get rid of the huge grin that was on his face.

She strengthened her Fire spell and waited for Randir to respond to it. After a few minutes in the desert heat, a Gate appeared.

"Have you called me with more information, Elder?" began Randir.

"On the contrary, I actually came to challenge you. You destroyed my house, and I want compensation for that." Without another word, she sent a burst of Light at Randir. Because he had not expected such a sudden attack, it hit him at full blast, but he did not budge.

"You are going to have to do better than that, Elder," he said as he threw his own fireball at her. She dodged it and summoned a Gate.

"Cameron, let's go."

Together, the two disappeared to re-enter Massachusetts, leaving a puzzled Randir behind them.

Cameron asked eagerly, "Did you do it?"

"Yes," she responded. "It was the same spell that I used to summon the Ring though slightly weaker. I believe that the other Elders will recognize it to be my tracking device of sorts. Randir will not be able to sense it, but he will find the Elders following his every move. No matter what he does, he will find us waiting for him."

Cameron nodded, impressed. "So, what do we do now?"

Elizabeth sighed deeply. "Now, we rest." They had reappeared near a hotel. "It has been a long day for both of us, and I shall allow the other Elders to take care of Randir for now. By the time he realizes what I did, we will both be gone, and he will not be able to track us. We can track him, but not the other way around. Would rather not have a Lord of the Shadows sneaking up on us."

"And what about…my training?"

"For now, I need to see how well you do without me. If we engage Randir tomorrow, I want you to take part as well. I have not seen you cast a single spell yet. Your training will begin when I have a firm understanding of your present abilities. For now, use spells when you can and learn from mine when you can. That is the way of the apprentice. Do you understand?"

Cameron replied with a grin, "Yes, master. I understand."

"Good. We will have an even longer day ahead of us tomorrow. Plus, I think it is time I talk to my daughter. She will wonder where I am if she has tried to call me." She took comfort in the fact there was no way Randir would know where she was, if he even knew she existed. Drage...he could probably protect himself at this point...she hoped. "It is time for her to know the truth about things. Then, I shall go and find Drage. Perhaps, he could offer some assistance if he has been practicing *mysteria*. The last time we talked, he told me that he refused to use any spells, but I could sense it when he was at home: He has been practicing ever since he returned from Gevás."

As they approached the door to the hotel, Cameron said, "How powerful could this Black Joker be now?"

Elizabeth responded simply, "More dangerous than a nuclear bomb, Cameron. In the past, he was called Loki, a god of chaos. While he was a manipulator, not a fighter himself, now...after his imprisonment, he is going to be angry. When cornered, he killed several mages with ease. It took many of the mages all they had to imprison him. If the Lords of the Shadows do free him, he could shake the very foundations of this world."

In the World of Dragons

The wind felt empowering beneath his wings. There was no ground beneath him, and thick clouds surrounded him. The setting sun gave these clouds an orange tint and was almost blinding to Draconis.

Sharl Vran was a world that consisted of air mostly with a large ball of fire at its center. By some strange force, there were several islands that floated in various locations throughout the gaseous world. Those islands held the Dragon cities for which Draconis was searching. He had relished this particular flight for several hours without coming across one of the floating islands.

He tried his hardest not to think about Gevás, or the Emperors of Light, or the Third Obsidian War. His worries were lost in the extravagant breeze. Each flap of his wings felt exhilarating. Every deep breath of air was a thrill, and every beat of his heart was a rapid rhythm. His golden, serpentine body stretched along the wind and displayed his elegant scales and sharpened claws. His thin whiskers billowed against his face annoyingly, while his claws were tucked against his body.

Finally, he managed to make out one of the islands ahead of him. Increasing his speed, he came closer and closer to the floating rock. There was not a city on the island, but there was a small forest. As he landed, he became more and more aware of how quiet the island was. He could not hear birds, running water, other Dragons, or even the wind itself, though he could feel its force against his body.

The trees were perfectly still as he walked among them. "What is going on here?" he asked the wind, not trusting the quiet. However, there was no response. His claws dug into the dirt below him. His blue eyes glanced down at the ground and searched for some sign or tracks. He was not surprised when he found nothing.

He opened his heart to *mysteria* and became aware of another presence in the forest. He wheeled around to face the being and could sense that a Dragon was hiding behind one of the trees perfectly. His claw went to his sword instantly, but the other Dragon noticed the motion and spun from behind the tree to attack Draconis with her own silver sword. Draconis barely blocked it with a back-handed grip.

The two blades held their position. The two Dragons, Golden and Black, stared at each other in the eyes. Draconis was fully surprised by his opponent's weapon, the twofold. His blue eyes gazed deeply into her red eyes.

His mouth grumbled the word, "*Lune*." Suddenly, the two Dragons were repelled from each other. Draconis, having been the one who cast the spell, recuperated quickly and attacked once more. The Black Dragon had expected the incoming slash and held her twofold so that Draconis's blade slipped into the space between the two blades of the twofold. With a wrenching twist of her blade, the Black Dragon twisted Draconis's own sword out of his hands, and his blade went flying into a tree. Draconis was utterly surprised to find her sword pointed dangerously at his throat.

"Who are you?" commanded the Black Dragon.

Draconis breathed heavily from the short skirmish. "My name is Rexam Draconis. As strange as it may sound, I just got back from another world. I've been gone for around a hundred and fifty years."

The Black Dragon smirked. "I would believe you, but there's one problem. I don't think there's any way that you could have escaped Cairon then. That would have been nearly impossible." Her twofold lowered slightly.

Draconis replied sternly, "I speak the truth. I came from one of the Imperial cities. I don't know what all has happened in my absence, but I came to see how I can help. I'm not interested in your games."

Now, the Black Dragon was stunned. She took a step backward and exclaimed, "What? You can't be serious!" Without wasting a moment, Draconis leaped to where his sword was and drew it in time to block another attack of the Black Dragon's twofold.

Dancing between the trees, the two fought again, blades clashing. Draconis allowed his attacks to flow smoothly into each other to create a whirling combo. The Black Dragon moved like a snake, dodging every strike. Within seconds, the Black Dragon disarmed Draconis a second time in the same fashion as the first.

She grinned, proud of her ability. "If what you say is true, Rexam, then why are you here now? It is too late for your kind. Cairon has eliminated almost every Golden Dragon in this world. For all you know, you could be the last one."

Although the comment enraged him, he growled, tensing. "I might be the last one, but if that is so, then I will do what the duty I have been given demands and fight Cairon as the last of my kind."

Then, he could not take it anymore, and a ball of Fire left his golden claws to attack the Black Dragon. The distraction gave him time to once again retrieve his sword.

However, before he could reach it, he felt a small nick on the back of his neck. He did not have to turn his head to know that the Black Dragon had just barely missed decapitating him. His sword flashed as it spun to attack the Black Dragon.

To his surprise, though, the Black Dragon was not behind him to finish the job. She was resting against a tree, relaxed. She asked simply, "Are you for real?"

"What do you mean?" As he spoke, he realized that his voice was becoming somewhat slurred.

"You would fight against Cairon? Even if it was just by yourself?"

Draconis stumbled as he approached the Black Dragon. "Of course, I would. I saw him once, and he did not kill me. I could survive another encounter, I believe."

The Black Dragon's red eyes widened slightly. "You have survived meeting Kusvor Cairon?"

Before he could respond, he began to notice that his vision was blurring as well. "What...what did you do to me?" he inquired with a fuzzy feeling in his head.

"My twofold is poisoned." Within merely a couple of yards from the Black Dragon, he collapsed.

When he finally awoke, he could hear the sound of waves washing over a thousand shells along the beach. As his blue eyes opened, he saw several thick clouds cover the night sky above him. The air was cool and felt nice against his scales.

Gradually, he rose to a sitting position and was amazed by what he was seeing.

He was in the middle of a bustling encampment on the side of a lake. To his left was the forest, and to his right was the white beach. All around him were Dragons of almost every color: Blue, White, Golden, Red, Brown, Silver, and Green. Then, he saw the female Black Dragon approaching him. Each of the Dragon races were being represented in this unusual camp.

He asked her perplexedly, "What is going on? I thought you were going to kill me."

The Black Dragon responded with an air of dignity, "No, how could I kill one of the remaining Golden Dragons?"

As he looked around and observed some of the Golden Dragons that were in the camp, he said, "Well, it does not look as if I am the last one, after all. You were testing me earlier, were you not?"

The Black Dragon nodded. "This camp…is dedicated to going against Cairon and overthrowing his rule. It is not that he has been a particularly terrible ruler. It is simply that he does not deserve the Dragon's crown. He took it by force, and that was not right of him. We are going to take it away from him and then give it to someone who better respects the Dragon's honor," she explained.

He slowly rose to his feet, still feeling dizzy from whatever poison had put him to sleep. "Why did you attack me in the forest?"

Her black tail curled around her feet in embarrassment. "You are the one who grabbed your weapon first. I was merely responding to your attacks. Don't accuse me for it!"

Then, Draconis asked the question that had really been bugging him. "Why are you here? Are you not one of Cairon's own kind?"

"I am, but I left the Imperial cities, hoping to find a Golden Dragon. I am actually the one who started this group. We are all the Dragons left who want to see Cairon removed. He killed and tortured hundreds of Dragons to gain personal power. Everyone here wants to see another ruler on the throne. I have led most of the raids."

"Raids?" inquired Draconis.

"Yes," stated the Black Dragon. "Occasionally, we attack one of the smaller Imperial cities to take their resources and their pride. It is a common method of attack for a Black Dragon, which is why Cairon will not see it coming. The past few raids have been mostly stealth missions, and, to our scouts' knowledge, Cairon has no idea what we've even been doing. If anything, he will only think it is the cause of a few Golden Dragons. He has been working rather sluggishly on weeding out the remaining few over the past few decades, and we are taking advantage of that mistake."

Draconis was thoroughly impressed by the success of these rebels so far. Despite overwhelming odds, they had become organized. They had made small victories with limited resources and limited training. It reminded him of the struggle that was occurring at Gevás at this very moment. It seemed like the chance to fight for what he believed in without having the complete obligation and subservience as he had in Gevás. Of course, he never minded serving the Emperors of Light, but it was a liberating feeling knowing that those obligations did not bind him here.

The Black Dragon turned to see a Blue Dragon approaching them. The Blue Dragon made a swift salute to the Black Dragon before saying, "Elani, we've found another Dragon in the forest. We think that it is a Silver. What do we do?"

The Black Dragon named Elani responded, "Hm…the Silver Dragons are always such wanderers. It should be productive for at least the first few missions. I shall see to this one personally. Lly, would you mind showing Rexam around the camp?"

The Blue Dragon named Lly nodded acquiescingly and gestured for Draconis to follow her along the beach.

He walked beside her and could not help but admire how glistening her blue scales were. He knew that Blue Dragons were masters of Liquid spells of the Element Water and usually lived on beaches such as these.

She began softly as she pointed to a part of the encampment, "Over there is where the captains meet. That usually includes Elani, myself, and a few others. You should be meeting them rather soon, I suppose. Elani said you were wanting to fight. Is this correct?"

Draconis nodded. "Yes, I would like to fight Cairon. What is the overall plan for defeating him exactly?"

Lly responded, "Well, Elani thinks that we should focus on taking his Imperial cities first and then aim for his fortress. If we forced the Black Dragons we captured to fight with us, then Cairon would be no problem." Her voice was confident yet soft. It made Draconis think of the quiet but powerful waves of the sea.

"That does not sound like a bad idea," began Draconis skeptically. "However, I am not so sure that it is the most honorable idea. Are you all just going to surround him and murder him on the spot? If you do that, you will be no worse than he is." He knew that he was not the best example of honor, but he also was aware that it remained a part of a Dragon's morality.

Lly interrupted as she pointed to another building, "There is where the blacksmith works. If you need a weapon repaired or constructed, see him." Then, she considered Draconis's words. "Rexam, your words carry a surprising amount of sense. I feel inclined to ask how you would lead this attack?"

"Well, I would definitely conquer the Imperial cities as Elani is doing, but then I would issue a direct challenge to Cairon. I would not hide behind an army in cowardice; I would be at the front. Of course, in order to effectively challenge him, I would have to remove his final supporters, the Dragons in the Imperial capital."

"And how would you perform that feat?"

"By diverting his attention. I suppose that the easiest way would be to act as if a different goal was in our minds, such as conquering more of the world first. If we try to expand our territory and leave him alone, he would only be angered by the action and send a large amount of troops to wherever we were pretending to extend our borders. Doing this would leave him far more unprotected, leaving me the opportunity to challenge him."

Suddenly, Lly stopped in her tracks. She turned her head to face Draconis. "You think you can take on Kusvor Cairon by yourself?"

Draconis growled, "I came here with the intent to stop him. I was a general in Gevás, one of the strongest fighters that world knows. Cairon *will* submit."

"Perhaps, I shall mention it to Elani. She told us that you claimed to have come from this other world."

Draconis nodded deeply. "Yes, that is correct. When Cairon attacked the Imperial city I lived in, I managed to barely escape him and went to an underwater world called Gevás. I have spent a century and a half there as a guard and a military general."

Lly's eyes widened. His military expertise was not what surprised her. It was his past that was of a great interest. He was from one of the Imperial cities. "Ah, I see…" she muttered, not revealing why she was so interested. "Please, let us continue the tour. Then, we may go and speak to some of the captains."

A question came to Draconis's mind then. "Lly, what about the other Golden Dragons? How did they survive Cairon's attacks?" He found it to be a rather important question.

A sigh escaped from Lly's lips. "They were not born in the Imperial cities. They were raised with other races. To be honest, they have never met Cairon in their entire lives. They simply want to fight to bring honor to the Golden Dragons."

"So…" Draconis began rather timidly. "I was the only survivor of Cairon's attacks?"

"Yes."

Elani spoke firmly to the other captains that were under the tent. A long table with a map on it filled most of the space, and the Dragons all circled it, studying it carefully. "The next city is considerably closer to the capital. We are going to have to make sure that we keep the operation as covert as possible. We are sending several spies to the area to help plan our exact strategy."

A Brown Dragon responded to the introduction. "How soon are we attacking, Elani?"

The Black Dragon turned her head toward the Brown Dragon and said, "It shall be in a week's time. We must prepare for this attack well, because it shall be a much more dangerous mission this time. We are going to need an adept set of archers to get rid of most of the guards and lookouts. Our soldiers need to aim for quick attacks that can disable the enemy. Volwyth, can you make sure that happens?"

"Yes, Elani," replied the Red Dragon. "How are we going to approach the city exactly? If it is close to the capital, then I am sure we will be spotted well before we actually strike."

That was the one part of the plan in which Elani actually lacked confidence. "That is going to be another objective of our spies: to cause several chaotic distractions throughout the city as we are approaching. Even if they spot us relatively early, their hands will be too full to be able to stop us altogether."

Draconis was thoroughly impressed by the plan. It seemed to be quite well thought out by Elani. That Black Dragon was certainly an interesting one. Her back was a particularly interesting physical attribute, Draconis decided, even for a Black Dragon. It was as if her back were divided into seven or eight large rows of scales. It reminded Draconis of a suit of armor with several plates of black metal overlapping each other.

Though Elani seemed to be quite a commanding individual, Draconis could see that Elani was hiding her true personality. Her whole demeanor seemed to be quite forced. He sensed a much softer, kinder, and even lonely Dragon beneath those armor-like scales.

Lly began, "Elani, one of our scouts at the capital has reported back to us and has revealed some interesting new information." All heads swiveled to face Lly. Draconis noticed that Lly was relatively highly ranked and regarded here. "It seems that there is an unusual storm hovering above the capital. Pitch-black clouds block out the sun but bring no rain or snow. The rumors have said that the blackness is a sign of Cairon's rebirth."

The Red Dragon Volwyth, along with everyone else, was completely perplexed. He tilted his large, horned head toward Lly, his deep voice resounding, "What do you mean by his rebirth?"

Lly swallowed nervously. "Our scouts have apparently discovered that Cairon claims to have found new powers, powers that can summon the darkness. The storm is supposedly his doing."

While the captains in the room were debating the truth in the claims, Draconis was debating how Cairon learned the ways of *mysteria*. While humans could have several strong Elements in their hearts, Dragons always had a sole Element they could utilize. That Element was dependent on the Dragon's race. For Golden Dragons, the Element was Fire, but more specifically, it was the form Flame. For Black Dragons like Elani and Cairon, the Element was the form Poison of Nature. Dragons were not really aware of the existence of *mysteria* or the Elements. They merely understood that each race could manipulate specific parts of nature. Draconis and Cairon were probably the only two Dragons in Sharl Vran who knew that, however. They were the only ones who could use an Element other than the Elemental form unique to their races. Although Dragons were generally aware of other worlds, they simply had no interest in them. Most Dragons had at least distrust for humans, and most of the other worlds had humans as their top inhabitants.

Draconis decided to volunteer some of his information. "Elani," he began. Everyone looked at him in surprise. He was still the new Dragon, and no one knew what to think of him yet. "I believe that these rumors are true, and I have proof that they are, as well. May I demonstrate?"

Elani's red eyes glared at the Golden Dragon. She was still not quite sure why Lly had insisted on Draconis's coming to this meeting. However, she knew that Draconis could probably prove his point. When she had fought him in the forest, he had been able to use some strange ability that repelled the two of them from each other. Nevertheless, she nodded in confirmation to Draconis.

Draconis walked to the middle of the tent and said, "While I was away these past few years, I learned about interesting abilities that all individuals possess: *mysteria*. It is in our hearts and is connected to our emotions. Every Dragon race is connected to an Element or form of *mysteria*. The Red Dragons have an affinity for Lava, while the Blue Dragons have an affinity for Liquid. The thing you do not know, however, is that that affinity has nothing to do with your race. It has to do with how you are raised and which emotions you feel. Red Dragons only *learn* Lava. It's the only thing they have ever tried teaching each other. We've been taught it has to do with our blood, but it's not. Anyone can use any of the Elements. Observe." He looked around and witnessed no reaction from his audience. Then, he muttered the word, "*Dlaez.*"

Instantly, three chunks of Ice hovered around him. This time, the captains gasped in shock. He continued his demonstration gladly, "As you can see, I am a Golden Dragon that can summon Ice. Now, I shall show you a spell that no Dragon is familiar with." Again, he whispered. "*Voe.*"

Air roared violently into the tent, causing papers to scatter and the tent walls to billow fiercely.

At this point, half of the captains were terrified, while the other half were quite impressed by Draconis's feats. Lly and Elani, however, were completely blank.

Elani inquired then, "Can you show us what Cairon did with this storm?"

Draconis was quite astonished by the question. Never before had he found the necessity to utilize the Element of Darkness. Therefore, he had never learned how to manipulate it. He shook his head in shame. "Elani, I can use Fire, Water, Wind, Earth, Nature, and Light, but I cannot manipulate the Darkness. I apologize."

Lly smiled slightly at Draconis, "Do not worry, Rexam. You have given us quite a bit of useful information here. We shall discuss what you have said and will summon you when we have more questions."

Draconis made a gracious bow and then exited the tent. He knew an order when he heard one, and he was not the type to disobey such orders.

He sighed as he walked across the beach. There was simply too much on his mind at the moment. In the distance, he saw the light at the blacksmith. Perhaps, he could volunteer his services for a few hours.

A few minutes later, the other captains left the tent. It was just Elani and Lly remaining. "Lly, would you walk with me, please?"

"Of course, Lani," replied Lly, using her nickname for her close friend.

The two Dragons began walking along the beach and observed the twinkling stars that shone above them. Elani began hesitantly, "Lly, this new Golden Dragon is proving to be quite interesting. If Cairon has truly learned of the abilities of *mysteria*, then we could be in a great amount of trouble."

Lly nodded softly in agreement. "You are right. It seems that our previous strategy might be ineffective against his new weapon, but we cannot lose now, Lani. What do you think we should do?"

However, Elani's firm composure began to soften. Her eyes drooped sadly. "I do not know, Lly. We have worked so hard to get where we are already, but it might take an even more immense amount of work to stand against Cairon now."

The Blue Dragon patted Elani's back to comfort her. "And what of the Golden Dragon? Could he be of a greater use to us?" Lly had found Rexam Draconis to be attractive with his well-polished, golden scales and thin whiskers.

Gradually, a thought occurred to Elani. "He-he shall be our secret weapon. He might be the answer to this new dilemma. Perhaps, Rexam could use his skills in *mysteria* to strengthen our own armies. Though Cairon is obviously much older than Rexam, he might have less experience in *mysteria*. We could win this yet." A smile began to spread across Elani's black face. Her red eyes reflected the starlight eerily, yet they revealed a sense of peace and satisfaction.

"Lani…he was from one of the Imperial cities."

The glow left Elani's eyes then. Her smile faded.

Lly continued, "Does he know what that means?"

Elani shook her head doubtfully. "I do not think that he does. He had to have been quite young at that time, much too young to know the governing laws."

"Are you going to tell him?"

Elani again shook her head. "No, if I tell him, then everything he does will be for completely different reasons. I want him to help us and fight against Cairon just as we are. If he knows the laws, that will only complicate things further."

The two were silent for a few seconds, and then Lly said, "What are you going to expect him to do while we prepare to attack the next city?"

"He shall train and teach. In the morning, we shall discover his strengths, his weaknesses, and what he has to offer us. It may be that, after a few battles, he could join us as a captain."

Lly was inspired by Elani's words. For the past few years, the two had been almost as close as sisters. The only odd thing about the relationship was the fact that she was a Blue Dragon while Elani was a Black Dragon. It was often frowned upon in Dragon society to get too close to a Dragon of another race, but Elani's campaign had been about breaking those segregations.

Lly's thoughts went back to the Golden Dragon Rexam. He seemed like an honest enough Dragon and a polite one, as well.

Elani, on the other hand, was thinking of how useful Rexam would be in defeating Cairon. He could be the greatest weapon against the black tyrant. Her only concern was that Rexam did not become too aware of the laws of Sharl Vran. Golden Dragons had a habit of being too proud and stupid.

The Compendium of Myriads

The three men stood in front of the massive metallic wall covered with tens of black computer screens. Though Marqest had known this computer for most of his life, Matthew was only slightly familiar with the technology, and Drage had never had the chance to even understand that much of it. He only knew what Matthew had told him about it.

The goliath technology looked as new and intelligent as it had five years ago. The mile-long and mile-tall chamber showed no signs of aging or breaking. It had remained just as they had left it.

Marqest beamed proudly at the all-knowing computer he had named COM, the Compendium of Myriads. Packed with information, COM could answer almost any question and do almost anything. Marqest had programmed it with a very unique feature: a mind. It was able to connect to *mysteria* in ways still unknown fully to Drage.

He called out in excitement, "COM, you may awaken now."

Instantly, each black screen flickered to life, revealing a digitized face that consisted of several blue zeros and ones. "Marqest, you have returned, I see."

Drage was truly appalled by the spectacle of the computer that could think of its own accord.

"Yes, I am back at last. I wish I had not had to leave you five years ago. However, I had other matters to which I had to attend. I pray that you have not been idle in my absence, COM?" Marqest asked hopefully.

All of a sudden, all of the screens except for one that displayed the digital face began shuffling through random images of Gevás over the past five years. "Indeed, I have not been idle, Marqest. Rather, I have stayed at my full potential, and now, you have come to me in order to learn more about the remedy to Dragenopn Helius's Heartbind."

While Drage was even more impressed now, Marqest and Matthew were not surprised in the least. "Yes, that is correct, COM," replied Marqest.

"Well, then, I hope that you understand when I say that it is by all records incurable by anyone other than the person inflicted. It is a connection between two hearts and cannot be severed so forcefully," COM explained.

Drage argued this point however. "What about Maris's death? Shouldn't that have gotten rid of the curse?"

COM countered, "Your logic is quite reasonable. However, one must take into account that even *mysteria* has a record of experiencing inexplicable phenomena. Also, it could be that though his body was killed, Maris's heart might have survived."

Matthew frowned in confusion. "How could his heart survive? That does not make any sense."

"The spirit, or soul as some call it, is the non-physical aspect of a being. There have been instances when a person was so strongly connected to a realm of a world that his or her spirit remained in that realm. You are an Earthan, so perhaps you shall be more familiar with the term 'ghost?'"

Drage could not believe what he was hearing. It was becoming too supernatural now. "Are you trying to tell me that I am being haunted by Maris's ghost?"

Marqest was also stunned by the idea. "COM, are you sure that this is a real possibility?"

"My statistics show that there is a 65.0% chance of the cause being from a spirit. Also, there is a 34.6% chance of the cause being entirely inexplicable."

Anger swept over Drage. He was becoming so tired of having other things control his life, and he was not pleased that a spirit was manipulating his heart. He stared up into the digital face on the screens. "Alright, how am I supposed to get rid of a ghost exactly?"

The silver walls echoed the sounds throughout the room strangely. After the eerie echoes ceased, the blue face replied, "There are several ways to get rid of a spirit, and to be honest, your Spirit Sword would probably do the job."

Drage held out his hand in curiosity, and the blazing, blue Sword of Destiny materialized by a beam of light in his outstretched hand. It was one of the tricks he had mastered over the years. "It can cut through spirits, too?"

Marqest spoke before COM had a chance. "Not exactly, Dragenopn. In actuality, the piece of spirit that resides in your Sword has enough power to physically combat any spirits it comes in contact with. Because your piece came from the Great Spirit, it will more than likely defeat the enemy spirit."

"The hardest task is not the defeating of Maris's spirit," explained COM in its neutral, robotic voice. "The hardest task is locating that spirit. I suppose that the greatest tracking device in this particular case would be your own heart, Dragenopn Helius. The closer you are to him, the stronger his pull will be."

Suddenly, Matthew became aware of the blue aura around Drage's Sword. "Hey, Drage, why is the Sword glowing like that? I do not remember it doing that before."

Drage shrugged in equal puzzlement. "It's been doing this for a while now. I don't know what caused it, though. It did this once before, when Maris had me in that prison on the Obsidian Plains."

"The piece of spirit is responding," muttered Marqest. "The brighter it glows, the more active it is at that moment. The piece of spirit in your Sword is understanding every word we say and is watching every action we make. I do not know why it is responding now, but it is, nevertheless." He stared curiously at the blade. "It must be sensing something…It protected you from Maris in the battle outside Apolis."

"The Sword of Destiny only allows those who affect the destiny of the world to wield it," called COM. Its mechanic voice resounded throughout the room. "It acts to protect those it chooses and to sever all ties to the physical world. Walls, rocks, storms, and even spells are broken before its sharp blade."

Most of what COM was saying was news to Drage. He had never learned that much about his own Sword. His father had left most of it as a mystery to him. He was finding the curse of Maris's ghost to be a far less interesting thing in comparison to the topic of the Sword of Destiny. "What else can you tell me about it?" he inquired anxiously.

"A thousand years ago, the Great Spirit, the central deity that watched over this world, was attacked by the Lord of the Darkness Dagan. The attack forced the Spirit to divide into five pieces. Each piece fled to find refuge, a guardian. One of these pieces attached itself to the Lord of Light Lux's own sword. This connection gave the sword great power, and the Great Lord Lux discovered many attributes to the Sword including its preference for those who hold the world in their grasps, such as the Lords of Light. Therefore, since that time, the Sword of Destiny has been an heirloom among the Lords of Light and has never left their possession."

Drage was fully intrigued by the short story. He had never truly heard anything about his Spirit Sword. "What else do you know about it?"

Marqest interrupted this conversation, however. "No, Dragenopn. We need to figure out what we are going to do about your Heartbind problem. COM, are you sure that there is not an easier way to track down Maris's ghost, if that is indeed the problem?"

COM seemed to analyze data for a few seconds before replying, "Marqest, my statistics are not revealing any flaws in my reasoning: His heart is the quickest way to locate the spirit. However, it might be advisable to explore the areas to which Maris enjoyed visiting. Perhaps, his spirit would remain in those areas."

Marqest's face flustered. "This is likely. However, we do not have time to go on such a search. Dragenopn, you must train now. Meanwhile, I shall try to find possible locations for Maris's spirit."

Drage was not enthusiastic about being further connected to this world, but as long as he was spending his time with Matthew, he supposed that it might not be as terrible as he had imagined. Perhaps, Marqest would find Maris's spirit. "Alright, Marqest, I suppose I can stay and train." Out of the corner of his eye, he noticed Matthew smile at his reply.

Marqest nodded in satisfaction. "Good." His scepter tapped the ground, and an icy Gate appeared. "This Gate will take the two of you to the doors of the Capital in Immyx." He pulled two permits from his robes. "Take these. You will need them to enter the Capital. I trust that one of you can find a decent enough military training facility there?"

A nod from Matthew was sufficient reassurance for Marqest. Together, Matthew and Drage entered the Gate. They were surprised at the warmth of the water. For Drage who had spent the past five years in Massachusetts, the water was too hot, but for Matthew who had been in the Western Continent, the water felt nice. The plains were covered in grass that waved in the undulating current and small hills that gave contour to the land. Then, the two beheld the spectacular, enormous city known as the Capital. Skyscrapers towered over the city walls, and the lights glowed through the sea. The booming music reached their ears from the city's depths.

As they approached it, Matthew sighed. "I'm glad you're back Drage. It's been a while."

Drage smiled warmly at Matthew. "Yeah, I know. This place changed me so much the last time I was here. I've spent the past five years hoping that this curse would just go away, but it's been affecting me on a regular basis. Everything I believed in before coming here was proven false when I arrived. My father lived in another world. You were really my half-brother, and Helen was actually my half-sister. It was possible to breathe underwater. I just…really don't think that I can do this, Matt."

Matthew put an arm on Drage's shoulder. "Hey, you're pretty forgetful, you know."

"Huh?"

Matthew comically waved a finger accusingly at Drage. "Five years ago, you made a promise to me: You said that you would stop being so depressing. You would be more optimistic. What happened to that Drage?"

A sigh left Drage's lips. "I don't know…"

"You have got to snap out of this state, Drage. You have got to quit feeling so sorry for yourself, too. Believe it or not, this war isn't about you: It's about control, freedom, politics, and the laws as they stand now. Whether you asked for them or not, you have responsibilities to this world, Drage, and you can't just ignore them." Matthew was typically not the kind of person who would lecture his best friend and half-brother, but nothing else seemed to work.

Drage's black eyes turned to stare coldly at Matthew. "Back off, Matt. You don't know what I went through five years ago." As soon as the words had left his mouth, he felt regret instantly. "Look, I'm sorry. It's this annoying curse."

However, Matthew already felt hurt that he had unintentionally pushed Drage so far. He tried to hide it by saying, "Don't worry about it." Matthew regretted what he had said and felt sorry for hurting Drage's feelings.

The two of them sighed as their walk progressed.

After several minutes in silence, they were at the gates to the Capital. The two guards at the doors asked to see their permits, which they provided indifferently.

The Capital was even more remarkable on the inside. The buildings were all towering skyscrapers, and a thousand aquatic vehicles drove through the water above the two young men. Glowing neon lights made the city seem like it was in a state of perpetual day. The city was warm throughout, and the neon rainbows all around masked the crime that happened beneath the city's streets.

"Wow, this is amazing," commented Drage in astonishment.

Matthew was equally surprised. "I can't believe I've been in Gevás for five years and have never been here before. This place is larger than Apolis!"

"Yeah, it's bigger than Boston and New York too."

"Now, we just need to find a training facility."

A few minutes later, they found a soldier and asked him. "Excuse me, do you know where we could find a military training facility around here?"

The soldier responded politely, "New recruits, huh? If you go down that street over there, take a right, and then walk for about three or four blocks, a nice facility will be the short building with the guards in front of it on your left. Got it?"

The two replied in unison, "Yes, sir." Then, they went about following the soldier's directions. However, they found that the directions were much more confusing than they had originally thought. The streets were not simply horizontal and vertical. Several diagonal roads intersected the road on which they presently walked. This arrangement made it difficult to find the first right they were supposed to take.

Drage complained, "Why couldn't this city be a little easier to understand? It's like a maze!"

Matthew agreed quietly. He was still quite upset for having spoken down to Drage earlier. Although elated to see his brother after so many years, Matthew was beginning to see the long-term effects of Maris's curse on Drage. How close were they now? Drage seemed…darker. "Let's ask that soldier over there," he said as he pointed to their left. When they were closer to the armored youth, Matthew started, "Excuse me, which way is the nearest training facility?"

"Training facility? I'm off duty now, so I suppose I can walk you there. It's been getting less and less safe around here."

"Less safe? How so?" inquired Matthew.

"Well," began the soldier. "Since the Third Obsidian War started, the Emperor Regin has been quite aggressive. He sees every attack as a personal one, and he spends less time on his usual level of strategy. His focus has been on crushing the exiles. In fact, he hasn't even cared about most of the affairs of the Capital. The guards have doubled by order of the generals and captains, but the crime has still been elevating. Things have been getting stranger and stranger. It's not as safe here."

"Well, why doesn't he start caring about his own people?" asked Drage.

"Everyone has their own opinions," stated the soldier. "Some say that it had to do with the assassins that killed everyone in his castle. Others say it has to do with the famous captain that left his service to work for Helio. I think it is because of the rumors."

"What rumors?" said Matthew.

"Supposedly, the Lords of the Shadows have come back. I know it sounds like a child's tale, but several people claimed to have seen a few days before the War broke out. What's more is that supposedly that captain that left us was with one of the Lords of the Shadows. I think they've been causing trouble in the Capital. Maybe even messed with the Emperor Regin."

Drage and Matthew were familiar with the term that was the folktale name of the Y'mordi. They had each had their encounters with the robed figures who possessed immense powers and immortality. The seven Guardians of Light had been destined to fight against the seven Y'mordi by an ancient Prophecy that had been made a thousand years ago.

"The Y'mordi were here five years ago?" asked Drage in perplexity. "What were they doing around here? None of the Guardians were on the Eastern Continent."

"I don't know what they were doing here, but I am staying out of it. For all we know, they are still lurking in some dark alleyway. Since they showed up, everything has been...tense." Then, he stopped walking. "Alright, if you go straight for a few blocks, you will find it. It is pretty well-guarded, so you can't miss it." He made a quick salute and turned back to the direction from which they had come.

Matthew and Drage looked at each other in wonder. Drage murmured to himself, "This War has affected everything."

"I'm as surprised as you are, Drage. I have spent the past few years with my dad in training. I think, though, that when we train to be generals, it will be a long process. We will need to be patient, and then, we can help this War end more quickly."

"I hope you're right," said Drage softly. From what he had heard, the whole world seemed to be in chaos. The Northern Continent was in civil war, and the Eastern and Southern Continents were combatting the Western Continent fiercely. "This War needs to end."

Matthew exhaled deeply. "I really need to get a license. Driving would be so much easier than walking the whole way there." He smiled.

Drage grinned slightly, and, for a second, he seemed like his old self again. "Y'know, that might not be a bad idea, Matt. I've had mine for a while now."

Matthew's arms folded in mock jealousy. "Hmph, showoff."

Drage pushed his half-brother jokingly, and the two kept walking amongst the colossal buildings. The irregular music was still blasting throughout the city, but the two discovered that the hum of the vehicles above them was much louder. Another interesting feature of the city was the brilliant electric lights that illuminated almost every corner of the Capital. Though it was day, the towering skyscrapers created monstrous shadows that swallowed most of the city, providing the need for the electric lights regardless of the time of day.

It did not take the two too long to find the military building they had been seeking. It was indeed a low building that appeared to be quite heavily guarded. It was snugly fit between two skyscrapers and gave it an almost comical appearance next to the behemoths.

As their feet began proceeding up the white marble stairs, one of the guards halted their progress. "What do the two of you think you are doing?"

Drage retorted, "We are here to train to be generals for the terra of Apolis."

The muscular guard laughed with another of his comrades. Their laughter was deep and mocking. "As if we would believe that! You are far too scrawny to be in the terra!"

Drage instantly became angered by the guard's words. Matthew placed a hand warningly on Drage's shoulder. "Don't do anything you will regret later," said Matthew softly.

"What will take for us to be allowed inside?" asked Drage heatedly.

The two guards laughed more before the first guard responded, "Alright, kid, I'll make you a deal. If you can beat me in a duel, I will let you in. Deal?"

A grin came across Drage's face. "Deal."

Y'tal was concealed fully in a black robe and hood that hid every feature of his face. A Gate appeared yards away in the highest hall of the black Palace of Shadows as another robed figure appeared. Y'tal spoke quietly, "What news do you have, Ixion?" Y'tal rested his chin on a gloved hand as he sat in the throne that had once held the Dark Lord Dagan himself.

Ixion was also in a black robe, though his features were by far less concealed. He had short brown hair and green eyes. Around his neck was a green jeweled pendant. After bowing to Y'tal, he replied, "My lord Y'tal, I have been watching the events at Apolis, and it seems that the Prince of Light has returned. He is on his way to the Capital to begin some form of training that the Emperor's Council wants him to do."

Y'tal responded simply, "Is that all?"

Ixion winced at the remark and commented, "No, sir. Also, the boy who was with the Prince five years ago, Matthew, is with him again. What would you like me to do? I could spy on him if you wished it." Ixion looked up from his bowing state.

"No, Ixion, that shall not be necessary. I believe that Y'dax shall take care of it this time. However, I think I have a better plan for you."

"Yes, my lord?"

Y'tal approached Ixion much to Ixion's fear. "I need you to remain in the Southern Continent. I want you to keep a watchful eye over the events of the Academy at Gryphos. One of the Guardians of Light is training there, and I want to keep her in sight at all times. More than anything, I want for the Guardians to not be distracted from this War."

Ixion murmured timidly, "But, m-m-my lord, what would distract them exactly?"

"Draconis," answered Y'tal. "He, too, is one of the Guardians of Light, and they are all connected somehow. With him being in Sharl Vran, the connection shall be much weaker, but it is there, nevertheless. I do not want the other Guardians to go to Sharl Vran and interfere with our takeover there. We want Kusvor Cairon to eliminate Draconis once and for all. Once that happens, the Guardians of Light will no longer be a threat to us, and our presence can be known to the rest of the world. Gevás will be ours for the taking. Shortly, three of the worlds shall be within our grasp." Y'tal circled Ixion like a vulture, anxious to feed, his voice a soft hiss.

"Three, my lord? I know about Sharl Vran and Gevás, but what about the third?" Ixion was always so perplexed by Y'tal's elaborate plans.

"Randir and Mali are trying to find a powerful ally on Earth known as the Black Joker. Perhaps, you have heard of it. If we gain that ally, Earth could be ours, as well." Y'tal knew Randir thought to gain that power for himself, but Y'tal also knew that

Randir underestimated Y'tal's power over him. Before Ixion could respond, Y'tal continued, "Now, Ixion, go to the Academy. You have your orders. Watch over Aria Newman, and if you can, kill her. However, even more importantly, stay hidden. You have a habit of being caught. If you can just report her activity to me, that will be enough."

Ixion could clearly remember the last time that Y'tal had punished him for his failure. Five years ago, his identity had been discovered by the Emperor of Light, Draconis, and the Prophet of Earth at the time. After that initial battle of the Third Obsidian War, Y'tal had tortured Ixion mercilessly, though he had been quite confident that Randir had received an even more painful punishment. "Yes, my lord," Ixion muttered nervously.

Without another moment's hesitation, Ixion left as quickly as he had come.

Y'tal was left alone in the darkness of the hall. "Xarden..." he whispered. As if the blue-robed Y'mordi had heard the whisper, Xarden appeared.

"Yes, Pullatus?" he inquired, using Y'tal's name for himself after the Final Battle of the Second Obsidian War.

Y'tal folded his arms behind his back and moved to one of the enormous glass windows that served as one of the walls to the hall. "I need you to go to the Capital. The Prince of Light and the son of the Prophet of Wind are at a military training facility. I need you to go there and keep me informed as to their whereabouts."

"Yes, Pullatus, but I must ask you why you need this done." Xarden knew that he was not being rude to Y'tal. It was his job to act as Y'tal's advisor. That was the position he had obtained when he had first become one of the Y'mordi. As the third ranked Lord of the Shadows, he wielded the Element of Water and was easily the wisest of the Y'mordi.

"I am quite concerned about the Guardians of Light," began Y'tal. His voice was high and childish, which had been a puzzle even to one as wise and intelligent as Xarden. "I do not want them interfering with the events at Sharl Vran. Keep an eye on those two."

Xarden nodded. "It shall be done, Pullatus." A Gate opened in front of him, and he stepped into the Capital in Immyx. He wondered which disguise he would use to hide in the Capital.

Y'tal, however, was thinking of how well everything was falling into place.

The Prophet in the Gardens

The city of Apolis was truly spectacular even to one such as Stehl who had been raised in the extravagant Capital. The golden buildings reflected dazzling lights across the city, brightening every corner of the place. Over the past five years, she had begun to love the city of light and its optimistic population. However, she had noticed that that optimism had gradually faded into distrust of the Emperor's Council. Although Master Valdridge was the head of the Council, she suspected that there was another manipulating the will of the whole group. The way they had ruled Helio the past five years indicated a love for battle, a passion for chaos too distinct from previous rulers.

She, too, had changed over the years. She brushed her blonde hair out of her eyes. For most of her life, she had disguised as a man in order to be able to fight for Immyx, and she was not used to her feminine appearance now. Her frame was slender, showing curves around her hips. Her new breasts weighed on her, making her posture cumbersome. She had found that women's clothes, and even armor, were much tighter on her figure. Her position too had changed. While she once held the title of Captain Terrell, she was now General

Stehl. Apolis's terra probably had around thirty generals, and Stehl was glad to finally possess such a high rank. Leading several battles over the years had earned her the title, and it was one that she held proudly.

However, she still felt an overwhelming discontent. The reason for her joining the terra of Apolis was not to rise in rank: it was to find and eliminate the elusive Enigma Brigade, the Emperor of Light's secret military organization that consisted of the most elite soldiers in Gevás. She had been there when the Enigma Brigade had slaughtered all of the servants in the Emperor Regin's castle. When Stehl had fought the Brigade, she had almost been killed herself, until the interesting Lord of the Shadows Randir had saved her.

Since then, revenge had been her primary goal. Of course, she still cared about Helio's cause and the Light, but the Enigma Brigade was a brutal vigilante group as far as she was concerned and needed to be stopped…even if vigilantism was required to do it. However, knowing the whereabouts of a secret military force that most people did not even believe in was quite difficult, even for a General.

As she walked through the golden city, she sighed in frustration. It had indeed been quite hard these past few years. She had not had many friends in the Capital, but for some reason, she felt more alone here than she ever had. It was such a strange and inexplicable thing to her.

She was presently approaching one of the military quarters where she had been staying. Being a general actually meant doing a lot less work as far as keeping up with others. She knew where all the captains under her command were, but other than that, she had nothing to do at the moment.

Her section of the terra had recently led a string of attacks on the Western Continent. However, several of the captains had complained of lack of rest, so General Stehl had applied for a leave. Considering it was her first request, the Emperor's Council had obliged her, and all of her troops were stationed at Apolis for the time being. She hated doing all this waiting. It was her greatest joy to be on the battlefield, and it was quite nerve-wracking trying to learn more about the Enigma Brigade.

She wished to search in the Palace of Light, but only a select few were allowed in there. It seemed to be the most likely place to be the headquarters for the Enigma Brigade, but she simply had no access to the Palace without direct permission.

She finally found herself at the entrance to the Imperial Gardens. This place was not where she had meant to go, but she merely sighed and entered the massive and magnificent Gardens. Having lived most of her life in the Capital, she had not been exposed to many natural beauties.

In fact, when the Lord of the Shadows named Randir had lain beside her to gaze at the stars, it had been the first time that Stehl had ever really seen the night sky as anything but a distraction or even a factor of war. For the first time, she had beheld true beauty. The moment was frozen in her mind. He had helped her escape the leader of the Enigma Brigade, and she had saved his life in the battle against the anima at the start of the Third Obsidian War.

Suddenly, she imagined that black-robed figure standing beside her with his spiked red hair and the scars and burns that laced his hard face. Surrounded her entire life by men, she had found the men of Immyx to be posers, adorning a mask of masculinity. With Randir, it seemed real. He had seen true battle, true pain, and true glory. About a year ago, she had finally accepted Randir to be just a fond dream, something that was completely unobtainable but still sweet and enticing.

"General Stehl? What are you doing here?" asked a voice.

Stehl nearly jumped when she heard the voice. She turned to see Master Valdridge walking in the Gardens as well, his robe brushing the small stone path that wound its way through the multi-hued coral of the Gardens. "Well…I was off duty, so I thought I would take a small stroll through the Gardens. The captains have the troops well under control. Forgive me, Master Valdridge. I will leave at once."

"No, no, you are fine," replied Master Valdridge with a slight smile. "I was just doing the same. Working in the Council is quite tiring, believe it or not."

Stehl was quite astonished that Master Valdridge was even talking to her. He was not only the head of the Emperor's Council but also the Prophet of Light. "Surely not, Master Valdridge. You do quite a good job in the Emperor's Council." However, she doubted her words. The Emperor's Council had slowly been losing the trust of the people of Apolis through their dragging out of this War.

The Prophet's expression was blank. "You are lying, General Stehl. I am not so blind as to realize this. The Council has fallen so much from what it once was. The Council was never meant to lead for so long. We need an Emperor of Light to take the Throne."

Red began to appear in Stehl's face in embarrassment, but she spoke honestly and almost bluntly, nevertheless. "Sir, forgive me, but why can we not elect an Emperor to take the Throne? If we are in such desperate need of one, why do we not act to gain one?"

Master Valdridge shook his head dismissively. "It is not that simple, I am afraid. In actuality, and try not to spread this around, the Prince of Light has indeed returned to Gevás. He is in training to become a general right now."

This news flustered Stehl even further. It had taken her years to achieve the title of general, and now, the Prince of Light was going to take a quick course and bear the title. That did not seem in the slightest bit fair to her.

Stehl's fury was noticed by Master Valdridge as he countered it, "Do not worry. It shall not be a long-lived title anyways. We are trying to convince him to take the throne as is his right and responsibility. If he does decently as a general, which I have no doubt he will do, then he may possess the confidence to lead Helio against the exiles as an Emperor."

Stehl, however, felt a strong urge to argue this point. "Master Valdridge, surely you would agree that leading a country is different from leading an army? I mean no disrespect when I say that a leader should appoint a general to take care of military affairs but should then leave the general to do what he does best. Other than that appointment, a leader should have no real connection to the military."

"I understand and agree, General Stehl," replied Master Valdridge in an attempt to calm Stehl. "However, this is not an act of promotion for genuine merit. We merely want the Prince to find faith and confidence in himself. If he does that, he might be more easily encouraged to take the Throne. It is true that there is a considerable gap between leading an army and leading a country, but you must remember that he is the same warrior that defeated Maris five years ago. He knows about fighting and would not be a complete dolt on the battlefield."

Stehl remained obstinate that Master Valdridge was wrong on this point, but she did not argue it this time. "I suppose that you do make a slight point," lied Stehl.

Master Valdridge again caught the general's lie. He sighed, "Well, at any rate, we still have a great amount of work to do. Although the West is falling, the Northern Continent remains in a state of utter chaos. Half of the Continent is not protesting the exile, while the other half is fighting it with every bit of power it possesses. Although the War has led the people of Apolis to question us and lose some trust in us, it has also solidified them. They are patriotic even as they curse our names in the streets. We are stronger."

"Is that a major reason for this War?" inquired Stehl somewhat accusingly.

"No!" exclaimed Master Valdridge in astonishment. This general was a much quicker thinker than he had previously thought. She was just as strict as when she had first arrived in Apolis five years ago, he realized. "If we ally with the exiles, the Eastern Continent would attack us. We cannot allow that."

For once, Stehl found that she agreed with Master Valdridge's words. "That actually sounds quite logical, sir. It would be foolish to choose the nonhuman exiles over humans."

Master Valdridge eyed her in confusion. "What are you suggesting, General Stehl?"

Stehl replied proudly, "Why do we have to endure this struggle? Those things are not human, so why must we share this world with them at all? Why not purify this world like Earth is?" Like many of the Eastern Continent, Stehl also had the firm prejudice against the nonhumans of Gevás.

The Prophet of Light was simply appalled by what Stehl was saying. He took a deep breath before replying, "General Stehl, I would prefer that you keep such opinions to yourself. I would rather your soldiers not start spreading such ideas around the Southern Continent. Thank you very much for your words of wisdom."

Before he could leave, Stehl said, "Excuse me, Master Valdridge, but I have a more personal issue I would like to discuss with you."

He did not want to speak further with her, but he felt that it would only be polite to repay the favor of an open ear. "Yes, General?"

Stehl hesitated for a moment. She had not honestly expected for Master Valdridge to listen to her. She also was unclear about his motivations. Still, it was the first time in a while she had such close contact with a member of the Council. "Well…I have a confession to make, and I need you to hear it not as the head of the Emperor's Council but as the Prophet of Light."

Now, his interest was quite piqued by Stehl's request. "Go ahead," he implored.

"Five years ago, I did not come here to become closer to the fighting. In actuality, I came here for the intention of revenge."

"Revenge, General?"

"Yes," Stehl continued slowly. "When I was a captain for Immyx, I happened to witness something quite horrible. A group of people came to the Emperor Regin's castle and slaughtered everyone there except for the Emperor himself." She noticed Master Valdridge's expression of shock. "I am not just talking about the soldiers and guards. I am talking about every servant, child, ambassador, and even relatives and friends of the Emperor Regin. I tried to fight the group, but they overwhelmed me." She chose not only to lie but also to hide the fact that a Lord of the Shadows had helped her.

"Why would they do something like that?" inquired the Prophet.

Stehl's eyes became cold then. "The leader of the group claimed that he wanted to have the Emperor Regin's support but did not want to engage in a political discussion. He wanted for both of them to be straightforward with one another, no games, so he killed everyone to show how serious he was."

"The group got away with it? I would think that the Emperor Regin would have had them executed for such a crime."

"That's just the thing, though. He couldn't. The group was…the Enigma Brigade." Her body tightened, realizing what she was risking. However, she knew that if he demoted her on the spot for treason, she would still pursue her goal just as fervently.

Now, Master Valdridge was quite speechless. If it was not for Stehl's well-earned title, he would have disregarded such an idea, but he could not ignore it if it was coming from a general. "Are you sure that your information is correct, General?"

Stehl's eyes bore into Master Valdridge's own, and she did not respond.

"So you came here in the hopes of hunting down the Enigma Brigade? That is an extremely dangerous and traitorous goal, General Stehl."

"Is it wrong?"

Master Valdridge admitted softly, "No, it is not wrong."

"I am wondering, Master Valdridge," began Stehl hopefully. "Would you be able to give me just some piece of information that I could use to track down the Enigma Brigade? I am not asking you to kill them yourself. I merely want to see justice done."

"I am afraid that I cannot help you with that, General." Before she could protest, he said somewhat forcefully, "It is not that I do not agree with you or that I do not want to see this justice done. It is that the Emperor's Council has no control or knowledge about the Enigma Brigade."

Now, it was Stehl's turn to be surprised. "What?"

Master Valdridge swallowed nervously. "After the Emperor of Light passed away, we tried to make communication to the Enigma Brigade to give them orders, but we only received a mysterious reply that they only follow the orders from the Throne of Light: The Emperor's Council does not command them in any way whatsoever. To this day, we have heard nothing of their whereabouts."

That revelation instantly crushed Stehl's theory about the Palace of Light. It also diminished most of her hopes of finding the Enigma Brigade. "Alright, forgive me if I said something out of line, Master Valdridge. I shall leave you."

As she proceeded to leave, Master Valdridge exclaimed, "Wait! There might still be a way." His eyes shifted uncertainly. "If the Brigade does not respond to the Council, then that means that it speaks directly with the Emperor. If they find out that the Prince of Light has returned, they will likely try communicating with him as soon as possible."

Stehl brightened at the implied suggestion. "So, if I go to where the Prince of Light is, I might have a better chance of finding the Enigma Brigade?"

Master Valdridge stroked his chin thoughtfully. "Well, it would be quite difficult for you to get there. You do have certain duties here."

Stehl's mind, however, was already made up for the moment. "In that case, I am already on personal leave. Where is the Prince of Light?"

Master Valdridge stuttered, "He is training at the Capital. I have no idea where exactly, though."

"It's not important. I will find him." As she bowed to leave, she said, "Thank you very much for your time, Master

Valdridge. You have been a great help. For what it's worth, I hope that you can get the Council back in order."

Then, she was gone. Master Valdridge felt as if so much had happened so quickly. More than the general's attitude, her final words of advice had been the most interesting aspect of the conversation. He felt as if the Council had been directed by someone other than himself, as if the past few years had been a vague blur of history. How had things become this chaotic?

Viso Tharlam of the Emperor's Council began walking through the alleyways of Apolis cautiously. His white robe slid silently along the ground. Since joining the Council, he had needed to have more of these stealth missions. It was of the utmost importance that the other members of the Council did not know what he was doing in the middle of the night almost every night.

Finally, he arrived at the graveyard. Thick fog covered the area, giving it a ghostly aura. Without making a sound, he approached the large gravestone that served as the marker for the grave of the Emperor of Light John Helius. Standing there already was a young man with extremely long crimson hair.

The red-haired man spoke quietly, "What news do you have for me, Viso?"

The much taller man responded, "Captain, the Council has brought the Prince of Light back to Gevás. He is training to become a general in the Capital."

Maksimilian, the leader of the Enigma Brigade, replied, "He is not the Emperor of Light yet, and therefore, Viso, he does not concern us. He has much to learn yet, as do you. Nevertheless, the Capital may be a place of interest to us." He would not admit it to Viso or the other members of the Enigma Brigade that he led, but he was desperately searching for the five legendary Spirit Swords. Though he had one, the Steel of Life, which granted immortality, he wanted the powers of the other Swords even more. Because of the Capital's massive size, he had avoided searching there, but the idea seemed to be a possible location of a Spirit Sword.

"Oh?" inquired Viso cautiously. He knew how easy it was to push Captain Maksimilian to do something cruel. "Might I ask why that is, Captain?"

"You may not, Viso," was Maksimilian's cold response. *"You know your place, so stick to it. I would hate to be responsible for anything that happens if you went too far."*

Viso took a step back fearfully. *"Yes, sir, I understand. Also, the Western Continent seems to be falling just as you predicted, Captain. However, the Dragon general disappeared on a 'personal leave' today. Do you think that that will affect the fighting in the West?"*

Maksimilian replied with a smile, *"No, everything is going as it should, Viso. The Dragon and the Western Continent are of no concern to us. We merely need to make sure that this world is prepared for the new Emperor of Light when he takes the Throne. We shall serve the Emperor of Light as the Light sees fit. That is the way of the Enigma Brigade, is it not, Viso?"*

"Yes, Captain, you are right." Viso was all too happy to agree with anything that his Captain said. This quick agreement was also why Maksimilian had trouble trusting Viso. He was not like Bryco or Tilgé who were quite trustworthy. Viso did not think for the Light. He only responded in a way that was subservient. Still, it was nice having eyes in the Emperor's Council. Although it did not give him particular power, it gave him more connections and knowledge.

"Viso, you are dismissed."

"Yes, Captain," murmured Viso as he left the Captain alone in the graveyard.

Maksimilian regarded the elaborate grave mournfully. *"This world is being thrown into chaos, your Majesty. The Light cannot wait on your son forever, either. I promise you, though, that I shall not allow your kingdom to fall. If I find the next Spirit Sword, I shall destroy your enemies. Every kingdom in your opposition shall weep before my power, and Helio shall accept me as its new ruler. The power of the Great Spirit will guide me into such a future if your son does not hasten."*

Then, a memory of his last visit to the Capital came to his mind. Two people still had a debt with him that needed to be repaid: the Y'mordi Y'ran and Captain Terrell. The two of them had been responsible for the deaths of four of his men five years ago. Perhaps, as a side goal, he could track down those two if they were still in the Capital. It would at least provide a goal for the other four members of the Enigma Brigade.

"Besides the Steel of Life and the Sword of Destiny, there are three more Swords out there. I must find them," muttered to himself. "No matter what the cost is."

The Hidden Archives

Aria woke up covered in sweat. The mysterious stranger Ace had haunted her dreams so many times over the past few years. She constantly imagined the dark-robed man chasing her, muttering in his soft voice a spell she could not quite grasp. Matthew had provided her with much information about him, but it was not enough. Ace remained a puzzle that needed to be solved. He had appeared several times throughout their adventures five years ago, starting with appearing on the beach on Earth and saving them from Shadows sent to kill them. Matthew had probably had the longest conversation with Ace, learning that he was seeking a place called Paradise. He went by several names, including the Wolf. At first, she had assumed this meant he was the Werewolf who lived in the Northern Continent, but Matthew knew that could not be the case because Ace's voice was much younger, and his heart was more guarded. Although she had spent countless nights scouring the books of the library in the Academy, a name such as Ace had never appeared. Not even the census records revealed anything. He truly was an illusion as he had claimed five years ago.

The problem was that the dark illusion was a nightmare that never went away.

Slowly, she began to rise from her hard bed. Living in the Academy had been a rough switch for her. Having stayed for months at the Palace of Light, she had become accustomed to having servants and living in luxury. Then, the rules had changed, and, if she wanted to get her position back, she had to enroll in the Academy. The Academy was an immense castle that seemed from the outside to be quite archaic, but the interior was a more technological and futuristic design. Every room had at least one computer, and every inch of the rooms was covered in silvery metal.

She made sure not to wake any of her three suitemates. It was surprisingly easy to get in trouble at the Academy. Leaving your dorm sector was against the school rules. Nevertheless, she had mastered the craft of sneaking around the place.

Carefully, she made her way to the desk at the far end of the room and grabbed her wand. For spells, she relied on using words much less, but the wand was still a useful tool to her. After a rapid gaze around the room to make sure that everyone was still asleep, she flicked her wand systematically in the water, and the Light bent around Aria, making her invisible to everyone but herself.

Using a few spells, the door to the side hallways opened without making the slightest sound or revealing any change in the lighting of the room. She crept into the hallways, pleased with her handiwork as the door shut just as quietly behind her.

The ivory-metallic hallway was well-lit, but her spells prevented even a shadow from appearing from her form. Soundlessly, her bare feet stepped along the cold floor, and the place was so quiet, she wondered if she was in a dream at this very moment. This occasion was not the first time she had tried to explore the castle a little more. For the past few years, she had been seeking a hidden part of the Academy's Archives. The Archives were the general libraries and databases that every student had complete access to at any time of day. However, when searching for the identity of the stranger named Ace, she had also discovered that there were holes in the Archives, as if the data were to be located somewhere else. Aria's theory was that another library was hidden in the castle somewhere.

After asking several of the professors at the Academy, she had decided that they were indeed hiding something. The answers were always different, from claiming the Archives were, of course, complete to stating that many files had been removed from the Archives hundreds of years ago. Even now, there were parts of the castle she had not explored. These nightly ventures had to be short. Classes were always early in the mornings, and she needed to get as much sleep as possible.

Along with seeking knowledge about Ace, she was also trying to learn about the ability of Gifting. It had been the Prophet of Earth Linda Daghda who had revealed to her that someone had given Aria all of his or her powers in *mysteria* in a process known as Gifting.

It was one of her goals to find out who had Gifted her. However, her studies made her goals quite difficult to achieve.

The first door was in front of her finally. Using a few spells, the door opened somewhat noisily. She winced as the clang echoed through the halls. If she was caught, not only would she be in trouble with the professors, but she would also have greater difficulty in trying to sneak out in the future.

She rushed into the next hallways and began running. As she ran, she strengthened the spell that silenced her movements.

Then, she became aware of another person in the hallway. It was a small boy. He was out in a white overshirt, just wandering the halls, a stuffed unicorn in his hands dragging across the metallic floor. She could not sense any *mysteria* coming from him, and he looked as if he were sleepwalking. Although she needed to get to where she was going, she felt sympathy for the boy. If he was caught, he would likely be in as much trouble as she would. Looking at him, she thought of what Drage and Matthew must have looked like when they were that young and helpless.

After looking around the hall to see if they were alone, her wand emitted a soundless blast of Force that knocked the boy back. In confusion, he looked around and was quickly embarrassed, though he could not see anyone.

She realized that he was too young to know his way around the maze of monochromatic halls, and she released another spell, a ball of Light that floated in front of the boy and began moving toward the dorm sector for the children. Entranced by the floating Light, the boy followed it comically, walking under the bright neon lights that cast his reflection along the pristine walls. Aria watched him leave fondly. She was not that young when she had met Drage and Matthew, but the boy's helplessness reminded her of how helpless the three of them had been. They played at the beach. They were always found together at school, chatting about books and films. They all had plans to make something of themselves when they were older. However, they could never have imagined what would happen to them that fateful night on the beach. Aria shook her head in amusement at the boy and continued on her search. She began to pass other sectors of the castle: the apprentice sector, the professor sector, the military sector, the Archives, and the dining sector. This castle could be a maze to those who had not spent at least two years in the place. She had already thoroughly explored each of those sectors. Her present sector was the technology design sector.

As she entered it, she took note of the large number of computers. The two tech sectors were bound to be full of the computers. However, her knowledge of Gevatian computers was quite limited. She could remember how skilled Drage was at using computers back on Earth. Thinking of her boyfriend made her wish that she was with him now. However, choosing to remain in Gevás had given her new responsibilities. Learning how to use *mysteria* properly was one of those. She despised being forced to learn something that she already knew, and the Emperor's Council was to blame in her mind. They had been behind the changes in the rules governing the terra. The Emperor's Council pushed away the issues the people of Helio had been fighting before the War and solely promoted the War, almost as a means of distraction. It worried her.

The sector was fully illuminated though no one was in it, which was quite an unusual thing in itself. The hallways were supposed to be extremely bright, but the sectors were only to be lit when someone was in them.

Aria opened her heart to *mysteria* and could not sense another being in the room. She was alone. Her eyes closed as she allowed her heart to delve deeper into the well of *mysteria* inside her. It was quite likely that any hidden areas of the castle would be hidden with a rather low-level spell, something that would be more easily concealable. She needed to be able to sense the slightest hint of *mysteria*.

She walked carefully through the room with her eyes closed. Her heightened senses allowed her to avoid stepping into desks and computers. Then, vivid colors flared in the back of her mind: reds, blacks, blues, and greens. A sinking feeling hit her heart. She quickly turned around and opened her eyes. There was another being in the hallway. The heart that she could sense was quite irregular. It was covered in Darkness, yet she could feel the Element of Water hidden beneath that dark cloud. The strangest observation was that the heart was not complete. It was as if she was sensing only half of a heart.

The figure appeared in the doorway, and she beheld a silver-haired man in a blue robe, wrinkles covering his face. The strength of the Darkness in his heart told her that he was one of the Y'mordi. Without thinking, she allowed her heart to unleash a variety of spells at the man who held the metal scepter in his hands.

Thick streams of Fire emanated from her wand. She allowed her spells of stealth to dissipate as she concentrated on her enemy. Dying at the hands of an Y'mordi would be far more terrible than any punishment from the Deans.

However, her spells were countered by the Y'mordi's torrential streams of Liquid, rippling through the water from the Y'mordi's scepter. Where the two spells collided, the water in the room began to boil fiercely.

Simultaneously, they both released their spells. As Aria prepared a shield made of Earth, the Y'mordi's scepter glowed a blue hue, and the water around them began to freeze to solid ice. Aria's shield, however, protected her from the Ice spell. She could feel the cold creeping in through the cracks in the Rock sphere that surrounded her. Waving her wand inside the sphere, she summoned a bolt of Lightning in the area outside her sphere. The bolt instantly shattered the Ice and arced to attack the Y'mordi.

As she released the spell of Earth, she saw the Y'mordi block the bolt with his scepter. Hopefully, that thunder would alert some of the professors. She was surprised that someone had not come already.

Her wand waved again, and several of the computers went flying through the water at the Y'mordi. Using the form Gravity of the Element Earth, he repelled the computers away from him. His scepter tapped the ground, and a blue wave of Stasis shot from its head.

Xarden had been thoroughly surprised by the girl's rapid and powerful spells. He had used a Gate to enter the Academy, and as soon as he had, that girl, the Guardian of Light, had attacked him. It was as if he had been expected.

He was by no means weaker than the girl, but he had simply not expected such a sudden attack or any attack at all for that matter.

Besides the girl's initial spells of Fire, he had been able to silence every spell and movement that they had made. Until the Guardians of Light were out of the way, secrecy was quite a high priority. He exhaled deeply. That girl had nearly given him a heart attack.

The girl with the brown hair was frozen completely under his spell of Stasis. Y'tal had said to keep an eye on the two boys, Matthew and Dragenopn, but he had needed to gain a few useful resources from the Academy, some information. Nevertheless, if he killed the girl now, the Guardians of Light would fall. The Y'mordi would be able to conquer Gevás without fear of opposition.

Before he could forge a knife made of pure Ice, he heard the sound of rapid footsteps coming from the hallway: Someone had heard those first streams of fire that the girl had created. Angrily, he tapped his scepter once more on the ground and sent a forceful surge of Lightning throughout the castle. The surge was controlled so that it would cause a loss of power in the Academy. That would leave the mages of the Academy scrambling around for a while.

Then, he realized that whoever had come in from the hallway was standing in the doorway. "Who's there?" the stranger called. Whirling his scepter, Xarden struck the man cleanly in the face, sending him flying. Xarden ran down the hallway, ignoring all spells of stealth. The darkness of the castle would protect him for now. All he needed was to steal a potion or two from the storage sector.

Suddenly, the whole world shifted. She had just been fighting one of the Y'mordi, and in a flash of blue, everything changed. Six of her professors were standing over her questioningly. She was also in one of their classrooms. Sitting up, she felt dizzy as the faces around her blurred and spun. "What? What just happened?" she asked, wondering if she had simply been dreaming what had happened. The room had all the tables pushed to the wall except the one on which she was sitting.

"We would like to ask you the same question, Miss Newman," muttered one of the professors with an edge of impatience. Then, she realized that the one who had spoken was actually the Second Dean, the third-in-command of the Academy. "We found poor Professor Leif knocked out with a bruise covering the whole left side of his face and you in Stasis with your wand ready."

"Stasis? He put me into Stasis?" she murmured. "Second Dean, sir, as hard as it may be to believe, it was one of the Y'mordi. I tried to fight him, and I guess…"

The other professors looked as if they did not know what to believe. Though the Y'mordi were tales of legend, they had just revived a girl from Stasis, a spell that was equally mythical. It had taken their combined efforts to release her from that spell.

The Second Dean growled low to the others, "Professors, would you leave us please?"

The professors bowed to the Second Dean and left the room. "Miss Newman, I am not usually the type of person to doubt a student, much less one as highly regarded as you. However, if you are trying to claim that an Y'mordi is hiding in this Academy, I am inclined to disbelieve you."

"No, sir, I am not claiming one is hiding here," she said as she scrambled for the right words. "You see, sir, he appeared by a Gate, and I just happened to be right where he was. My heart was already open to *mysteria*, so I thought that the best idea would be to fight him, and any noise I made would bring the other professors to help me."

The Second Dean hissed angrily, "You are a liar! First of all, only one sound was made in that whole time. Professor Leif said that he had heard what sounded like flames, and that was all. Even the security cameras reveal a strong spell of Flame erupting in mid-water, but those were the only sights and sounds that were on the camera. Second, why were you grasping *mysteria*? What were you doing out of your sector?"

Now, her mouth remained shut. She did not want to have to give up her nightly explorations of the castle. It was the closest thing she had come to a challenge over the past five years. She had found the training easy, and she had picked up all the lessons in no time. Plus, her exploration was the only way she would learn about Ace and the Gifting. "Sir…I—"

Suddenly, the doors to the room opened. Standing there was Mistress Leona. "Second Dean, I understand that she is your pupil, but I would like to speak with her in private if you do not mind."

Mistress Leona could be quite a formidable woman as Aria had learned. She was not surprised when the Second Dean bowed to the Prophet of Nature, his face flustered, and left the room. She was surprised, however, that Mistress Leona had heard of the events already. How long had she been in Stasis?

"Mistress Leona, what are you doing here? Do you know how long I have been in Stasis? I just now got out of it."

The Prophet closed the doors behind her. "Aria, the Grand Master Dean is the one that contacted the Emperor's Council. It was sometime last night. Listen: I do not have much time here. The Council has several affairs to attend to right now, and the affairs of the Academy are not a concern of ours. Nevertheless, I came to tell you to be careful. If the Y'mordi are indeed showing their presences here in the Academy, then they are likely trying to find you. The one that came last night likely was at the wrong place at the right time. They are still trying to remain hidden to the rest of the world."

"Then, how am I supposed to defeat them if they are not going to show themselves? Can I really stay here?" countered Aria with worry.

"I do not know what you should do, other than carry protective barriers at all times. You really need to be careful from now on."

"Mistress Leona…before you leave, I think I need to tell you something. You might be able to help me with this problem I have been having."

"Can this not wait, Aria?" said Mistress Leona in exasperation and impatience.

"No," said Aria at what she considered the Prophet's rudeness. "I think that a part of the Archives are hidden."

The Prophet grinned slightly. "What do you mean hidden? You are probably just not using them correctly. Have you not been here long enough to learn, Aria? I never had a problem with them when I was here."

"I don't think you understand, Mistress Leona. I have found holes in the Archives, data that should exist but just doesn't. The reason I was out last night was because I have been spending many nights looking around the castle for a secret room or something. I think that the Academy is hiding some of its greatest information."

The Prophet's face brightened. "You are clever, Aria. The Prophet of Earth was wise to take you as her apprentice five years ago. I sometimes think that the Council's decision was wrong in forcing you to study here. Nevertheless, I suppose that I should tell you that you are right in your theory. Some of the Archives *are* hidden. I know, because I found them once."

Aria's eyes widened in shock. "You found them?!"

Mistress Leona nodded. "Yes, and I will tell you more, too, if you can promise to keep it a secret. The Academy keeps the information hidden for a reason." Though she had guarded much of that knowledge for all of her life, she was confident that Aria would find it out sooner or later anyways. The Prophet was well aware of Aria's stubbornness and did not doubt that the Guardian of Light would be able to find it. She was merely shortening that search.

Aria nodded eagerly.

"The hidden Archives are all contained in the form of data. What's more is that the Academy itself is the program that can run those sets of data."

"What do you mean?" Aria asked with a frown.

"This castle was once just a regular school, but after the Obsidian Wars, the interior was rebuilt to not only be metallic but to be a computer in itself as well. The Grand Master Dean is the only one who is supposed to know how to utilize the computer's full capabilities. Not even I know everything about the system."

"Well, how do I access the data?"

"The input module. It's at the top of the central tower." Aria was quite familiar with the tower. It ran through the middle of the castle, and its peak was the highest point in the Academy. It had such an amazing view. "The reason no one has found it already is that it is bewitched to be both invisible and untouchable."

Aria was even more puzzled by the term. "Untouchable? How so?"

"It is a somewhat difficult Earth spell that makes any substance or spell go right through the module, meaning that a person could not accidentally stumble upon it."

"How interesting…" Aria said as she considered the cleverness of the spells.

The next night, the elevator hummed as it went straight up. Aria nervously bit her nails. She had been waiting for this moment for five years, and it had been under her nose the whole time. What information would she find? Who had Gifted her? Who was this Ace character that had brought Drage, Matthew, and herself to this world? The questions came one after the other.

Before she knew it, she was at the top of the mechanical spire. She halfway smiled as she stepped out of the elevator. She had always pictured the ascent of a tower to be a long and arduous walk up several flights of stairs, and here she was taking an elevator. It closed and lowered behind her. A mechanical floor sealed the hole where the elevator had stood seconds ago. She had been here once before, but all the tower offered was a good view of the icy plains of the South.

Then, she was alone in the circular room. An iron railing lined the rim of the room to avoid accidents, and the chilling current swept around her.

Her excitement rose as she embraced more of the power of *mysteria*. She traced the floor with her keen sense but was disappointed to find nothing. For several minutes, she stood in the same position looking around the room for the invisible input module. However, nothing was near her. She could not make out the slightest hint of a spell.

Giving up, she leaned against the railing behind her and looked out at the frozen plains of the Southern Continent. To one side, she could see the rest of the city of Gryphos, but the city was of no interest to her. It was not the golden city that Apolis was.

Gradually, she began to release her *mysteria*, but then, she felt it. It was merely a spark, but she sensed it nevertheless. Her heart reached out for more *mysteria*, and then, it became clear: The module was not *in* the room. It wrapped around it like a second railing for the upper half of the room.

She drew her wand and pointed it at the outline. Focusing on several of the Elements at once, she began trying to lower the defenses that surrounded the machine.

Mistress Leona had said that it would respond to one's verbal commands only once the spells were disarmed, so Aria was pleased to find that the spells were easily dissipated.

The computer screen encircled the entire room, from rail to ceiling. She had never before seen such a large computer nor one so circular. "Computer, access Archives," rang out her voice, revealing her great excitement.

"Password?" requested the mechanical voice.

Aria was taken aback. Mistress Leona had never mentioned there being a password. She sighed miserably. It was not going to be as easy as she had thought. Then, she began guessing passwords that might allow her access to the hidden data of the Archives, prepared to open a Gate the second an alarm might go off.

Squirrel in the Trees

The white horse charged through the shadowed forest. Her panicked breathing was muted by the pounding of her hooves into muddy ground, kicking up clouds of muck into the sea as she went. Her wild eyes looked up to see the trees stretch straight toward the sky like black claws ripping a hole in the clouds. She knew the forest well enough to avoid the occasional fallen tree or rock, but her caution was waning as she heard her pursuers gaining on her. The place had been her home for her whole life, but now she had no choice but to flee. The others from her once peaceful village were either dead or fleeing as well. The griffins that had attacked them were quite skilled in battle and had defeated even the adept anima, the animals that could shift into humans, of Lilian's village.

Hopefully, her knowledge of the forest would protect her and allow her to escape the clever beasts that were chasing her. However, griffins were not known for quitting. On the contrary, they were quite persistent creatures. She knew that she might have to fight them if she could not outrun them.

Turning suddenly, she faced her attackers, and her elegant white mane rippled in the strong current of the Northern Continent. Her silver eyes were bright and mystifying, while her front hooves lifted high into the water. An aggressive neighing sound left her mouth as she faced her opponents.

The griffins were unique creatures. They had the bodies and legs of a lion and the head and wings of an eagle, their hands and feet a combination of human hands and eagle claws. Unlike Dragons, griffins had no skill in *mysteria*. Using the powers of their hearts was too complex for them, but they were masters of the sword. The three griffins charged at Lilian, and to her, they were quite fearsome. Equipped with steel armor and deadly swords, the griffins flew between the trees to get to her.

When her hooves hit the ground, vines emerged from the earth and sprang at the flying griffins. Although the vines managed to entangle one unlucky griffin and began to drag it into the crack in the earth from which the vines came, the other two griffins hacked at the plants and proceeded toward Lilian.

In irritation, she stomped another hoof on the ground, and tendrils of Lightning snaked around the two griffins, electrocuting them in their armor. The two smoking bodies fell to the soil in a heap.

A single tear rolled down her elongated snout. She had hoped that her village would not be affected by the civil war that had occurred between Astra and Hurale, the two kingdoms of the Northern Continent. Hurale had pledged to Maris's cause five years ago and stuck to his philosophies of freedom. Together with most of the Western Continent, Hurale had hoped to remove the laws that exiled the nonhumans.

However, Astra had chosen to remain loyal to the Emperor of Light in Helio and his laws. Lilian and most of the villagers she had spent her life with agreed with Astra's queen's choice. Despite their love for each other and their hopes of future independence, they knew that such would not be achieved by fighting the Light and the kingdom that represented it. The most shocking surprise had been when the forces of Helio did not come to Astra's aid when Hurale began the civil war.

Her father, another horse anima, had enlisted in the terra of Astra once the war had started. He had done it to "protect his little girl," he had said. Three months later, a messenger had come to the village and informed her of his death on the battlefield.

Since then, she had been the village leader, although young for an elder, and had protected the village to the best of her abilities. In spite of her strength, a battalion of griffins had snuck past her defenses and decimated the village. She knew that several had escaped, but she was more aware of the vast number of anima that had been killed.

All of a sudden, a high-pitched voice echoed in her mind, "Don't worry, Lilian. I'm sure that a lot of them made it out okay."

Lilian was quite stunned to hear that familiar and childish voice now. However, she was also glad to hear it. Her mind replied, "Senagul, you escaped. I am glad to see that. Have you seen anyone else?"

The squirrel anima scrambled up Lilian's leg and stood with his arms crossed against his furry white chest. "I told you to stop calling me that! Call me Sena!"

Lilian gave Senagul a rather stern look, and the child squirrel finally relented. "Oh, alright. I saw several of them going further south to the other village. My family is a tree or two over from here." He dropped his angry pose and crawled up to stand on Lilian's head with his tiny paws grasping her white hair. "Why do you look sad? Everything will be fine."

The white horse smiled up at the little boy squirrel that was standing on her head. "I am just worried about the others. What can we do? Our homes are gone…"

The squirrel leaned over so that his grinning face was staring right into one of Lilian's silver eyes. "Don't worry. I'll take care of us. No griffin would stand a chance against Sena the Warrior!" He held a fist up challengingly. Then, he saw the griffins that Lilian had defeated. "See, Lilian? The two of us could make a great team: I'll scare them out of their feathers, and you can fry 'em!"

Lilian chuckled at Senagul's proposal. Though the squirrel was quite enthusiastic, she simply could not feel the same way.

They had lost many of their friends in that attack. "You said the others went south, Senagul?"

Sena straightened his posture and ran to Lilian's back. He sat down as his tail twitched in irritation. "I told you to stop calling me that..." he mumbled.

As she tilted her head, she saw Sena's family in the trees above them. "Excuse me, Lara," she called to the mother squirrel. "Would you mind if all of you sent a search party back to the village? I want to make sure that we have not left anyone behind. Also, can I borrow Senagul? I need someone to lead me to the other village. It's been several years since I have last been, and I know that your family goes there often."

The mother squirrel Lara responded with a nod and leaped with her mate and other children to the next tree.

Her head turned to face Senagul. "Sena, do you think you could show me the way to the village? I do not actually remember the way." Over the past few years, she had remained in her own village and had not gone to the other village. Most of Astra consisted of these small villages, and several were quite closely knit, but her village was not one of those. They were only ever in communication with the one to their south.

Brightened by Lilian's using his preferred name, Senagul gave a rapid salute to the white mare and leaped onto a nearby tree trunk. He clumsily scrambled to one of the lower branches and called to Lilian with his mind, "Follow me!"

Several hours later, Lilian had found no one and only had the rapid blur of brown and white fur above her as a guide. "Sena, how much further? Surely, we are almost they by now?" She was not becoming tired. She was, however, getting anxious to see the others and discover how many had survived the attacks of Hurale's griffins. Only once had she ever left her family and friends. That had been when she had gone from the Northern Continent to the Western and Southern Continents with Marqest and Matthew.

Though those times had been exciting yet terrifying adventures, she preferred living a calm life with her village.

Now, however, she no longer had that luxury. Hurale was winning the civil war, and peace was not an option. She knew that once she regrouped with the others, they would have to plan how to keep each other safe. Lilian would have to join the terra as her father had.

Senagul responded with his usual high voice. "It's not too much further! Mom says that it's not good to whine either!"

Lilian smiled in agreement, "That's right, Sena. You have a smart mother."

Senagul nodded his tiny head rapidly, "Uh-huh!"

The trees went past them at nearly lightning speed. Her hooves pounded the ground with every step as she galloped through forest, sunlight barely piercing the trees. She breathed in the water deeply, and then she felt another presence amongst the trees that was keeping pace with them. Her heart rose in her chest anxiously. Was it another survivor?

She opened her heart to *mysteria* and felt it drop down once more. It was a griffin. Her mind reached out to Senagul alone, "Sena, we are being followed. I need you to stay hidden high in the tree but watch me. If something happens to me, keep going to the village and tell them. Do you understand?"

"Yes, Lilian," was Senagul's stuttered response as he scrambled to get higher into the tree on which he had stopped. Lilian turned to face the direction where the unseen griffin was. The whole forest was silent for a moment. The current softened, and not even the animals in the treetops were making their usual noises.

Then, the griffin appeared from behind a tree. Its razor-sharp beak opened, and he spoke. "Anima, I mean you no harm." His voice was raspy and deep.

Lilian snapped, "Then, why have you been following me?"

"I only have the intention of finishing a job I had a few hours ago. If you are not from the village to the north, then I have no business with you. I have been seeking survivors." The griffin regarded Lilian cautiously, trying to figure out if this anima standing so calmly and comfortably in the forest could have escaped the raid and stopped here randomly in the woods.

It dawned on Lilian that the griffin had obviously not been part of the group that had been actively chasing her. Nevertheless, he was one of those who had killed many of her friends.

As her fury rose, the current strengthened. Seeing what was happening, the griffin drew his sword and prepared to block whatever spell Lilian was summoning.

Suddenly, a bolt of brown and white shot down from the sky onto the griffin. With a terrified scream, the griffin dropped his sword and frantically tried to remove the creature that was clawing at his face, the ball of fur dodging the swipes of his talons.

Once the bolt leaped off the griffin's light brown body, Lilian released a surge of Lightning to envelop the griffin. The bolt of fur moved to stand on the back of the smoking griffin. "See? I told you we make a great team, Lilian! Heehee!" He put his fists on his waist and struck a comical, heroic pose as he beamed up at the white horse.

Lilian shook her head and scolded the young squirrel, "You could have gotten yourself killed, Senagul. Next time, do as you are told. Your mother will hear about this." She made her voice as stern as she could, though she was in all honesty glad for Sena's help. The griffin had not seen that particular attack coming.

Senagul lowered his head sadly. He could tell that Lilian was upset with him. "I'm sorry, Lilian. I didn't mean to make you mad." His optimism decreased considerably as he dropped his proud stance. Sparkling tears welled up in his beady black eyes. His tiny lower jaw began to tremble.

Lilian could not help but feel sorry for the little creature. She simply could not stay mad at him. "Just try to be a little more careful next time, okay?" She managed a weak smile. Hopefully, that griffin had not found any of the survivors.

The squirrel smiled back up at Lilian and wiped the tears away with one slender paw. "Okay. Are you ready to keep going? I'm ready when you are."

Lilian nodded encouragingly. For the past two years, the small squirrel anima had loved being around her, and his parents trusted Lilian enough to allow Senagul to stay under her protection. If anything, they thought that perhaps Lilian would be a positive influence on him. Plus, it got him out of their hair every once in a while.

She had watched over him fondly and had enjoyed satisfying his growing curiosity in the world around him. Senagul had become considerably attached to Lilian in the form of an annoying little brother. However, he was always optimistic, and that could brighten her life almost any day. "Let's get going, Sena."

"Actually…" began Senagul hesitantly. "I was wondering if I could stay on your back for a little while. To be honest, my paws are kind of hurting." He did not like to complain, least of all to Lilian.

"Alright, can you point me in the right direction first? Then, you can rest for a while. Sound good?"

Senagul beamed warmly at Lilian. "Yeah, the village is that way," he said as he pointed one meek clawed finger to the south and a few degrees east. "It should only be an hour away now." He yawned deeply, and then, he leaped onto Lilian's immaculate, white back and curled into an innocent ball with his tail wrapping around him. Sleep came instantly.

Her hooves traversed the ground at a slower yet even pace, so as to cover plenty of ground without disturbing Senagul. As she galloped, she noticed the current shift to the east. Like Senagul, she, too, was getting quite exhausted from their excursion. Most people took a night's rest on the way to the village. Although she was built for long runs like this one, it was rather tiring. Her form was muscular, the product of years of fighting for her village. Now, though, her body felt spent.

"We will be there soon," she muttered, more to herself than to the squirrel that was sleeping on her back.

It actually took her two and a half more hours to get to the southern village. Her pace had overall been slower than she would have liked. She admitted to herself, however, that was likely because of her not wanting to wake Senagul.

Two lizard anima who were guarding the village approached her. "Are you the village elder from the north?" they asked.

Lilian panted heavily from her trek. "Yes, I am she. Has anyone else returned from my village?"

The guards nodded grimly, "Yes, there were a few. Come with us. We will take you to the elder here."

Lilian interrupted them first, however. "Actually, can you take this boy to where the others are? He is pretty tired right now." She gestured with her head to the squirrel anima. "Sena, it is time to get up. This guard is going to show you to where the others are, okay?"

The half-asleep boy was too tired to argue and scampered off of Lilian and onto the ground. He walked steadily with the reptilian guard.

A brilliant aura of white light surrounded Lilian as she transformed from a white mare to a young, thin woman with quite long, snowy hair and a white robe to match. Her face was round, and her skin was pale and without blemishes. She had grown into this much taller appearance three years ago, and she had been considerably glad of the change. Although the animal form grew at a regular pace, an anima's human form developed in sudden stages, more like a spider shedding its skin for a new one. "Take me to the elder, please," she requested.

The lizard stood and transformed into a lanky but scaleless man with no hair on his head and green eyes that perfectly matched the color of his scales from his lizard form.

The elder was an old crane. Her hut was kept warm by a scorching blue fire in the back of the building, and miscellaneous vials were scattered across the room. The old woman croaked sadly, "It was the griffins, then?"

Lilian nodded with equal grief. "Yes, elder. We never saw them coming. They snuck past our defenses somehow." She looked down and to the side. "I am quite ashamed of my blunder to be honest."

The elder waved a hand dismissively. "No, it is not your fault. I have no doubt that you did everything that you could. I believe, however, that the greatest concern now is what to do."

"What to do?"

"Yes," replied the elder with a nod. "It is likely that Hurale's troops will attack this village next. They will not rest until all opposition is crushed. What they do not realize is that they are only helping the people in the East and South by eliminating us, not rebelling against them. This world is getting tired of our kind, and we are suffering."

Lilian countered the idea strongly, "We can still stop them, though. We will not be exiles forever, elder. I know that the people at Apolis will get rid of that law. I have seen their Prince, and I am sure that once he takes the Throne, we will be fine. He would not want us killed."

"You put too much faith in the humans. The point remains that this village is not safe, by any means. The griffins will come here next, but this time, they will be killing two groups: the survivors of your village and my village. There is simply no point in fighting."

Anger faded out of Lilian. She remembered her initial training in *mysteria*. The trick was to empty oneself of all emotions and be ready to feel anything at a moment's notice. If she responded with anger at this elder, then any hope for negotiation would disappear. She had to approach this matter more calmly. "Elder, I am sure that we could go against them and protect this village. If you are sure that they are coming, then we can stop them. We cannot give up hope now."

The elder grumbled something incoherently.

Before Lilian could ask for the elder to repeat herself, she became aware of a Darkness moving outside the village. She rose suddenly.

The elder's head also turned to where the Darkness was located. "Something is moving out there, is it not? Tell me this: did you lead them here on purpose?"

Lilian rapidly twisted her head to look at the elder. "What? Are you accusing me of bringing the griffins here? I would never have done such a thing! I had no idea they were following me!"

"You did this on purpose. You are a traitor. You have condemned us all." The Elder seemed to draw into herself, lowering her head in utter submission to the oncoming attack.

The horse anima could not contain it any longer, and she stormed out of the domed hut. She began roaring out instructions immediately. "You!" she called as she pointed to a nearby armored goat. "To the entrance of the village! We are under attack!" Her voice elevated as she addressed the standing anima around her, all confused about the forces of evil they sensed around their village. "Everyone! Get to your positions! We are under attack from the griffins! If you want to survive the night, you need to grab a sword and get out here!" The response was immediate: all of the anima, from the ones who had been standing still and looking at the village walls to the anima who had been running around in panic, leaped into action. Many ran into the closest huts and grabbed rakes, swords, poles, and anything else they could get their hands on that would suffice. With someone to unite them, they felt a fire burning in their hearts. They felt strong.

If this village's elder would not stand up for the village, then Lilian would. The white glow surrounded her once again as she transformed into a horse, allowing her to focus entirely on *mysteria* and not be distracted with keeping up her human form. Her neighing was a deep battle cry that resonated through the village, and she charged forward into the night with her heart ready to cast any spell she might need.

One dilemma was still puzzling to her however: Why was she sensing Darkness? Griffins were not masters of spells, so what was causing her to sense such a dominating and active aura? Then, she saw that they had a Dragon with them. This battle was going to be much more difficult than she had previously imagined.

A few yards away, Senagul rolled over in his sleep, dreaming about fighting griffins and monsters just like Lilian had on so many occasions. With Lilian having cast a spell to help him sleep better, his furry ears could not pick up the struggle that was occurring all around the village. Carefully, his bushy tail began to curl around his wearied body.

Sacrifice

B ecause Draconis was awake quite early and before most of the people in the camp, he decided to take a stroll along the white, sandy beach. The ocean before him reminded him instantly of Gevás, with its atmosphere of water. However, he found himself surprised that he did not miss it. As his talons clawed at the sand, relishing its grainy texture, he realized how much he had missed the air, the sky, the wind. It was relaxing to feel that soft breeze against his face. Behind him, he could see the rows of tents that marked the rebels' camp. The beach extended along a lake. The other side was lined with trees.

The morning sun began to paint the cloud-filled sky a multitude of bright colors that caused Draconis to smile broadly. In Gevás, the water made the sky blur somewhat. Here, however, everything was crystal clear.

He stretched his muscles casually and felt the soreness in them. Although he had been training in the ways of the sword for years, he had not expected such a vigorous routine of battle training as Elani had shown him the past few days. In Gevás, he had been adept in the Way of the Dragon, but here, his form was easily defeated by Elani's deadly twofold.

Along with the swordplay training, he found it necessary to teach several of the Dragons how to utilize the full potential of *mysteria* in the span of a few days. Of course, he had taught them the less destructive Elements first: Water and Earth. Learning even the simplest spells came as a surprise to the students and onlookers as well. The idea of a Dragon manipulating an Element that was not unique to his or her race was still a bewildering concept to many of them.

The Black Dragon Elani had been exceptionally pleased when he had shown the Dragons a particularly useful spell: how to summon Gates.

After days of this preparation and training, the time of the mission had come at last. Today was the day that the Dragons would raid one of the Imperial cities.

While taking another deep and relaxing breath, he noticed the Blue Dragon in the distance who was standing pensively in front of the sea. He leisurely continued his walk until he was standing beside Lly.

"Rexam, what are you doing awake this early? You know you have a long day ahead of you, do you not? I had thought that you would have prized sleep much more by the end of the week."

Draconis countered gently, "The world in which I have lived for the past century and a half was an underwater world. I have not felt the air in my face since I was last here. I enjoy even the simple act of walking around the beach. After Cairon is taken care of, I want to go back to that world. I have so much unfinished business there that I cannot ignore. Therefore, I am going to make the most of my time here."

Lly's eyes widened for only a second in astonishment. She had thought the Golden Dragon would stay with them even after Cairon was defeated. It never occurred to her that he would have the slightest intention of returning to Gevás. "Ah, I see."

"You like the sea, do you not? That is how Blue Dragons are, if I remember correctly." As Blue Dragons had lived for centuries in lakes and ponds, they had developed advantages:

more deeply webbed hands, long, slender wings that can tuck tightly against their bodies, and pointed snouts that cut through the water.

Lly nodded as she turned her head back to the vast sea in front of them. "Blue Dragons are the only Dragons capable of breathing underwater. We love living under the sea. It is a completely different world under there. It has a life all its own." Her eyes betrayed a sparkling love for the shimmering water.

The Golden Dragon offered a grin as he said, "Maybe one day, you could come to Gevás. It is the underwater world I told you about. At first, it seemed amazing to me, but I suppose that as the years went on, I became used to it."

Lly responded, "That makes sense, Rexam. Perhaps, one day, when this is all over, I would like to see such a world. I can honestly say that I have not given much thought as to what I will do when the world is righted. I am not one to plan or think ahead so far as that. Thank you very much for your offer." Though she was trying not to reveal too much emotion, she was genuinely glad that Draconis had made such an offer. The sea was a thing of enchantment to her, and the offer that Draconis had made to her was now something that she anticipated eagerly.

Draconis decided to attempt to gain some information from Lly then. "Pardon me for asking, but do you think you could tell me a little bit about Elani? She seems to be quite an interesting character, but she is not one to approach on personal affairs. However, I have noticed that you and the captain are somewhat close, am I not correct?" He found his interest piqued regarding the mysterious Black Dragon. He knew that somewhere beneath her aggressive exterior, there was a softer Dragon.

"We are. We have known each other for a long time, Rexam. I suppose that I can tell you that Elani is a lot less hard than she appears to be. She is not as heartless as she tries to make everyone believe. Elani is devoted and loyal but not to the point where she is allowing others to think for her."

Draconis nodded. "Yes, I could tell that she was quite independent." It was then that the sun was at the perfect angle to reflect onto the sea, creating a million diamonds of light on the water's surface. While Lly was entranced by the illuminating display, Draconis was enthralled by something else.

As the water shimmered, so did Lly's blue-scaled body. Draconis found himself admiring the serpentine curve of her figure and the calm eyes that were taking in the glow of the sea. That same glow reflected onto her scales and created a beautiful display of light on her pale chest.

Suddenly, her eyes moved to look at him. Embarrassed, he straightened his form and looked out at the sea quickly. Though he did not see it, a grin formed on Lly's lips. She said softly, "You might want to get ready. Elani will be awake soon, as well." As she left him, she gave him one last sidelong glance.

Once he was sure that Lly was no longer looking, he buried his scaly head into one large claw. He could not believe how rude he had just been. Then again, Lly had not reacted badly to him. He shook his head. The last thing he needed to do was read more into something that was likely to not exist.

With a sigh, he began walking back to his tent. Today was definitely going to be a long day.

Lly approached Elani that morning in an incredibly positive mood. "Lani, the dawn is here. Would you like for me to awaken the troops?"

Elani's red eyes opened in bewilderment, "You sound quite happy, Lly. Why is this?"

Lly gave her friend a sly smile and left the tent.

Elani gradually rose from her hammock. As she stretched her back, each muscle felt alive and fresh. She was ready for this day. It was time for one of their most effective raids yet.

She walked to the back of her tent and found her nicest set of armor. Like her scales, it was a solid black and perfectly smooth, meant to deflect any blows. Although the craftsmanship of the armor made it seem sharp and dangerous, she could see her reflection clearly on its surface, perfectly polished ebony.

The past several years, she had become hardened. As a leader, everyone had looked up to her. The weight of responsibility had made her limit her more personal side, unless she was around Lly. The only thing in her mind was the goal of defeating Cairon. She remembered when Cairon had first conquered the capital. Almost every Black Dragon was delighted by his conquest, but she had seen the wrong in his actions and wanted retribution. The Black Dragons had defied the natural order. The Divine Dragons of the Heavens had pushed them down to a certain caste, and, while Elani was against total exile, she did not like the way that Cairon had completely upset the natural balance of Sharl Vran. The Golden Dragons had done nothing except maintain their birthright. Cairon was a villain.

However, now that the Golden Dragon Draconis was on their side, defeating Cairon would be much easier. Depending on the success of today's mission, the capital would likely be the next target. She had been making Draconis work to his maximum over the past week. She had personally taken care of his battle training, and watching him teach other Dragons about using the mystical force he called *mysteria* had been quite interesting as well. The successful results, however, were even more impressive. Draconis had effectively taught around thirty Dragons how to manipulate various spells. The Gates had been the most useful spells. Her plan was to use those to transport the troops to and from the battlefield. The element of surprise would be theirs, and that was an advantage that she had never imagined having. This new plan removed much of the risks on the spies' parts.

As she equipped her heavy armor, she realized how anxious and nervous she was. This battle could either cripple everything she had worked for over the years or turn the tides of this struggle fully against Cairon. Every raid up to this point had merely been a thorn to Kusvor Cairon, hardly a blow. This time, however, if they won, Cairon would find himself at a disadvantage: it was a stronghold of resources. Besides having a command post right beside the capital, the rebels' amount of resources would increase almost exponentially by taking this Imperial city.

Finally, she brushed back the tent flap and beheld the dazzling sunlight. This attack would have to occur in the morning. Where they were planning on attacking, the sun would be to their backs at this time and in their enemies' eyes. Much to Elani's surprise, this particular strategy had been one of Draconis's own. His military tact was clearly more developed than hers, and for that reason, she envied him, but she noticed that the Golden Dragon was not trying to take her position. He was subservient to her, yet he was an instructor and leader for the rebels. Despite his dominant and often aggressive personality, she was not intimidated. She felt proud to have him as an asset here.

Around her, she watched as her troops began assembling for the day's mission. She held her helmet at her side and began heading toward the blacksmith. By now, her twofold would be well sharpened.

Several tents away, Draconis arrived at his sleeping quarters to see that the blacksmith had fulfilled his requests. Before him was a full set of green armor. The blacksmith had been justifiably perplexed when the Golden Dragon had made the proposal. It was mostly chainmail, but green cloth connected many of the pieces of the suit. He preferred the lighter armor as compared to the heavy armor that most Dragons used. He had a strong favoring of versatility in a battle. His finesse in fighting did not come from his strength: It came from his skill and speed.

He handled the material fondly as he inspected it. Every link of metal was immaculately made, and the cloth was as durable as he had wished it to be. The blacksmith had truly outdone himself. Draconis found himself wondering how Elani had happened across such a gifted individual.

As he suited himself for the upcoming mission, he noticed the other item in his tent. It was exceptionally thin sword. The blade was gold, yet it had occasional stripes of green running across the thin metal. Beside the sword was a note. In utter perplexity, Draconis bent to grab the note and began to read it:

"Rexam, I know that you only asked for the armor, but I have been watching you in your training, and I realized that one of your disadvantages in combatting Elani is the weight of your sword. It takes little to no effort for her to disarm you using her twofold. If you want to stand against Cairon and his Black Dragons, I decided that you would need something...more appropriate. I call this blade the goldfoil. It has nowhere near the strength of your previous weapon, but it as light as air, and the shape of the blade prohibits the twofold from disarming you. Good luck today!"

Draconis smiled at the kind note and considered the gift. He had never heard of a Dragon using such a thin sword. The twofold had equally thin blades, but at least it had two blades rather than one. Plus, the twofold was curved sharply at the end. This goldfoil was far simpler.

Nevertheless, he felt as if the blacksmith's judgment probably had some truth in it. At the same time, though, he was not prepared to go into battle with a new weapon.

Then, an idea came to him: He would ask Elani to train with him once more before they left for the city. With a rush in his step, he strode to where Elani was. It seemed that the other soldiers were preparing for the mission as well, so that meant that Elani was probably almost ready to leave. He hastened his pace. Although the battle was a few hours away, he wanted to test this new blade first.

When he arrived at Elani's tent, no one was there. Anxiously, his sapphire eyes began scanning the camp for the Black Dragon, and finally, he found her in the distance. She was standing at the blacksmith's tent. With a pleasant rumble vibrating in his chest, he performed a mighty leap and allowed his wings to carry him to Elani.

"Can I help you, Rexam?" said the Black Dragon calmly. Her red eyes studied him curiously.

Draconis nodded. "Yes, Elani. I was wondering if you would train with me one more time before we left."

A sly smile crept across Elani's face. She could sense something different about the Golden Dragon other than his uniquely colored armor. Draconis obviously wanted to test out his new armor, or something of the like. "Very well. Shall we do it here? We really do not have that much time to waste."

Draconis nodded appreciatively. "Here is fine." Then, he noticed that Elani's twofold appeared to be completely new. Both blades had been polished and sharpened. He swallowed nervously as they stepped a few yards away from the blacksmith's tent. He was not surprised to see that the red-scaled blacksmith was watching the two in an almost anxious excitement. More Dragons started to crowd around, excited to see two experts in battle combat each other in full armor.

Without warning, Elani lunged at Draconis, her twofold flowing into the dance of battle. Equally rapidly, the Golden Dragon drew his goldfoil, blocking Elani's attacks. The tiny weapon vibrated every time the twofold met it. He struggled to maintain a tight grip on it, but, after a few of Elani's aggressive combos, he became more used to it.

"What a puny weapon, Rexam," Elani said in an attempt to provoke the Golden Dragon. She decided the training was merely a means of testing his new weapon. Rather than aiming for speed, she increased the strength she put behind each strike. She smirked as he stepped backward, failing to maintain control over his sword against her onslaught. As they pressed toward the ring of Dragons, some of them stepped back, anticipating being run into. Draconis growled and planted his feet, and he forced himself to regain some control, although he was still entirely on the defensive. In an attempt to push the training further, she struck downward at his sword, preparing to disarm him. She hesitated for a moment to allow Draconis an opportunity to strike, and then her twofold lifted at just the right angle to allow his sword to fit between the parallel clawlike blades. With a jerk of her wrist, she attempted to wrench the goldfoil out of his hands.

However, both Elani and Draconis were surprised to find that the sword was small enough to avoid the twisting twofold. His blade continued its momentum, and he only just stopped it in front of her snout. Her red eyes widened.

"You are the first Dragon to have ever beaten me in combat, Rexam."

Out of the corner of his eye, he could see the Dragons cheering and the blacksmith beaming with pride in his handiwork. He had been right: the goldfoil was entirely effective against the deadly twofold. The other Dragons departed.

Elani sheathed her weapon and gave a warm smile to Draconis. Though she had been defeated, disappointment in herself was not among her emotions. Rather, she was proud that Draconis had managed to become a more adept fighter through the use of his new weapon. "Good job, Rexam. We really must go, now. We are running out of time."

Draconis gave a silent bob of the head in acknowledgement and proceeded to follow her back to the rest of the troops. As he sheathed the goldfoil, he was in shock of what had occurred. For a second, he could have sworn that he had seen through Elani's hard and seemingly heartless shell. He could have sworn he saw a soft and gentle heart beneath.

"Prepare the Gates!" called Elani's commanding voice.

As many of Draconis's students in *mysteria* began summoning several Gates across the campsite, Lly stood and strode over to Elani with a smile on her blue-scaled face beside her.

"Lani, this is going to be our strongest blow to Cairon. Today, we are going to change the world." She felt quite optimistic about this battle. Years of planning and working were finally going to show amazing results.

The Black Dragon did not avert her eyes from the troops. "Lly…we have been close friends for a long time. I will tell you now that if something were to happen to me on the field, you are to take my place as leader. You know what this is rebellion is about more than anyone else here. For years, you have served as my eyes, ears, and sword. I—"

Lly shook her head in confusion and exasperation. "What are you talking about, Lani? Nothing is going to happen to you. We have the perfect battle planned. What are you worrying about?"

Elani lowered her dark snout and muttered, "A long time ago, a wise Dragon told me that the day another Dragon could defeat me in a battle of the sword would be the day that I died. I do not know if I necessarily believe him, but he was a well-reputed wise Dragon."

"It does not matter. You have not been defeated, and I doubt you will today. We have the element of surprise after all."

"You do not understand, Lly. Today, Rexam defeated me."

Lly's first reaction was of admiration. She was quite impressed by Draconis's skill. No one had ever managed to stand a chance against Elani when she had the twofold in claw. Gradually, she realized what Elani was implying, however. "Nothing is going to happen to you, Lani. Everything will go as planned. Even if Rexam had the luck of beating you, a weaker Dragon will not be able to perform the feat. Do not let your shaken confidence be your weakness today."

Elani was inspired by Lly's words, although she still had some reservation. The last thing she wanted to be was one of those ironic stories of war. "You are right. Thank you." Then, she noticed that all of the Gates had been summoned. A nod of her head signaled to the flagmen who were standing beside the Gates.

The uniformed flagmen flew into the air, and simultaneously, the red flags were raised high so that every Dragon could see the crimson command. Rapidly, the entire army of Dragons began charging into the Gates. The only sounds were the stomps of their scaly feet and the metallic clanks of the shifting armor.

In the charge, Elani and Lly could make out the Golden Dragon Draconis. He did not stampede recklessly as the others did. It was a controlled sprint that made his body move as little as possible. He seemed to glide across the field. However, both of them could see the intense passion that was alight in his eyes.

It was time for battle.

As soon as the Gate disappeared behind him, Draconis recognized the city in which he was fighting. He had been here before, but with each passing second, the city was being altered by the tides of war. Already, several corpses of Black Dragons littered the ground, and his students continued to unleash a barrage of fireballs around the city. Towers and buildings were broken and cracked, although they retained their golden luster. He recognized a plaza that was once a market, a corner that once held a training ground, and a shattered fountain that was once the favorite place of his family to stop and listen to the music in the courtyard.

Suddenly, an archer appeared on the battlements of the city. With one outstretched hand, Draconis summoned a bolt of Lightning that sent the Black Dragon flying. As more archers appeared, the rebels shot a few Lightning bolts toward them, imitating their golden leader. When a few guards came rushing out of a tower, Draconis buried them beneath an Earth spell in seconds. Some of the rebel Dragons split off to clear out some of the buildings.

In the distance, he could clearly see the central fortress. To take the city, they would have to conquer that fortress. "They are taking shelter in the fortress," said a voice beside him. He turned to see Lly running beside him. They both smiled at each other as if they were not in the middle of a battlefield right now. "We should probably fly ahead."

Draconis nodded as his wings lifted him into the air. "What about Elani? Where is she?"

"She is covering the rear. She believes that the greatest priority isn't winning, but keeping her people alive."

A look of puzzlement spread across Draconis's face.

"For Elani, part of being a leader means leading us into a better life."

Draconis considered what this might mean in the midst of battle. "So, if a retreat was made, she would be at the lead of that?"

Lly nodded. "That is right. However, no one thinks negatively of her for that choice. No one doubts her courage, and we know her intent is always to help. She is the brains behind this operation. While she is a strong fighter, it is her spirit and her intelligence that has led us this far. It is no selfish desire that puts her at the front of a retreat, but the desire to preserve all of us."

Draconis thought only positives of Elani. She was by all standards an effective leader. On Gevás, he would have quickly harassed a captain who did not cover the rear during a retreat. On Sharl Vran, though, the logic of leading a retreat seemed reasonable. As his sapphire eyes drifted over to Lly, he saw a Black Dragon darting toward them. It wielded a twofold.

In an almost impossibly sharp turn, Draconis soared over Lly by mere inches and drew his goldfoil at the same time. The thin blade barely blocked the twofold in time from slashing Lly's side.

The Black Dragon was obviously shocked by the appearance of a Golden Dragon. With a snarl, it struck drown at Draconis's head, but the goldfoil blocked the blades again and slashed at the Black Dragon's stomach. The Black Dragon nimbly dodged the strike. As it pulled its arm back to swing again, Draconis heard a sudden roaring sound. However, he ignored it and continued to fight his enemy. Before he could get another attack in, the roaring intensified, and all of a sudden, a stream of Water engulfed the Black Dragon and held him. Without hesitation, Draconis performed a horizontal slash through the water, slicing the Black Dragon in half.

When he turned around, he saw that Lly had manipulated the water in a nearby fountain. Impressed with Lly's quick thinking, he smiled again at her. She glided over to him and said softly, "Thank you for saving me, Rexam."

For the first time, he became aware that Lly might actually have feelings for him. The look in her eyes revealed that much. Draconis's battle-ready expression melted before her, and his smile portrayed a feeling of fondness. It was then that Lly realized that Draconis had feelings for her as well.

A deafening explosion interrupted the moment. They jerked their heads toward the sound, and their eyes widened.

Torrents of black smoke shot out from the windows and doors of the fortress like immense arms. These thick columns began crushing the front members of the army. It was as if the smoke solidified upon impact, smashing and killing any Dragon it touched. Draconis growled in both anger and fear. Cairon had indeed learned how to use the various Elements of *mysteria*, and he was using them as weapons of malice. The Dragons' screams were muffled by the smoke, and the Dragons not crushed began to panic. The effect was instantaneous, and Draconis knew that not even he himself could cut through this spell.

Elani shouted, "Retreat! Retreat!" The rebel Dragons immediately escaped through Gates, and the Dark arms hurried to crush as many as it could before they fled.

In a fury, Draconis rushed toward the fortress. His wings beat faster than he had ever flown before. Lly called out his name as she chased after him.

He desperately reached for the Light within his heart and forced that energy outward. His whole body began to glow with a golden light, and the Light acted as a shield around him. One of the black arms shot from the fountain and arched up into the air before descending again to crush him, but it dissipated once it came near the golden aura. Lly gasped a few yards behind him.

She exclaimed fearfully, "Rexam, we need to get out of here!"

A deep voice rumbled from the depths of the fortress, "King Cairon told us that we would find a Golden Dragon here. He never told us that we would find two."

Draconis was quite surprised by this comment. He looked around and was even more stunned to see that the Dragon behind him was Golden. "Lly?"

A sad expression lit her face, "It's just a spell. I am a Blue Dragon, but can you not see it now? This was a setup. We were expected."

"Why are you disguising as—?"

"Silence!" roared the voice from the fortress. A black arm shot out and pulled Lly into a dark window.

"Lly!" called Draconis, and, as he did so, worry piercing through his focus on the Light, his aura of gold faded. Another black arm reached out and enveloped him. As it dragged him into the the black void, the overwhelming power of Cairon's Darkness closed his consciousness.

Hours later, Elani was pacing in the forest, frantically trying to come up with a way to get Lly and Draconis back. What had happened back there? Cairon would pay for what this tragedy.

She angrily slashed a nearby tree with her twofold, and the trunk collapsed onto its side. On the other side of the woods, she heard Dragons still wailing and bemoaning those who were lost. Thankfully, Cairon had no idea where their camp was. They were safe. The next question, however, was what to do next.

She had already sent spies back to that city to try to find out where Lly and Draconis were, but she had not heard back from them yet.

Suddenly, her anger subsided, and she was left with only sorrow. A few tears began rolling down her cheeks. "Lly, where are you?"

1,000 Years Ago - 2

"So cold…"

"Soldier? Are you awake?" said a voice.

"So cold…" he repeated.

The voice called out to someone else, "Quick! Healer, will you raise the temperature?"

The soldier's eyes opened slowly, and the light above was almost blinding to him. He was shivering under golden sheets. In the corner of the room, he could make out a healer. She was pressing several buttons in the wall panel. As she did so, he noticed that the temperature of the room was increasing. His shivering gradually decreased.

"Soldier, can you hear me?" said the voice.

The soldier turned his head to see a uniformed man standing there. "Who are you?"

"My name is General Paldas. I was assigned to watch over you while you were out."

"Out? Where am I?" His eyes scanned over the room in wonder.

"You are in the infirmary in the Palace of Light. You were found several weeks ago with a White Dragon."

The mention of the White Dragon brought all of the memories back to the soldier. "Kohana! Where is she?" He sat up quickly and began calling to her with his mind as he had done weeks ago. *Kohana! Kohana! Are you there?*

"She is here in the Palace. She has been in as much of a coma as you. His Majesty, the Lord of Light Lux, wants to know what happened to the force you were with, and how you ended up on the Southern Continent with a White Dragon and a sword that followed you all the way."

The last piece of information was quite perplexing to Tatsu. Suddenly, he heard a voice in his mind, *I am here, Tatsu. I have just woken up as well. Something feels strange, does it not?*

Tatsu also felt something unusual blooming within his heart. He was noticing that he could almost feel what Kohana was feeling. He reached out for that feeling even more, and he closed his eyes as he did so. Those emotions began to grow in his heart, and when he opened his eyes, he found quite a surprise.

He was no longer in the infirmary. He was in a large, circular room with a high ceiling. As he scanned the area, something caught his attention: white scales. His gaze snapped downward to see the claws of a White Dragon. It took him several seconds to realize that those claws were his. When he moved his arm, the claw moved as well. Entirely disoriented, he felt his heart race.

Kohana? What is going on?

I do not know. Somehow, our bodies have switched. Tatsu looked around for Kohana, but he realized she must be in his body, still in the infirmary. *Who is this noisy man in here? He reeks of skander and spice.*

When Tatsu laughed, it came out deep but soft at the same time. *That is General Paldas. We are in the Palace of Light.*

Kohana grunted. *Well, how are we doing this? I can feel your essence deep inside my heart. This is rather unusual.*

That is how I think I did it. I reached out for your heart, and we sort of…switched places, I think.

Kohana attempted the feat with some concentration, and instantly, they were switched back to their regular bodies. Kohana was back in the large room in her serpentine body, while Tatsu was in the infirmary on the bed.

"Soldier, are you alright?" repeated General Paldas.

Tatsu nodded slowly. "Yes, sir."

The General sighed and then asked hesitantly, "Are you well enough to walk? His Majesty would like to speak with you as soon as you are ready."

"I can make it."

The General brightened. "Very well. Your clothes are over there," he said as he pointed to shelf on the near wall. Meet me outside the infirmary in a few minutes." Before he reached the door, he stopped suddenly and added, "Oh, and by the way, your sword is among your possessions as well. Would you mind satisfying my curiosity? How did you get it to follow you while you were in a coma? We never saw it move, but...every time we stopped, it reappeared beside you."

Tatsu was even more perplexed and curious now. He could sense Kohana's surprise as well. *Did you hear that, Kohana?*

Yes, Tatsu. I think that if you try you could hear and see what I am observing as well. Something happened to the two of us. When the Y'mordi stabbed you, he left, but a strange light hit the sword, and that is all that I remember...How are we even still alive?

Tatsu remembered, too. How was he alive? He had been stabbed in the chest. He pulled the sheets back, and there was only a scar where the sword had entered his body. The wound had healed completely.

An hour later, Tatsu was walking in the coraled Imperial Gardens. The Great Lord of Light had not been that helpful. After recounting what had happened to his comrades and how he had met Kohana, the Great Lord of Light had concluded that Kohana had simply been one of Dagan's plans for a future weapon, a Dragon to be molded into a fearsome assassin. As a result of this knowledge, the Great Lord of Light decided to put Tatsu back into the terra immediately, and Kohana would be trained in Apolis until she could fight on her own. The plan was for the two to be separated. Their meeting had only been a coincidence.

In frustration, he kicked a nearby pebble. He had not spoken to Kohana since that unfortunate meeting. Nevertheless, they could each feel what the other was thinking. They were terrified, furious, miserable, and lonely. The spiritual bond between them made them connect on a deeper level than either had ever known another being. They shared body, heart, mind, and soul, and that connection was more comforting than alarming. They knew they were never alone. Everything they faced, they faced together.

A metallic clank resounded in his head. He halfway closed his eyes so as to see through Kohana's eyes without switching places with her. The door to her large room was opening, and several troops entered. One spoke, "Alright, Dragon, we're gonna begin your training in one of the arenas. Come with us please."

Tatsu could sense Kohana's reluctance. He whispered into her mind, *Kohana, go ahead with them. I will meet you at the arena. I can follow you there. I can honestly spend most of the day with you. The Great Lord of Light gave me one more day to rest if I needed it.*

Kohana's hesitation subsided slightly. *Very well. Thank you, Tatsu.* She then began following the men.

Tatsu realized then that Kohana did not have the same sense of responsibility that he had. For years, he had been an excellent soldier in the Lord of Light's terra, but she had been brought up in a tiny prison. The most horrible part was that she was going to end up doing exactly what Dagan was planning to do with her. Understanding Kohana's sadness so intimately made him share the same emotions, but he knew that he could do nothing about the situation. As he exited the Gardens, he discovered that his new bond with Kohana allowed him to know how close he was to her. His heart acted like a tracking device of sorts.

None of the people he passed paid any attention to him, though many people had already heard his story. Apparently, over the past three weeks, word had passed around the city of what little information was known about Tatsu and his dangerous mission in the Eastern Continent.

This city of Apolis was absolutely spectacular with its grassy lawns and golden houses. He had been to Helio's capital only a few times in his life, and he had always been at the military base to the north in Mashan Telis.

Then, he saw her. The White Dragon was as beautiful as he had remembered. However, he had to admit that her glow was not as magnificent as it had been in the moonlight. As soon as he came closer, Kohana turned her head to smile down at him, but the troops that were with her began yelling at him. "The Great Lord of Light demands that you stay away from the Dragon!"

This news came as an offense to both Tatsu and Kohana.

"I do not think that you understand how little the Great Lord of Light's power over me is, soldiers," grumbled the White Dragon.

In an attempt to both change the subject and show how little he cared what the soldiers said, Tatsu began, "So, where is the training arena?"

Naturally, the soldiers were baffled as to how Tatsu could know that this was where Kohana was being taken at this exact moment. However, the soldiers did not try to force them apart again.

One stuttering soldier said, "The training arena is this way." He led Tatsu and Kohana in that direction, leaving the others troops dumbfounded by their blatant disobedience.

That was interesting, said Kohana, impressed. *How did you know they would not try to stop us?*

I didn't. It was a little of blind faith, responded Tatsu with a sigh.

*Hmmm…*grumbled the White Dragon pensively.

Within a few minutes, they were at one of the massive training arenas. The whole area was simply a large patch of dirt. It was nothing phenomenal, but it usually sufficed. In the rear of the arena was a great deal of training equipment, but Tatsu doubted that any equipment for Dragons could be found there.

Then, Tatsu saw one of the Great Lord of Light's Loyal Servants approaching. It was the Servant named Hector, he believed. Hector was the Great Lord of Light's personal servant and bodyguard. The servant was well-known for his long katana. "His Majesty the Great Lord of Light Lux has requested for me to supervise this Dragon's training. If I remember correctly, he ordered that you stay away from this Dragon, did he not, soldier?"

"All due respect, sir," mumbled Tatsu. He knew he was already overstepping his bounds. "The Great Lord of Light gave me one day of rest, and I would really like to spend it with Kohana."

"Your orders are clear, soldier, and you would be wise to follow them. Leave."

For the first time in his life, Tatsu felt underappreciated. He had done everything right with the terra over the past few years, and he had not seen a rise in salary, or a promotion, or any sign of gratitude. "No, sir. I think that I shall stay."

Hector's pale face contorted in silent rage. He turned to the other soldiers that were there. "Men, take this soldier to the Labyrinth."

Before the men could even think about moving, the White Dragon snarled ferociously and stepped between Hector and Tatsu. "You shall not touch Tatsu. He has done nothing wrong, and therefore, he shall not be punished."

The servant snapped back just as fiercely, "Silence your tongue, Dragon!"

For a second, both Tatsu and Kohana could feel a force deep within Hector. It was the feel of *mysteria*, and it was the feel of something far more mysterious. Kohana's mind revealed its identity: *He is one of the Y'mordi.*

Instinct took over as Tatsu unsheathed his Sword and charged at Hector. "Traitor!" roared Tatsu angrily.

The katana blocked the attack, and Hector used his free hand to blast Tatsu backward with a sphere of Light. "How am I the traitor? You attacked a Loyal Servant!"

Kohana replied coldly, "And you are one of the Y'mordi."

When the terrified soldiers began to flee the arena, Hector unleashed several bolts of pure Light that held such intensity that the soldiers turned to black ashes as soon as the Lights were near their bodies. "You are right, Dragon. I am one of the Y'mordi. And being such, I give you a choice: Will you come with me to the Dark Lord Dagan? Or will you stay here and allow me to kill this soldier?" In a flash of Light, Hector appeared beside Tatsu, and then both of them reappeared several yards away from Kohana. Tatsu's Sword had fallen, and Hector was holding Tatsu several feet into the water by his throat. "What is your choice?"

Kohana was appalled and did not know what to do. Then, Tatsu's voice rang clear in her mind, *Hold on to your body tightly with your mind. I have an idea that might work.* Kohana did as she was instructed as she felt Tatsu reach for her heart. However, she refused to give it up.

Everyone was baffled when Tatsu disappeared completely. At the same time, Kohana could feel his presence just as strongly, but it was inside her own heart that his essence existed.

Tatsu?

Kohana, I think that I understand our bond a little more now.

Kohana opened her mouth in surprise. *Where did your body go?*

I don't think it went anywhere really…I don't understand it fully, but it still exists somehow. She felt his confused emotions turn to rage. *For now, we fight!*

Kohana did not need to be told twice. A wave of Ice appeared and rushed at Hector, but the elusive Y'mordi leaped over it as if it was nothing.

Though his essence was buried in Kohana's heart, he could still utilize many of Kohana's abilities, including her refined sense, and using it, he noticed that the Sword that was still lying flat on the dirt had a unique aura to it.

What is different about that sword?

Kohana responded, *I am kind of busy!*

Indeed, she was fending off many blasts of Light from Hector with shields of Ice, which were nearly ineffective against the forceful strength of his attacks.

Tatsu focused on shifting his essence back into the physical world, and as he did so, he materialized onto Kohana's back. She gasped at the unexpected weight. "I'm right here!" he called as he slid down her tail to grab the Sword. He turned just in time to see Hector's spell shoot toward him. Not only did the spell not touch him, but it also disappeared entirely in front of his Sword. "Huh?"

Hector, however, was equally stunned. He reattempted the spell, but it faded before the Sword once again.

Kohana, noticing Hector's astonishment, cast another spell of Ice. This time, she summoned jagged icicles from the ground to pierce the Y'mordi. Hector moved out of the way of the spell in time and then blocked an icicle before using a Force spell to revert one icicle straight toward Kohana.

Tatsu shouted, "Kohana, switch!" She opened her heart to his heart, and he did the same. His military instincts moved his now serpentine body reflexively to avoid the icicle and then charge at the Y'mordi. His claws swiped at the Y'mordi but found only water. These Dragon talons were deadly sharp and could easily have ripped the man in two, but the Y'mordi was just as quick as the Dragon was. Despite being in an unfamiliar body, the increased strength and speed were easy for him to manipulate when combined with his training, something that Kohana lacked.

Kohana, though she was in Tatsu's body, was able to still summon her spells of Ice to attempt to freeze the Y'mordi. She suddenly became aware of the strength of the Sword in her human hands. Gradually, it began to glow white under her willful *mysteria*. Then, the energy released itself from the Sword and shot out at the Y'mordi like a bolt of lightning, and when it hit him, another surprise occurred. She could no longer sense his heart.

He held up his hand to cast a spell, but nothing happened. It was as if his heart's *mysteria* had been disabled. Frowning, Hector ground his teeth in instant panic.

Tatsu and Kohana switched again, but this time, they did not need to communicate the wish. It was simply understood through each other's hearts. Kohana approached the blonde-haired man. "You are under arrest, Hector."

Tatsu nodded in agreement.

"I do not know what you did or how you did it, but it is not as powerful you would think." He held up his hands again, and suddenly, a Gate made of Darkness appeared. "We Y'mordi have our hearts connected to the Darkness. It is not that we have a lot of Darkness in our hearts. It is a connection." Then, he was gone without a trace.

Days later, Tatsu explained many of his ideas of the bond to the Great Lord of Light, but he was not with Kohana at the time. Hours after that meeting, he rode on her back around Apolis as a watchman. Excitement and contentment filled his heart. The Great Lord of Light had finally allowed Tatsu to stay with Kohana.

"Kohana, I think I understand it now."

"Good, enlighten me, please," pleaded the White Dragon anxiously.

"The Great Lord of Light told me that the reason Dagan was not at his fortress was because he was trying to kill the Great Spirit." This revelation was a shock to both of them. The Great Spirit was supposedly the only living thing on this world when it had been found. It was the source of Gevás's ability to sustain life. In essence, it was the spirit of Gevás. "When he tried, something happened. The Great Spirit actually divided itself into five pieces. These pieces have been flying to different parts of the world and inhabiting swords. The Great Lord of the Light calls them Spirit Swords. They cannot be broken, and each one has interesting abilities. One of his swords recently gained one of the pieces as well. His Sword can cut through anything, and I think that when we were attacked by that Y'mordi three weeks ago, one of the pieces entered my sword."

"So, your sword is possessed by a piece of the Great Spirit?" asked Kohana skeptically.

Tatsu nodded. He, too, had been skeptical at first, but more and more evidence of it kept arising. "I think that my Sword has the ability to resist *mysteria*. You saw how the Y'mordi's spells just disappeared before they could even touch the blade, and then, when you cast a spell through the Sword, it stopped him from using *mysteria*, though I doubt that that will last forever."

Kohana was still confused. "What does the Spirit Sword have to do with our bond?"

"When the Spirit touched the sword, what were you doing?"

Kohana's tail twitched in embarrassment of the topic. "To be honest, I thought you were dead, so I was just…holding you."

Tatsu did not reveal how special he felt for having such a great friend. "Then, perhaps, because you were touching me, and the Sword was in me, its energy connected the Sword to both of us and connected me to you."

"I suppose that your theory does make some sense," replied Kohana hesitantly.

Tatsu relished the strength of the current that swept around him as Kohana flew. The night sky was alight with stars, and Kohana's white scales shimmered as they had that night three weeks ago.

"Kohana, I think we should stay with the military. The Great Lord of Light promised me that we would be treated as an independent unit. We belong to no particular group, and we get some of the best assignments. With our powerful bond, we would be unmatched on the battlefield."

The White Dragon sighed deeply, "If it is what you want…"

Tatsu could sense her disappointment. He gently stroked the scales on her neck, "What is wrong? I thought you might enjoy getting a chance to fight against those who imprisoned you for so long."

"I would, but at the same time, I just want...I want to be free, I think. I do not want to have to follow someone else's orders all the time."

"I hate to tell you this," started Tatsu sadly. "But I think that in life, regardless of who you are, someone is always above you."

Kohana's eyes lowered. "I understand. I shall be fine. Do not worry about me."

However, Tatsu could still feel that her sorrow was unabated. An idea came to him as a smile widened across his face. "Alright, I will make a deal with you."

"Hm?" was Kohana's curious response.

"Once we bring Dagan down, it will just be you and me. No matter how much we are needed, we won't stay in the military. We won't even stay in the South. We will go to the north where they say a hundred colors light up the shimmering night sky. What would you think about that?"

A tiny smile appeared on Kohana's snout. "It's not too warm there, is it?"

Tatsu spoke in a loud and exaggerated voice, "No, of course not! It is so cold up there! I would have to have five or six layers of clothes just to survive!"

Kohana's smile grew. "Well, then, in that case, it's a deal, but I would not invest in too many clothes if I were you. I doubt you have the money, and besides, I will make sure you do not freeze even if I have to learn how to create one of those annoying Fires."

Tatsu bent low to Kohana's neck and wrapped his arms around it. Her body felt so warm against the chilling current. He wanted this starlit moment to last forever. They both did.

Above the Streets of Boston

Randir sat down on a mountain ledge and buried his face in his hands. Mali appeared via Gate right beside him. Randir's muffled voice came up to Mali, "The Ring is making this incredibly difficult, wouldn't you say?" The wind swept against them coolly, rippling their robes.

Mali responded morosely, uncertain of where they were, "I would. We have been searching for almost two weeks, and so far, we have not learned anything new. This Black Joker could very well be a myth."

"That is what makes it more frustrating: Obviously, the Black Joker is real. The head of the Ring of Elders said as much, and they are interfering with my progress at every step. They stopped us at the pyramids. They stopped us in New Orleans. Every single time we pick up even the slightest bit of strong *mysteria*, they are right on our tails. If only this world were as small as Gevás, the search would be infinitely easier."

Mali considered Randir's words for a moment before saying, "You know, perhaps, it is not so much of a matter of finding him in the present."

"What do you mean?"

Mali put a hand thoughtfully to his pale chin. "Well, you said that he was imprisoned by the Ring a long time ago. If we could find out when they imprisoned him, we might be able to search this world's history to see if such a struggle existed and where it would have or even could have occurred," he explained.

Randir was thoroughly impressed by Mali's logic. "This makes sense, Hector. However, how would we go about learning the history of this world? Also, I doubt that the Ring will tell us how long ago it was anyways. Sure, if we had the information, it would make the search easier, but we just can't find that info." This dilemma was quite exasperating.

A malicious grin spread across Mali's face. "Perhaps, it is time to get the Ring to talk a little more. The next place we go to should be one that we attack. Whichever of the Ring comes, we can make them a spur-of-the-moment offer: save the village and reveal information about the Black Joker or allow the city to die."

Randir grunted. "You are starting to think like Y'tal."

Mali's smile faded. "Well, if you've got—"

The red-haired Y'mordi shook his head. "Your idea is at least something. We shall try it. Do you know a city that would be reasonable to attack?"

"I think I have a city in mind."

"Will it be an influential enough place that the Ring will notice it and react accordingly?" Randir inquired.

Mali nodded. "Yes, and it will likely require the attention of the head. If it does not, then that will be fine, as well."

"Very well, Hector. Let us go then." As they left the isolated mountaintop, Randir found himself missing the seas of Gevás. He had been on the dry world of Earth for too long. He had heard from rumors that this planet was made up of mostly water, but he did not believe it. All of the cities were on land and usually in low places. At least the mountains had precipitation. Although he preferred the heat to the cold, he also preferred the seas to the dry earth. A flame that spread through the seas was a marvel, but a fire in a desert is nothing spectacular.

The wind whirled violently around the two black robed figures as they soared several miles into the sky above Boston. Randir was amazed by the roar of the vehicles that were like tiny ants below him. Goliath skyscrapers filled the field of vision in every direction.

"Would you like to do the honors?" Mali said softly.

Randir lifted his head up to observe the somewhat cloudy sky. His hands reached up to the graying heavens, and the clouds seemed to multiply and darken. The entire sky became swarmed with the dark haze. As a warning signal, he let his mystical sky release a few basketball-sized fireballs down upon the city.

Before even those spells could hit the ground, they dissipated into black smoke, and one of the Elders appeared on the opposite skyscraper. Without hesitation, this Elder released a spell of Lightning.

While Mali deflected the bolt with his katanas, Randir allowed even more fireballs to rain down on the civilization below them. The Elder struggled to extinguish the fiery spheres. As the Elder was doing that, Randir and Mali used a Gate to appear beside the Elder.

Randir spoke with his usual deep and scratchy voice, "Listen, here, Elder, if you summon any of the others, this whole city will be incinerated. If you answer our questions, we will let you go about your business."

The Elder had dark reddish-brown hair. His choice of a leather jacket and worn-out blue jeans revealed his young age to the two Y'mordi.

"You are surely not one of the Elders, are you?" asked Mali incredulously.

Without giving a response, the young man retaliated with a spell of Poison of the Element Nature. The purplish cloud had no effect on the Y'mordi as Mali tried to slash at the boy with his katanas. The boy used his tiny wand as a shield. A slight spell of Force was enough to block each slash. Then, he noticed that he was backed up against the edge of the skyscraper. He looked down a couple thousand feet to see the ground nervously.

Randir mocked, "You are not scared of heights, are you, boy? Where are the Elders? You can't honestly expect me to believe that they sent a boy to do their work for them."

This provocation seemed to work as the young man began counterattacking with a flurry of spells. However, the boy did not seem to be angry. Rather, he was cool and collected. Therefore, his spells consisted more of Liquid and Ice rather than Flame and Lava. These attacks were more frustrating for Randir because his heart of Fire was more susceptible to such spells. He had to try a little harder. Even with Mali helping him, this boy was proving to be a greater challenge than either of them had expected.

In an attempt to give Randir some time to recuperate, Mali sent a blast of Light at the boy, but the boy blocked the spell and took the moment to create a more powerful spell. Several streams of Liquid shot from his wand and targeted the Y'mordi's eyes, mouths, noses, and ears. As he performed this act, he stepped aside in case either of them began casting spells wildly.

The Water spell both blinded and began drowning them. On Gevás, they had the Dark Lord Dagan's old protection that allowed them to breathe in air just as Gevás gave them the ability to breathe underwater, but here on Earth, they could only breathe air. While Mali struggled and grasped his throat in vain, Randir stopped his panic early and cleared his mind and heart. Then, he allowed more fireballs to fall from the sky. This smart move caused the boy to release his spell on them so that he could eliminate the Fires.

Without taking the time to breathe, Randir summoned his hammer and slammed it against the boy's chest, sending him flying off the building. Then, both Mali and Randir stood there choking painfully as they tried to get the water out of their lungs.

Within seconds, the boy appeared again through a Gate. Several blasts of Force were emitted from his wand and pushed the two still struggling Y'mordi off the building. Shifting his attention, the boy rapidly cast spells of Ice that eliminated the fireballs that Randir had summoned seconds ago. A few of Randir's spells grazed and burned the sides of the skyscrapers, but none managed to reach the ground. The boy seemed intent on not wanting civilians or their vehicles attacked down below.

When Randir and Mali reappeared on the roof of the skyscraper, Randir was truly angry. His red eyes seemed to be exceptionally ablaze at the moment. In a mad dash, his hand appeared in front of the boy's bruising chest and turned like a doorknob. Then, he stood straight on the other side of the boy as if he had gone completely through him. Before he could perform the finishing move of the Heartlock, a voice whispered, "Do not do it, Randir."

Standing there on the roof with the three of them was the head of the Ring of Elders. Randir grinned in satisfaction. "If you give me the information I seek, then I will free this boy. Tell me: Is he your son? He was with you at your home, and he was with you at the desert. Is he your son?"

The Elder shook her head. "No, he is not my son. He is my apprentice, and I can assure you, Randir, that if you hurt him in any way, you will have much to pay."

"Elder, if you tell me when the Ring imprisoned the Black Joker, I will dispel this firestorm. If you can tell me more than that, I will allow your apprentice to live as well."

"Sure, I can tell you when," smirked the Elder to everyone's surprise. "It was several thousands of years ago. I was lying to you when I told you before that it was just a few years ago. The Black Joker was causing chaos from the dawn of civilization. With each generation, the Ring of Elders has lost more and more information about the Black Joker. I have told you all that I know now. To be honest, I am not even sure that he ever existed. I just did not want to take the risk of him being real and then you finding him."

Randir, Mali, and the boy were all dumbfounded. Randir tried analyzing her words for some kind of lie but sensed none.

The Elder repeated, "Let the boy go. I have told you everything that I know, and if you do anything else, then you are not only wasting your time, but you are wasting my time as well. Leave this world. I grow weary of your antics. It seems that you would give the Joker himself a run for his money." She was in a highly sarcastic mood. Though her apprentice's life was at stake, she knew that Randir was not so cruel as to do something like that so heartlessly.

Randir snarled back, "I grow just as weary of your antics, Elder. Why do you not cower before me? I have threatened this boy, your family, your home, and your world, yet you never flinch. Why do you not tremble before my power?"

The Elder relaxed. "You helped my son. Although your heart may be filled with Darkness, you still do have a heart."

Randir dispelled the Heartlock and muttered, "Who is your son? You told me that I helped him twice, but I do not know to whom you were referring. I think that that mystery is even more puzzling to me than the mystery of the Black Joker."

With a sigh, the Elder decided to tell Randir after all. "My son is Dragenopn Helius, the Guardian of Light and Prince of Light. You saved him from your comrade there on an island to the south of Alerris, and then you saved him from Maris on his way to Apolis."

"Your son is Dragenopn? That is interesting…" murmured Randir. He could not believe that he was being considered less frightening because of a few small actions. Had he really fallen so low? He turned as if to leave and then added, "Do not for one second think of me as softer than the others. I helped him so that I would see Maris fall. I serve the Darkness not the Light. There might be a day when I see benefit in killing your son. Do not think I favor him." Then, a portal opened before him, and water poured from it and spiraled around the Gate. The two Y'mordi disappeared into it.

Mali exclaimed, "Why are we here?!"

"Because I think I have an idea as to how we can find the Black Joker after all," Randir explained as they began striding across the ashen plains of Heaven's Isle.

"Oh?"

"I remember that the Prophet of Water once had a master computer buried under this island somewhere. It was supposedly very intelligent and might even have the history of Earth recorded in it. If the Black Joker was imprisoned thousands of years ago, then it might actually have the information that we need."

"Yes, that sounds like an effective plan. I am curious as to how you are aware of the actions of the Prophets though. The Prophet of Water disappeared when Mentiris was around, and he just reappeared when Maris did."

A glint appeared in Randir's eyes. "You forget that I, too, am a Prophet, the Prophet of Fire."

Mali knew of many of Randir's roles. Randir was a Prophet, a Guardian of Light, a Lord of the Shadows, a General, and a former king. Thirsty for power, Randir had sacrificed his crown and his wife for immortality. Now, Randir was trying to give up his immortality for peace. Mali admired Randir for his constant ambition, but he could not imagine the price Randir had to pay for power. Mali started a new thread of conversation, "It must have been hard…killing your wife."

Randir stopped dead in his tracks. "What brought this up, Hector?"

The white-robed Y'mordi could sense Randir's anger and grief and even regret. "It's just that…Well, I know that I cannot know everything that goes on in your head, but I know that you have thought about her almost every day. When you look up at the stars at night, do you still see her? Even when she was alive, you told me something: 'The stars are my promise to come back to her. Every time I see a shooting star, I am one step closer to being with her.'"

A sigh left Randir's cracked lips. "The Dark Lord Dagan gave me a choice: to serve the Darkness and have eternal life and power or die a miserable death with the ones I loved. I made the wrong choice. Even now, a part of me yearns for more power, but even more than that, I just want to fade out of existence. I want to see her again. The stars are no longer enough for me."

Mali responded softly, "You are not wrong for that desire. It is not my place to say if you were even wrong in making that decision as you did." Randir opened his mouth to protest, but Mali held up a signaling hand. "Victor, my master is the Darkness, and I have only had one master since then. My greatest trait is my love for loyalty. Your problem is not that you are always on the wrong side: It is that you can never pick a side."

Silence was Randir's response. After a few seconds of hearing only the current sweep past them, he began walking forward. His bare feet crunched the charred remains of a once beautiful field of crimson flowers. In his mind, he began wondering about Mali's words. Was lack of loyalty the cause for his misfortune? He had never considered the idea. For almost a thousand years, he had considered himself an outcast. Perhaps, Mali was right: he had never chosen a side.

Then, he caught the glimmer of a few buildings in the distance. "There…" he muttered, deep in thought.

Mali followed Randir cautiously. Although he was becoming closer and closer to his old friend, he was well aware of Randir's unpredictability. He did not want to be on the receiving end of Randir's flames.

The buildings of Heaven's Isle steadily came closer and closer into view until they were within arm's reach. The doors were rusting, and vines had begun creeping up the metallic surfaces.

"Are you sure that it is here?" inquired Mali without expression.

Randir only responded with a slight nod. He reached out for one of the doorknobs but then stopped. "Someone was here recently. It was probably one or two weeks ago, but someone was here."

Mali slowly opened his heart to *mysteria* and then sensed the area around them. Randir could feel the spell sweep around the entire island. "I do not sense anything," concluded Mali. "Whoever it was is gone now."

With a noisy creak, Randir opened the door and beheld the shadowy staircase behind it. With a snap of his fingers, a miniscule yet bright Flame appeared in his hand. He began to descend the spiraling staircase with Mali close behind him. His heart could feel the chill that was prevalent in the underground building. It had the feel of *mysteria* and more specifically Water. "I can still sense the Prophet of Water. Perhaps, it was him who returned here recently."

"You might be right. I can't help but feel something else, too, though."

Randir did not turn to face his friend, "Hm?"

Mali hesitated before saying, "Well, I could almost sense a few of the Guardians of Light. If I am not mistaken, I believe that it is the same scent that the Prince of Light and his close friend had." Whereas Pullatus could sense many things in the Darkness, Mali possessed a similar ability through the Light. He compared it to smelling. Every light had a specific scent to it, and he could distinguish these scents.

"The Guardians of Light? Why would they need to use this computer?" Then, a thought came to Randir. "Why is the Prince not the Emperor of Light yet? It has been several years, so who has led Helio till now?"

"Well…" Mali kept forgetting how little Randir knew of the present time. He had been in Stasis for several years. "The Emperor's Council has been managing the affairs of Helio since the Prince of Light disappeared."

"Disappeared?"

Mali nodded. "Yes, after the battle, the Prince of Light disappeared. Y'tal made us look all over Gevás for him, but we could never find him."

Randir shook his head. The Prince of Light was not what he needed to be worrying about right now. Finally, they reached a point in the staircase where there was a door. The stairs continued their descent further, but Randir decided to try this door first.

It was a massive room with an exceedingly high ceiling. The space was both vast and dark. Mali summoned his Light, and instantly, the room was filled with a bright silvery Light. The only signs of darkness were the two shadows that accompanied Randir and Mali.

In the distance, they could see a large computer screen with an equally wide keyboard. The screen was dark, and the water around them murky from no one being here in years. As they approached the computer, Mali's sandaled feet clicked on the metallic tile.

"Computer, respond," demanded Randir.

Suddenly, a digital, blue face appeared on the screen. "It is an honor to meet you, Lord Victor Ferro."

Randir, however, was more surprised that the machine worked than at the computer's knowledge of his name. "What can you tell me about the legendary figure known as the Black Joker? I have been seeking information as to his whereabouts on Earth, and I only recently discovered that the Ring of Elders imprisoned him thousands of years ago. Do you know anything else?"

Several screens split from the one, covering the massive wall, and the face enlarged to fit all of the screens at once. The face was plain, blue, and pixelated. The mechanical voice spoke then, "If the Black Joker is indeed real, Lord Ferro, then he was imprisoned on Earth. The legends say that was a master of causing chaos, and this means that he would have been at a place where he could effectively cause such complications without people being actively aware of his use of *mysteria*." Then, three of the now nine screens showed a map of Earth. Several red blinking dots appeared on the map. "Here are many possible locations of the Black Joker."

Randir and Mali were amazed at the number of possibilities. There could easily have been over a hundred dots on the map. Mali asked, "If you had to guess his location, which one of these would it be?"

Suddenly, one of the red dots grew on the map, and all of the screens transformed into a single image of many huge blocks of stone arranged into unusual formations. "Go to this place known as Stonehenge, and you might find the Black Joker. However, I must warn you that the Ring of Elders has been watching over this place particularly closely over the years. It might be a reasonable idea to do something about the Ring before you begin excavating this site."

Randir's eyes gleamed at the sight of the colossal rocks. As Mali and he left the computer, Mali whispered to Randir, "That computer seemed a little strange, would you not agree? For a thing that helped the Guardians of Light, it seems a little odd it would help us, too."

"You are right. I think that it will be in our best interests to alert Y'tal to the presence and knowledge of this computer when we see him again. Perhaps, we could use it further to our advantage."

Unexpected Meetings

The Capital was even duller than he had expected. There had been no rumors of a mystical Sword or any skilled warriors. All the gossip was about the Emperor Regin, crimes in the city, and even the Lords of the Shadows. It was quite frustrating. Maksimilian had sent a few of the Brigade to search for Captain Terrell and Y'ran, but he had not even heard back from them yet.

He could not help but wonder if they would have had better luck if they had stayed in Apolis. Nevertheless, he knew that they would still need to spend a lot more time there before they could say for certain if no Sword existed there.

Gently, his hand traced the hilt of his own Sword, the Steel of Life. Though it gave him immortality, it was useless as a weapon. He craved another one.

Then, a knock came to the door. "You may enter," Maksimilian said softly.

Tilgé stormed into the room with his face red with anger. "Maks, we have scoured this city time and time again, but we have found nothing! How much longer must we wait before we can breach the fortress. It's obvious that the Emperor Regin has what we need. Why can't we just go in there and take it from him?"

Maksimilian's voice stayed calm as he spoke, "Because we are not sure that he has what we need. I feel the need to ask you, though, Tilgé, if you yourself know what we need."

Tilgé's angry demeanor subsided. "Captain, we serve the Light and its leader, the Emperor of Light. That is our goal."

"So, tell me," continued Maksimilian as he stood to approach the window of his hotel room. "What is it that we *need*?"

Tilgé responded promptly, "We need an Emperor of Light."

A crooked smile appeared on Maksimilian's youthful face. "Exactly. Find me the Prince of Light. I have reason to believe that he is here in the Capital. I would like for you to do this now."

Tilgé bowed. "Yes, Captain."

Maksimilian smirked. "You are clever, Tilgé. I am sure that you can find the Prince without any aid from me. Go now," he demanded. With another bow, Tilgé exited the room.

With a deep sigh, Maksimilian rose from his chair and prepared to explore the city on his own. In his trunk, he found a mud-brown robe. This robe was loose enough that it took little work to make it cover his lengthy crimson hair. He draped the hood over his face in order to disguise himself even further. He was confident that no one would recognize him from his last visit, but nevertheless, the last thing he wanted was to start rumors about the Enigma Brigade. The less people believed in the military force, the more of an enigma it actually was.

As he stepped out into the misty streets of the Capital, the blaring music annoyed his ears. He had always despised the Capital. It was a place of filth and vermin. Such a place was not for the Captain of the Enigma Brigade, but it was a place of Darkness, and that required his attention unfortunately.

He was inclined to think that Tilgé was right, however. If a Spirit Sword was to be found here, it would likely be in the Emperor Regin's fortress. That would also be where Captain

Terrell could be, as well. As for Y'ran, he would likely be where the Captain was. All signs pointed to that castle, but one fact prevented him from attacking it. The Eastern Continent was a major aid to the Obsidian War right now. If Helio lost that support, the exiles might stand a chance. The last thing he needed to do was to upset the Emperor Regin while representing the Emperor of Light.

Nevertheless, there were good chances that it might come to that if more proof became available.

His feet carried him to the center of the city where the castle of the Emperor Regin resided. He had heard rumors that the Emperor had fallen ill. Their king had not left his castle for a long time now. Maksimilian felt curiosity about this mysterious illness. A sickness that the Emperor Regin's greatest healers could not take care of within months? This did not bode well.

A noise caused him to turn his head. It was the sound of laughter. As he approached the sound, he realized it had simply come from a tavern. An idea sparked in his mind, and he entered the tavern.

This pub was small yet held a good thirty or forty people. The stench of drinks and sweat filled his nose, and the buzz of conversations about local disq players gave him a headache. When he sat at the bar, the young, slender bartender asked energetically as he wiped down a glass, "What can I get for you?"

"Information, please," replied Maksimilian softly. "I am going to give you a list of categories, and for every category you can give information on, I will give you two Imperial favors. Deal?"

Now, the youth's mouth seemed to water greedily at the prospect. "Alright, sir, go for it."

A corner of Maksimilian's mouth rose in a half-smile as he dropped a bag of gold onto the counter. His voice became a low whisper. "I need information about what has happened to the Emperor Regin, anything about where the Prince of Light is, news about the Lords of the Shadows, where Captain Terrell is, and any information whatsoever about any exceptional swords." He added in a hiss, "And I need my asking this to be kept discrete."

The bartender stroked his chin thoughtfully. "Well, let's see…No one knows anything about the Emperor Regin. No one goes into the fortress, and no one comes out, so I only hear rumors on that one. The Prince of Light officially returned to Gevás a few weeks ago. Apparently, he was on Earth. So, I would guess that he is in Apolis right now."

Maksimilian countered this statement, "Actually, he is here in the Capital somewhere. So far, you have been unable to help me with two of my categories."

The young man looked appalled and began to panic. "Uh-uh-well…Anything you've heard about the Lords of the Shadows are probably false. There were one or two reports of them when the War first started, but everything else is just rumor and speculation. Terrell left the Capital once the War started. If I remember right, he went to work in Apolis."

This news did come to Maksimilian as a shock. "Apolis?"

The bartender brightened, noticing that he had indeed given some useful information. "Yeah, yeah! Some say that he might have been responsible for what happened to the Emperor Regin. They say that he left so that he would not get caught!"

Maksimilian grunted, not believing the explanation. Nevertheless, if Captain Terrell was in Apolis, how had he not known it sooner? "Continue," he muttered.

"Well…as far as any exceptional swords go…I remember hearing about a massive sword several years ago, when the War first started."

"Go on," encouraged Maksimilian, his interest piqued.

"I've heard whispers that the sword could bring its wielder good luck, but I don't know if that is actually true or not." Though he sounded quite skeptical, Maksimilian was eager to hear more.

"Where is it?"

"Well…I think that the sorcerer Maris was the one who had it."

He felt his heart sink then. "Maris?" He was familiar with the Sword of which the bartender was speaking. It was known as the Behemoth, a Spirit Sword that would grant luck to whoever could lift its heavy weight. Why would a piece of the Great Spirit choose to bless Maris, the one who incited the exiles into rebellion against the rest of the world?

"Yes, sir," replied the bartender.

"Thank you," murmured Maksimilian distantly as he handed the young man four Imperial favors. Without another word, he left the tavern.

Maris had been killed and taken by the Y'mordi. Where could that Sword be? Would the Y'mordi have it?

With his curiosity about the Emperor Regin abated, he decided to simply stroll through the streets aimlessly. He had a lot of thinking to do.

Several hours later, night fell. Maksimilian finally sighed dejectedly and sat on a nearby bench. He was wracking his brain so hard that he was getting a rather annoying headache. He massaged his forehead methodically but found no relief.

Suddenly, a green light appeared from beneath his robe. As he opened it, he found that the source of the glow was his Sword.

When he looked around the street, the only people he saw were a handful of guards across the road who were busy talking amongst themselves. He unsheathed his Sword, and it was indeed glowing a bright green hue. "What is going on here? Are you awake at last, Spirit? What has caused you to react so?" As he moved the blade around experimentally, he noticed that when he moved it forward, it glowed even brighter.

Puzzled, he pointed it to where the guards were standing on the stairs to a two-story building, and the tip of the Sword held an even more intense light. In wonder, he sheathed the Sword and walked to the guards, his shoes tapping against the stone road.

One of them noticed him coming and called, "What can I do for you, sir?"

Maksimilian regarded the building they were guarding but could not identify it. "What building is this?"

Another guard responded, "This is a military training facility. If you are interested, I would recommend coming back in the morning."

"Or maybe in a few weeks," remarked another mockingly. "This facility is already pretty full."

"Allow me to introduce myself," began Maksimilian coldly. "My name is Captain Maksimilian. I would like to enter this building immediately."

One of the guards tensed and reached for his weapon to assert some level of dominance and security, but Maksimilian was quicker.

He drew his katana and used a spell of Light simultaneously. In less than a second, all of the guards were dead around him. He wiped the bloody blade on their uniformed bodies. He hated having to use that katana. Unfortunately, his still glowing Steel of Life was useless in battle: it granted him immortality as long as he never used it to harm another. He would much rather have a more powerful sword, a Spirit Sword, that could actually be used in battle, like the Behemoth.

After sheathing the sword, he opened the door to the military training facility and felt his own Steel of Life start to vibrate, though the glow had disappeared. He pulled back his hood to reveal some of his red hair. To his left, he saw a wide staircase. He walked up it and stepped onto the second floor. As he walked along the area, the windows on both sides of this hallway revealed several training rooms.

Then, he saw another figure in the hallway with him. The person was in an unusual blue robe. This figure was looking out at one training arena, but as soon as Maksimilian got close, the sword's vibrations stopped. His heart remembered this person.

He was one of the Y'mordi.

"So the rumors are true," Maksimilian said.

The man in blue turned to look at him. "I am afraid I do not know what you are talking about." This man had a hood over his face that hid his features.

"My name is Maksimilian."

At the mention of the name, the Y'mordi jumped back, holding out a gloved hand, summoned a long, silver scepter. Snarling, he waved it once and released a wave of Ice to freeze the Captain of the Enigma Brigade.

Maksimilian dodged the chilling spell and lunged with his Light-fused attacks: each attack moved at lightning speed with this combination, making his body a golden blur on the battlefield. Though the Y'mordi was able to block every attack through his connection to the Darkness, he did not have time to produce a counterattack. It did not take the Y'mordi long to realize that he needed to leave here. As Maksimilian backed him up to the window, the Y'mordi summoned a Gate behind him and fled into it.

The enraged Captain shot a final blast of Light, but the Gate closed before it could hit the Y'mordi. Instead of hitting its target, it merely broke the glass window behind it. The sound of the alarm was enough of a signal for Maksimilian to get out of there.

By the time he reached the stairs, there were several guards trying to climb up them to find him. With one explosive Light spell, the stairs were cleared, blasting the guards into different directions, and he ran out the front door and into the dark streets of the Capital. Using his spell of Light to make him move at the speed of light itself, practically becoming an anthropomorphic form of light, he was able to evade his pursuers and hide in an alleyway. Nevertheless, he stood there panting heavily.

A smile lit up his face. The Y'mordi were here after all. That also meant that Captain Terrell was probably here as well. Knowing that was a relief. They still had much work here in the Capital. He decided then that it would probably be in the Brigade's best interests to invade the fortress.

However, he also realized that many preparations would have to be made. If they could explore the fortress without having to alert the Emperor Regin as to their presence, it would be a perfect operation.

Xarden stood atop one of the higher skyscrapers in the Capital, seething with rage. He looked down at the traffic of flying vehicles and the neon lights below. This day had been the second time in two weeks that he had been ambushed. First, the Guardian of Light had attacked him at the Academy, and now, Maksimilian of all people had found him.

How had Maksimilian survived all of these years anyways? The last time that Xarden had seen him had been during the Second Obsidian War almost a thousand years ago. He was obviously not an Ancient, one who could grow old but lived perpetually through mysteria: *Maksimilian had maintained his youthful figure. Somehow, Maksimilian had cheated death, and Xarden intended to learn the source of this power.*

As his anger began to fade away, he decided that Maksimilian had not been looking for him. It had been simply an accident. However, the fact remained that he, Maksimilian, was alive.

Xarden could remember that the red-haired man had been one Lux's most favored generals and had often been declared an amazing war hero. That meant that he had likely fought in the Final Battle. So, how was it possible that Xarden had just seen him once again in a military training facility in the Capital? Y'tal would have to hear about this mystery.

First, though, he needed to watch the two Guardians of Light here. They were nearing the end of their training, and he needed to know what the two boys were going to do first. Once he found that out, he could go to Y'tal and submit a full report.

He laughed deeply then. "Pullatus's plan will work perfectly. I am confident that he will find the third Great Servant soon. Sharl Vran is becoming ours, and if Randir succeeds at unleashing the Black Joker, we shall have Earth in turmoil as well. If I can get rid of just one Guardian of Light, then Gevás will fall."

As he looked out upon the enormous city, he felt a soft pang in his heart. The smile faded from his face, and he closed his eyes to observe his heart more easily. Beneath the layers of Darkness that was characteristic for any Y'mordi, he found the remnants of a shattered heart.

According to the Dark Lord Dagan, Xarden had once been a part of another person, a weaker person who did not want whatever strength he did have. Xarden could not remember what he was before that shattering of his heart. The Great Lord of the Darkness knew, however. He had claimed that Xarden's only strength was the ability in mysteria. *Whoever Xarden was before had found a way to literally divide his heart into two pieces. Because the heart is greater than the body, the new piece created its own physical form. Somewhere out there, another like Xarden existed, broken…unless that other half had already died over the centuries. Xarden had no idea what the other person looked like.*

He released a sigh as he realized how unlikely it was for that person to be alive.

In Gevás, people believed that when the body died, the heart would go to its true Element's realm and reside there as a spirit. This way of afterlife was an ideal contentment and happiness for the spirits supposedly.

Xarden's chief concern was of what would become of him when he finally passed: He did not have a full heart. Would he become a spirit in death? Or would he merely cease to be?

"Heh, what does it matter to me? The powers of the Darkness will protect me. I don't even need to worry about death. It's Hothead that needs to worry about it. If he fails on Earth, Y'tal will have his head." While Y'mordi were always brought back to life from death, Y'tal knew ways to make that death as painful as possible. Xarden had always despised Randir passionately, almost as much as he disliked Ixion. Randir was always so sudden in his actions and resisted any form of order. What he lacked in wisdom, he replaced with his craving for power. Randir was a mindless machine. Why had the Great Lord of the Darkness given Randir the rank above Xarden's?

His head shook as he thought back to his broken heart. He could have sworn that the girl from the Academy had looked straight into his heart. It had felt as if he had been entirely naked before her. Every emotion and thought was open to her. It concerned him considerably what she could do with her knowledge of him. If she had indeed seen his half-heart, perhaps, she would use that against him later. He had no idea what she could possibly do with that knowledge, but she was a Guardian of Light. He did not trust her with his one vulnerability.

She would need to be eliminated. He grimaced as he realized that Ixion was supposed to be watching her. That meant that the job would probably never be accomplished. Ixion made an excellent spy and scout. Also, in battle, he was a fearsome fighter with his knives, but against people who were particularly skilled in mysteria, *he always failed. It had been his bane against the Prophet of Earth and the Golden Dragon years ago.*

He created a gentle chill in the water around him, and the unbearable heat of the Eastern Continent subsided.

The dilemmas of Maksimilian, the girl from the Academy, Randir, his half-heart, and the Guardians of Light raced through his head as he analyzed them. "All will come into place…" he whispered. "This War will tear Gevás apart."

Tilgé was astounded by what he had just witnessed. Maks had fought a random person and then failed to subdue the stranger. From what he had seen, the person had been robed and skilled in the mystic arts. Despite the apparent skills, however, the mysterious figure had disappeared, leaving Captain Maks to fight off several guards.

The whole incident had been quite unusual. Tilgé had only minutes before learned that the Prince of Light was in this training facility, and then, as he had been about to give up and leave, he had seen Maks climb the stairs to the second floor. Tilgé had followed him curiously and had been dumbfounded by what had occurred.

The first thing he concluded was that his Captain had attacked a stranger. The second was that his Captain had not defeated the robed man. Something was definitely wrong with this scenario, and he knew he could not ask Maks: the Captain would probably kill him for it.

Lost in his amazement, Tilgé became aware of another person, the Prince of Light. The Prince was standing with another man who looked to be slightly older. Without pausing, Tilgé approached the young man. He could not believe that this man was the Prince. He had seen pictures over the years, but seeing him in person made it even more incredible. The Prince looked too young to be as great as the stories claimed.

"Excuse me, your Majesty, may I have a word with you?" Tilgé began politely. Though he was usually sharp with his tongue, he knew how and when to place respect on one's words.

Aria's Discipline

"The Sword of Destiny?"

"Password invalid," replied the computer in its droning, monotonous voice.

"Guardians of Light?"

"Password invalid."

Aria scratched two more phrases off her extensive list of possible passwords for the input module of the Archives. Two weeks had not brought her any closer to discovering the password. She had spent every night here in the top of the central tower, yelling at the circular rail that separated her from simply yelling at the Southern frozen landscape, though the security around the Academy had become even tighter since the Y'mordi had snuck into it. Guards had been stationed everywhere even at night, and the cameras were even more enhanced, so that they could locate invisible objects. Aria had had to create a more complicated Light spell in order to stay hidden: She had used Light to create an image of the area around her and then set that image around herself so that the cameras saw everything but Aria.

"*Mysteria?*"

"Password invalid."

Crossing out another attempt on the metal sheet, she sighed in frustration. She gently laid down the sheet before leaning against the railing.

One of the most perplexing factors of this whole ordeal was the fact that Mistress Leona had not given her the password. It was not likely that the Prophet had forgotten that particular fact. However, she could have just as easily not mentioned anything about the input module, so obviously, the Prophet thought that Aria could figure it out somehow.

It was not as if Aria could simply talk to Mistress Leona either, though. The Prophet was busy with the War and was probably stationed in Apolis. She did not have time to meet with a student at the Academy. Furthermore, she had already told Aria everything she was willing to offer.

Why had Mistress Leona not told her the password? It was so mind-boggling.

"Aria Newman," she tried desperately.

"Password invalid," repeated the machine.

Somehow, she had the feeling that she was on the right track, though. Maybe, the computer password changed depending on who was trying to unlock it. If so, it was a password that would be somewhat personal to her, yet it would be something influential. "Dragenopn Helius?"

"Password invalid."

"Shut up!" she roared violently as she unleashed a serpentine stream of Flame from her wand. "Shut up, shut up!"

Suddenly, she heard the elevator shifting in the center of the floor: Someone was coming. With a flourish of her wand, the input module disappeared along with her own body. The cylindrical elevator appeared then, and its floor aligned with the floor of the roof.

With a quiet hum, the doors opened, and an elderly man stepped onto the top room of the tower. The elevator shut behind him and then lowered. It took Aria only seconds to realize that the person before her was none other than the Grand Master Dean himself. Though she had never seen him in person, Aria had seen multiple pictures of him throughout the Academy: Every student was required to know who the Grand Master Dean was in case he or she did come across the all-powerful Dean.

The Grand Master Dean was in charge of all affairs of the school and superseded all others in the Academy. Besides his dominion of the school, he was a well-regarded and quite influential man in Gevás.

The old man with the bald head and white goatee stepped forward, silver robs motionless despite the waves, and silently dispelled the invisible barrier around the input module. Aria put a hand over her mouth. The worst thing that could possibly happen to her would be getting caught up here by the Grand Master Dean.

The machine started in its digital voice, "Password?"

A raspy, deep voice emitted from the man's throat. "Tatsu and Kohana!" he bellowed.

Tatsu and Kohana? What is that? Aria thought in perplexity.

"Password confirmed," was the input module's response.

Aria's eyes widened.

The circular computer spun rapidly around the room, causing the water to swirl around them. Suddenly, the mechanical blur started to glow blue with light. As it slowed again, the walls to the tower seemed to be made of the ceiling-to-rail blue panels that gradually rotated around the room. The glaring blue screens illuminated the space to full brightness, yet Aria could make out glimpses of the outside through the thin slits between the screens.

Aria was taken aback by the phenomenal technology that surrounded her. Never before had she seen machinery as advanced as what she was seeing now.

"Ms. Newman, you may release your barrier now," grumbled the Grand Master Dean.

"Huh?" Aria looked down at herself in embarrassment and fear, yet she was still invisible.

"Mistress Leona told me that you would be up here for a while. She told me to expect you the next time I came in the middle of the night."

With an embarrassed blush in her face, she removed her invisibility spell. "Sir…I—"

The Grand Master Dean raised a hand to silence her, and she complied. "Ms. Newman, I have known since the power outage that you have been coming here every night. What I do not understand is why you have so desperately sought the secret records of the Archives."

Aria began hesitantly, "Grand Master Dean, sir…it's just that I've been…" Then, she realized what the old man had told her: Mistress Leona had trusted him with what she was doing, and he had done nothing to stop her. Her heart relaxed slightly. She was not about to be expelled or worse. Instead of apologizing, she decided to simply ask for help. "Sir, when I first came to Gevás five years ago, I learned that somebody had Gifted me when I was born. However, I was never told who did it."

The Grand Master Dean looked skeptical. "You thought that the Archives would tell you that?"

Aria shuffled her feet nervously. "Yes, sir…And there is something else, too…"

"Yes, go on," implored the old man.

"There was a man…He is the one who brought Drage, Matthew, and I to this world five years ago. He saved us from the Y'mordi that night…And then, I met him again in the Imperial Gardens in Apolis. He is the one who encouraged me to try to lead a part of the terra. Then, he talked to Matthew. We all learned a lot from that conversation. He called himself Ace. Matthew told me that he had listed off several other nicknames he had: the Remnant, the Seeker of Paradise, the Wolf, and the Shadow. When I had talked to him, he called himself an illusion. He told me that he should not exist. I want to know who he is and why he helped us."

The old man stroked his goatee thoughtfully. "I am not familiar with most of those names…"

"Most, sir?"

"Yes, most," replied the Grand Master Dean. "I have heard of the Seeker of Paradise…once. Perhaps, the input module can help you after all." He gestured with a flourishing hand for Aria to ask the module her questions.

Aria gave the old man an appreciative nod, and her eyes went to the multitude of screens. "Computer, can you tell me anything about the Seeker of Paradise?"

Suddenly, one of the screens displayed a black and white sketch. There was a young man wearing light yet decorative armor, emblazoned with black symbols. Despite his appearance of a soldier, Aria noticed that there was a deep and almost soft look in his eyes, a look that revealed hardship and sorrow. Around the man were five large circles. Each circle held an interesting symbol, and beyond the circles and around the corners of the sheet was a fascinating image: It was a beautiful meadow with flowers scattered across the grass, and birds flew amid the partially cloudy sky. Aria could almost feel the warmth coming from the sun in that background.

"What is this?" she asked in awe.

The computer responded, "600 years ago, there was a man who claimed that a place known as Paradise existed. He claimed that this beautiful place would appear when all the worlds were Resolved. One day, he simply disappeared, and this sheet was found on his desk."

Aria's eyes traced over the strange figure in the image. "Could that be Ace? Did he travel through time?"

The Grand Master Dean raised his brow. "You think that he traveled 600 years to reach you?"

Considering the idea made her lower her eyes. "No, sir. That would be illogical. Still, there has to be some connection."

"Perhaps so," commented the Grand Master Dean.

Suddenly, she looked up to face the old man. "Excuse me, sir, but may I ask why you did not come up here sooner if you knew that I have been here every night for the past few weeks?"

"You have not sensed it, then?"

When he saw Aria's puzzled expression, he explained, "Ms. Newman, ever since the power outage, I have sensed a dark presence in the Academy. I do not know if it was the same one that you confronted, but there is indeed an Y'mordi in the Academy even as we speak."

"An Y'mordi? No, I have not sensed one anywhere since then, sir."

"I have not been able to pinpoint its location, but I have had a general area. Over the past few days, it has moved closer and closer to your dorm area. I think that, with the full protection of myself and some other Deans, tonight would be the best time to have you moved to another area."

"Another area, sir? Where would that be?"

The Grand Master Dean sighed heavily. "Ms. Newman, there are many people here in the Academy that think that you are not disciplined enough for a mage. There are even several Deans that possess that mindset." Aria's face began to pale. She could not believe how much doubt there was. She had known that there were students and a few professors that thought that she was weakly disciplined, but she had never imagined that the Deans shared that sentiment. "Nevertheless...on the grounds that you have been apprenticed by two Prophets, passed one of Mistress Leona's silly trials, led sorcerers in the Emperor of Light's terra, challenged the Y'mordi, and done well in many of the more advanced courses here at the Academy, I deem you fit to graduate now with a general *mysteria* discipline, no examination required."

In disbelief, Aria put her hands to her mouth, and her blue eyes widened. She could not believe what she was hearing. She had been planning on spending several more years at the Academy in order to graduate, but the Grand Master Dean was offering her an immediate discipline, the equivalent of an Earthan degree. Then, her mind went back over what she had just heard. "Wait, did you say a general *mysteria* discipline? I was trying to get a discipline in the Elements." She knew that a general *mysteria* discipline was more like *mysteria* appreciation. It covered a lot of theory and history and not so much actual practice.

"I am sorry to disappoint, Ms. Newman, but a discipline in the Elements is a much tougher discipline, and the final examination in that mandatory—"

Aria interrupted here, "Well, then, may I take that examination?"

The Grand Master Dean immediately flustered at the outrageous prospect. "I mean you no offense, Ms. Newman, but the final examination for the Elements is near impossible for someone of your level. I am not exaggerating in the least when I say that it takes several years purely devoted to studying for this examination in order to pass it."

Aria countered, "And I mean you no offense, sir, when I say that if you can have the examination prepared by tomorrow, I will pass it."

A gradual smile appeared on the Grand Master Dean's wrinkled face. "Yes, Mistress Leona did mention something of your willfulness when you first came to the Academy five years ago. She told me that when you had your mind set to do something, you usually followed through with it." He sighed, excitement tinged with uncertainty. "I will have the examination ready by tomorrow afternoon and a short graduation ceremony immediately after your results come in, assuming you do indeed pass it." He said the last bit more as a question directed at Aria to which she nodded in response.

"If you do not mind, sir, I would like to stay here with the input module and use it to prepare for the examination."

The old man nodded gently and said as he walked back to the elevator, "That is fine as long as you do not attempt to access the *hidden* sections of the Archives again tonight." With this request, he gave Aria a quite stern look. "Also, when you are done for the night, I would like for you to lock the computer again. You can use the exact same password."

"Tatsu and Kohana?"

The Grand Master Dean nodded. "That is right."

As the elevator rose, Aria inquired, "What are Tatsu and Kohana? I do not think that I have heard of them, sir."

The Grand Master Dean turned his head to face the young woman. "You do not know Tatsu and Kohana?" He shook his head. "Then again, you were not raised here, so I suppose that it bears some logic. Have a seat. I think that this is a story you might enjoy hearing, and I would like to tell you before you graduate tomorrow." Then, under his breath, he muttered, not without confidence, "If you do indeed succeed."

Aria complied and looked up at the Grand Master Dean as the elevator arrived behind him. He waved a hand, and it stayed in place while he talked.

"1,000 years ago, there was a skilled fighter in the Great Lord of Light's terra. His name was Tatsu. In battle, there were few that could compare to him. Many people said that on the battlefield, he became one with his sword in a way unlike any other. He was one of the greatest swordsmen to ever enter Gevátian history. One day, the Great Lord of Light sent him with others on a mission to attack one of Dagan's fortresses. As soon as they entered the fortress, an Y'mordi decimated the force, and Tatsu was trapped under the bodies of his comrades, crushed under their weight. However, even as the Y'mordi left he heard a voice."

"A voice?" Aria was entranced.

"Yes, a voice that told him to be still. Not seeing a better option, he listened to the voice, and sure enough, the Y'mordi left the pile of corpses. He followed the orders of the voice, and it led him into a safer part of the fortress. Finally, he found the source of the voice: an elegant, beautiful White Dragon. Dagan had imprisoned her for the purpose of being a formidable weapon of war." Aria could tell that the old man had told this story multiple times. He had a certain feel about him and this story that seemed almost ancient.

He continued, "After freeing her, the two escaped the fortress, with Tatsu using his keen military intellect and the Dragon using her skills in *mysteria*. They rushed back to the Great Lord of Light, but they were stopped by another of the Y'mordi. Using Tatsu's own sword, he killed Tatsu but left the

Dragon. The White Dragon wept over her rescuer's body, and that was when it happened."

"What happened?"

"A piece of the Great Spirit appeared and entered that sword. That explosion of power created a unique bond between Tatsu and the Dragon. Besides keeping Tatsu alive, the Great Spirit's power connected the two physically and emotionally. Just through mere wish, the two could move their hearts between their bodies and therefore switch places. They could hear each other's thoughts and feel each other's emotions.

"The Great Lord of Light then decided to use this magnificent bond to his advantage and sent the pair to fight in the War."

"Tatsu and Kohana," Aria commented.

"Right. They were easily some of the most feared warriors on the battlefield. As a pair, no one could beat them, and in fact, no one ever did defeat them. They were unstoppable. When they switched places in mid-battle, Tatsu could utilize Kohana's Dragon physique to tear enemies to shreds, and Kohana could manipulate intense abilities in *mysteria* through Tatsu's Sword, his Spirit Sword."

"So what happened to them?" Aria inquired, unable to contain herself any more.

"Well, in the Final Battle, they were leaders. Thousands of Shadows were killed by their fury. Even Dagan was enraged by the presence of the Dragon that had once been in his possession. However, because they were so close to the front line, they got the worst of it…"

"That mysterious blast?" Aria winced as she said it, remembering when Draconis told her, Matthew, and Drage the story of the Battle that ended the Second Obsidian War.

"Yes. When Dagan and the Great Lord of Light fought, 'a colossal wave of silvery light spread across the land and roared throughout time and space.' That is what the legends say. Only a few survived that Battle. Everyone closest to Dagan and the

Great Lord disappeared completely, including Tatsu and Kohana. Everyone else was found dead."

Aria felt the hint of a tear in her eyes.

"The saddest part about the whole story is that many say that Tatsu made a promise to Kohana before they died. He promised that after the War was over, the two of them would go away together: They would be free from the politics, the fighting, the struggling. They would be free to live on their own, just the two of them."

Aria nodded her head solemnly, "That is a sad story."

"In Gevás, we tell our children that story. It has a strong message to it: Life is full of tragedy. Sometimes, you just have to accept it."

Again, Aria winced, though this time, it was due to the brutality of such a message. She had been raised to be optimistic about life, not to "accept" the world. She had been taught to be ambitious and strive to make the most out of life. "Why choose that as your password?"

The old man smiled at her, "I want the Academy to be just like Tatsu and Kohana. No matter what happens to the world, I want the Academy to persevere. This community should fight with its last breath until the very end, even if only doom can be found after it. For decades, I have wanted to change the symbol of this Academy from the griffin to a White Dragon with a sword in hand."

"Pardon me for asking, but why haven't you?"

"For now, we are griffins. We do not have the need for the strength of Tatsu and Kohana yet. When the time comes, we shall raise a new flag. I shall not inspire new strength prematurely." He gave one final smile to Aria before saying, "Now, I must leave to make tomorrow's preparations. I trust you will know where to go?"

Aria gave a slight nod, "Yes, sir. Thank you very much for everything. You have been a major help to me."

"It was my pleasure. You know, I once had Mistress Leona as my apprentice. After meeting you, I am convinced that you may very well have more potential than she did. I wish you the best of luck tomorrow. Oh, and I shall arrange for someone to move your things in the morning. I do not want you returning to your dormitory. There is no telling when the Y'mordi will strike." With that being said, he stepped into the elevator, and it hummed as it disappeared beneath the floor.

A grateful smile came across Aria's face. "He genuinely thinks I can do it." Defiantly, she commented, "I will show those other Deans how disciplined I can be."

Then, she set about learning as much about the Elements as she could from the input module. It was well into the morning before she got any rest.

Standing in front of five Deans, Aria breathed deeply, struggling to remain calm. The Grand Master Dean, usually not present for such examinations, sat at the end of the table, as an equal judge to the other Deans here, allowing the Dean of *Mysteria* to dictate the exam.

"Aria Newman, you stand before us to initiate your examination in the discipline of Elements. Are you prepared to take this examination now?"

"Yes, Dean Alcar," Aria responded.

"As you probably know, I am to give you overall instructions of the examination, regardless of whether you are intimately familiar with the rules or not."

"Yes, Dean Alcar."

She watched the other Deans shift uneasily in their seats. Taking the examination so suddenly and without warning or preparation with an advisor was not unheard of, but certainly rare. "The examination consists of two parts: an oral examination and a demonstration examination. The question-and-answer section will consist of a hundred questions regarding the Elements. This section will be given to you by all five of us, with each us of having decided upon twenty questions a piece. Some of the questions will require simple answers, while others will require full explanation. You have an hour to get through this portion of the exam." The Dean of *Mysteria* took a deep breath, showing his boredom with having to recite the instructions for what seemed like the hundredth time. There were usually a small handful of students who were disciplined in the Elements every year. The examinations differed between each Discipline, but Dean Alcar had been doing this for so long, the task of presiding over examinations was more of a chore. "The second section will involve each of us having five tasks for you to complete in this room. You will have up to two hours to complete this portion of the examination. Passing the examination requires correctly answering at least 80% of the questions and successfully performing at least four of each person's tasks. Do you understand the instructions as they have been presented to you?"

Aria nodded. "Yes, Dean Alcar. I am ready to proceed."

"Very well," Dean Alcar said as he sat back down. "Who would you like to begin questioning you?"

"Dean Scyllma, please."

Dean Scyllma was a tall, spindly woman with a tight face that exaggerated her pointed nose and thin lips, making her look like a dark-skinned, furless fox. Compared to many of the other Deans, especially in this room, she had a peculiar sense of fashion, preferring tight clothes with decorative, pointed pieces extending from her shoulders and down her front. She was one of the twenty-five regular Deans at the Academy. She taught several courses on spellcasting, one of the few professors who could easily manipulate all five of the primary Elements. Standing, she began, "Aria Newman, as your first examiner, I want to cover some basic, general knowledge questions first, and then some specifics regarding individual Elements."

"Yes, Dean Scyllma." Despite the nervousness crawling inside Aria's gut, her face only conveyed calm repose, her posture straight and her hands down at her sides.

"Excellent. First, list the possible Aids to manipulating *mysteria*."

Aria took a deep breath before beginning, staring intently at the Dean. "Incantations, wands, rods, orbs, scepters, rituals, and Convergence, Dean Scyllma."

"Good. Can you explain the difference between a wand and a scepter in the manipulation of *mysteria*?"

"Wands help with concentration and building form for spells. Performing the proper motions with each spell requires complete and total focus, allowing mages to have a physical act to focus on to help bridge the gap between *mysteria* and the physical world. Scepters, on the other hand, are reservoirs of power. They can increase the efficacy and intensity of spells. However, they do not make spells any easier to cast, like wands do."

Dean Scyllma smiled, her thin lips seeming to split her head in two. "How is one verified to be a Prophet for a certain Element?"

Aria smiled, having known this answer from her lessons with Mistress Leona. "Prophets are the only ones able to transform themselves into their respective Elemental Spirits."

"Can you name for me at least three of the Elemental Spirits?"

"Yes, Dean Scyllma. Nature's Elemental Spirit is the Unicorn. Fire's is the Dragon. Water's is the Serpent."

The questioning went on for the full hour, switching between each of the five Deans. Aria found herself quizzed on the emotions associated with each Element, the Prophets, and even the Elemental connections to the five Spirit Swords. As she switched over to the demonstration part of the exam, she was required to perform simple tasks, such as lighting multiple candles at once and growing a tree from the floor, and complex tasks, from creating a thunderstorm in the examination room to completing a Healing spell.

By the time it was the Grand Master Dean's turn to give her tasks, she felt an overwhelming sense of relief: the exam was almost complete. The Grand Master Dean stood and spoke in his low, raspy voice, his knuckles pressed against the long table. "Ms. Newman, for your first task for me, I want you to forge a sword. In one step, please."

"Forge a sword?" Aria's eyes widened. "Do you mean to make a sword out of an Element?"

"No, Ms. Newman. Forge a steel sword."

She lowered her gaze in consideration. Forging a sword would require having the block of steel and then using spells to melt and shape the steel. She could imagine a multi-step process but not a way to do it in one step. It would require creating the steel and shaping it at once. Gradually, she realized the Grand Master Dean was asking her to manipulate two Elements at once. "I…" she started and then shook her head. Looking at Dean Scyllma, she asked, "Dean Scyllma, may I borrow a second wand?" The Dean rose and offered her a wand in confusion. As Aria looked over the faces of the other Deans, she realized they were as perplexed as she was by the Grand Master Dean's difficult task. Grabbing the wand, Aria held out her own wand at the same time, a wand in each hand. Closing her eyes, she began waving each wand in different directions, tracing two very different designs into the water. One hand traced the movement for Rock, while the other traced the design for Lava. In front of her, a molten ball of steel appeared, and it condensed and elongated into the shape of a hilt and blade, the form white-hot. The spell complete, the Grand Master Dean cast a cooling spell, and the steel sword between the Deans and Aria hung in the water. The blade was crooked and not particularly sharp, but the task was complete.

The Grand Master Dean proceeded to give her tasks that required combining Elements. She had never before had to try manipulating two Elements at once. It required more concentration than she had ever attempted. It was not an impossible task, but it was certainly more advanced than was asked of students at the Academy, usually reserved for mages that pursue research after completing their education. She was sweating by the third task. Each of her performances became sloppier and sloppier in form; still, each task was completed.

With a tremendous grin on her face, she shook the hand of the Grand Master Dean, which generated several claps from the audience of several of the Deans and professors who had taught her over the years. Even Mistress Leona and Master

Valdridge were there with a proud smile. Though the few Deans and professors that supported her were cheering her eagerly, many others were simply dumbfounded by what had just occurred.

Aria took the sheet that held the proof of her mastery of the Elements discipline. As she stepped away from the Second Dean, she ran over to Mistress Leona and could not resist giving her a hug. She was surprised to note that the Prophet was hugging her back. The current moved around them. They had held a small ceremony outside on the grounds.

"Excellent job, Aria," Mistress Leona said.

"You knew that this would happen, didn't you?"

Mistress Leona shook her head. "I did not plan any of this. I knew you would solve the password."

"And the Grand Master Dean?"

"Well, yes, I told him that you were going to be up there looking for it, so that he knew where you were in case something happened. If the Y'mordi were to return, I wanted him to know that you would be safe up there using the input module."

However, Aria only shook her head. "I am glad it is over, and I can finally do something with this War now."

Master Valdridge regarded Aria in wonder, "Oh? And what is it that you intend to do now?"

Aria finally released Mistress Leona, and she beamed with pride as she said, "Well, first, I am going to find the sorcerers who served under me, and then we are going to find Drage and Matthew if they are done with their training. We are going to put an end to this War. From what I have heard, the Western Continent is almost defeated, am I not correct?"

The two Prophets nodded. Mistress Leona added, "Now that you have completed your training here, I can certainly install you again as the Wand Master, 2nd Class you were years ago, but I cannot make the troops who were once under you leave their new posts."

Aria nodded but did not address the comment. "Since the West still remains a nuisance, my troops and I shall extinguish what few flames there are in the West before moving on to the North. I know Astra is having some problems. We need to get to Apolis, so I can find my sorcerers."

Without hesitation, she summoned a Gate and was almost welcoming the cool current of the Southern Continent. For the first time in five years, she felt like the world was at her fingertips again.

Green and Blue

D rage had been marveling at the blue glow to his Sword only seconds before the glass window above the square arena shattered. He and Matthew ducked out of the way of the glass, hearing it crack behind them. As they glanced back up, they saw guards rush down the hallway that ran across the edge of the arena above, overlooking them.

"Look," Matthew said, gesturing toward the Sword, and, gradually, they watched as the glow of the Sword of Destiny faded.

"What was that?" asked Drage as he scanned where the window had just been. He could have sworn that he had sensed someone using the powers of Light.

Matthew was silent as he tried to hear what was going on above them.

Then, Drage felt it again, "There, someone is definitely using Light. Come on!" He ran to the door into the main hallway, stepping outside into the streets. The two brothers were appalled to find that most of the guards were sprawled along the ground groaning. They seemed to be fine, just in pain. Suddenly, a voice spoke.

"Excuse me, your Majesty, may I have a word with you?"

Drage regarded the man with the gray robe with annoyance. He grumbled, "I should not really be called that as of yet. Trust me, if you start that, it will only cause more problems for me. In fact, whatever problems you have, you should just bring them up with the Emperor's Council. They seem to know what they are doing." He knew that the Council had things far from under control, but he did not want random people to start relying on him since he was not even the Emperor.

Matthew nudged him in the ribs painfully with his elbow. "Drage, whether you are Emperor or not, you are still the Prince. Would your dad want you to treat people like that?"

Though Drage wanted to argue, he could not help but see the logic in Matthew's words. He turned to address the robed man, "Look, sir, I am not trying to be rude, but I really don't think that I can help you."

The man, however, was not swayed by Drage's initial words. "Oh, allow me to introduce myself. My name is Tilgé. I am just wanting to have a few words with you in private." He eyed Matthew nervously.

Drage's expression grew quite dark, then. "I am sure that whatever you have to say can be said in front of Matt. Go on. What is it you want?" His tone was becoming harsher, which only made Matthew more wary of his half-brother.

Finally, the man snapped, "Look here, Prince, I am on strict orders, so I need you to come with me. The Captain is expecting us." He made as if to grab Drage's arm, but Drage resisted.

"Captain? Who is that supposed to be? I am busy training here. I do not have time to see any captain."

Tilgé had a look of utter shock and rage. "You may be the Prince of Light, kid, but you are not the Emperor yet, and until you are, you are going to follow the orders of Captain Maks, see?" Suddenly, the man drew a dagger from his robe.

At seemingly lightning speed, Matthew whipped out his staff and knocked the blade out of Tilgé's hand. Drage was able to barely sense that Matthew had used a Time spell to perform the feat. Even after training with his half-brother for almost two weeks, he was still impressed by those fascinating spells.

"Who is Captain Maks, Tilgé?"

"He is the Captain of the Enigma Brigade, the force dedicated to protecting the Emperor of Light and serving the will of the Light!" roared Tilgé with spit flying from his mouth full of decaying teeth. This uproar gained several looks, but before anyone could come closer, Matthew froze all Time except for in the area where the three of them stood.

Tilgé was left speechless by the display of Matthew's power. Drage continued, losing his patience, "Now, you are going to need to explain this a little better to me. The Enigma Brigade?"

For the first time in his life, Tilgé was afraid of someone besides his Captain. "Yeah…the Enigma Brigade was made after the Wars to protect the Emperor of Light, and it has done its job well ever since then."

Matthew shook his head in confusion. "Why has no one heard about this Brigade?"

"Because it's a secret," snapped Tilgé. "Only the Emperor of Light and his Council are supposed to know about it, and even they should only be in communication with the Captain of the Brigade. Your speaking to me now is probably the first time that a Prince of Light or Emperor of Light has spoken to a member of the Enigma Brigade who is not the Captain in several hundreds of years."

"Well, why does the Captain need to speak with me? I am not the Emperor yet." Drage's fists clenched as he became more and more irritated with the man.

Tilgé's thin lips spread into a crooked smile. "That is why he needs to speak with you. We need an Emperor. Without that, the Enigma Brigade does not have a purpose. We need you to take your place as Emperor of Light."

Matthew noticed Drage clenched his fists, but he placed a comforting hand on his half-brother's shoulder. "Drage, relax a little. We can handle this."

Slowly, Drage relaxed his hands and his shoulders and replied, "Alright, where is this Captain?"

Tilgé brightened at the change in response. "He is waiting at a hotel. Come with me," he implored.

Matthew nodded encouragingly to Drage. "I can let time continue once we get out of the building. We should be back in no time, and then we can explain why we were gone. I am sure that they can make an exception for the son of a Prophet and the Prince of Light, right?" He offered a friendly smile to Drage, but Drage did not return it.

As they stepped into the warmth of the night, Tilgé began to notice how different Drage was from other Emperors of Light he had known. This one had a considerably darker personality. He could not help but think of Emperor of Light Mentiris from a century and a half ago. Though Tilgé had not been around then, Maks had talked about him nonstop. Could this Prince of Light be as influential and formidable as Mentiris had been?

Matthew released his spell of Time and frowned at the uncomfortable warmth of the Capital. He had become more used to it over the years: He had been living in the Western Continent which was probably a little warmer than it was right now, but he still missed the cool water of the Southern Continent.

"So what did you say your name was?" inquired Drage, attempting to make light conversation as they walked. "Tilde?"

Tilgé frowned in both anger and disappointment. "No! My name is Tilgé! Till-gay! It should not be that hard to remember, and I would hope that you never forgot it, too!"

Both Drage and Matthew could tell that this character was quite easy to upset. Nevertheless, Drage felt as if the man needed to learn at least some respect, so he commented, "Y'know, for a man dedicated to serving the Emperor, you sure are quite disrespectful." Drage smirked as they walked down the alleys between buildings.

Tilgé rounded on Drage and looked as if he was about to grab his dagger, but then he remembered what had happened to his blade. His face paled slightly when he realized he had no weapon on him. In shame, he lowered his eyes, "Forgive me, your Majesty."

Though Matthew disagreed with Drage's approach, he did not say anything. He had to agree that the man had been considerably rude. "How much further, Tilgé?" he asked softly.

The many in the gray robe did not avert his eyes from the ground. "Oh, just a few minutes, I think."

Drage changed the subject. "What kind of a person is this Captain?"

Luckily for Drage, this topic was one that Tilgé felt quite comfortable talking about, and it instantly brightened the Brigadier. "Captain Maksimilian is a fierce leader and formidable soldier. He always looks out for the good of the Brigade and the will of the Light."

"Why is it that my dad never mentioned anything about him?" asked Drage.

"The Captain and the Emperor of Light did not communicate much until the start of this War. There was never much of a need to, really. The Captain is a great politician himself; there was hardly a need for the two of them to meet regularly." Tilgé beamed at this remark. His favorite attribute of Maksimilian's was his aggressive and abrupt methods in conversation and politics.

Matthew smirked, "A great politician? How can anyone be a secret politician exactly?"

"Many leaders possess much respect for the Enigma Brigade, given the right persuasion."

Matthew and Drage grimaced as they understood what Tilgé was referencing. Before either of them could say anything in protest, they noticed the blue aura coming from Drage's scabbard. Drage pulled it out and saw the Sword of Destiny was glowing again.

Tilgé's eyes shone greedily. "Is that…?"

"The Sword of Destiny…it's doing something again," Drage muttered.

"It must be responding to something nearby," Matthew remarked.

When they stopped in front of a shabby building, the Sword was glowing more intensely. Tilgé was amazed by the shimmering blade. He could only imagine how phenomenal of a weapon it could be, and it made him crave the Sword even more. Nevertheless, he knew that the time for such desires was not at hand. He opened the door to the hotel and allowed the Prince of Light and his half-brother to enter.

As they ascended the creaking stairs, the Sword's aura was now almost blinding, and it began to vibrate, which was quite unusual. Then, Tilgé stepped forward to knock on a door.

"You may enter," called a voice from inside the room.

Tilgé muttered gruffly to the two, "Wait here, got it?" He entered the room alone and began, "Hey, Maks, I brought the Prince of Light, but he brought his friend along, too."

A soft yet confident voice responded, "Well, then, invite them in. Do not be rude to your future leader." The words came as a blow to Tilgé considering he had been scorned by the Prince already.

"Yes, Captain," he murmured as he went out into the hallway and said quietly, "The Captain would like to see you." He led the two into the barely lit room, and Drage and Matthew marveled at how homely the room seemed. A set of fine clothes hung neatly in the open wardrobe, and a pile of old, rusty books rested on a trunk at the foot of the bed.

Then, they saw the man at the window. He was wearing a golden robe with a crimson bird on its front. To match his red bird, his long hair that bore the same shade went down slightly below his waist. He turned his head to face the Prince of Light and revealed his bright green eyes. "It is a pleasure to meet you, Prince Helius," he said with a bow. "I have heard much about you over the years. My name is Maksimilian."

Drage gave Maksimilian a polite nod and replied, "Pleased to meet you, Maksimilian. Tilgé has told me a lot about you. May I ask what has called your attention to me, Captain?" There was a glint in the Captain's eyes that alerted Drage not to anger or disrespect this man.

Maksimilian gestured to his small table with four chairs encircling it. "Please have a seat." When he noticed that Tilgé was going to join them, Maksimilian gave the man a stern look, "Tilgé, you are dismissed." This reproof came as a shock to Tilgé, and his look of wounded bewilderment quickly became a jaw-clenched glare directed at the two young men. Before his face could become any redder, he stormed out of the room, but he made sure not to slam the door behind him.

The man with the long red hair continued, "You will have to forgive Tilgé. He is quite the selfish man and does little for others."

Matthew replied with a calm tone, "He did not seem to be too bad of a person."

Maksimilian grimaced at the judgment. "I am familiar with the Prince's name, but I do not believe that I know yours. You are a friend of the Prince, I am assuming?"

Drage could sense the tension between the two immediately. Matthew nodded as he said, "Yes, sir. My name is Matthew. I am Drage's half-brother."

"Half-brother? I see." An amused smile formed on Maksimilian's lips. "Anyways, your Majesty, I requested an audience with you for a specific reason. This War is getting out of hand."

Drage frowned in perplexity. "We have almost defeated the exiles in the Western Continent, though, haven't we?"

"Almost, yes. However, we are coming across their stronghold there now. It will be the hardest battle of the War more than likely. Believe it or not, the progress in the West has decreased quite considerably since the Dragon left."

"The Dragon?" inquired Drage in disbelief. "Draconis?"

"Yes, that is his name. He requested an emergency leave. I suppose that I do not begrudge him any, however. For years, he has done his duty, so I can agree that he needed the time off. However, the Western Continent is not my primary concern."

Drage interrupted him here. "Excuse me, but do you know what has happened to Draconis?"

Maksimilian was actually quite stunned that the Prince was more interested in the actions of the Golden Dragon rather than the force of the Enigma Brigade. "I believe that the official report read that he went home on an emergency leave. I do not know what home is for a Dragon, though."

Matthew guessed, "He probably went to Sharl Vran."

"Sharl Vran?" Drage asked.

"It is the world of Dragons. My dad told me about it. I wonder what caused him to go there," commented Matthew in equal confusion.

The man with the red hair interrupted this topic. "Excuse me, your Majesty, but I believe that the real concern is not the West, or the Dragon, but the North. The exiles there are in a civil war at the moment. If we can take it, that will cut some of the West's supplies."

Drage retorted, angry at the change of topic, "Oh? And what would you suggest me to do about that? I cannot do anything until I complete my training here first."

Maksimilian snapped back, "And will you take the Throne then?"

To this question, Drage had no answer. It depended on if he could find Maris's spirit. Hopefully, Marqest would help with that search a little more, but over the weeks, Drage and Matthew had heard nothing from the old Prophet of Water.

"Well then, I suggest you listen to my proposal."

Drage's black eyes glared into Maksimilian's green eyes. "Alright, I am listening."

Maksimilian could not believe he was being talked down to by someone so young. His instinct was always to punish those who disrespected him. Maksimilian's fingers were struggling not to reach for his katana, but he knew that he could not raise a weapon to the Prince. With a deep breath, he calmed himself. "The Enigma Brigade has for centuries served the Emperor of Light, but seeing as there is not one, it makes it quite difficult for us to do our job."

"Go on."

"I want for you to lead the Enigma Brigade into battle against the rebel exiles of the Northern Continent. If you can successfully lead at least one battle, then I can legally promote you to the status of General. Though my rank is called 'captain,' I am the leader of the entire Brigade. The Emperor of Light granted me that power long ago."

Both Matthew and Drage were instantly wary of this proposal. Matthew inquired, "Why would you want this? You could lead the Brigade into the battle more effectively than either of us could. Why?"

The Captain took another deep breath and replied calmly, "I want you to take the Throne, your Majesty. Making you a General puts you one step closer to accepting your place. The Council has done a horrible job of leading your kingdom, and I have been realizing the past few days that I am not the one who can change this chaos. Only you can do that." Before Drage could protest, he continued, "Believe me, I do not want someone so young and inexperienced to be the Emperor, no offense, your Majesty, but I find that even those who are old and experienced are incompetent. For your information, I also have reason to believe that someone is manipulating the Council from the inside and is responsible for the poor quality leadership of the Council. Valdridge is appearing to be the source of this nonsense."

Drage tried to calm himself as well as he said softly, "I shall worry about the Council when that time comes. For now, I shall take you up on your offer. If the Enigma Brigade is ready, then we shall fight in the North. I do not want any time to be wasted. However, I shall encourage you to leave the politics to someone more adept at handling them than yourself." Drage could tell that Maksimilian was young, and he meant to make sure that the Captain knew his place.

However, the man did not reveal any anger and merely nodded. "Yes, your Majesty. The troops are ready when you are."

Matthew remarked, "That quick?"

"Yes, they are ready at a moment's notice. That is the way of the Enigma Brigade."

"Well, then, we are going to the training facility we have been staying at to pick up a few things, and then meet us in front of this building in an hour with the rest of the Brigade," commanded Drage sternly.

Maksimilian responded with a sole nod.

Then, Drage left the room with Matthew close behind him. Matthew began whispering to his half-brother as soon as the door was closed. "Drage, there is something off about this. I am sure of it."

"I feel it, too," Drage agreed. "There was definitely something that he was not telling us, but whatever his motives are, we still have much to gain from this deal. Whatever he had hoped to gain from us, he only half-gained. Had to push him down a notch."

Matthew nodded at that statement. "You are right about that." He regarded Drage with caution. "You have changed a lot since you were last here." He was becoming worried about his best friend's mental and emotional state. He did not know what to do.

Drage responded coldly, "As I have changed, so has this world. What I used to be was not strong enough to lead Helio, but what I will become once Maris is out of me fully will be more than enough."

As they went down the stairs, Matthew replied, "Did you never think that perhaps it would not be that bad to lead with that piece of Maris still within you? I think that you can be strong and still protect your heart from Maris's control. Every once in a while, I catch a glimpse of the old you, but…you've changed. I think that you can do it."

"It is not that simple," snapped Drage. They exited the hotel in silence. Once they were halfway to the facility, Drage sighed and said, "Hey, that guy with the red hair…"

"Yeah?" Matthew said with a brow raised.

"He had a Spirit Sword."

"What?"

"That man," Drage explained. "Maksimilian had one of the Spirit Swords. That was why my Sword was responding as we got closer to him. I could just barely see the green glow of his Sword, and I am sure that he saw mine."

Matthew looked thoughtful then. "So, you think that he might try to take your Sword? Hm, he was very interesting. He seemed a little too young to have been the Captain of the Enigma Brigade and the wielder of one of the Spirit Swords." When he saw Drage's accusing look, Matthew shrugged. "I am just trying to say that you would have to be pretty important to have one of those Swords. It is likely that he inherited that Sword like you did. Still, I am curious as to how he got where he is now."

Drage nodded in agreement. "Perhaps, we will ask Tilgé later."

"I don't think that that will happen," remarked Matthew with a shake of his head. "He seemed pretty upset when Maksimilian kicked him out. If looks could kill, we would have been dead once his eyes fell on us."

Maksimilian's fists clenched as soon as the door shut behind them. Those two had treated him the way that he had wanted to treat them. He had hoped that by the time they had left that they would be under his thumb wholeheartedly. He was infuriated to find that the tables were turned with Drage ordering him around.

However, he had learned a lot from the encounter. For one, he had learned that the Prince of Light had indeed inherited the Sword of Destiny. He had decided years ago that he did not desire that blade. Its strength came in its ability to reduce friction, but its weakness was that it had restrictions, a code of conduct. The Sword would not cut easily through people or through weapons in the heat of battle. He had to admit that the Sword of Destiny was an amazing weapon compared to his Steel of Life, but it was simply not worth the trouble of obtaining it. Perhaps, if he gained the others Swords, it would be beneficial to take the Sword of Destiny, but until that time, there would be no true benefits. The weapon was more of a kitchen knife than anything, a tool.

Shaken by his encounter with the Prince of Light, he put a bony finger on the hilt of the Steel of Life. This simple gesture seemed to bring him a form of comfort and rejuvenation. He had always wondered if this feeling of relief was simply a mental trick or if the Steel was actually giving him more vitality.

Then, he remembered Tilgé's anger. Maksimilian grunted in frustration. That short-tempered man was beginning to be a nuisance. He intended on having a talk with his second before they moved to the North. Hopefully, after that talk, Tilgé would improve.

Maksimilian's next concern was of the fortress here in the Capital. He still had the intention of searching it before he was done here. He stroked his chin, deep in thought. "Very well. I shall wait until after the attack in the North. I shall take just two or three of the Brigadiers. That will make it a more covert and easily accomplished mission."

As he rose, he summoned the slightest ounce of mysteria, *and the red phoenix on his chest glimmered brightly. Within seconds, the rest of the Enigma Brigade appeared in the street outside of the hotel. His smile broadened. "Let us see how much you have learned, Prince of Light. Let us see if you are as incompetent a leader as your father was."*

An hour later, Drage and Matthew approached the hotel, each carrying a small tote bag on his shoulder. They were stunned by the spectacle of the Enigma Brigade. Though it was quite a tiny force, they were formidable in their stoic poses, all in formation.

Drage put his hands behind his back as he remarked, "Five men? This is the finest that can serve the Light?"

The Brigade did not hesitate in their response, "Yes, sir!"

Though Matthew winced at the unexpected reply, Drage stood perfectly still. "Good," he said softly. Then, he stepped up to the soldier on the far left. "What is your name, soldier?"

The soldier responded with a stern voice, "Sume, sir."

Drage stepped over to the next soldier and gave a demanding look, and without waiting to hear the question, the second soldier said, "Bryco, sir."

He continued in this fashion and learned the names of the other Brigadiers: Maksimilian, Viso, and Tilgé. Both Matthew and Drage were astonished to find that a member of the Emperor's Council was also among the Enigma Brigade. Drage found himself wondering if Viso was behind the corruption of the Emperor's Council, but he did not dwell on the thought.

"Let's move out," he commanded, and then Sume created a Gate of Light. Before Drage and Matthew stepped into the Gate, he added, "Keep in mind that Matthew is not my second. He is my equal. If you get an order from him, treat it as if it came directly from my mouth. Understood?"

In unison, the Brigade responded, "Yes, sir!"

With Drage, Matthew, and Maksimilian leading the Brigade, they entered into the warm current of the Northern Continent. They were immediately met by screams and roars. As they looked around at the scores of dead bodies in terror, they realized that they had stepped right in the middle of a battle with mages and gunmen firing all around them.

It was Matthew who brought everyone to their senses again. "Quick, aim for the griffins. Treat them as the opposition!" Without waiting a second longer, the Brigade struck. A barrage of Flame and Force spells danced across the grassy plains at the armored creatures who all divided to dodge the attack, only some of them succeeding.

What had signaled him as to the enemy was a face he had recognized amongst the melee: Lilian. Though she was in her horse form, somehow, he just knew that it was her. She happened to be fighting the griffins. Then, he saw the massive Silver Dragon that she was fighting as well.

Drage called, "Maksimilian, Bryco, target the Dragon! Target the Dragon!" The two instantly responded, and Matthew joined them to help Lilian. Drage did not recognize the anima, which was only logical, considering that he had never officially met her. Nevertheless, he went to aid Tilgé, Sume, and Viso.

It took little effort for Drage to defeat the griffin with his skillful swordplay, the Way of the Dragon allowing him to dance across the field, and Tilgé and the others were able to finish off many of the griffins from that point.

Matthew, Lilian, Maksimilian, and Bryco were having a rougher time defeating the opponent of the Silver Dragon. Every time that Matthew tried to manipulate the flow of time, he found an unexpected resistance. It was as if the Dragon were preventing him from casting any Time spells. After a quick examination of the Silver Dragon's heart, Matthew found this idea to be true: the Dragon's true Element was of Wind, and he could sense a Time spell that kept time steady, unable to be altered. Nevertheless, he swung his staff as fast as he could and managed to hit the creature multiple times at nearly crippling strength.

Maksimilian's rapid attacks went hand in hand with Lilian's vast array of spells. The Dragon was truly struggling now that he had to time his defensive spells with blocks and parries. In fact, the Dragon was so distracted by the effort that Bryco managed to follow through with several slashes, which caused great amounts of blood to pour from the Dragon's silvery hide.

Finally, Matthew saw a weak spot in the Dragon's Time spell. With all of his might, he broke through the spell and immediately slowed down time for the Dragon alone. Maksimilian's, Lilian's, and Bryco's slashes all connected with the Dragon at once, and Matthew released his spell. The Dragon went flying backwards into the water, and blood sprayed from its flailing corpse in torrents. After a few more seconds, it stopped its thrashing and roared sadly across the vast sea. Lilian approached the head of the beast and transformed into her human form in a white aura.

As she stroked its scaly head, it spoke deeply, "Forgive me, creature of Gevás. My master cursed me with Darkness: I could not control my actions. They call us Silver Dragons wanderers, Dragons without a place to call home. I heard the whispers of a return of the Golden Dragons, a hero. His name was Rexam Draconis. Can you tell him? Can you tell him that—," but the Dragon did not finish his sentence, nor did he finish that choking breath. He was gone.

As the griffins retreated into the woods, the Enigma Brigade pursued, casting spells as they went. Drage and

Matthew stood side-by-side over Lilian, Matthew relieved and Drage concerned.

"He mentioned Draconis," commented Drage. "I am starting to think that we need to check on him, Matt."

"Prince Helius…Matthew…what are you two doing here?" asked a bewildered Lilian with her soft voice.

It was then that Matthew noticed how beautiful she looked now. Five years ago, Lilian had been only a little girl. Now, she appeared to be as old as Matthew was. "We came to help end the civil war here," he responded.

She smiled gently as she said, "Thank you then. I am glad to know that Astra has not been forgotten by his Majesty. I only wish that you could have come sooner. Much has happened lately. You only just came in time to save this village." She gestured behind her to the village that everyone had fought to protect. It had remained intact, no damage.

Matthew squinted at the sight in confusion. "That's not the village you came from, is it?"

Lilian shook her head. "No, those same griffins destroyed my village earlier today. I would guess that only half of us survived the raid and made it here. However, they followed us and brought the aid of that Dragon."

"Did he speak the truth? Was he possessed by the Darkness?" he inquired softly.

Lilian nodded. "Yes, I think so. There was a massive cloud of Darkness around his heart that alerted me to the invaders' presence, but when he was fading, the cloud disappeared altogether. It did not gradually vanish. It was removed. I think that whoever his master was is probably out to get Draconis based on what some of the survivors have said."

Drage cursed violently and stomped away in frustration. Before Matthew could follow him, he felt a hand grab his arm. He turned to see Lilian staring straight at him.

"I just wanted to repeat my gratitude. I do not know how you knew where we were or how you knew we needed help, but you saved many lives by coming here when you did. Thank you."

Matthew smiled warmly and felt the slightest blush fill his cheeks. "You're welcome," he replied. He found himself admiring her white, flowing hair and silver eyes. Those eyes were like diamonds.

Suddenly, he noticed that there was a mass of brown fur on her head. Then, the mass spoke, "Hello, there! Nice to meecha!"

Matthew was dumbfounded. "Is that a squirrel on your head?"

"Oh?" Lilian's eyes looked straight up, and she grinned. "Oh, this is Senagul. What are you doing in my hair? I thought you were still in the village?"

The squirrel anima crossed his tiny arms comically. "I told you to stop calling me that," he grumbled.

Unanswered Prayers

The sun filtered in through the cracks of the ceiling and revealed the clouds of dust that filled the room. That same sunlight painted the room in many colors through the stained-glass windows that made up the roof of the ancient temple.

This particular room was circular and held a thick altar in its center, occupying most of the room. Two gigantic stone torches were on either side of the altar, and blue flames filled them. On the altar, various fruits and meats existed along with a few goblets of the drink called bubbler.

"Oh, remnants of the Great Spirit, hear my call! I pray to you now."

The voice came from a scrawny man who was knelt before the altar. He looked as if he had not eaten for days, yet he was offering the food on the altar to the Great Spirit.

"You allowed my family to be taken away by the armies to the South, and I have been left with nothing but an old suit of armor. I have fought against the intruders who fight in the name of the Light as I believe you have willed me to do."

His blonde hair was cut quite short, and he wore rusty armor that covered legs. Beside him were a dented helmet and the top half of his armor. Salty tears lined his scarred cheeks.

"You have taken everything from me, and I seek to be made anew. A thousand years ago, an evil man broke you into five pieces, and I grieve for your suffering. I want to relieve you of your pain. Allow me to end these monsters who would destroy your temple. Give me the power to fight back!"

However, his desperate prayers rang emptily throughout the Temple of the Spirits, as they had every time that he had returned to this exact same spot. The only sounds that accompanied his calls were the crackle and snap of the azure flames that surrounded the altar.

In the throne room, two Y'mordi spoke. "Heh, the two kids left for the North. They were with the filthy Enigma Brigade," explained Xarden with his arms folded across his chest. His old age had no effect on his light remarks.

Pullatus did not react visibly, but he said, "That is good. Are they trying to affect the fight there? They are fools if they think that they can change all that much so quickly."

"Yes, that is their goal. However, I believe that a complication has arisen," he began tentatively.

The small man did not respond.

Xarden continued with hesitation. "I believe they encountered the Dragon that you requested the Great Servant to send to the North. In his death, he revealed some of the goings-on in Sharl Vran. My spies reveal the Prince of Light is considering going there, despite his duty here. What would you like for me to do?"

At first, Pullatus was silent. Then, he strode past Xarden, which sent chills up Xarden's spine immediately, and approached the door to the hallway. "It seems that the Guardians of Light are mobilizing. Even Ixion has had problems locating the Guardian whom I sent him to watch. I am beginning to doubt that the Y'mordi have the power to affect the iron wills of the Guardians of Light. However, I think that it is time to add another pawn to the board."

"That would be a wise move," commented Xarden. *"Who can play that part?"*

Pullatus stood at the door with his back to the elderly man as he spoke, *"The Darkness has spoken of a name to me. There is a man to the West who seeks the power to annihilate his enemies in the Southern Continent."*

"Oh? Does this man have what it takes to do so?"

Pullatus shook his head gravely. *"No, but I think that he might be able to distract the Prince of Light. His mind is weak and will be easily molded. Nevertheless, I think that we can give him the power that he seeks."*

Xarden smiled wickedly as he realized what Pullatus was referencing. *"Shall I take care of this man, then?"* he asked eagerly.

"No, I want you to keep your eyes on the Prince of Light and aid in the spread of this man's tales. I want him to be a legend before he has even struck. Do you think that you can handle that, Xarden?"

With a nod and a bow, Xarden returned to the Water Realm of Gevás through his icy Gate.

Pullatus opened the door to the hallway and entered the next room. It was a grandiose ballroom of sorts and held an archaic chandelier that dangled lifelessly from the black ceiling. The Dark Realm was the only realm of Gevás that had the colossal Palace of Shadows. Though the Great Lord of the Darkness had possessed many such castles in the Water Realm, the Palace of Shadows had been his true home.

When the Great Lord of the Darkness had fallen in the Final Battle, Pullatus had taken control of the Palace. Not even the other Y'mordi knew all of the dark secrets that he kept hidden in this place.

At his heart's will, a thousand Shadows filled the room and bowed before him. *"Go to the Great Servant of the Darkness named Kusvor Cairon. He shall need your aid soon."* He summoned a Gate without so much as lifting a finger, and the Shadows swarmed into the Gate that released bubbles of air into the Palace. Then, he called upon eleven more of the Shadows. *"Come with me. We are going to answer a man's prayers. Look your best, for you are all going to be my dark angels now."* As if it was under their control, black wings sprouted from the hazy bodies of the Shadows, and their features became more solid, giving each one an even more humanlike visage.

The man's tears finally dried. "Great Spirit, I shall leave you now. Bless me with the power to do what I must today." Gradually, his head rose, and standing on the altar was a figure shrouded in black. He staggered backward in shock and exclaimed, "Who are you? How did you get in here?" Then, he noticed the black angels that were encircling the entire room. "Are you...the Great Spirit?"

The figure responded, though his hood did not move from its position that hid his face fully, "No, but I act upon its behalf. For a long time, I have heard your prayers, and the Great Spirit has sent me to grant you your ultimate request." He held his hands up in show of his generosity.

The blonde-haired man's eyes widened. His tears became tears of joy then. "Do you speak the truth? Has the Great Spirit finally answered my prayers?"

"However, the Great Spirit has a request for you at the same time," the figure said as he crossed his arms. "He wants you to lead the exiles of the Western Continent against the forces of the South. Most of all, he wants you to kill the Prince of Light. He is a scourge on the face of the planet, and you must eliminate him. Is this understood?"

The man smiled gratefully, "Yes, sir. It is understood."

"Good. What is your name, soldier?"

The man stood then and maintained a posture that revealed his pride and honor. "My name is Gaspard. I am a swordsman."

Beneath his hood, the figure chuckled softly. "That is very good." From his robes, he summoned a massive Sword. As if it was weightless, he tossed it to the man, and Gaspard barely caught it. The blade was immense and heavy. It took all of his strength just to carry it. "This blade is known as the Behemoth. Though it is quite large, it shall grant you the skills of the thief and the gambler: it grants you luck. As you wield this Sword, the odds will stay in your favor, and you will find that those who once denied your might will now serve under you proudly." As a wide, dark Gate appeared above the figure, the angels flew into it, and the figure repeated, "Eliminate the Prince of Light, and the Great Spirit may be willing to reward you further." Then, he, too, rose into the Gate that had been as large as the room itself.

Gaspard was alone in the room. Experimentally, he attempted to raise the Sword above his head and found it nearly impossible. "The Behemoth, huh? Appropriate name…" When he found on his second attempt that raising the Sword too high would be impractical, he decided to change his form to the way of the Shark, focusing on hurling the sword amid punches and kicks. The weapon was quite fitting for the form, and it meant the amount of work he had to do would be considerable, but the slowness of the blade's attacks would not be a problem.

As he practiced, the Sword began to produce a golden aura. With each strained slash in the water, he began to realize that the Sword glowed brighter when it was closest to the altar of the Great Spirit.

Cautiously yet curiously, he approached the altar with the Behemoth in his hand. The Sword began to vibrate, and suddenly, a voice whispered in his head, "Lies…lies, Gaspard…Do not obey to He Who Listens to the Voice of the Shadows. Lies…lies, Gaspard. Lies…" Before the ominous, silent chant could continue, he stepped backward, clenching his ears.

"Get out of my head," he murmured. He had finally seen an angel of the Great Spirit; he had no intent of doubting this wonderful gift. He could not understand what the words meant, and he did not return to that altar again. The voice ceased as soon as he stepped away from it.

Then, he heard a voice come from the main hallway. Dragging his Sword across the stone ground, he opened one of the giant doors and beheld an army of rebel anima. One hesitant bear anima approached him. "Please pardon us. We were just looking for somewhere to stay for the night."

Gaspard turned his head back to face the altar where he had been worshipping only minutes before. Either the Great

Spirit had granted him an opportunity, or the Behemoth was demonstrating its luck.

When Pullatus returned to the Palace of Shadows, he dismissed the Shadows that he had summoned and then addressed the short man who had arrived as well. "Why are you here?"

"My Lord…my Lord, I came to report to you. The girl has left the Academy. She graduated."

Pullatus sat back in the colossal throne. "Hm, it seems that the Grand Master Dean was suspecting you then. I am assuming then that you have lost her entirely?"

Ixion bowed multiple times. "Please forgive me, my Lord! I will not make that mistake again!" He silenced immediately when he saw Pullatus's raised hand.

"Fear not, Ixion. It is of little consequence. Actually, I have a different assignment for you." He did not react when another Gate appeared, and Xarden entered the Palace of Shadows. "Ixion, I would like for you to begin spreading rumors in Apolis that a new General is leading the forces in the West: His name is Gaspard, and he is a fierce swordsmaster. I need for the Council to send the Prince of Light into that struggle as fast as possible." Before Ixion could reply in his high voice, Pullatus commented, "You are dismissed."

Ixion bowed as he left.

"Y'tal," began Xarden hesitantly. "I am sorry for coming back so early. To be honest, I had forgotten to tell you something rather important before we departed."

"Oh, and what might that be?" inquired Pullatus, his patience wearing thin.

Xarden noted the impatience in Pullatus's voice and said rather quickly, "Do you remember Maksimilian from the Wars?"

Pullatus responded with a silent nod.

"He is alive, Y'tal."

The leader of the Y'mordi leaped to his feet. "What?" he said somewhat forcefully. He was trying his best to contain his emotions. "I could have sworn that he died in the Final Battle."

"No, sir. What is more is that Maksimilian is the Captain of the Enigma Brigade, I believe. He was wearing the crest and everything. He looked as young as he did back then, too. He has not aged a day."

Pullatus was dumbfounded at first. After a few seconds, he replied, "Maksimilian has returned but not as an Ancient. This information is quite interesting, Xarden. Do you have any more information about him?"

Xarden shook his head. "No, sir."

"Well, then, once you have successfully spread the word of Gaspard's attacks, I would like for you to investigate Maksimilian's doings. I have never expressed an interest in the Enigma Brigade, but I have found reason to investigate them now. Is that all, Xarden?"

"Yes, Y'tal. I shall leave you now."

Once Pullatus was finally alone again, he sat down again. "Maksimilian, you have revealed yourself at last. How long did you think you could hide from the Y'mordi? It has been almost a thousand years. Come to think of it, this Gaspard fellow reminds me a lot of you, or at least what you used to be. Neither of you seem to realize that the Great Spirit is gone. All that are left are five remnants in the shape of metal swords. The Great Spirit is gone."

Moonlit Lake

"Lly...Lly? Are you awake? Lly?"

With a noisy and painful groan, Lly opened her eyes, and she became aware of the chilling wind that was brushing forcefully against her scales. Her eyes snapped open as she breezed past the pink clouds of the sunset. Her head whipped around several times in panic before she realized that she was in an uncomfortable metal cage. Above her, three Black Dragons carried her cage as they soared through the dusk. She suddenly became aware of her extreme thirst. It felt as if she had not drunk any water for days.

"Lly, over here!"

Lly turned to the sound of the voice and saw Draconis in a cage beside her. She staggered over to the bars. "Rexam, what is going on?"

Draconis had been awake for a few hours already. However, he had learned very little in his time awake. He, too, was quite thirsty at the moment. "I do not know, Lly. I think that they might be taking us straight to Cairon," he explained grimly.

"We lost the battle…" said Lly with a downcast expression. She had been so optimistic about the attack, but somehow, it had gone all wrong.

Draconis decided then to get over his nervousness, and he reached a claw out to Lly. Her tear-rimmed eyes looked into his, and she gave a faint smile as she accepted his hand and gripped it tightly. He said, "You should not have done it, Lly." He glanced over her golden body in worry. She had disguised herself as a Golden Dragon just before they had been taken. "Let us hope that they do not find out."

She clenched his claw tighter. "I could not let them take you alone, and if changing the color of my scales could change that, why would I not take that chance? You saved my life in that battle. Thank you." Her blue eyes twinkled brightly in the twilight glow of the setting sun.

Draconis's small smile was his response. "We need to figure out how we are going to get out of this mess, though." He observed the legion of Black Dragons that had taken them. "It appears that many of them are getting tired. You can tell by their slow speed. It is as if they are struggling."

"That means that we shall be stopping soon. Considering how far we were from the capital, it should take us another day at least. So, our stop will only be a temporary one." Although their voices were rushed, they did not have to be quiet as the force of the wind carried their voices away from their captors above.

"And that will be the most opportune moment to escape."

Lly was puzzled for a moment. "Can you not use your powers to get us out of here?"

Draconis lowered his head in shame. "No, there was a group of seven people from the world of Gevás that had extraordinary powers. They are called the Y'mordi, and I believe that they are helping Cairon. I think that they taught him how to use *mysteria*, too. They have bewitched these cages, so that I could only cast spells inside the cage." Occasionally, their cages banged against each other, sending them sprawling.

"Then," Lly managed as she tried to sit up again, "*you* should be able to get out of here right?" When Draconis gave her a look, several cold tears streaked down Lly's face. "Rexam…"

He interrupted her then with a broad smile on his face as he whispered, "I promise you, I'm not going to leave you. When all of this is over, I am going to take you to see Gevás. It is a fantastic world, and it is completely underwater. You do not have to worry about breathing, and the coral reefs are breathtaking."

Lly's eyes closed as she daydreamed about the place that seemed too good to be true. The stinging wind blew their tears away, and they leaned against the sides of their cages with hands together.

A few seconds later, they heard chattering amongst the Black Dragons above them. Simultaneously, Lly and Draconis looked forward, and they beheld a gray and dreary island in the sky. Towering mountains dotted the island's surface, and dead valleys occupied the spaces that connected the rocky crags. Lly and Draconis surveyed the land to see if there were any lakes or streams to quench their thirst and found only one.

They swooped over the island and landed in one of the gravel-covered valleys. When one of the Black Dragons approached the two cages, it said, "We are stopping here for the night. If you try anything, King Cairon will wipe out the rest of the rebels including the Dragon Elani."

Both Draconis and Lly were appalled that Cairon had learned of Elani's name. How much else did Cairon know about the rebels? The Black Dragon unlocked the cages, and Draconis and Lly stepped out of the cages hesitantly. Immediately, one of the Dragons put manacles around the prisoners' claws. The same Dragon led the two of them to a lonely tree that resided in the valley and connected the manacles to the thick trunk to prevent any possible escape, though Draconis knew that it would take little effort for him to break the tree.

As soon as they were alone, Draconis began whispering, "Alright, I am going to create a Gate, and you are going to get out of here. You need to tell Elani that Cairon knows about the whole operation. You need to warn—"

His words were cut off by a stern glare from Lly. "I will not leave you as you did not leave me. We are in this together, no matter what happens, Rexam."

Draconis shook his head. He could not believe how stubborn yet attractive this Blue Dragon was. Sighing, he admitted his intentions. "I want to face Cairon alone. I have wanted it that way for a while now. It is only right for me to be the one to fight him, I think. I saw him on the night that he began the raids, and he let me live, but he killed my friends and my family. I ran away to another world and have been there for all of my life. I cannot keep running away. I have to face him. I have to know why he spared me, and I have to take the Dragon Crown from him. Perhaps, Elani could be the new ruler of Sharl Vran. Once in the castle, it will be easy for me to break out and find him."

"No," murmured Lly as she shook her head as well. "Elani could not be the ruler. The law states that fact."

Draconis was perplexed instantly, "The law? What law would that be?"

"Even Cairon has paid some attention to that law and has not taken on the full privileges of being the King. He has limited international affairs and even some trading policies. If anything, he is an unofficial King, and he knows that, though he will not admit it. When this world was new, because of the fight between Golden and Black Dragons, the Divine Dragon of the Heavens defined the order of the Dragons. The Black Dragons were designated with one small area, and the Golden Dragons inherited the world."

"So what?" Draconis was astonished by this news. The segregation in Sharl Vran was far worse than he had originally thought. "You and I both know that Elani would make a great leader. Why could we not simply amend those laws after we defeat Cairon?"

Lly retorted, "The fact that an actual heir exists."

"An heir?" Now, he was dumbfounded.

"The laws of Sharl Vran state a hierarchy. It is a system that defines who has the right to take the Dragon Crown. It starts out with the firstborn son of the King, and then it spreads throughout various lines of the Imperial family."

"I thought that Cairon killed everyone, though."

"He did," explained Lly sadly. "Every last member of the family was indeed killed. However, the law did not stop with the Imperial family. It goes on to say that a leader of one of the Imperial cities can take the Crown." She continued quickly before Draconis could interrupt again. "And after that, any citizen of one of those Imperial cities is the heir," she paused before adding, "as long as the Dragon is a Golden Dragon."

Finally, he realized what she was hinting at exactly. "You mean to tell me that I am the heir to the Dragon Crown? You cannot be serious. There are other Golden Dragons that survived."

"No, Rexam. The ones who are with us had never been raised in the cities. That is how they are still alive. They had never been affected by Cairon's raids. You are the last surviving candidate for the Dragon Crown."

A memory echoed in the back of his mind, "*Six, an heir and self-made outcast dressed in gold.*"

A thousand excuses to not take the Crown came to his mind all at once, but in a second, he dismissed the thoughts, and he was calm again. "If what you say is true, then it must be me who fights Cairon. My duty is indeed here." He was having trouble figuring out how could justify permanently leaving Gevás at the same time, however. He still had a debt to Lord Bral Helius that could not be repaid until his death. Still, he now saw a duty here he could not ignore.

Lly beamed at what Draconis was saying. "You will make a fine King, Rexam, but you are a foolish Dragon if you think that I will let you fight Cairon alone. You may have the right to fight him, but you are not the only one. I will fight, too, and I am confident that Elani will know of our plan shortly."

"What makes you confident of that?"

"She will notice that you have not returned, and nor have I. I am sure she believes either of us is perfectly capable of escaping these dolts on our own."

Suddenly, one of the Black Dragons to which she had just referred called out, "Hey, be quiet over there! No talking!"

The two ignored the Dragon and merely spoke more softly. Lly licked her parched lips thirstily. She was beginning to feel a little hot now that they had not been exposed to the cool wind in the sky. "Lly, it will be much harder for me to fight Cairon if I have to worry about protecting you, as well. Surely, you understand that?"

Lly nodded confidently with a smile. "I do understand that, but that does not change my mind. My fighting may not be as advanced as yours, but, if we are together, it will not matter. I have not known you for long, Rexam Draconis, but my heart feels as if it is meant to be with yours." She almost blushed saying that. "You are an amazing Dragon, Rexam."

His heart skipped a beat at her gentle words. When he noticed how shy she was feeling, he decided to share more of his feelings as well. "Lly, I hope you will not think any less of me when I say…I think I love you."

Her smile was so large that it was beginning to hurt her face, yet she felt an immense, warm feeling inside her heart. "I do not know that you could do anything to make me think less of you. I—" Before she could finish her statement, she swooned, and her vision blurred. In a heap, she collapsed.

"Lly? Lly, are you alright?" he asked frantically. He called out to the Black Dragons, "Hey, we need to get her some water over here. She's sick!"

The Dragons were relatively quick to respond, used to following orders at the spur of the moment without actually thinking about whether or not they should follow said orders, and they unchained both Draconis and Lly. With a soaring leap, Draconis scanned over the island, and finally, he saw a small pond. He called down to the Black Dragons, "There is a pond that way!" In rapid response, the few Black Dragons lifted Lly up into the air and followed Draconis to the pond that he had mentioned.

He took her from the Black Dragons and laid her in the refreshing pond. In mere seconds, her eyes fluttered open, and her tongue lapped up the water. She mouthed the words, "Thank you," as she attempted to stand.

Draconis turned to the guards and snarled, "Would you mind giving us a few minutes?"

The guards looked at each other, utterly perplexed by the request. One of them said gruffly, "Remember what we said. Any claw out of line, and Cairon will decimate your rebel friends." Then, they turned away and flew back to the camp. Dracons rolled his eyes. *Dolts.*

Draconis turned back to Lly, but she had already dived into the depths of the pond. In confusion, he went after her. Though being in Sharl Vran removed his abilities of breathing underwater, his experience in Gevás had strengthened his lungs, so he could still stay underwater for a long time.

Then, he saw a serpentine shape at the water's depths. He surged downward and forward so that he was only a few feet in front of Lly.

The water was crystal clear, and somehow, her beauty was magnified extraordinarily by the sparkling water around her. She lowered the spell that made her gold, and her blue scales shone brilliantly from the starlight that shimmered down into the lake. Her blue eyes sparkled magnificently. Her body and tail were splayed out so that Draconis could see every curve and angle of her body. However, Draconis's focus was on her face.

Her sapphire eyes met his, and for the first time in his life, all thoughts of duty, of pride, and of war melted from his mind. The only thing that mattered to him was this moment, this moment of pure contentment and peace and love.

Lly was admiring him as well. His golden scales sparkled like the reflection of the sun on the open sea, and his strong muscles were almost bulging from his body. Though his figure was that of a warrior, his eyes were soft. She could see his love for her in those massive sapphires, and he seemed to be a figure from a dream, but she knew that this moment was real, and she wanted it to last forever.

Then, Draconis choked for a moment. He had allowed some of the water into his lungs. He tried to hold his breath for a little while longer as he began swimming to the surface, but he was stopped. He looked down to see that Lly had stopped him. Gently, she pulled him back down to almost touch the sandy bottom of the pond. She put his face in her delicate hands and pulled herself closer to him.

Their eyes closed as she gave him the breath of love, the kiss of life. With a tender claw, he caressed her neck affectionately. She pulled her head back and wore a faint smile as she mouthed, "I love you too."

At the meager campsite, two of the Black Dragons began arguing, "When do you think they will be back?"

"How am I supposed to know? It was your idea to let them stay there."

"Well, what was I supposed to say? 'No, now get back in your cage'?"

A third Dragon joined in the conversation, "Both of you need to give it a rest. I am sure they will be back shortly. I think they care too much about their rebel friends to do anything stupid. They will be back. I guarantee it."

The first responded, "Well, I just do not see—Wait, do you feel that?"

Under Cairon's training, they had learned a few tricks of the Darkness, including being able to sense other spells. The other Dragons stood then.

Suddenly, a Gate appeared, and the Y'mordi twins stepped into the campsite. "Where are the two Dragons? The Dragon King said that you had them here," snapped one of them impatiently. Sarn had truly begun to hate Kusvor Cairon for his petty orders and requests.

One of the Dragons started, "Well…. Uh…One of them was actually passing out, so we took them to a pond just over that mountain and—"

The Y'mordi did not let the Dragon finish his sentence and whipped out a long, edged chain. In milliseconds, the rapid chain decapitated the unlucky Dragon. "Imbeciles!" she roared. "Where are they?!"

In a scrambling rush, the others took to the wind and led the Y'mordi twins to the pond.

Draconis continued to chase Lly around the bottom of the pond playfully, jealous of her natural ability to breathe underwater. She would let him get close before shooting ahead of him at lightning speed.

Every time he ran out of breath, she would approach him shyly and breathe into him for a few minutes that felt like eternity to them. Neither of them had ever felt so free in their entire lives. They wanted this feeling to never end.

Suddenly, he sensed the Darkness: there were Y'mordi approaching. He gestured frantically for Lly to follow him to the surface, and she did in perplexity. When they reached the air, he breathed it in deeply, and he saw the dark blurs that were headed toward them from the campsite.

The two of them rushed to the shore.

"Lly, remember, we are not trying to escape. We will just play dumb, okay?"

Lly nodded carefully. "Very well. What is it?"

Draconis remembered that Lly could not sense things as he could. "The Y'mordi are here," he answered with some fear. He could not fathom what had warranted their arrival, but it could not be a good thing.

"Are they to be feared?" inquired Lly with a hint of worry.

"No, just play dumb. I am just wondering why they are here at all."

Without a sound, the Black Dragons landed alongside the two Y'mordi. The twins pulled back their hoods to reveal their blonde hair and green eyes. Arnim scowled visibly. "I was under the impression that you had two Golden Dragons."

Everyone turned to stare at Lly: She had not replaced the spell that made her appear gold. Draconis gasped, but before he could do anything, Sarn struck with her chain. It became like a solid spear when she threw it due to her spells of Wind. Once the metal went through her chest, piercing her ribs and coming out through her back, Lly collapsed.

"Lly!" Draconis called as he knelt beside her. Her blood instantly began to stain his scales.

With another spell of Wind, Sarn repelled Draconis from the Blue Dragon. "Unless you want to end up like her, I suggest you pay attention, Dragon." To emphasize her point, she kicked at Lly's heavily breathing body.

"Stop that, witch!" roared Draconis. In a wretched fury, he released a fireball that Arnim blocked with a six-foot-tall wall of solid Earth. Knowing that the Black Dragons must have his goldfoil somewhere on them, he struck out at the Y'mordi with his claws slashing.

Though everything was happening so quickly, in his mind, time had slowed. He could feel each of Lly's fading heartbeats echo within his own heart.

Suddenly, the water from the pond rose up with a deafening crash and engulfed the Y'mordi and the Black Dragons, trapping them in a watery sphere before they could react. Draconis could sense that the spell was Lly's doing. He ran over to where she was lying and knelt beside her. "Lly, can you hear me?"

Her blue claw went up to his face, and she stroked it with the back of her claw. "Yes, Rexam. I can hear you. Now, I want you to hear me." Her voice was soft and as gentle as ever, yet it seemed to be fading, becoming weaker as the blood poured down her body, trailing down both her sides. "When you defeat Cairon, do not be angry with him."

Draconis argued, "But he is responsible for—"

Her claw went to his elongated snout to silence him. "Ssh. Do not be angry with him for a new age in this world needs to be founded not through hate but through peace. Do not grieve me until then either. There is a time to grieve and a time to celebrate and even a time to fight. But no matter what happens to me, you, or the rest of the world, you have to keep going. Live for the future."

Rivers of tears rolled down Draconis's face. "Lly, you are going to be fine. Do not give up. Not now. We are so close to beating him!" The twinkling light in her eyes began to fade. He bent his head low to her chest as he whimpered, "Do not leave me."

Her claw stroked his face again. "Never," she muttered.

Then, the Water spell broke, and Draconis felt the water hit his legs. The Y'mordi charged at Draconis. A spell of Force knocked him away from Lly's failing body. Arnim quickly summoned manacles to ensnare Draconis's claws and feet.

Before Draconis could do anything, Arnim blasted him with a Rock that knocked him out cold.

In the recesses of his mind, he was still calling out to Lly even as her heart's once lively beat diminished to a final halt.

A Black Dragon's Tears

Elani did not know why she was feeling so sick to her stomach this morning. She had eaten perfectly healthy food the day before, and no unsettling events had happened recently either. She strode over to where the healer's tent stood and called the healer's name politely. He finally came and was only able to offer a few repulsive herbs for medicine.

With the bad taste still in her mouth, she headed to the blacksmith's tent. That was where she was going to meet with the other leaders. They needed to finalize a plan of action to both rescue Lly and Draconis and attack Cairon. Once they did that, those plans would start to be carried out fully. Also, she was expecting to hear from a few of her spies as to the whereabouts of Lly and Draconis within the next few hours. All signs were already pointing to Cairon's keep in the capital, but she wanted to make sure.

Her solid black claws crunched the sand softly beneath them as she walked over to the blacksmith's tent. Most of the captains were already there, and their faces all forlorn. Though she had tried to avoid it, she noticed the gap where Lly had once stood. All the soldiers were exhausted, and morale was at an all-time low.

She began without betraying any of her worried emotions, "I come to you for ideas. What would you suggest that we do? It is obvious that we have a traitor or two in our midst. Someone alerted Cairon to our attack on the city. That is the only reason that we failed there. Lly and Rexam are still missing, and Cairon only seems to be getting stronger."

A Green Dragon responded tentatively, "If there is a foul spy among us, then the only thing we can do is not to inform the troops of our actions."

"But," added a Brown Dragon. "We need to also double our defenses. Any traitor can still inform the enemy as to our decreased number of troops. We cannot afford to be struck in the middle of the night. We can work on placing wards and making more troops take on guard duty."

Elani nodded, accepting the idea gladly. "That sounds like a reasonable idea." She addressed one of the White Dragons, "Can you ensure that such a defense is put into place?"

"It shall be done, Elani," responded the Dragon.

Volwyth the Red Dragon inquired, "That takes care of the defenses, but what are we going to do about weeding out the traitor? And what are we going to do about Lly and Rexam?"

"I believe that Lly and Rexam are going to be okay. Regardless of what was done to Rexam, I believe he could have escaped and arrived here by this time. Something tells me he has another goal in mind."

"Would he have done so? Really come back if he could?" argued one Dragon.

Elani snapped back, "Of course he would have! He is a Dragon of honor."

The blacksmith said from the back of the tent at his forge, "Then, it could only stand to reason that he does not intend on coming back. He is going to fight Cairon on his own."

"And Lly would not let him take all the glory either," grumbled Elani in frustration. "We might have to meet them at Cairon's fortress."

The Green Dragon replied, "That sounds reasonable enough. So, is Cairon the next step? Are we finished with all of the raids? We are going straight to the capital now?"

All eyes moved to Elani, and she did not speak for a moment. "That is why I have summoned all of you. I am ready to end this if all of you are."

Volwyth exclaimed boldly, "I am with you until the end, Elani. I was with you when you began this with Lly, and I am not giving up now. Lead us as you have done so well in the past." Then, he did something completely unexpected. He knelt before Elani, his wings flattened, his one knee pressed into the grass softly. Everyone stared at him in surprise: kneeling was the greatest show of honor and loyalty a Dragon could display.

The Green Dragon smiled before saying, "He is right, Elani. Though you have striven to give all the rebels a voice here, we have always agreed. Everyone here has a profound trust in you and your words. Whatever you choose to do, we will have faith that is the right thing to do." Following Volwyth's example, she, too, knelt.

Much to Elani's amazement, every captain bowed down before her. Her head whirled around observing every Dragon who was pledging his or her allegiance to her. Although she had already heard their faith in her, she had never seen such an expression of commitment. Disbelief, appreciation, love, and determination came over her in a wave.

Elani's face curved into a smile as she said, "Today, we shall get rid of Kusvor Cairon once and for all."

This time, Elani chose not to use the Gates, and instead, she chose to go by flight. She wanted to intercept her own spies if she could.

Meanwhile, she had arranged for many of her captains to start investigating any possible candidates for the treachery among the rebels. She wanted to take no chances of this operation. There was simply too much to risk.

She inhaled deeply as she began worrying about what could have happened to Draconis and Lly. She had grown so close to the Golden Dragon, and she always had a close relationship with the Blue Dragon. Though she believed that they were both alright, she found a lingering doubt in her heart.

No Dragon flew beside her in the gorgeous, blue sky. They all flew behind her. It was the first time she had ever led the front of an assault, but she wanted to ensure she was the one to bring down Cairon. He had caused her enough suffering. Everyone knew it would be Elani who would defeat the Black Dragon King.

They had not been travelling for long when she saw two dots in the distance. With a quick signal to the troops behind her, the force sped forward. Her heavy armor actually began to clink because of the incredible velocity of her flight.

She gradually began to identify the figures they were approaching. One was a Silver Dragon, while the other was a Red Dragon. They were her spies. She sighed in relief and signaled for the rebels to relax their pace.

When the spies finally caught up with the force, each went to one of Elani's sides. The Red Dragon spoke first, out of breath, "Elani, last night, Rexam was brought to Cairon's dungeons. There was a gash on his head, but he looked fine other than that."

Elani sighed in relief. At least he was not dead. "And Lly? What state is she in?"

The Silver Dragon answered this question softly, "Elani...she was not there. We looked everywhere, but we could not find her anywhere. We were going to ask Rexam himself, but we could not get any closer to him, and there were guards approaching. We are so sorry, Elani..."

Elani swallowed dryly and muttered, "Do not worry. I shall be fine, and I am sure that Lly is, as well. We will find her soon. Fall into rank. We are heading toward Cairon's keep now. We will end this struggling tonight." She had already spoken with her captains, detailing the plans for the siege.

While the Red Dragon immediately followed Elani's orders, the Silver Dragon remained at Elani's side. The Black Dragon was instantly puzzled by this defiance. "Are you well, Ulrill?"

"No," the Dragon responded softly. "I know that the Blacks and the Golds have been fighting for centuries, but what about the Silver Dragons?"

"What do you mean?"

"All of the Dragon races have developed the thinking that the Silver Dragons are inferior to the other races. We are called wanderers, troublemakers, rogues, Dragons that do not belong amid Dragon society. How often have you heard of a Silver captain? Or a Silver mayor? Sure, there are some of us that probably are inferior to other Dragons, but why do those select few represent the entire race?"

Mid-flight, Elani was stunned by this sudden topic.

The Dragon continued more softly, "I would not bring this up now…but with the end approaching, I know changes are on the way. While most of the Dragons have rights to gain, the Silvers do not."

To be honest, Elani had always considered the Silver Dragons to be wanderers as well. Each Dragon race had a unique place that it felt more comfortable in than others. For example, the Black Dragons preferred caves, while the Green Dragons preferred the forests. Many said that this system of preferences was an evolutionary trait: Dragons liked to be well-hidden amongst their surroundings. She had always been taught that the Silver Dragons had no such place: They roamed the world freely.

She replied pensively, "Perhaps, it is simply that no Silver Dragon has stepped up to show otherwise."

The Silver Dragon suddenly took on a look of murderous anger. "Believe me, Elani, there are those that have tried. I will be the first to admit that the Black Dragons had it far worse off than the Silver Dragons, but you are blind if you think that we have not seen our share of hatred as well. The difference is that your kind was hated. Mine was treated as a joke. Truly, there are more Dragon races than just Golds and Blacks, and marginalizing Silvers is almost as bad as openly hating your kind." Without another word, the Dragon retreated to his position in the ranks.

Elani remained puzzled by his words. She shook her head, as this dilemma was not her concern. She needed to worry about Lly, Draconis, and Cairon.

She repeated the signal to increase their speed, and the rebels flew faster than eagles through the morning light.

He groaned as he awoke. At first, all he felt was the cold of the dungeon cell. Then, he became aware of a throbbing sensation in his head. When he tried to move, he found that his legs and arms were chained to the stone wall. He pulled as hard as he could against the chains, but they would not budge, and it only caused his head to hurt worse.

"Lly…Lly, are you there?" he asked hopefully. However, he was not surprised to find that no answer responded to his voice. He had no trouble in recalling the events of the night before, and despair washed over him, filling his core.

Though he could not open one eye, the other eye could see a glimmer of light in the lonesome cell. There was a hole near the top of the cell several yards away. He could barely make out the light of the morning seeping through that brick-sized hole.

Draconis breathed out heavily and thought back to what Lly had said before she died. It had been powerful advice for one so close to death, yet he was not sure that he could follow it. More than anything, he wanted to be angry at Cairon. He wanted to destroy that Black Dragon, but he found that, for some reason, he could not. He could feel his stomach plummet as he thought about Lly and her final words. He was torn between a burning rage, that desire to have the sweetest vengeance against Cairon, and a mournful obligation to obey Lly's dying wish.

He prepared to summon mysteria, *and he immediately felt the dark powers that filled the castle. As he prepared to dissolve the poorly constructed lock on his cell, a thought came to his mind. What about Elani and the others? Doubtless, they would be on their way here to rescue Lly and to defeat Cairon. Even if he was able to get out of this cell, there would be no way to break through Cairon's internal security with its wards and guards and make it to the throne room without alerting Cairon himself and allowing him to escape. His only hope would be to wait for Elani and the others to arrive at the capital.*

He sighed again as he imagined Lly with him there at the bottom of that lake. She had kissed him, and he had kissed her. It had been the happiest moment of his life, and he had been able to tell that it had been hers too. His heart ached to feel her tender touch again, but he knew that he would never be able to feel that again.

His eyes closed, and he dreamed of Lly as he passed out once more.

Volwyth approached Elani unsurely. "Elani, the others are getting tired. We are going at a hawk's pace. Surely we can rest a while?"

When Elani gave him a determined glare, he countered, "Hey, you know that I am never one to argue or complain. I am voicing the opinions of those around me."

Then, her stern façade lowered. "Forgive me, Volwyth. I suppose I am just worried about Lly and Rexam. Very well. We shall rest somewhere for a few hours, I suppose. Perhaps, I need a brief rest as well." Even as she spoke, she saw an island up ahead. "Look there, Volwyth. Relay to the force that we will be stopping there."

Volwyth immediately began roaring her commands to all of the rebels, and other captains repeated the orders to those around them, so that it took only seconds for the large force to hear those commands.

The island appeared to be uninteresting to many of the rebels, but to the White Dragons and Elani, this place looked beautiful. While the White Dragons preferred living in the mountains, Elani anticipated seeing some amazing caves here. The whole place appeared to be rocky mountains and gray valleys. Elani could barely make out one or two tiny ponds on the island's surface. The whole of the rebels swooped down on the island like a volary of birds.

Immediately, tents started to be erected. Elani countered this construction at once. "We will not be staying here long. So do not even bother setting up the tents. We are here to rest for a while. I want my troops well-rested. That is all."

When a few of the younger Dragons groaned, their captains scolded them. Elani walked away from the camp once she realized everything was under control. She simply had too much adrenaline rushing through her to be able to rest as the others could.

As soon as she was out of sight of the others, she did something that she did only in private. She went on all fours and began charging along the mountainside. Many Black Dragons had the ability to run faster on four legs than they did on two, but the ability was unique to them due to a slightly different skeletal structure. Still, that special quality further grouped Black Dragons in with the animals, and it was a source of embarrassment for Elani. Running, she considered the differences between the Dragon races. Perhaps, that Silver Dragon was right: the culture of the Dragon society had evolved to possess too many wrongs. The laws needed to change as did the Dragons' way of thinking.

Then, she tripped over a soft, black mass. Her body went tumbling forward, and her sharp claws tried to grasp something that would stop her from moving as much, but all of the rocks were small and loose. Finally, she was brought to a stop, and she noticed that she was bleeding from snout to tail from scratches she had gained from running through the woods.

She grumbled as she walked back to where she had just been. She was stunned to find that she had tripped over a rotting Dragon carcass. It had been a Black one. It looked as though a spell had slashed it all over. She looked past the corpse and saw a gorgeous lake. She wished that Lly could have seen this amazing body of water.

She saw two other Dragons nearby. They were drenched in water and were also Black Dragons. What had happened here? There did not appear to have been any struggle, so what had caused two Black Dragons to drown while not being in the pond? Her eyes scanned the area in wonder.

Suddenly, she saw it: Lly's dead body. Ignoring the black corpses, she ran over to her best friend. Though Lly was also drenched, she had a gaping, bloody hole in her chest. "Lly…" Elani muttered as she held Lly's head in her black claws. "What happened to you?" A few tears rolled down Elani's dark snout and dripped from her rounded nose. A part of her core wanted to scream out and berate the wind that swirled around them, but all she could manage was harsh, choking sobs. She had seen Lly's face smile, laugh, cry, and roar. She had never seen it so empty, so frozen—so lifeless. She held Lly close. "They did not want you, Lly…You could have come back with the others, and this would never have happened." Elani sniffed miserably. "But you wanted to protect him, did you not? You wanted to be with Rexam, the future Dragon King. I am sure he tried to protect you, too. You could have come back with the others…This would never have happened."

Then, the stronger sobs came, and she could not contain it anymore. All of her years of appearing strong for those who served under her shattered around her. All she wanted now was just to hear Lly's voice again, to hear her comment on the magnificence of the water, to hear her talk about how peaceful the world would be once Cairon was brought down.

Her cries lasted for a few minutes before she finally stood. "You always loved the water, Lly. This is the best that I can do for you." Carefully, she laid Lly's sapphire body into the water of the lake and watched her sink to its chilling depths. With a bloodstained claw, she wiped away some of the tears from her face.

She stood slowly and began to walk back to the others when she saw a glimmer of gold. Her head turned to see that one of the dead Black Dragons had Draconis's goldfoil. Shakily, she stumbled over to the Dragon and took the goldfoil from the body. Her hands shook as she tried to strap the blade and scabbard to her own belt. She intended on give it back to Draconis the next time she saw him.

Then, she continued heading back to where the rebels were resting. She chose to walk the rest of the way, and she took her time about it as well. She felt as if she was in a daze, and her clawed feet stumbled along the rocky ground.

After a few minutes of this stupefied staggering, she reached the top of the last mountain, and she could see all of the rebels clearly below her. She felt so strange. It seemed so odd to her that the most important person in her life could die, and the rest of the world would be perfectly content with that tragedy. What is more is that the world could not only be fine with it, but that it could also move on as if nothing had happened.

While some Dragons were curled up on the few smooth and flat rocks that existed, others were talking quietly amongst themselves and laughing. Surrounding the rebels, a few guards were watching the skies to ensure that no enemies were in sight. There were even a few scouts that were roaming the mountains cautiously.

The wind howled deafeningly around her, and her wings were almost forced backward as she strained to keep them shut against her body. The sun peaked overhead and began to warm up the mountainous valleys.

Going against the force of the wind, she flew forward and down to land in the middle of the camp without so much as making a sound as her feet touched the gray stones. A passing Dragon saluted her timidly and then ran off among the tents to talk to another. She realized she probably still looked as if she had been crying, but she did not care if the marching soldiers saw her. Lly was worthy of those tears.

Then, she called out, though her voice was already breaking with a sob still in her throat, "To the wind! To the wind!" With only a moment of hesitation, the Dragons took to the sky and flew into formation.

Volwyth approached her nervously. "Elani? You've just arrived. Did something happen?"

Elani looked at Volwyth, and he could see how swollen her eyes were. He could see the traces of tears on her snout, and on some level, he understood what had happened. He gave her a sympathetic nod and soared upward to take his place above the island.

"Lly…" she whispered. "You did not die for nothing. I will make sure of that." Then, she, too, spread her wings and flew forward to lead her army of rebels against the tyrant Cairon.

Helen's Reunion

Elizabeth drove through the northeastern United States highways, both hands gripping the steering wheel tightly. From what she had sensed and heard, the Lords of the Shadows had left Earth and returned to Gevás. Though she had spoken the truth of her lack of knowledge to Randir, she had not given him the few reasonable guesses she had of the location of the Black Joker.

Now, she knew it was time to talk to someone else, someone who needed to know the truth about herself. Although Elizabeth had never told Drage, Helen had been having problems in school over the past few years due to certain uncontrollable phenomena, such as cuts and scratches healing overnight without a mark, knowing when particular people were nearby even if they were out of sight, and, on one occasion, a rival spontaneously bursting into flames in class when Helen stared at her. Elizabeth had recognized these phenomena as the symptoms of someone who possessed a great deal of *mysteria* but having never used it intentionally. However, she had chosen not to tell Helen of her potential abilities due to wanting Helen to stay out of the world of *mysteria*. Apparently, that was no longer an option.

Now that the Black Joker was on the Y'mordi's minds, she felt that Helen needed to know how to protect herself in case something were to happen.

She pulled into one of the many parking lots of the college, and the car came to a steady halt. With a soft sigh, she opened the door and headed toward the dormitory that Helen had told her where they would meet, and Elizabeth found herself thinking about what had happened the past few weeks to prompt this meeting, especially her mysterious, new apprentice Cameron Kane.

That young man had been trapped by the Y'mordi in Boston, and she had almost arrived too late to help him. She had hoped she would not have needed to give Randir any more information, but it had been the only way to save her apprentice. Over the weeks, Cameron had learned many things about *mysteria*. He had much potential, but he lacked a certain control over his heart. *Mysteria* seemed to pour from him like a flood even when he was casting the simplest of spells.

She approached the building with her black leather purse dangling from her shoulder. She was dressed in a pink-and-white plaid button-up and tight jeans, easily blending in with the college crowd, despite her age.

Helen came out of the dormitory to greet her before Elizabeth was even close to the doors. She had long, brown hair and blue eyes. Elizabeth felt as if she was standing in front of a mirror. Though Helen's hair was much longer than her own, the two appeared to be twins.

Seeing her daughter put a broad smile on her face. The two embraced each other tightly. It had been several months since they had last seen each other.

Helen began, "So what brings you here, Mom? What's up?"

Elizabeth looked around anxiously before saying, "Do you have somewhere we could talk in private?"

"This is your idea of private?" she asked skeptically.

They were sitting at a small table in the middle of the college's carpeted and dimly lit cafeteria. Hundreds of people filled the space. Helen responded with a shrug, "No one will be able to hear us, and we couldn't use my room, anyways. My roommate was still there. Besides, surely, you're a little hungry?"

Elizabeth shook her head with an amused smile. "Alright, fine, Helen. Listen, this is going to be really hard for me to explain, but you need to listen very closely, and perhaps, things will make sense."

Helen noticed the serious tone in her mother's voice, and she nodded in understanding.

She took a deep breath before she began, "Helen, you know those…strange phenomena you've told me about? The ones where you started to think you were a bit crazy?"

Helen nodded in hesitation. "Yeah? What about them?"

"Well…you're definitely not crazy. Helen…there is a force that exists called *mysteria*. It is a lot like the magic you see in movies and read about in books."

Helen raised an eyebrow with an amused grin. "Wait, you're talking about spells and stuff?"

Elizabeth raised a hand and said, "Humor me for a moment. *Mysteria* is real, and I can prove it to you." Without hesitating for even a moment, she pointed to one of the passing students, and spontaneously, the food on his tray caught fire. He gasped and dropped the tray. As soon as the tray hit the ground, the fire disappeared.

"Whoa," was Helen's astonished remark.

"Still don't believe me? Allow me to demonstrate this again." She pointed a finger at the glass of the window closest to them, and it shattered outward. Students leaped from their seats and exited the cafeteria in a screaming panic. Helen was half-tempted to join them, disbelieving what was happening. Within seconds, every student had left the building, leaving Helen and Elizabeth alone.

To further demonstrate her point, Elizabeth stood and waved her hand in front of her. The glass repaired itself and looked as if it had never been broken. She turned to her daughter and asked, "When people look at the cameras later, they will just see students leaving the cafeteria. The window never shattered as far as the cameras go, and they won't even show us talking right now. Do you believe me now?"

Helen stood and was shocked, amazed, and confused all at once. "I do...but I would like some more explanation please."

"In every heart, the force of *mysteria* exists. It is connected to our emotions and serves as the connection between our hearts and the world around us. Some people are born with a more concentrated amount than others, especially those who are trained or have the blood of a mage in them."

"Okay, I am following you so far."

"You once told me that weird things were happening to you. You could sometimes guess the weather, and it would be accurate. When you were angry, lights would brighten to almost blinding proportions. When you were calm, the air itself would seem to chill. When you were—"

Helen responded somewhat angrily, "Okay, okay, I get it!" Then, she realized how loud she had spoken. Her voice softened, "Look, this is all a little surreal, y'know? I'm a little pissed you haven't told me sooner, and you've let me think I've been imagining all of this."

"Helen...do you want to know where your brothers went five years ago?"

A dumbfounded expression appeared on Helen's face as she nodded silently.

"This is probably going to be harder to believe than it was to believe in *mysteria*. There is more than one world in this universe. There are five actually. Each world is based on its own Element: Earth is from Earth; Waldann from Nature; Sharl Vran from Wind; Menx from Fire. I am from the final world of Water. It is called Gevás. This world is also where your father lives."

"My father...is alive?" Helen asked in utter disbelief. "He is really alive?"

Elizabeth nodded sadly. "Yes. However, John Helius is not your real father, more like your stepfather. John was my second husband. Your father's name is Derek. He is alive in Gevás even as we speak. Also, Matthew is your brother by blood. He was not adopted."

Helen sat down with a hand to her mouth. "Why? Why did you never tell us? Why didn't you tell us any of this?"

Elizabeth crouched in front of her daughter and grasped her hands. "Listen, Helen. I raised the three of you away from *mysteria* and the other worlds so that you would be raised better. I wanted you to develop yourselves mentally and socially. On Gevás, people are placed into the military very early. There is a lot less freedom in that world. John agreed with me that it would be best to raise you all here."

"And what about Drage? You said that John was your second husband. Was Drage—?"

"Yes, Drage was my only child with John. John was not just a random person in Gevás though. He had the title of the Emperor of Light. He was the king of a whole country there, and Drage is the heir to that throne even now. Drage, Matthew, and Aria were sent to Gevás five years ago because there were terrible people trying to kill them. Sending them to Gevás was the only way to fully protect them. They learned a lot about that world, and John was killed in a battle they fought in. Somehow, throughout all of their adventures, Matthew and Aria decided to remain. Drage came back of his own accord. He does not think he is ready to be the king there right now."

"So, you're telling me that my brother is a prince?" inquired Helen incredulously.

"Yes."

"Okay, I'm trying to process all of this." One part of this whole explanation was still bugging her, though. "Alright, so why didn't you tell us about the whole family thing? Why all the secrecy about that? You could have easily told us the truth, so why didn't you?"

Tears began to well up in Elizabeth's eyes. "That was John's wish. He did not love Matthew as much as he loved Drage and you. He was wrong for it, but that hatred was part of him. He loved Drage because of the similarities between the two of them. John wanted them to be the perfect father and son around Gevás. Though Derek is your father, you have always looked just like me. John thought you were so beautiful. He accepted you as his daughter but not Matthew as his son. He made me promise despite my protests to make it clear that only Matthew was adopted into the family."

"Poor Matthew…" whispered Helen distantly.

"I hated keeping it from the three of you, but I had made the promise. John would come and visit every once in a while, though he never came when the three of you were around. He wanted to make sure everything was going well."

"So…what happened between you and Derek?"

"It was just one big mistake," Elizabeth said with tears rolling down her cheeks. "I slept with John one night, and I regretted it, but then, Drage was born…and I couldn't…John had a Palace, Helen, a Palace! He had money and power, and Derek had a shack in the woods. Staying with John was doing the right thing for all of you! I had no feelings for him. I stayed with him because of you! Please forgive me, Helen. Please, please forgive me." She sobbed into her hands, elbows on the table, until her daughter sat beside her and gave her a comforting hug.

"Mom, it's okay. Of course I forgive you. Nothing has changed between you and me, okay?"

Elizabeth quickly quit her crying and dried her eyes as fast as she could. She was not the type to break down like she was at the moment, and she did not want to continue it any longer. "I'm sorry, Helen. It's just…"

"It's fine, Mom," Helen offered. "Don't worry about it. What I want to know now is why this is all coming up now?"

Elizabeth dried her eyes further as she said, "The same people who were trying to kill Drage, Matthew, and Aria have come to Earth. Not only are you and I mages, but I am also the head of an organization called the Ring of Elders. It is a council of mages that defines the rules for using *mysteria* on Earth. Being a lawyer has merely been a side job, as hard to believe as that may be. Those people are seeking the power of an ancient demon that caused chaos here thousands of years ago. He is known as the Black Joker, and the Ring of Elders at that time imprisoned him somewhere on Earth. These people seek to free him. I was worried that if something happened, you wouldn't be able to defend yourself. Helen...I want to teach you how to use *mysteria*. Do you want to learn?"

Helen smiled nervously, still processing everything, "I would love to."

Cameron sat in the cheap hotel room near the college, anxiously waiting Elizabeth's return. He had been thoroughly disappointed with himself after the duel with the Lords of the Shadows. Though he had tried his absolute hardest, he had failed against those two opponents. It had taken a lot of encouragement from Elizabeth to get him out of his state of momentary depression. Even then, he was embarrassed by her having to try to cheer him up as well.

He hated being weaker than others. Ever since he had met Dragenopn Helius, he had constantly been surrounded by those who were more skilled than he was. However, he had to admit that being Elizabeth's apprentice was quite beneficial to his learning. Already, he had learned spells that he had never dreamed of using. The Elements seemed to be infinitely more versatile to him.

As the sun started to lower in the horizon, he rose impatiently and went out into the parking lot. Casting a strong spell of Light, he made himself and what he was about to do entirely invisible. It was a simple spell that bent all light around him, and it was among his favorites.

Then, he began practicing his Wind spells. All of the cars in the lot, about eight or nine, hovered above the ground, and straining, Cameron attempted to simulate a light tornado. The cars rotated around him, and it took all of his concentration to focus on the different points of contact he was making with his spells. The rotation increased in speed, but his concentration did not waver. The tornado became a whirling blur of colors, and the wind created from it pushed against him. Pressing the spell even further, he attempted to lift the cars even higher and spin them faster. This level was the furthest he had ever gone, and he was scared to push it more.

He could remember what Elizabeth had taught him: the only way to get better is to push the extremes a little every now and then. Cautiously, he created another thread of *mysteria* that lifted the nearest tree as well and placed it into his whirlwind. He gradually relaxed his spells and returned everything to where it had been only moments before, but a cloud of dust and dirt still remained in the air. Using a few blasts of Air, Cameron swept the dust away from the parking lot.

Exhausted mentally, he sat down on the ground and tried to sense where the Lords of the Shadows were. However, they were too far away for him to be able to pinpoint the location.

As he glanced out at the busy interstate, he thought about where he finally was. He had spent years seeking the Prince of Light in the hopes of either joining the terra or serving as his apprentice. Instead, he had been raised to the status of apprentice to the head of the Ring of Elders. He felt honored and grateful toward Elizabeth. He pulled his leather jacket tighter around him then to ward himself from the cold around him.

Perhaps, one day, he would rise in the ranks and become an Elder as well. First, he needed to prove himself further. He felt as if the connection between master and apprentice was still quite weak. He wanted for Elizabeth to see him as a strong sorcerer, a mage specializing in battle spells, rather than just a general mage. However, altering that image would be rather difficult.

Suddenly, he felt something in his heart: The Y'mordi had returned. They were here on Earth again. Summoning a Gate, he left the area to find Elizabeth. It was not too hard to find her either.

He was stunned when he saw what appeared to be two Elizabeths in the vast cafeteria. One appeared to be younger and had longer hair, but the two still looked considerably similar. The younger one was probably Elizabeth's daughter, he decided.

Elizabeth turned to face her apprentice, "What is it, Cameron? You were supposed to stay at the hotel."

Helen regarded the man cautiously. "Mom, who is this?"

The reddish-brown haired young man spoke quickly to Elizabeth, "It's them: They're back. Can you sense them?"

Her face turned extremely pale as soon as Cameron began speaking. "They have breached the barrier…" she muttered distantly.

Cameron shook his head. "What do you mean? What barrier?"

"Cameron, there are more dark secrets in this world than the Black Joker. A few centuries ago, there was a malicious witch who plagued all of Europe. It is true that she was nothing compared to the Black Joker, but she was fearsome nevertheless. She manipulated rulers and ruled herself for a time. Her dark magic had no sole equal. The Ring imprisoned her as they had the Black Joker. They imprisoned her in Stonehenge, and that is where the Y'mordi are at right now. They are going to free Morgana."

"But…that's impossible. Morgana was just a story. Surely, she was not real?" However, Elizabeth's stern look was enough to make him believe otherwise. "You are serious…What can we do to stop them?"

Elizabeth shook her head rapidly. "Nothing, the two of you need to stay here. The Ring will take care of these fools once and for all." She summoned a Gate right there in the middle of the cafeteria.

"Mom, what's going on?" exclaimed Helen, still confused by the whole ordeal.

Cameron added, "Elizabeth, I can help. Let me come with you!"

"No, Cameron. Stay here. You have been a good apprentice so far, and now, you must learn obedience. Stay here." She turned to her daughter. "Helen…if something happens to me, I need you to find Drage and tell him. You will both need to get out of here. Go to Gevás. Cameron, you can show them the way, I am assuming?" Before she could receive an answer, she was gone.

Helen looked down at her hands curiously at the new wand her mother had given her. "What is going on?"

Cameron looked at the young woman who looked exactly like her mother. "Is your name Helen?" he began nervously.

She nodded, "Yes, I'm Helen. You are Cameron?"

"Yeah, I am your mother's apprentice. We actually just met a few weeks ago. I showed up probably around the same time that the Lords of the Shadows did."

"And are you from that other world, too? Gabas?"

Cameron laughed at the mispronunciation. "No, I am from Earth actually. To be honest, I wanted to go to Gevás though. I was wanting to be a sorcerer there, but the Council would not allow it. I went to your brother to override it, but he...wasn't exactly helpful."

Helen thought sadly about her brother. "Yeah, he was never the same since he came back from Gevás five years ago. He came back...I don't know...hollow. Sometimes, he would laugh again, but usually, he was always so quiet. He still made friends and all, but I don't think his heart was in it anymore."

"Huh? What happened to him five years ago?"

"I don't know. I only found out about *mysteria* and Gevás today. It all still seems so farfetched. But I just saw you appear and my mom disappear into thin air. I have seen a guy's tray spontaneously combust and glass shatter and then repair itself. It all seems so...bizarre." She glanced down at the floor, not sure what to make of these new truths.

He could not help but ask, "Do you have the powers too?"

Experimentally, she tried one of the tests that Elizabeth had given her with the wand. As she closed her eyes, a palm-sized flower appeared in the air in front of her wand, and it hovered there. In those few seconds, Cameron could sense Helen's heart's true Element of Nature. She gradually opened her eyes and was dazzled by the white flower in front of her. "Magic...is real," she whispered to herself.

Cameron decided to offer her some help. "Try opening yourself more to *mysteria*. You have had that feeling inside of you your entire life. Reach out for it, and let it fill you." Helen closed her eyes acquiescingly. He could sense her heart blossom like the flower had. "Relax..." his voice called enticingly. "Don't lose that feeling. Just direct it. Allow it to flow out of you."

Her wand began to shine a green light, and the flower multiplied into four flowers, then twenty, then a hundred. It took only a few seconds for the cafeteria to be filled with the white petals. Her eyes opened once more, and they sparkled as she beheld the spectacular mass of white flowers she had created. They floated and swirled in the air, like light snow frozen in place. "It's so beautiful..."

"If you think that is neat, watch this," claimed Cameron boastfully. Using spells of both Light and Darkness, he dimmed the lights around and inside the building, so they were left in the dark. Then, he made Helen's flowers gleam with their own white light.

Helen's eyes sparkled as she watched the cafeteria become bathed in that pearly light. "Cameron...this is amazing..." she said, mouth agape in awe at the beauty of the scene.

To further impress her, Cameron cast the Wind spell he had been practicing only minutes before, and the flowers began hovering around the two of them like fireflies in the night. Helen reached out to them with a bright smile on her face, and she was surprised when one of the glowing flowers landed in her outstretched hand. Then, it was gone as it rejoined the others.

Together, the two of them craned their heads upward and observed the whirlwind of blossoms around them.

Their amazement was ended by the sound of police sirens in the background. Instantly, Cameron's focus faded, and the room lit itself once more. The flowers faded into dust, and they could see the campus police pulling into the parking lot.

Helen exclaimed, "What are we going to do? What will happen if they find out about the *mysteria*?"

Cameron shook his head doubtfully. "That is unlikely. They will not know anything." As he waved his hand, the air in front of them seemed to shimmer. In reality, he had bent the light once more so that the police could not see them through any of the windows. "Now, they cannot even see us."

Helen repeated, "What are we going to do?"

"To be honest, I am a little worried about Elizabeth. I don't know what it is, but I can sense something happening. Something is wrong, but I can't identify it."

"In that case," Helen began with some confidence returning to her voice. "We need to go where she is and help out."

Cameron countered, "I am afraid that it is not that simple. Elizabeth is my master, and she gave me a clear order to stay here. I can't just go against that."

"Wrong," argued Helen as she pointed a threatening finger at Cameron's face. "She might be your master, but she is my mother. Do you think she would be madder at you for allowing something to happen to me or for disobeying her? I can figure out a way to get to her on my own. Would she want for you to allow me to do so by myself?"

Cameron was dumbfounded at her stubbornness. Then, he heard the police open the doors to the cafeteria. He shifted the spell so that it surrounded the two of them. Then, he created a Wind spell that canceled out the vibrations of sound around them, so that the police could also not hear what they were saying. "Helen, you are a hard woman to argue with."

Helen smiled broadly. "I know. Now, let's get going. Let's help my mom."

Cameron immediately summoned a Gate, and he warned Helen, "Be careful when you are going into it. I have heard that it helps to hold your breath when you go through a Gate for your first time."

"A Gate?" repeated Helen as she observed the gaping hole in space with interest.

"Yeah, it connects two spaces together. They're how a person can travel between worlds, realms, and time."

She put a cupped hand over her mouth and nose as she stepped into the Gate. Cameron watched the policemen enter the area where they were hidden. He cast a light spell of Force that knocked over a chair on the other side of the room, and the distraction gave Cameron the time to drop his illusions and exit through the Gate. The rocky pillars Stonehenge stood on the other side, storm clouds swirling above.

The Nightmare Returns

The few weeks that Stehl had been in the Capital had proven to be entirely useless. All signs of the Enigma Brigade were simply gone. She had investigated every hotel, inn, and alleyway, but she had found absolutely nothing.

It had come as quite a surprise to her when the occasional rude man would come up and say something he learned to regret immediately about the size of her breasts or how soft her hair looked. Stehl had been brought up in the military and would not stand for any pig male to talk to her like that, regardless of how attractive he thought she was.

As she walked down the neon-lit streets, hands in her pockets, she began to feel quite dejected and lost. Then, something caught her eye. She turned to see the very tavern where she had first met that Lord of the Shadows named Randir. A small part of her hated Randir because of his past life—though another part was infatuated with him. He had at one point been the Lord Ferro that ruled over most of the Eastern Continent during and before the time of the First Obsidian War. He had been responsible for the policy that dictated that women were not allowed to join the military. Of course, she knew that to this day many women were serving in the military, but they were all under the guise of males. It was simply amazing what a black market mage could do to one's appearance.

As the memories swept over her, she entered the tavern slowly, and she could hear her shoes tap against the wooden floor. She stepped up to the bar and requested impatiently, "Hey, I would like a fizzer please."

The bartender was stunned by the extreme desire. "A fizzer?! Are you sure, madame?"

Stehl gave him a cold, hard look, and he relented.

As he fixed the drink, he asked, "Had a pretty rough day, then?"

"Yeah, it was bad enough, I suppose. I've been looking for some people for a long time, but every time I get close, they slip out of my grasp. It's quite frustrating actually." The bartender handed her the esteem-building drink, and she began to chug it down thirstily. The bartender merely gaped at her.

"Who exactly are you looking for?" offered the bartender nervously.

Stehl set the drink down and wiped her mouth a with her sleeve. "The Enigma Brigade," she answered somewhat loudly, which generated many looks from around the crowded, dimly-lit tavern.

The bartender leaned in close to her over the bar and whispered, "That is quite a claim, madame. What makes you think that such a group, assuming they were real, would be here in the Capital of all places? Surely, they would be in Apolis."

"Not necessarily. They serve the Emperor of Light, and if the Prince were here, then wouldn't the Brigade follow him here?" She took another deep drink before saying, "This tavern has been around for a while, has it not? I have been here so many times…"

"Are you sure? I don't recall ever seeing you around here."

Stehl smiled distantly as she swirled a finger around the rim of her glass. "Yeah, I'm sure. It's just been a really long time. It was probably before you started working here. It was when this whole War started. I've been hunting them down ever since."

"I hate to break it to you, madame, but the Enigma Brigade isn't real. How could you possibly hunt them? Besides, every rumor about them says that they are the Emperor of Light's finest warriors. No offense, madame, but what makes you think that a woman like yourself could stand a chance against them?"

Stehl rounded on the man instantly. "What did you say?! You know, women can be just as good if not better than a lot of men at fighting!"

The bartender grinned as the seedy customers laughed around the room. "Forgive me, madame, but you are just not making sense now."

Her rifle moved so fast from under her cloak, it created a swishing sound as she raised it into a ready position. A shot rang out from it, and the whole room cringed, but when they saw that the bartender had not been shot, they relaxed. Then, they realized that she had not been aiming at the bartender. She had been aiming at a round dart target in the back of the room: She had shot it perfectly in the center, what they called "hitting the serpentseye."

At first, the tens of patrons' mouths dropped. Seconds later, the applause began.

Stehl turned toward the bartender. "I think you would like to amend your previous statement, sir."

The bartender was as white as a sheet at this point. Although he was tempted to argue that being a good shot did not make you a good fighter, he was not about to anger a lady with a gun who had been drinking and who *was* a good shot. "Yes, madame. A woman can fight as good as any man," he said, almost at the point of stuttering in fear. At his statement, the room burst once again into cheers.

A smile formed on Stehl's face as she finished her drink and then slammed the glass onto the bar. "That is how it is done, gentlemen!" she roared, the fizzer finally taking its effect on her.

Suddenly, a little boy ran into the tavern screaming, "The troops from the West are back! They've been hurt really bad! Come help!" Then, he was gone.

Everyone in the room exited as fast as they could, and Stehl joined them in the panic as they rushed toward the gates where a bloodied and limping navy was entering the Capital, trudging through the streets in search of respite; she found herself anxious to join in some kind of action, some kind of purpose.

It did not take long for a group of healers to appear with floating stretchers beside them. Those that were too weak to stand were placed on these, while the people from the tavern aided those who merely had difficulty with walking to follow the healers to an infirmary.

Stehl managed to find one that looked like a General and went to his side. When she noticed his limp, she put his arm around her shoulder and she began to help support his weight. "Sir, what happened?" she asked eagerly.

"Eh, thank ya," grumbled the portly man with the scratchy voice. "We were doin' fine fer a while, but den dat new guy came outta nowhere."

"New guy?" inquired Stehl.

"Yeah, da new guy. Goes by da name Gaspard. He go about claimin' he is da servant o' da Grea' Spirit. We tol' him he was out o' his mind, 'n' den he say dat he was gonna rip us apart…'fer yer blasphemy' he say."

"Gaspard? Is he a new captain or something for the Western Continent?"

The General nodded sadly. "Yeah, so he is. Came out o' nowhere. Da terra didn' stan' a chance, doh. Dat sword o' his is mighty fierce. Dat ting is probly taller dan you or me. But dat guy knew 'ow to use it alright. Dat dere was da way o' da Shark. Dat's fer sure. An' all we had left was ta take Saldir, too. We 'ad jus' taken Rulia. Da West was almost ours. Now we 'ave dat new guy ta worry 'bout."

She began to lead him after the healers. He looked like he had a pretty nasty leg wound. She asked him curiously, "So what happened ta…er…what happened *to* you?"

The General gestured down toward his leg. "Eh, dis? Ah, dat's nuttin'. His troops had some pretty po'rful artillery. Mos' o' us didn' 'ave very safe landings into da Capital. Piece o' one guy's ship's shrapnel got me."

"Oh," she replied sadly. "Well, the healers will have you fixed up, I'm sure."

"Now, what do a youn' woman like yerself be doin' out here at dis time o' night?"

Stehl blushed at the question, much to her own surprise. "I've been asking myself the same question. I've been looking for somebody, but I am beginning to think that that person is not here."

Unexpectedly, the General placed one large, hairy hand on Stehl's shoulder. "Don' give up hope yet. Ya very well migh' fin' whoever yer lookin' fer. Don' give up hope." The General looked onward as they approached the infirmary. "If dis new guy keeps up at dis rate, we will 'ave quite a bit o' trouble real soon. What's more is dat he put a boun'y on da Prince's head."

"The Prince?!" exclaimed Stehl in shock. "Why is he doing that?"

The General shrugged and winced as he did it. He could feel a bruise still stinging on one of his shoulders. "No one knows. But he wants dat Prince. Claims da worl' would be free from evil if da Prince were killed."

Strangely, Stehl felt sorry for the Prince of Light. Though she had associated the Enigma Brigade with the Prince, she could remember how young the Prince had been when she had seen him fight in the first battle of this War five years ago. "Poor kid…" she whispered. "I actually saw him once. I saw him in the battle against Maris."

The General's eyes widened in shock. "Ya were der? I wish I had been. I only joined da navy when dey were lookin' fer good pilots. I t'ink dad I saw 'im once, too. It were around dat same time, too. Short little lad wit' brown 'air and a fancy little sword. I sold 'im one o' me boats," he said proudly.

They trudged into the white-marble infirmary with others ahead of them and behind them. As one of the healers relieved Stehl, she decided to walk with the man and at least say goodbye to him before she left. "Well, it was nice meeting you, General…?"

The large man gave a toothy grin, "General Silverpike's da name, but you c'n call me Mirah. Spelled em-eye-ar-ei-eich, but said like mee-rah. It was nice meetin' you too, Miss…?"

She smiled amusedly as she replied, "My name is Stehl. I am a General of the terra in Apolis."

"Eh, really?" exclaimed Mirah. "Well den, it was indeed a pleasure ta meet ya, General Stehl. Best o' luck ter ya, an' I 'ope ya find yer friends."

Stehl smiled even wider. This man had the most interesting and comical personality. "Thank you, Mirah. Good luck to you, too. Look me up after you get out of here, and maybe we can go get a bubbler or two."

"Ya got yerself a deal, Miss Stehl!" replied Mirah as he gave her a final salute.

She returned the salute and left the infirmary, feeling infinitely better than she had previously. She thought back to what he had said. Perhaps, she would find the Brigade here after all. She had to admit she was not as familiar with the enormous city as she had once been, and a few weeks was hardly enough time to find a small group of people in such a place.

Suddenly, she stopped. She remembered the last time she had been this happy, like she had someone she could be open with: she had been with the Lord of the Shadows Randir. She had told herself time and time again to stop thinking about him. It was a relationship that could not work under any circumstances, yet her heart kept thinking about him. She hated that her heart was so tied to him.

"Randir…you have caused me much grief…almost as much as the Enigma Brigade has, so why have I not been seeking you instead?" she asked herself quietly.

As she sighed, she thought about the General she had met a few minutes earlier. Mirah Silverpike seemed to be quite eccentric for a General of the navy, and he was certainly not shy. He was humorous, well-mannered, and easy to talk with.

Furthermore, he did not treat her like a piece of meat to salivate over like half the dogs in this city. He had provided her with incredible news about the War. Was it getting as bad as he had claimed? It made her feel considerably guilty for hunting the Enigma Brigade when she could be helping win this War.

She had found that one of the strangest things about this War was the disunity in the minds of the people. Many of the people in the Southern Continent, Apolis included, were against the War. They had developed the notion that the exiles deserved their own rights, too, as if they were humans. However, the people of the Eastern Continent knew how ignorant the nonhumans could be and were fighting this War wholeheartedly. She was glad that the Emperor's Council agreed with the East on this matter. She had heard from many soldiers about the barbaric nature of the exiles and their zombielike personalities. Even when she had fought them for a brief time in that battle against Maris, she could tell how primitive the creatures were that she had been fighting. Many used their claws and fangs to kill others and would not use the civilized weapons of a sword or even a gun.

Those creatures, the nonhumans, disgusted her. Of course, everyone who had been around her for most of her life had shared her feelings of hatred and disgust toward the exiles. Their opinions had always been that the Emperor Mentiris had been too light in his punishment of the nonhumans.

As she sighed a second time, she finally decided that she would spend some more time searching for the Brigade in another part of the Capital. First, she attempted to quit thinking about the exiles, the War, Randir, Mirah, and everything else. She needed to focus on the Enigma Brigade and tracking them down.

She could remember that the Brigade had worn robes of gold, but the leader of them had worn a golden robe with a tremendous red bird on the front. That leader had been the one who had attacked her: the Captain. That enigmatic man with the red hair had almost killed her and likely would have if Randir had not stepped into the fray. She could picture that serene face. That Captain had hypnotic green eyes and the calmest look on his face, as if none of the killing he had committed had shaken him in the slightest.

Just thinking about that smug smile on his face made Stehl clench her teeth. The current was warm as it moved around her, and she felt something change in the water. Looking around between the buildings, she wondered what it was. It was quiet. The neon lights did not extend down this alley, and the darkness swallowed her with each step. Whether it was coincidence, luck, or maybe she truly sensed something, she had a feeling that something was in one of the nearby alleys.

Her eyes darted around the area, scanning for any signs of movement, but she could find none. Cautiously, she walked around the area, making sure that her feet made no sound on the hard ground. She called out, "Who's there?" No one answered her, however.

Suddenly, a clanking sound rang from an alley behind her, and she whirled around at the same time she drew her rifle. A fat and hideous rat scampered out of a trash can and ran past her. She grimaced in disgust and looked around a final time. She was alone after all.

Sighing, she saw something move in the shadows of the night. Her head snapped in that direction. For a second, she could have sworn that she had seen a golden robe, the kind of robe that the members of the Enigma Brigade wore.

Then, she saw the golden glimmer a second time. There was a figure in one of the alleys, and it moved rapidly down the dark corridor and turned into the next.

Instantly, she chased after that golden-robed figure and followed it cautiously through several of the alleyways. She made sure not to step too noisily, and she always watched her step to avoid running into the scattered trash of the alley that would both alert anyone as to her whereabouts and cause her to slow down. After turning several sketchy corners, the blur of gold vanished.

She looked in all directions, but she could not see the figure she had just been chasing. Hesitantly, she continued in the direction she had been going, her breath sharp and labored, and she was amazed to find that she was now standing in front of the Emperor Regin's castle. She had not thought that she had gone so far as the castle, but she was standing there, nevertheless. Her head cocked sideways in confusion as she neared the front gate.

Then, a truly gruesome sight met her eyes.

The guards that usually stood watch here were all dead on the ground with small puddles of blood forming around them. Their weapons were still in hand, though there did not appear to have been any struggle whatsoever. The gates were creaking as they began to close: Someone had only seconds ago killed these people and went through the gates. Stehl ran forward and barely made it through the crack between the gates before they shut and locked themselves mechanically. She could hear the bolts sliding back into place.

"What's going on here?" she muttered to herself.

Then, she turned to face the castle. It was a massive building that had once been quite spectacular and silvery, much like the Palace of Light in Apolis. Now, vines crisscrossed their way up the metallic walls, and rust had formed in various places. Even some of the windows were shattered. However, she could make out lights emanating from several windows around the castle.

As she stepped forward, the nightmare continued. She could see a trail of blood drops leading to the front door of the castle, and she approached it hesitantly. She felt as if she was stepping backward into the past. She put a rough hand against the door with a pang of terror. When she opened that door, would she see the same massacre that she had beheld five years ago when the Enigma Brigade had attacked everyone in the Emperor Regin's castle?

The next question she asked herself was, "Am I sure that I am ready for this? This time, I don't have a Lord of the Shadows to save me…"

"What is ya talkin' 'bout, Miss Stehl?" said a voice from behind her.

She whirled around with her heart pounding from the sudden surprise to see General Mirah Silverpike standing before her.

"What is wrong wit' ya, Miss Stehl?"

Stehl smiled in relief. "Mister Mirah, I have a confession to make to you, though you will probably consider me to be crazy. The people I have been looking for are the Enigma Brigade. Several years ago, I lived here in the Capital, and I loved this city very much, but one day, the Enigma Brigade came to this very castle and killed almost everyone in it: servants, guards, and even the Emperor Regin's family. It was horrible. Since then, I have vowed to avenge him. I have vowed to get rid of every last one of the filthy murderers. That is why I joined the terra in Apolis, and that is why I am here now." She looked Mirah up and down. "What about you? Is your leg alright?"

Mirah responded. "It din't take da healer long to heal me, jus' a few secon's. I heard a few people talkin' 'bout ya an' da Brigade, an' I started worryin' 'bout ya. I follow yer fer a while, an' I found you at da gates over dere. Is ya alright, Miss Stehl?"

Stehl smiled, "Yeah, I think so, but you saw those guards that were just killed. I think that the Brigade is here."

Mirah responded as softly as he could, though his voice still rumbled considerably, "Well den, Miss Stehl, I t'ink we should go in dere an' make sure dat nuttin's wrong, wouldn't ya say?"

Blue Rain

Matthew embraced Drage once again in front of his tent that morning. "Hey, take care of yourself over there, okay?" They had all been quite astonished when Master Valdridge had appeared the night before and congratulated Drage on his performance in the battle. Master Valdridge had then gone on to explain that the fight in the Western Continent was gradually reversing itself due to the actions of a man called Gaspard. When Master Valdridge had explained more about Gaspard, Drage knew that he had to go and fight in the Western Continent and help there rather than aid Draconis. The last thing he wanted was for people to start dying for him. If Gaspard wanted to fight him, Drage was ready for him.

"Alright, I think I can do that," responded Drage warmly. "You and Lilian can take care of everything here, right?"

Matthew nodded confidently. He had honestly hoped that the Enigma Brigade would stay with him, but they vowed to protect only Drage. Though Maksimilian and two others had disappeared with the claim of having important matters to attend to, the remaining two decided to stay with Drage as he went to the West to claim a small army. "While we are trying to end this fight, you take care of Gaspard. When you're done, let's meet back here, and we will go and help Draconis together."

"Sounds like a plan," replied Drage. Although Drage seemed to be slightly like his old self, Matthew could sense the underlying sadness that overwhelmed his half-brother. He could sense it in Drage's tone.

"Good luck," Matthew said softly. "You can do this."

"Thanks, Matt."

Then, Master Valdridge summoned a Gate and encouraged Drage to step into it. Together, Master Valdridge, Drage, Tilgé, and Sume left the Northern Continent and arrived in Rulia of the Western Continent.

"He shall be fine, Matthew," encouraged the gentle voice behind him. "You would not place your confidence in someone blindly, and I am under the impression that you place a great deal of confidence in your friend. Therefore, it can only stand to reason that he shall be fine."

Matthew turned to see the beautiful horse anima Lilian. "Thanks, Lilian. I needed to hear that. I guess that I am a little concerned about his curse problems."

"Was that man the friend you talked about years ago?"

Matthew cringed as he remembered Lilian's connection with Maris. It had been a master and apprentice relationship, and Matthew struggled to find the words to explain without sounding offensive or disrespectful. "Yes, I told you about the curse before. When he fought Maris, he found his Light for a few moments, and that Light eliminated most of the curse that was inside of him, but for some reason, it was never completely destroyed. That is why he refuses to become the Emperor of Light: He does not think that he can lead while he has that piece of Darkness inside him."

Lilian shook her head, puzzled. "How can that be? If Maris is gone, then how can he still have a hold over your friend? That does not make any sense."

"You remember Marqest, right? He believes that Maris's spirit is still wandering in this realm and is maintaining the hold of the curse. He is supposed to be looking for his ghost right now."

"Maris did not move on? That is unfortunate…" Lilian muttered as she lowered her head mournfully. "If he did not, then he would be in one of two places that would have been close to him: near our village or around his grave. He cared for the village. So, if he is not there, he might be trapped by his grave. I have neither seen nor felt him around our village, and, besides, that place is gone now. The griffins destroyed it," she said with a hint of bitterness and resentment in her voice.

"So, you think that he is around the grave in Apolis?" To this question, Lilian merely nodded. Nervously, he stepped forward and placed a shaking hand on Lilian's shoulder. He had never been very skilled when it came to approaching women. That was Drage's specialty, if he recalled. "Look, I'm sure that Maris was a great guy before the Darkness messed with him. If he is still in this realm, then maybe he just wants to apologize. If he is bearing some hatred, then the Darkness might still be affecting him, as well. As for your village, once this civil war is over, you'll be able to build it back bigger than ever. Don't worry about it."

When she turned to face him, a gleaming smile was on her face, and she replied, "Thank you, Matthew. Perhaps, you are right. Maris could not be miserable now. The village will come back, as well. There is no reason to lose hope."

Matthew decided to press the philosophical issue, smiling, "But what if we can't change things? We cannot stop plague, disasters, or even death. Don't we have to accept those things?"

Lilian smiled back at him. "Not necessarily, Matthew. Most people in a way blame themselves for tragedies beyond their control. A mother wishes she could have been at home the day of the fire. Maybe, she could have saved those who had been in the house at the time. A man wants to kill the person who robbed his family and murdered his best friend. He takes it upon himself that that responsibility is his, as if he holds the fate of that story in his own hands, as if his killing that person would set things right. Every day, people blame themselves for the wrongs of the world. One should live every day with hope."

Matthew found himself inspired by Lilian's optimistic words. Before he could reply, a voice squeaked several yards away. "Hey, Lilian! Lilian! Everyone's ready when you are!" Both Lilian and Matthew turned to see Senagul the squirrel anima approaching.

Matthew brushed a hand through his dark hair as he asked in wonder, "So what is with the squirrel? He's definitely interesting…"

Lilian laughed at Matthew's puzzled expression. "Senagul is his name. He is quite energetic, but he helps out with a lot of errands, and he provides the villagers with some of his good spirit."

"And I'm quite the heroic soldier, too!" exclaimed the squirrel as he clambered up Lilian's white robe to stand on her shoulder. They had met each other the previous day already, but Matthew was still not used to the squirrel anima.

"So, do you ever change to your human form, Sena?" asked Matthew, using Senagul's preferred name. "I've never seen you change."

Sena stood proud and tall as he said, "That's because I look much better in this form. Lilian always says, 'Anima are not humans that can turn into animals. We are animals that can turn into humans.'"

"That's reasonable logic," agreed Matthew. "But what if you need to be taller to reach something? Surely, there are times when it is more beneficial to be a human."

Lilian responded to this question. "Yes, there are times. However, many do not create such a strong balance between their human and animal forms. It usually leans one way or the other. Very few try to stay completely balanced between the two. We find ways to make do with our animal forms at times. Sena can climb up most things if he cannot reach them as a human to get what he wants. However, with my being a horse, I find it much easier to be a human most of the time, though I absolutely despise the appearance of myself as a human. I look dull and uninteresting," she said as she gestured to her whole body.

"Not at all!" Matthew exclaimed. "You look beautiful!" He had not meant to say that, but it was already out of mouth. It did not take long for his face to begin turning deep red.

Senagul broke the awkward silence, "Oooooo, you have a crush on Lilian!" With a giggle, he scampered back to the ground. "Lilian, everyone is waiting on you." Then, he left.

Matthew rubbed the back of his neck and began with an embarrassed laugh, "Kids…they think the craziest things, huh?"

Changing into her horse form, she asked, "Do you think I am beautiful, now, Matthew?"

His expression became hard then as he responded to Lilian's half-accusing tone. "Of course, I do. You look just as beautiful as a horse as you do in your human form. Did you think that I would think you were ugly as a horse?"

This time, Lilian was embarrassed. "I'm sorry. It's just that there are so many people that hate us anima. I did not know if you had even the slightest similar characteristic to those people."

Matthew offered a smile as he said, "Hey, it's fine. Let's get going. We have a war to end and a kingdom to defend."

"Yes, you are right," Lilian agreed as they ran to the others.

At their first stop for the night, seeking one of the enemy posts of the North, Matthew was appalled at the fact that there was not a spare tent to be had. Reluctantly, he asked Lilian if he could share with hers. He was even more amazed at the size of her tent. After he laid his bag on the floor of the tent, he commented, "The weather was horrible today. The rain was miserable and cold." The idea of rain in an underwater world still came as a surprise to him, but he had become somewhat used to it as the water they breathed was less dense than the rain that poured down on them. The most fascinating characteristic of the rain in Gevás was that it was a shimmering shade of blue. Though it was beautiful, it was usually quite cold, too cold for Matthew.

Lilian remarked, "Oh, really? I found that it was considerably refreshing." Many of the people from the Northern Continent found the water there to be warmer than Matthew thought it was.

Deciding to give Lilian some privacy before they retired for the night, he said, "I'll be back in a few minutes. I am going to check on the others." She nodded as he exited the tent.

His shoulders felt extraordinarily better. Carrying that bag all day was exhausting and wore down on his back muscles. The blue rain began to pour again, and he lowered his head miserably so as to not get the cool rain in his eyes. He popped the collar of his cloak so that it touched the back of his neck. This technique prevented the rain from going down his back.

Supposedly, they were nearing one of the enemies' outposts. They planned on getting there the next day, but so far, they had not found any signs of them. He was really hoping that they did not have another Dragon. He was not confident that Lilian and he could defeat one alone.

Thunder roared in the distance, and he noticed a few of the younger villagers jump in fright. It was remarkable that a whole village was having to fight like they were now. There was not a safe haven for even the young in the Northern Continent, and it was not as if they could send the young to Apolis or somewhere: The law prevented such a transferal. The nonhumans were exiles now.

All of a sudden, a blur of brown came rushing at him in the dark. Matthew reached for his staff, but the blur got to him first and crawled up his side. He jumped back in shock and fell to his back in the mud. Senagul was sitting on Matthew's chest with the most innocent expression on his face. "Hi, Matthew. What are you doing up? It's starting to rain again."

Matthew sighed in relief. "I was just going for a walk, Sena. What are you doing? Shouldn't you be going to bed now?"

Senagul's tail twitched guiltily. "Yeah…but I couldn't sleep. I was actually kind of wondering…"

"What?"

"Could I sleep with you?"

Matthew wanted to laugh so badly at the comical and cute nature of the squirrel anima, but he merely smiled. "I don't know. I'm in Lilian's tent."

Senagul leaped with excitement. "That's fine! Lilian lets me sleep in her tent all the time…or at least in her house…"

"Alright, alright. First, you're going to have to let me up, though."

Puzzled, the squirrel looked down to see that he was indeed standing on Matthew's chest. It was as if he had been completely oblivious to the fact that he had basically attacked Matthew seconds ago. "Oh, sure!" Acquiescingly, Senagul leaped off Matthew, and the dark-haired young man rose to find that he was dripping with mud.

"Oh, great…" muttered Matthew. "Lilian is not going to want me to walk into her tent like this. Come on, Sena."

The squirrel climbed up Matthew once again and sat on his shoulder. He pulled Matthew's collar down to shield his own body from the rain. As Matthew felt a single drop of rain go down his cloak and roll down his back, he shivered.

As he approached the tent, Senagul said, "I'll go and get Lilian. You, wait here." Then, he scampered off his shoulder and ran across the mud to enter the tent.

Lilian came out seconds later in an almost see-through night gown with amusement. Matthew felt simply humiliated as he said, "I kind of fell in the mud. Do you think you could get me a cleaner shirt out of my bag?"

"You can come inside," she replied. "I will use a Force spell to get rid of any dirt or mud. It's not a problem."

"Are you sure?" he asked.

She nodded in response.

He entered the tent with his clothes soaked brown and blue. He watched as Lilian created a green fire in the water. Senagul was already curled up in a ball on Lilian's blankets, fast asleep. Lilian herself went to bed as well, leaving Matthew alone in the dim glow of the green fire.

As he pulled off his cloak and shirt, he shivered again. He looked around the massive tent wonderingly and finally saw a wooden rack next to the second sleeping bag that Lilian had prepared for him. Gratefully, he bent down and placed the freezing clothes on the rack.

When he rose, he sensed a presence behind him, and he turned to see Lilian standing there.

"Wha—?" he began, but Lilian interrupted him by placing a soft finger on his lips.

"I wanted to thank you once again for all of your help the past two days. I do not think that I could have managed without you, and even if I had, I would not have been able to lead the others the way that you have. Even Senagul, as young as he is, thinks you are amazing."

A smile came over Matthew's face. "It was nothing. I am sure that you could have done—" Again, she put a finger to his lips.

"Also, I wanted to thank you for thinking that I am beautiful. You are the first person who has ever complimented me on my looks as both a horse and a human. By the way, Senagul told me what you told him earlier today."

"Huh?"

"He told me that you said I was cute," she explained.

Matthew's eyes widened. "I didn't—"

"Do not worry, Matthew..." She hesitated before saying, "I think you are cute, too." She put a soft hand against Matthew's bare chest and felt the muscles there. "You are strong, Matthew. You have such a nice face and a muscular body to match it, but it would not hurt if you gained a little more hair." As she said that, she winked slyly. "Matthew, I do not know why you came, but you are like an angel to this village. I hope you realize that." Her hand brushed down his chest as she moved past him.

Then, the green light vanished, and Matthew could sense Lilian return to her bed. All of a sudden, he remembered to breathe, and he found his heart was racing.

He was the kind of person that believed in true love, and he did not know if Lilian was meant for him or he for her. However, he felt an overwhelming desire to watch over and protect her no matter what happened.

He lay down on his sleeping bag and stared up at the ceiling as he thought about the horse anima a few feet away from him.

"The General Gaspard would like to have a word with you," cried a high-pitched voice outside the tent. In a second, the green flame returned, and Lilian and Matthew stood.

When they opened the tent flap, they were horrified to find that there were griffins holding every villager at swordpoint. Many of the villagers were crying, especially the younger ones.

The voice repeated, "The General Gaspard would like to have a word with you."

The small man with the black robe was straight in front of them. He grinned wickedly.

"Ixion..." Matthew growled. "What's going on here? Gaspard is to the West, not here."

"Nevertheless, he would like to speak with you."

Lilian asked quietly, "Who is this man?"

Matthew replied equally softly, "His name is Ixion. He is one of the Y'mordi, and he is trying to get me to go with him to see Gaspard. He plans on luring Drage out, using me as the bait." His tone was calm yet had a rough edge.

Ixion continued, "If you refuse to come, we will kill every last villager here. Do you really want to be responsible for their deaths?"

He was torn: save the villagers or protect Drage? At the threat, Matthew stepped forward, but Lilian grabbed his arm. She called out to Ixion, "If you take him, then I will unleash a spell so strong, it will wipe out every one here."

The Y'mordi laughed deeply. "You think I care what happens to these griffins? They are nothing but tools to me."

At this remark, the griffins looked at each other in anger and resentment toward their leader. "They can die, too."

Suddenly, another voice roared from the camp, "Hear that, griffins? Your leader is willing to dispose of you. Are you going to stand for that? Is that what you are fighting for? Poor leadership?" All heads turned to see the elder crane speaking to the enemy. "Shall we rise up as one against this? If we can't unite over our exile, we can at least unite against this dark scum."

Instantly inspired by the words of the crane, the griffins changed their targets. Their anger was apparent, and they immediately charged at the Y'mordi. Ixion moved surprisingly quickly in his shock. After creating a massive Gate in the water above the tent, he unleashed a powerful Gravity spell that launched himself, Matthew, Lilian, and the tent into that Gate.

Rise of the Phoenix Regiment

The golden buildings of Apolis were as brilliant as ever, and the soft current was still freezing to her. She strode into the crowded headquarters of the terra and instantly went to the secretary, "Where are all the sorcerers that served under me?"

The secretary did not look up from her computer and said simply, "Name, please?"

Aria retorted, "Look at me when I am talking to you." The secretary's head snapped up at the command.

"Oh, Ms. Newman, I'm so sorry. I-I was not expecting you today."

"I do not want your excuses," snapped Aria coldly. "I want you to find the location of those who served under me five years ago. Can you do that?"

"Yes, madame. Hold on one second."

Mistress Leona stepped up beside Aria and whispered in her ear, "You know, it is quite unlikely that you will be able to locate them as a single group anymore. They have all been reassigned to other regiments."

Aria replied, "Well, then, we are going to have to reassign them once again."

The secretary began, "Ms. Newman, they have all been moved to different areas. Most of them are fighting in the Western Continent, and others are here in Apolis. Also, some are on leave, while there are some who were killed."

"In that case, I am going to need you to get in contact with each of those who are on leave or elsewhere, and get them to come here. Regardless of where they are, they are more needed with me. We are going to put an end to the fighting in the West, and I am going to need my sorcerers to do it. If it helps, tell them that the Phoenix has returned." With that being said, she turned away from the secretary without awaiting an answer. Mistress Leona followed her in an admiring surprise.

Once they stepped outside, Mistress Leona asked her, "The Phoenix? Is that your symbol now?" Her face betrayed her utter amusement at the idea.

Aria responded seriously, "Yes. It was the symbol of the Light Brigade a millennium ago. It is the symbol of the Enigma Brigade now. It was on my robe five years ago when I dueled your husband in that trial. My heart's true Element is Fire much like a phoenix, and we shall take the symbol and bring it back into power, into the Light again."

Mistress Leona added, "And from which ashes are you arising?"

Without missing a beat, Aria replied, "The Prophet of Fire's."

"Excuse me?"

She explained, "The last time that there was a Prophet of Fire was before the Wars. He was a king in the Eastern Continent named Lord Victor Ferro. Since then, many people have tried to gain the title, but I am going to do what all of them failed to do. I am going to be even better than Ferro was all those years ago. I shall spend the next few years training to become that."

Mistress Leona paled at the thought. "But that is crazy. You are too young to be a Prophet. You are…you are going to try to do it, are you not?"

Aria nodded solemnly. "I am, but it will take me a few years to be ready for it. I have heard that many who have tried died mysteriously. I want to make sure that there is not a spell that I do not know."

"That is a powerful albeit reckless goal, Aria. Anyways, what do you plan to do, now? It will take your sorcerers several hours to arrive."

Aria sighed as she replied, "I suppose that I need to find Drage and Matthew. Once I get the troops, we are headed there immediately, and it would help to actually know where he is. Do you have any ideas?"

"Yes, actually, in the Council meeting this morning, we decided that the Prince of Light needed to be put on the front lines. There is a new General in the Western Continent who is asking for the Prince's head. So, he should be somewhere in Rulia right now."

Relieved, Aria smiled. "That is good to know. That saves me from one task that could have been frustrating. Now, I suppose the next thing to do is to find Master Marqest. I need to talk to him about a couple of things that have been on my mind."

Though Mistress Leona was slightly offended that Aria was not choosing to talk to her, she responded, "Master Marqest is probably in the Palace somewhere. He usually spends his time in one of the libraries there. He seems to think that it is a good place to study. Quiet, he says."

"Alright, thank you!" Without another word, she ran off into the distance, and Mistress Leona watched the determined young woman as she ran. Aria was such an interesting person, always able to defy limits in unusual ways.

"Master Marqest, there you are!"

"Eh, Ms. Newman, what are you doing here? I thought you were at the Academy in Gryphos," replied the old man. His long gray hair flowed behind him, and though his face was wrinkled, his eyes were lively. His overall demeanor made him seem younger than he really was. "Does Mistress Leona know you are here? She will have a fit if she knows you ran away from the Academy again."

"No, Master Marqest, I actually graduated yesterday. I have a mastery in the discipline of the Elements."

"How is that possible?" asked Marqest with a curious frown on his face. "The school year has not ended."

Aria replied, "No, sir, but the Grand Master Dean decided that I was ready to graduate, and he allowed me the exception of doing so this early. I am preparing to join in the War."

Marqest nodded without any surprise on his face, "I see. So, what can I do for you then?"

Hesitantly, she inquired, "Sir, you are an Ancient, are you not?"

"I am."

"How much do you know about the Y'mordi named Y'dax?"

"Y'dax?" repeated Marqest with a puzzled expression. "I know that he is the oldest of the Y'mordi and specializes in the Element of Water. He uses a metal scepter. I know a couple of historical battles in which he fought, but what are you looking for in particular?"

Aria began softly, though she was sure that no one could hear her, "He came to the Academy one night, and I challenged him. As I fought him, I learned something interesting about him."

"Oh?"

"I only sensed half of a heart in him. At first, I had thought that it was merely a really small heart, but then I realized it truly was half of a heart. It is hard to explain, I guess…"

Marqest shook his head. "No, you are making perfect sense. It is indeed possible to split one's heart, or at least it was. To this date, I have only known of four people to split their hearts, not counting Y'dax, that is. The legendary pair Tatsu and Kohana were such people. Then, Bastion and whoever his partner was also split their hearts."

"Wait, Tatsu and Kohana split their hearts?"

Marqest nodded. "Yes, that was the reason for their magnificent bond. Somehow, a piece of the Great Spirit sliced their hearts in two, and instead of fixing themselves, two pieces of the hearts switched places, giving each one the abilities and thoughts of the other. It was how they could switch minds."

"Alright," said Aria, trying to take in all this new information. "Who was that other guy you mentioned?"

Marqest paled at the question. "Bastion…was my brother actually. You see, I fought in the beginning of the First Obsidian War, but he did not. To be honest, Bastion was a lot like me, so it is a wonder that we did not talk that much. Nevertheless, he joined in the War a few years later, and when I saw him again, he possessed only half of a heart. He would not explain anything to me or even to whom the other half went. Unfortunately, I do not know that much about the ancient ability, but since then, I have not heard of any other occurrence of the technique. For all I know, Bastion could have had something to do with Y'dax's knowing how to split his heart."

Aria sighed, almost disappointed with the little information that Marqest had given her. "Well, then…There is something else I would like to talk to you about actually," she said softly.

"Oh? And what would that be?"

"I guess that I am a little curious as to the state of Drage's curse. Were you able to heal him at all?"

Marqest's head lowered sadly. "No, I am afraid not. We believe that Maris's spirit is still lurking around here somewhere, and I have been trying to locate it, but that has been difficult. Participating in the Emperor's Council along with keeping up with this War has kept me quite busy. It is hard finding the time to search for a spirit."

Flustered with slight anger, Aria replied, "So, you are just going to let him suffer?"

"It is not like it is a simple task. The easiest way to find the spirit is for Drage to merely sense its presence nearby. He is the most effective tracking device for that spirit. There is nothing that I can truly do for him until this War is finished. Believe me," Marqest explained, and Aria could see the sincere look in his eyes. "I want to help him. He brought me back into the life of the world again after I had been cooped up for over a hundred years. I really do want to help him. It's just that I have so much responsibility now…"

Aria nodded her head respectfully to the Prophet of Water as she said, "Well, thank you very much for your time, Master Marqest. I will leave you alone now."

"Attention!" she roared over the chitchat of her sorcerers in front of the Palace of Light. In response, the sorcerers snapped into the attention stance: feet together, back straight, shoulders back, head up. The conversations had come to an abrupt halt, and all eyes were straight forward.

Aria commanded again, "Present arms!" In one second, every wand was raised centimeters from every sorcerer's face in salute, and in the next second, the wands were lowered to point at the ground. Each movement was crisp and uniform, and Aria was impressed. The sorcerers in the terra were so well-trained and disciplined. They had been taught well the meaning of respect. "I have been led to believe that many of you were reassigned to other regiments." She glanced over her motley regiment of troops proudly. "Doubtless, you have learned of calculating strategy, careful attacks, and even defeat under the command of whomever you have served over the years." She noticed that several of the sorcerers were eyeing her phoenix-decorated military robe. "Today, we are all going to the Western Continent, and we shall eliminate this foolish man they call Gaspard. This regiment shall rise up from the ashes of these five years. As I am the Phoenix, so are all of you Phoenixes."

Without using a word or even her wand, she summoned a large Gate in the water. "Come, my Phoenix Regiment. Let us end this nonsense. Forward march," she demanded, and her sorcerers proudly stepped in time and marched into the Gate.

Before Aria walked into the Gate, she turned around and gave Mistress Leona a polite nod. "See you soon," she said.

"Until next time," Mistress Leona replied.

They arrived in the middle of an enormous military camp, troops practicing formations among the tents. As soon as one of the camp's guards approached her, she ordered, "Take me to Drage now." As the guard paled and nervously began to lead her further into the camp, she commanded to her own sorcerers, "Halt. Do not move a muscle until I return."

The camp was filled with several scores of soldiers, and she could not sense any signs of strong *mysteria* around the area. Her sorcerers were the only ones around the camp besides her and Drage whom she could sense several yards away from her.

The guard acted as if he was going to escort her into the tent, but she demanded softly, "I can take it from here, soldier. Back to your post." The soldier muttered something incoherent as he stumbled away in confusion. Aria was tempted to shock him with some unpleasant spell or other, but she thought better of it.

Then, she pulled back the flap of the tent and entered. She saw him looking over a map in the back of the tent. His brown hair spiked up considerably, and he was quite a bit taller than he was five years ago. "Drage," she started.

Slowly, the young man turned to face her. She could see how dark the irises of his eyes were, and it stunned her. Suddenly, a warm smile appeared on his face. He stepped closer but did not move to embrace her. He merely held his arms out in welcome and eyed the sorcerers behind her. "Aria, what are you doing here?" he asked.

She smiled back as she responded, "I brought my Regiment. We are here to help you, Drage."

"I think that that is the best news I have heard in a long time, Aria. I thought you were supposed be in the Academy, though?"

She came closer to him. "I just graduated yesterday. What are the plans here?"

Without answering the question, Drage suddenly embraced Aria in a soft hug. Aria could feel his heart grow lighter then. When she hugged him back, that light increased. He whispered into her ear, "I keep hearing him. His voice tells me everyone's problems. I can sense their emotions all around me. Soldiers that pass, troops screaming in the healers' tents, parents scared they might not see their kids…it's a Darkness I just can't get rid of."

His fear and sorrow surrounded her like a cold blanket. For a moment, she could sense a Darkness inside him, but she must not have sensed its depths: she could not sense Maris inside of it yet. She felt a profound sympathy for him. "Drage, listen to me," she said soothingly. "The Darkness may be strong, but your Light is far stronger. Your blood is the blood of a generation of people who devoted their lives to protecting the Light. You can do this." She smiled and whispered, "I believe in you, and I love you."

Drage lifted his head and stared into her beautiful blue eyes with his black ones, searching her own to read her emotions. "I love you, too, Aria." For a moment, the Darkness subsided. He stood back and turned to regard his maps. "Aria," he began, changing their focus. "This new guy Gaspard has one of the Spirit Swords. I am sure of it. I don't know how he did it, but I think he has Maris's Behemoth. The problem is that this guy actually knows how to use it."

When she tried to remember the massive Sword, she said, "Maris used that in the battle, right? Well, Randir killed him, and then they disappeared. So, the Sword would have to be with the Y'mordi, right?"

Stunned by the revelation, Drage replied, "I had never even thought of that. That means that the Y'mordi are likely behind this guy. That would explain his sudden rise to power. I would be willing to bet anything that the Y'mordi have been spreading lies about him, too. There is no way that one guy could become so famous in the middle of a war. I was starting to wonder where those guys were."

"The Y'mordi? There was one or two at the Academy. I know for a fact that Y'dax was there, and there might have been another, too. What are they planning?"

Drage folded his arms in frustration. "It seems they might be trying to still get rid of the Guardians of Light. Draconis had an emergency, so he is out of the picture. You said they were at the Academy, more than likely to kill you. Now, they are trying to get a random person to come after me. They give him a Spirit Sword, and he is all-powerful." All of the death threats worried him, and, then realization dawned on him. "And there was a Dragon in the North that was possessed by someone and tried to kill Lilian. More than likely, the Y'mordi were behind that, too. Have you heard anything from Marqest?" The Guardians were in serious danger, he saw.

Aria was dumbfounded at Drage's explanation. "Uh…yeah, he has been holing himself up in the Palace. He's been saying that it is because the Palace is much quieter."

"That's a lie," snarled Drage. "He knows the Y'mordi are after us, so he probably has the whole place warded with several spells. That's what he did on Heaven's Isle, too." With a sigh, he added, "The Emperor's Council wants me to fight Gaspard."

"And there must be a traitor in the Council…it's a setup," muttered Aria in understanding. "So, what are we going to do?"

Drage replied, "It is going to have to be on my terms. Likely, the Y'mordi have the whole battle rigged, so that means I have to undo their work at the last minute. I am going to have to challenge Gaspard on a personal basis."

"Are you sure that you can do that? Do you know anything about Gaspard's fighting experience?"

"No," Drage answered. "But I know mine. I can beat him as long as he does not start using advanced spells." He remembered his fight with Cameron Kane back on Earth. If Gaspard was a sorcerer, that could cause some complications. Besides, I have the Sword of Destiny. I will be ten times faster than him in the fight."

Aria was still doubtful, however. "That may be true, but he has luck on his side. That is the gift of the Behemoth. It will be his luck that you trip on a rock at just the right time. There are so many factors in a battle. You have to worry about terrain, timing, weather, offense, defense, predicting, and a million other things. You barely defeated Maris years ago, and that was only because you used *mysteria*. Your Sword protected you, and Maris was not much of a swordsman. What makes you think that you can defeat Gaspard?"

He blinked, staring into the canvas of the tent, before he responded, "I have done a lot of wrong to this world. I have to try, Aria. If I had stayed and become Emperor of Light, this War might not have escalated to the point it's at. If Gaspard wants to challenge me, then I have no choice but to try. I have faith that I can do this."

Hearing his optimism made Aria think about the tragic legend of Tatsu and Kohana and the Grand Master Dean's words about its message. "Drage...you don't have to repair what you've done. Sometimes, tragedy happens. You just have to accept it..."

Drage glared at her all of a sudden. "I know you do not believe that, and nor do I. But before I can even think about fighting Gaspard, I need to worry about regaining what parts of Rulia he has taken."

"Your Majesty!" called a voice at the entrance of the tent.

Drage and Aria turned to see a man in a golden robe. "What is it, Sume?"

"There are some sorcerers in the camp, sir, and they refuse to move. We are trying to move some of our heavy artillery, but those sorcerers are not budging." Then, Sume caught sight of the phoenix-decorated robe of Aria. His eyes widened in surprise at the ancient symbol. Nevertheless, he did not comment on it.

Before Drage could do anything, Aria ran outside the tent and cupped her mouth as she yelled, "Phoenix Regiment, to me!"

Instantly, the tight formation of her sorcerers charged toward her, and they resumed their attention stance once they were in front of her. Both Drage and Sume were fully astonished by the promptness of her troops.

"The Phoenix Regiment?" inquired Drage. Then, he, too, noticed the phoenixes that curved around her robe elaborately.

"Yes, Drage. They refer to me as the Phoenix, and in my eyes, they are phoenixes as well. They are the fourth branch of Apolis's military."

"The fourth?" said Sume innocently. "What is the third?"

Aria gave the man a stern look. "Do not play games with me. I know very well that you are a member of the Enigma Brigade. It is not half so well-kept of a secret as you would like to think. You verified that for me when you were admiring the phoenixes on my robe."

Drage commented curiously, "The fourth branch? No offense, but don't you think it is a little small to be a whole branch of the military? Looks like just another twenty or thirty women."

"How large is your Enigma Brigade?"

"Point taken. Tomorrow, we will have our first battle. See Tilgé for my battle formations, and the two of you can work out where your 'phoenixes' are going to be." Then, he went back in his tent to continue planning for the battle ahead.

The Divine Dragon
of the Heavens

He woke up when he sensed her nearby: Elani the Black Dragon. Instantly alert, his eyes snapped open. She was really close, and knowing that filled his heart with hope. As his eyes scanned the dark cell, he realized he needed to get out of there, now. As he frantically tried to break the chains that held him, he found that they were as unbreakable as before, and Draconis decided to try something else.

Summoning feelings of anger and passion, he created Lava that ate through the metal links around his claws. The chain melted, and he massaged his aching wrists. Silently, he approached the iron bars that confined his cell, and his heart opened itself even further to *mysteria*. There was one guard on the other side of the hallway, and Draconis created a bolt of Lightning that instantly destroyed the guard.

The bars melted away before his Lava spell, and he found himself free at last.

The unlit, wet stone hallway was silent as he moved along it. Occasionally, his feet splashed softly in some unseen puddle, but other than that, there was not a sound. He sniffed the air in caution, and the reeking stench of death filled his nose. He was completely alone in this dungeon.

As he widened his area of sense, he became aware of multiple beings below him. His foot tapped the ground lightly, and he could feel how hollow the ground was: There was another floor underneath. Wondering who could be on the lower floor, he strengthened his sensing spell, and he found that the imprisoned Dragons were all dying. Their fading and weak emotions washed over him sadly, and he realized that he had to find a way to get down there without alerting Cairon as to his escape.

"*Eldra,*" he whispered. A great Light appeared and illuminated the dungeon floor. His mouth gaped at the sight. Every cell was packed with rotting Dragons of different races. He did not want to believe that he had been in a similar cell for a little over half of a day. When he turned around, he saw that the puddles he had stepped in were those of blood. He felt like vomiting over the stone floor, but he focused his thoughts on finding the exit.

Finally, he saw the small, wooden door, and he treaded toward it carefully, making sure to watch where he stepped this time.

The black oak door opened with a noisy creak, and Draconis began descending the crumbling stone stairs that let to even lower levels. He was not sure how far down he was already, but he decided that it could not be too far as he had been able to see a small light from his cell.

As he came to the next door, he refocused his sensing abilities and tried to see how many guards were on this next floor. However, it was far too difficult to distinguish between that many hearts, especially when he sensed both enemies and allies. His greatest desire at the moment was to have just one sword. Unfortunately, the Black Dragons who had taken him and Lly still had his goldfoil. He felt almost naked without a blade on him.

Ignoring caution, he slammed the door open into a hallway and began throwing fireballs at every guard he saw. While the first few surprised, unfortunate Black Dragons were roasted, the others began to retaliate with their deadly twofolds and spells of Poison that emitted clouds of toxic gas.

Draconis dodged the first twofold attack that came at him and then slashed that Dragon's throat with his bare claws. Using that momentum as he continued spinning one foot, his body crouching low and then rising as it turned, he took the twofold from that Dragon's claws and blocked the next attack with it. However, he did not have the finesse with this weapon that the others had. He managed to block several of the attacks before being slashed in the side by a twofold that he had simply not seen. It was only a slight wound, but it stung anyways. At least it did not have the poison that Elani made all her own troops use. He silently wondered how these Black Dragons had even obtained the twofold: from what he had heard, Elani had been the one to help re-develop the ancient blades. Perhaps, some of Elani's troops over the years turned traitor.

Rapidly, he unleashed several bolts of Lightning at once without aim, and many of the Black Dragons went down. He noticed two remaining, and he used an Air spell to blow away and dispel the green clouds of Poison. Two massive fireballs finished those remaining Dragons, and Draconis looked around in shock.

This floor was another dungeon, and in each cell, there were dying Golden Dragons. Cairon had imprisoned these poor Dragons and allowed them to die. Angrily, Draconis summoned three liquid streams of Lava that streaked down the hallway, melting every iron bar they found.

The eyes of the freed Dragon glistened with tears as they began to exit their filthy cells. A Nature spell breathed life back into the Dragons as their hunger, thirst, tiredness, and wounds were healed. One Dragon at a time, the mass of Dragons began to cheer for their rescuer.

Draconis was stunned speechless by the crowd. Finally, he pointed to one young Dragon and asked, "Where are all of you from?"

The Dragon replied, "We were from the mountains to the south. We had been living there for centuries, but Cairon finally found us a few days ago. We don't know how he did it, though. We've been so well hidden there."

"Everyone!" roared Draconis furiously. "Kusvor Cairon has plagued the Golden Dragons for long enough! A Dragon named Elani has been leading a group of rebels against Cairon for years, and she is almost here now! Will you fight alongside Elani and I as Dragons of honor? Or will you run and hide as you have done for the past century and a half?"

One bold Dragon exclaimed, "The Divine Dragon of the Heavens promised us the world, and it is ours by right! I say we fight!"

This response generated a cheering roar that gave Draconis the answer he had been looking for from them. Creating an extremely large Gate, he called, "Go, then! To war!"

The Dragons were comparable to a swarm of some flying insects as they soared into the Gate that led to outside the fortress. They did not think about who was freeing them or why. They did not question the magical portal that allowed their escape. They merely knew honor, and they were prepared to do what they could to aid their rescuers.

Before he could follow the other Dragons, Draconis felt something pulling at his heart. Somewhere below him still, he could sense a spell. He was simply puzzled by the feeling, because he could not sense anybody below him now, but a spell was in place nevertheless. It felt vaguely like Light, but he was not sure. He closed the Gate and headed back to the staircase.

Elani did not reveal her surprise at the fact that there were scores of Golden Dragons already attacking the Imperial capital as she and her troops arrived. Her black head turned to her troops as she roared, "Attack!"

The rebel Dragons dive-bombed in a V-formation into the hive of Black Dragons that already were struggling to keep up with the Golden Dragons' ferocity. Draconian cries from all sides filled the air, and the stench of their hot blood spilling across the city filled the Dragons' noses, making their own blood boil in rage. One of Elani's spies sniffed, approached Elani, and said, "Are you ready to see the dungeons?"

Elani nodded, disappointed she would have to miss this battle. Nevertheless, she needed to find Draconis before he went after Cairon on his own. She assumed since all these Golden Dragons were free, he must have been the one to release them.

Suddenly, a Black Dragon escaped the melee and charged at Elani screaming, "Traitor!" Though she had never met this particular Dragon, she was sure that the claim was made simply because of her black scales. Once the Dragon was close enough, Elani's spy attacked with the Lightning spell that Draconis had taught him. Elani smiled with pleasure as the black creature dropped instantly.

"No, you are the traitors," she muttered. "You are the ones who went against the laws. You reversed the order." Her red eyes scanned the pitch-black clouds overhead with dread, sensing the evil forces needed to conjure such Darkness. If Cairon had indeed gained the power to create such a phenomenon, they might be in a lot of trouble. She shook her head. There was no way that she was backing out now. Lly did not die for nothing, and neither of them had worked for so long on this rebellion for nothing either.

Suddenly, a bolt of lightning lit the darkened sky. The deafening thunder roared around the capital, and a torrent of rain began to pour from the massive black clouds. To make matters worse, a tremendous wind began to howl in the sky, making even the simplest of flying difficult.

Elani snarled as she said, "Alright, take me to the dungeons. I need to find Rexam." Her spy shot downward at intense speeds, and Elani followed her, wingbeat for wingbeat.

Draconis stepped into the immense hall with interest. Because it was completely dark, he summoned a small Light to illuminate the hall. He was amazed to find that the hall held several elegantly painted murals etched onto the walls.

He approached one of these murals and was entranced by the fine art. The mural displayed a Golden Dragon and a Black Dragon fighting. Admiring the image, he traced a claw delicately across its surface. "These paintings were made so long ago…They even feel ancient. How have they stayed here for such a long time?" When he opened his heart to *mysteria*, he could sense a faint spell that was clearly preserving the art, but even that spell was fading away.

The Black Dragon in the mural was wielding the forbidden twofold, and the Golden Dragon was wielding a simple sword. Suddenly, he remembered seeing the image a long time ago.

"Rexam, have I ever told you the story of the war that the Golden and Black Dragons fought centuries ago?"

"No, Gramma. Tell me! Tell me!"

"Well, let me get my book…See? Here it is. This all started when—"

"—the eight Dragon tribes were at war. The leaders were the Golden Dragons, but—"

"—one day, the Black Dragons created a fearsome weapon known as the twofold. It had two blades coming from its hilt, and they were tipped with a deadly poison that could kill you once its sharp edges touched you."

Draconis could remember it all so clearly now. He had been talking to his grandmother as a child about the story. This same image had been in one of her storybooks.

All of a sudden, he heard a voice behind him, "We won that war, Rexam."

He turned swiftly and found Elani standing there with a Silver Dragon beside her. She whispered to the spy, "Go back to the others now." The Silver Dragon left.

"The Black Dragons won?" he asked in slight shame and wonder.

Elani nodded. "Yes, the twofold was the greatest invention in Dragon history, but your kind disagreed. They thought we were scum for creating a weapon that finally undermined their own."

The two moved on to the next mural. It held a Golden Dragon as large as a mountain and a much smaller Black Dragon whose height probably went up to the Golden one's knee. "Is that the Divine Dragon of the Heavens?" asked Draconis as he admired the colossal Golden Dragon.

"Yes, it 'came from the heavens' and challenged our leader. It banished all of my kind to live forever in the caves of the south, and the Golden Dragons were chosen to rule over the world, because they were the same race as it was. Many believe that legend is completely false, but regardless of its truth, it has shaped this world," Elani explained.

Draconis faced Elani with a sorrowful expression on his face. "Elani…I am so sorry…Lly—"

"I already know," interrupted Elani with an equally sad expression. "I found her body and gave it a decent burial. I hope you tried to take care of her."

"I did," Draconis pleaded, seeking her forgiveness. Somehow, he felt that he needed at least that in order to accept Lly's death. "I truly did…We were there in the lake, and then, the Y'mordi came. She had let her disguise drop, and they…"

"It is alright, Rexam. I believe you." Her tone was mournful but forgiving. "I only wish I could have been there at the end. We had been through so much together, and I know that she cared about you…No, I know she loved you. To be honest…I loved you, too, but I wanted her to be with you. I knew she deserved you far more than I did. Did she tell you how much she cared about you?"

Draconis nodded simply. "She told me many things, Elani, but I am still not sure if I can stay here after this is all finished. I think the memories will be too hard for me to bear, Elani."

She nervously placed one of her claws on his as she said, "Rexam, I do not know what all Lly told you when she died, but it was always her greatest belief that one should not waste his or her life mourning another's death or trying to avenge such either. She said that it is not a form of accepting or forgetting. She claimed that mourning was simply a form of learning and using that knowledge. You cannot run away from her memory, Rexam. You do not have to embrace this idea of death either, though. You only have to keep going."

He sighed in understanding as he grasped her claw and said, "I know…It is just easier said than done, I suppose. Maybe, I will stay here, but I am scared of being alone again. Meeting Lly was the first time that I ever…really connected with anybody."

Elani offered softly, "Rexam…I know that I could never replace Lly…I know that more than you do probably…but maybe you and I could stick together. Maybe, we would both be alright if we had each other."

"Maybe, you are right…" replied Draconis with uncertainty. He did think that Elani was quite attractive, and he had to admit that Elani had certain personality qualities that he admired, but he agreed with her that it would be hard to fill the hole that Lly had left in his heart.

As he opened his heart, he felt that Light spell he had been seeking down here. It seemed to be coming from the mural itself. "That is odd…" he muttered in profound interest.

"What is it?" inquired Elani, unable to sense anything.

He noticed a spell of Light affecting the mural. Although he tried to think of a use for a Light spell on this painting, he could not identify one. Cautiously, he began to remove the spell. "There is some strange spell affecting the mural…"

Finally, the spell snapped, and Elani and Draconis gaped at what they saw. The Dragon that had been black was now gold, and the Divine Dragon of the Heavens was now silver. Hurriedly, they ran over to the previous mural, and Draconis found the same spell altering its image. Once he dispelled it, the Golden Dragon became black, and the Black Dragon became gold.

Elani murmured, "The legends were all wrong. Someone deceived us…"

Draconis nodded in astonishment. "It's true that the Golden Dragons and Black Dragons were at war, but the Golden Dragons had used the twofold, not the Black

Dragons." They went back to the mural with the Divine Dragon of the Heavens. "The Divine Dragon of the Heavens was not even golden. He was a Silver Dragon. This whole time, the Silver Dragons have been treated as nothing more than scum, but they were the chosen ones, not the Golden Dragons. It even shows the Divine Dragon of the Heavens fighting a Golden Dragon here." Draconis's jaw lowered in shock and sorrow.

Elani growled, "Someone tried to cover this up at one point." Her fists clenched, and her fangs ground against each other in fury. Everything they had ever been taught was a lie. "And it was likely a Golden Dragon." She looked down at the ground, unable to keep looking at the mural. "Perhaps, Cairon was right for doing what he did."

Instantly, Draconis snapped at her, "No, Elani, his way was not right, and nor was King Vran's. None of the kings of the past have been right. This segregation should never have happened. We have to stop him now."

Another voice spoke from the depths of the hall. "We can't let that happen, Draconis."

Draconis was not surprised in the least to find Sarn and Arnim standing there. Elani asked quietly, "Are these the ones who killed Lly?"

"Yes, but they cannot die like we can. They have the ability to come back to life, no matter what happens to them, so revenge is pointless, Elani."

"That is fine. Lly would not want me to be vengeful. I am glad that ripping them apart will not be considered revenge. Shall we?" she asked, invitingly.

Draconis nodded.

"Oh, you might need this," she said as she offered Draconis his goldfoil. He took the thin weapon, thinking about Lly. It was hard for him to believe that centuries of a single mindset had been entirely wrong. He could not help but think about how differently everything might have been if he had stayed in Sharl Vran rather than leaving to Gevás. Lly might have still been alive, too.

The two Dragons charged at the Y'mordi, Golden and Black, fighting alongside each other.

Sarn instantly released several sharp discs of Force. Both Elani and Draconis dodged these, and Arnim began shooting at the two Dragons with her two revolvers. Draconis barely managed to block the bullets in time.

Elani came at the Y'mordi first, and her twofold slashed dangerously at them, but Arnim created a wall of Rock that blocked the twofold and caused Elani to be knocked backward by the recoil of her weapon hitting solid rock.

As soon as the wall was lowered, Draconis emitted a stream of Flame to engulf Arnim, and Sarn used a whirlwind to direct the red Flames away from her sister. Then, she summoned her own chain to fight. The chain cracked like a whip as it reached out for Elani's neck, the Black Dragon dodged it nimbly and ran at Sarn. When Arnim tried to protect her sister by shooting at Elani, Draconis used Force to repel Arnim's bullets.

Thinking quickly, Sarn used Air to make her chain perfectly straight and solid and swung it downward, knocking Elani to the ground.

Before Arnim could finish the Black Dragon off, Draconis roared in a raging fury. He had already lost Lly, and he had no intention of losing Elani as well. He charged at Arnim and dodged two bullets that went whizzing mere centimeters from his golden snout. His momentum caused him to land two feet from Arnim, and he chose to do a dramatic backflip that allowed his sharp-clawed feet to kick the guns out of Arnim's hands. As soon as his feet landed, he kicked off from the ground to lunge at Arnim. She had not seen the needle-like blade of the goldfoil as it entered her robe and pierced her chest. She emitted a deafening shriek then as her bleeding body crumpled. She fell face down on the stone floor, and her sister went running to her side. "Arnie, can you hear me? Arnie?" She gave the two Dragons a nasty glare as she summoned a Gate and dragged her sister into it. She yelled at Elani and Draconis then, "You'll pay for this!" She was gone.

Although Draconis had doubts that was the last he would see of those two, he breathed a sigh of relief and turned to Elani. He gave her a comforting nudge, "Alright, are you ready to go against Cairon? I would not hold it against you if you wanted to help your soldiers."

Elani chuckled, "As if I would let you have Cairon all to yourself? I have been planning on this day for over a century and a half, and you think I would give it up? My soldiers can handle themselves, especially with those Golden Dragons helping them, which I am assuming was your doing, somehow?"

"Yes," replied Draconis with a nod. "They were imprisoned here, and so, I freed them. I could not just let them die there. Also, I am not sure if I told you or not, but I have my own score to settle with Kusvor Cairon. When he attacked my city years ago, he spared me for some reason, and I have to know why he did that. It has been the question that has plagued me the most for my whole life."

"That is understandable, but do not think that my right to fight him is any less than yours. While you have had one small question in the back of your mind, I have devoted years to planning his defeat."

Draconis nodded acceptingly. "Very well. Let us leave here." He summoned a Gate above the city and above the skirmish, and the two of them went through, instantly drenched by the warm rain. The echo of the pounding thunder roared around them, and the blinding lightning revealed the tangled fighting mass of Dragons below them. "There!" Draconis exclaimed as he pointed to the front door of the fortress.

The two flew as swiftly as they could and had to dodge several Black Dragons who tried to strike them with their twofolds.

As they came near it at top speed, Draconis shot out a ball of Lava that melted a hole in the door wide enough to allow both of them passage into the entrance hall. They dove into the gap and landed roughly on the tile floor of the fortress.

While they dripped water everywhere on the tiles, they observed the demonic architecture of the fortress. Sheets of black mist covered the floor, walls, and ceiling, giving it the appearance of the clouds that were now blocking the light of the sun outside the fortress.

Elani whispered, "The throne room is this way, Rexam."

As they approached the next colossal door, they found themselves holding each other's claw in nervous anticipation.

Draconis asked hopefully, "Together? For Lly?"

A smile came spread on Elani's black-scaled face, "Together, for Lly."

He released her claw and opened the door with a spell of Force. Together, they entered the throne room and beheld the Black Dragon that stood at its center. His ebony armor was like a suit of obsidian plate armor, his body rippled into rough ridges. His pointed shoulders extended, making him seem much larger than he actually was, and his open jaws revealed rows of razor sharp teeth. His red eyes thinned into slits as they bore into the two intruders' facades.

Draconis snarled, "Cairon…"

A Choice

At his army's campsite, under one of the meeting tents, Drage began hesitantly equipping the armor that Tilgé was recommending him to wear. He had never worn armor in his life, and he did not like the weight of it restricting his movements. Though he was not fighting Gaspard today, he still had to fight several people who would probably be proficient in the ways of the sword. The silver armor was dull and unpolished. Like much of the equipment that his troops had, it was battered and worn. "Tilgé, why do you insist that I wear this piece of junk? It's uncomfortable and heavy."

The Brigadier said, "Believe me, I don't think you look any better for it, but do you really expect to be able to protect yourself from every attack in this battle? Let's say a piece of shrapnel comes at you, or a stray bullet is headed your way, or a sword just barely scrapes you, or—"

"Okay, okay, I get the picture. Still, it is not like this cheap metal is really going to protect me from all of that. One bullet will be all it takes, Tilgé."

"Perhaps," snapped Tilgé. "But what if it at least slows the bullet? It could be the decision between life and death in that case. Now, stop your grumbling."

Sume offered, "At least, you will not have to wear it when you are fighting Gaspard. Today, can you not use your Sword to slice through people's swords anyways? Does the Sword of Destiny not have the ability to cut through things effortlessly?"

Drage replied with a sigh, "It does but only for certain things. Its personality finds that cutting through an enemy's weapon or armor is cheating, so I will find as much resistance as you or Tilgé would. I suppose that Tilgé is right. I am in as much danger as everyone else." He finished strapping on the last few pieces of armor, and he felt like an anchor on the bottom of the sea. He commented, "I look ridiculous."

Tilgé nodded and left the tent with a scowl on his face.

"Such an unpleasant person…" muttered Drage.

Sume agreed, "Yes, he has been in a rather foul mood lately. I do not quite know what has been bugging him, however."

Drage regarded the middle-aged Brigadier in interest. "Hey, Sume, how long have you been in the Enigma Brigade?"

Sume looked up at the ceiling of the tent as he tried to recall, "I suppose that in a few months, I would have been in the Brigade for…sixteen years, I believe."

"Oh, wow, what made you want to join?"

"I did not. The Brigadiers are chosen by the Emperor of Light alone. Not even the Captain has the say over who is in the Brigade. Your father is the one who recruited me. He must have seen some potential in me, but the Captain does not think that much of me. He usually has me do the lower level missions," he explained.

Drage felt sympathy for the man. "Have you ever wanted to leave the Brigade, Sume?"

He shrugged his shoulders, unsure, "I suppose that there have been times that I wish I was not in it anymore, but I do not really have a place to go back to. I was never close to my family, and I never got married or had kids. Sometimes, the

Brigade gets pretty rough, but I get the job done, no complaints, and it keeps a roof over my head and a solid income. I guess that ultimately I like my job."

Hearing those words made Drage feel a little better about the man and the Enigma Brigade in general. He felt that Sume was an honest enough man that understood well the concepts of duty and responsibility. Drage liked this man much better than Tilgé or Maksimilian. He had not had the chance to truly know Viso or Bryco yet, however.

"Your Majesty," began Tilgé as he entered with a sarcastic tone. "Your troops are ready for you."

"Already? I thought it would take them at least another half of an hour."

Tilgé grunted as he left once again. In frustration, Drage stuck out his tongue at the man's back. He then faced the mirror. "I still look ridiculous. I can't go out there like this." Then, an idea struck him. He imagined the armor that a knight from the old stories would wear, and that image became real around his armor. The metal began to shine, and the dents appeared to not exist. It not only looked brand new, but it also seemed to be a completely different set of armor. "Well, Sume? What do you think?"

Sume looked doubtful as he replied, "Well, your Majesty…it is fake…"

Drage rolled his eyes. "Well, of course, it is fake, but the troops will not know that. You will, Aria and her troops will, but that will be it!"

"In that case, it looks splendid, your Majesty."

Drage beamed then. "Thank you, Sume."

When the two of them stepped outside, they were both astonished to see the whole regiment in perfectly straight lines, their bodies erect. Drage was quite impressed by the organized structure of his troops. Occasionally in the formation, he could make out red-robed figures without swords. He decided that these were members of Aria's so-called Phoenix Regiment.

Trying to appear as solid and strong as his soldiers did, he walked to the front of the mass with Tilgé and Sume at either side of him. He approached Aria who was already at the front. "Our scouts said that there is a medium-sized force to our east. We should encounter them within an hour or two. Are your troops ready?"

"Yes, they are more than ready," she replied.

"Good." He turned to face the regiment and called out, "Forward march!"

After three hours of marching through the forests, Aria moved to Drage's position in impatient frustration. She had come here to help, to fight, but Drage's strategy seemed to be getting them nowhere. "Drage, we have not seen any enemies around here. Are the scouts sure of what they reported?" asked Aria wearily.

"They are sure. What puzzles me is why they have moved…In a few minutes, we will stop, and I want your sorcerers to try to scan the area as wide as they can with *mysteria*. Though the scouts could provide better info, I am sure that yours could get some info much quicker."

Aria nodded softly. She did not like Drage commanding her troops directly so often. Her intention in coming was to help him, not for him to take over completely. Nevertheless, she could sense his high stress level, so she decided not to bring it up. Several quiet moments passed. "Um, how is the curse doing?" she inquired tenderly, hoping he had some good news.

Drage was silent at first, but then, he responded, "It's about the same. It's not strong, but I can still feel him. I can look inside my heart, and I see Darkness. It feels like a poisonous taint that clouds my heart. Look, five years ago, I tried to kill Matt. Can you believe that? I tried to kill him. It took everything in my power to stop myself. If this curse worsens even slightly, everyone could be in danger of me. That is why I can't become Emperor until it is gone."

With a sympathetic sigh, she could see how much this dilemma plagued Drage, and she wished more than anything that she could help him, but she simply did not know what to do or even say. "Drage…you'll get through this…" She looked down at her feet, trying to imagine what Drage must be going through. Then, she raised her head and added, "No, we'll get through this."

He looked at her in surprise.

"We are in this together, Drage. I am not going to give up, and nor are you. You have been gone too long for you to just disappear again when this War is over. You're going to be the Emperor of Light just like your father. Please, don't give in, Drage."

She was quite astonished when a fond smile appeared on his face. "Aria...thank you." He leaned his head closer to hers and kissed her on the lips. It was a short moment, but in that time, Aria saw a fountain of Light inside Drage's heart, buried just beneath the Darkness. She smiled lovingly at him.

Tilgé snarled, "This is not the time to be playing games, your Majesty. The enemy could be anywhere."

Before Drage could respond to Tilgé's remark, they all heard a scout in the distance coming back from a venture. "Your Majesty, they are in the forest to our north. They are trying to circle around us."

Drage understood instantly, "They are going to attack us from behind," he muttered. "Company, halt!" he roared over the crunching steps of the formation. He stepped into the middle of the front line and called out, "Follow my right arm with your eyes only!" He raised his arm, acting like a visible midpoint for the regiment. "I need for everyone who is on my left to move ten yards to your right! Hurry up!"

As the troops followed his commands, Aria rushed to his side. "Drage, what are you doing?"

"I am controlling my enemies' movements. Aria, I need you to take those troops way over there further south, just out of sight of this very spot. In half an hour, charge to the northeast. I am going to take these troops and continue on our regular path."

"But that—"

"—is a really good idea," commented Sume who had suddenly appeared beside the two of them. "When the enemy attacks Drage's half from behind, your half will be attacking their rear, and they will be perfectly trapped. It is reversing the trap. That is brilliant, your Majesty."

Drage replied cautiously, "I would not be so sure. If they were attempting this plan, then they were either underestimating us, or they have another idea that they have not revealed yet. However, I have a couple of tricks up my sleeve just in case. For now, Aria, you need to quickly get them further south. We have no time to lose. Sume, come on, let's go."

Thirty minutes later, Drage, Sume, and Aria's sorcerers could sense the enemy troops sneaking to their rear. He was waiting for the right moment, and finally, he sensed them come within sight and prepare to charge.

"Reverse formation!" he roared, and the entire regiment reversed itself and faced the enemy that was seconds before at their backs. Using a Gate, he moved to the front of the formation once again. "Charge!"

He could immediately sense his enemies' stunned reactions to the sudden attack. As he ran, he held out a hand, and the Sword of Destiny materialized into it in a flash of blue light. He and the front line of his regiment rammed straight into the front line of the enemy, their blades crashing against those of the enemies' and their war cries rang out until the entire skirmish was a din of proud cheers and dying screams. The intertwining mass of bodies swarmed around Drage, but Drage was a flower amid the storm. His Sword moved in the way of the Dragon, the form that Draconis had taught him long ago. The shimmering, blue blade never stopped moving, and nor did he. Both Sword and soldier were blurs on the battlefield, his heart void.

Sensing every movement with his heart, he parried away many of the slashing swords of the rebel anima. Those attacks that he could not block scraped harmlessly against his armor. He was sure that he was going to hear an "I told you so" from Tilgé later.

He could clearly hear many of his riflemen shoot into the fray, and the sound of those bullets was deafening as they shot past his head and brought down many of the enemies he was fighting.

Then, he felt Aria charging at the rear of the enemy, and he smiled as he continued his assault. Greater surprise emanated from the enemies' hearts. This battle would be easily won, he decided. As both Drage's force and Aria's force attacked either the side of the enemy, Drage began to realize that the two would ideally meet in the center unless a surrender was made. Now that he was thinking about it, it was odd that the enemy had not surrendered already.

As he pushed through the enemy's ranks, cutting down rebels with ease, he finally saw why a surrender had not been made. One of the Y'mordi stood in a clearing in the middle of the enemy's forces. The blue-robed man held out his staff challengingly to Drage who had just entered the clearing. "Prince Helius, it is a pleasure to meet you. My name is Xarden."

"The pleasure is all mine," retorted Drage as he began to circle the Y'mordi with his Sword lowered to point at the ground but made to protect his legs. "To what do I owe such a visit, Xarden?"

"Heh," chuckled the old man. "I find that I am quite a generous person, Prince Helius. I am here to present you with a choice, and the choice is yours alone."

Drage ducked as a fireball came shooting over his head. "Alright, I am listening."

"Good," Xarden began. "I know of two important locations for you. One is a little to the south of here where Gaspard is waiting to battle you and your soldiers. The other is even farther to the east. It is where Maris's spirit is kept."

Drage's dark eyes widened at what Xarden was saying. "Where is he?" asked Drage furiously.

Xarden's grin widened. "Here is where your choices lie. Gaspard will find your troops even if you do not face him by tomorrow morning. I am going to open a Gate that leads to

Maris's spirit's location, but it will only be open for a short time. You can either fight with your troops against Gaspard, or you can go after Maris's spirit. That is your choice."

Angrily, Drage rushed at Xarden with his glowing Sword of Destiny. Xarden blocked the attack with his scepter and then released a blast of Force that sent Drage flying. Before Xarden could attempt an attack at Drage, he found himself fiercely blocking spells from another attacker.

Aria and two of her sorcerers had made it through the rebel anima to the center, and the three of them were casting offensive spells at a remarkable rate. While one of the sorcerers was creating blasts of Force that rippled through the water and near-lightning speed, Aria and the other sorcerer were releasing balls of red Fire at Xarden. Though there were a few yards between Aria and Xarden, the Phoenixes were able to push Xarden back.

Strangely, Drage became aware of another spell that affected the area. What was even more surprising was that it was a Light spell. He reached out for it with his heart and found that Xarden was controlling it. Suddenly, he felt the Darkness rise up in him and slice through Xarden's Light spell.

Instantly, all of the rebel anima lost their illusions, and they returned to their Shadow forms: Xarden had disguised an army of Shadows as anima.

Before anyone could react to the revealed illusion, the Sword of Destiny began to glow even brighter. As it brightened, Drage thought he felt a voice inside him. "*Open your heart…Let my Light fill you…*" Though his mind wanted to resist the beautiful voice, his heart relented, and he was amazed to find a flood of Light beyond his heart's reach. His heart connected to that source of power, and he felt that light fill him and surge throughout him.

The Sword of Destiny seemed to explode with brilliant, blue light, and every Shadow cringed under the dazzling illumination. Gradually, they began to fade into black mists due to the intensity of the Sword's aura.

When the light finally faded to a dim glow, all of the Shadows were gone, and Xarden had disappeared as well.

Although all the troops were cheering their victory, Drage was perplexed. He observed the Sword of Destiny carefully, wondering what had just happened, but the blade provided no answers. He traced his fingers along the shining metal, entranced by the still fading glow.

After setting up camp in the forest again, Aria, Drage, and Tilgé debated their next plan of action. "What did he say?" Aria demanded.

"He offered me the choice of fighting Gaspard or getting rid of Maris's curse," Drage explained.

"Well," argued Tilgé. "Of course, your Majesty should fight Gaspard. Think of your people. Without you, Gaspard will keep on killing others, and then people will lose so much faith in you that getting rid of your curse will not matter to them."

"Oh, come on, you can't be serious!" exclaimed Aria angrily. Ever since the battle had ended hours ago, she had been on edge. She was not sure if it was because of the overwhelming spell that Drage had somehow cast or the fight with Xarden or even the disguised Shadows, but she felt uneasy nevertheless. "Drage has had to bear this curse for over five years. Don't you think he needs this taken out of him already? He wants to get rid of it so that he can lead everyone effectively. He is doing it for his people!"

When Tilgé opened his mouth to further argue his point, Drage interrupted quite loudly, "Enough! Xarden said it was my choice alone, and I am starting to see why. I couldn't possibly let anyone else make the choice for me." He leaned against one of the enormous trees of the forest. "There's so much at risk, regardless of which one I choose. I could have this curse ended tomorrow morning if I chose that option, but people might die if I am not here."

Aria squinted at the young man against the tree. "Drage, there is something different, isn't there? What are you not telling us?"

Drage turned his head and looked at her for the first time since the battle. Her eyes widened at what she saw. "Drage...your eyes..."

His eyes were as blue as her own were but far more sparkling. They resembled diamonds in every way. He asked her softly, "And?"

When she opened her heart, she found that the Darkness that had been lurking around Drage's heart was gone. "Drage, is the curse gone already?"

"No, but it fell considerably. The Sword of Destiny...It spoke to me, Aria. It grabbed a hold of my heart, and I felt its strength. I felt its Light, and I think that that Light damaged the curse a lot. Maris is buried deep within my heart now. I have learned that it does not take too much time for that Darkness to spread and consume. I have to get rid of it now before it grows any more. I can't take this feeling. It's unbearable, and it's a risk I refuse to take."

Tilgé asked curiously, "Were your eyes blue before?"

Drage shook his head. "They have never been blue a day in my life. At first, I thought I was staring into the glow of the Sword when I looked at its metallic surface, but my eyes really are blue, though, now. Something has changed inside me, and I don't know what it is."

Suddenly, Sume joined them and interrupted the conversation, "Pardon me, your Majesty, but there is an old man in the camp who wants to speak with you."

"What?" said Drage in exasperation.

"He says he is Matthew's father. Would you like for me to send him away, sir?"

"The Prophet of Wind is here?" Drage muttered to himself. "No, Sume. Tell him I will be with him in a few minutes, alright?"

"Yes, sir."

Ivory Armor

Maksimilian had left the Prince of Light with hardly a word. He had become tired of the Prince's ceaseless orders. Also, he had been ready to investigate the fortress in the Capital ever since they had left.

When they arrived in the Capital, he spoke quickly to Bryco and Viso. "We are going to try to make this as quick as possible. The sooner we can leave, the better. We need to scan the area one final time, however, and make sure that neither Captain Terrell nor the Y'mordi are lingering on these streets."

Viso asked in puzzlement, "Shall we not disguise ourselves, Captain?"

"No, Viso. Both of you, meet me at the front gates of the fortress in twenty minutes. Be on time, or you shall be left." Then, he began strolling casually down the dark streets of the Capital with his gold robe flapping in the current.

Viso and Bryco looked at each other and shrugged before going their own ways around the city.

Bryco had always marveled at the massive size of the Capital. Born and raised in Apolis, he had never experienced the rough life of living in such a dangerous yet lively place.

Each sketchy building towered over him, and the blaring dance music rang throughout the dark city with its infectious beat.

However, he knew that living in such a place was beyond his means. Being a member of the Enigma Brigade was a lifetime responsibility that was not easily abandoned, for Maksimilian was not a man to be crossed, and besides, he stood as the third-in-command of the Brigade, with Tilgé being second. He had never envied Tilgé for his title, though. Bryco knew that the only reason that Tilgé was indeed the second-in-command was due to his avid support of Maksimilian's methods. Though he had been in the Brigade decades longer than Tilgé and Viso, Bryco had never thought Maksimilian's unusually cruel methods to be justified.

He shook his head and tried to block out his thoughts against Maksimilian. Not many people ever went against the Captain, and those who did usually found themselves in trouble; Bryco did not want to be one of those who ended up dead. Though Maksimilian was a horrible and malicious person, he was a great leader and knew how to convince others, even if it was by quite unorthodox means.

As he passed several of the skyscrapers, he extended his sensing ability through the steel walls but could not find any trace of the Y'mordi. The place seemed to be free of Captain Terrell and his Y'mordi friend. It had been five years. Bryco had trouble believing that anyone could evade Captain Maksimilian for that long, but nevertheless, the evil duo had done so.

Aside from losing four of their members those five years ago, the Enigma Brigade had remained quite solid. Maksimilian led, Tilgé acted as his greatest assistant, Bryco came for most important missions, Viso acted as an ambassador amongst the Emperor's Council, and Sume usually handled the dirtiest work that Maksimilian had to offer.

Bryco could remember when he had first been recruited into the Brigade. Being a swordsman in the terra had not gained him any particularly new praise, but when he had implemented spells of Light into his swordwork, making him a blur on the battlefield, Maksimilian was the one to notice and recommended Bryco to the Emperor of Light. Though he was only third-in-command, Bryco had been the only one of the Brigade that Maksimilian had personally recommended. This thought always put a smile on his face.

Viso wandered the streets aimlessly. He doubted that they would find the two people who had eluded Maksimilian five years ago. What were the chances of finding those exact same people in the exact same spot? Nevertheless, Viso had to admit that the two vagabonds had not been seen elsewhere. No matter how hard the Captain had looked, the Y'mordi and Captain Terrell had remained unseen.

As he strolled the streets with hands in the pockets of his robe and a calm look on his face, he heard a commotion in the distance. Careful not to be seen, he snuck through several side alleys to find out what was going on.

There appeared to be a naval regiment returning from a battle in the Western Continent. The soldiers all appeared to be quite bloody and beaten. Many healers ran toward them to take care of the wounded soldiers, and then people from a nearby tavern came to help. He smiled warmly at what he was seeing. There was still such Light in the world, even in a rotten place like this one, with all its taverns, its crime, its neglectful ruler, and its whores. He had always preferred the civilized nature of Apolis. He would not have been able to stand living here.

He sat there on the sidewalk for a minute and decided to watch the regiment until the twenty minutes were spent. In his mind, there truly was not a better way to use his time. He knew he could defend his use of time to Maksimilian.

After watching the soldiers for several minutes, he decided that it was probably time to go on and head to the fortress. He knew it would not take him too long to get there, and he turned into one of the main trash-laden alleys.

All of a sudden, he watched as a robed woman came closer to him. For some reason, there was something familiar about this woman, but he could not understand why. Sensing her bestial instinct to hunt, he ran into the next alleyway, but as soon as he did, he could hear her rapid footsteps trying to keep up with him. Fear overcame him: this felt different. It was not simply a battle. He was actively being hunted. He sensed her rage, her fury, her desire to kill, and he ducked into a side alley to hide behind a trash can.

He was even more stunned when a rat jumped out of the metal can, making a loud banging sound. Cautiously, he opened his heart to *mysteria* and sensed that the woman was still there, waiting for him. Angrily, he summoned enough *mysteria* to try one of Bryco's favorite spells, the ability to move at the speed of Light.

He maneuvered his way through the alleys, losing her with ease. Out there, in the maze of the streets, he could sense her heart beating rapidly. Something was familiar about her, and he knew he had been right in his instinct to flee, and not fight.

With a sigh, he created a Gate in the next wall he came across, and he transported himself into the fortress's entrance hall. He knew he was already late.

Maksimilian and Bryco stood in the lower levels of the fortress, where a white mold grew on the slick walls. The water was murky all around them, and the cool temperature brought even Maksimilian to a slight shiver. Bryco had created a small Light that floated near his head unless he directed it to go somewhere. With a sigh, Maksimilian drew his own Steel of Life, and he was amazed to find it was glowing green as it had when he found the Y'mordi in the military training facility.

"The blade…It is reacting to something, it seems…"

Bryco, however, had never been informed of Maksimilian's possession of a Spirit Sword, and he asked, "Sir? What do you mean by reacting?"

Maksimilian hesitantly decided to trust Bryco. "You are curious, Bryco. Be wary of that curiosity. It can be a dangerous thing," he spoke that quite calmly and allowed Bryco to pale in fear before adding, "Nevertheless, I suppose I shall explain. Are you familiar with the five Spirit Swords of legend?"

"Yes, sir, but I do not know every one of the Swords. What about them, Captain?"

The Captain of the Enigma Brigade raised the green blade to his face, hypnotized by its warm light. "There was one Sword that was wielded by a remarkable General and noble during the Obsidian Wars. That Sword had an interesting ability, the ability to make life eternal. However, it had a restriction: the blade could not be used to kill any living thing."

"Are you trying to tell me that the sword in your hand is *that* Sword?" asked Bryco in fascination.

"Yes, Bryco, and I am also telling you that the General of whom I speak was me."

Bryco's eyes became large then as he realized what Maksimilian was saying. "You-you're an Ancient?"

The Captain shook his head in frustration. "No, you fool. An Ancient still ages, just remarkably slowly. This Steel of Life keeps my life and age sustained. I have been in the Enigma Brigade for a long time, Bryco. No Emperor of Light ever figured it out, as I rarely even meet with the Emperors, and when I do, I have not always had to give my name. I do not intend for one to ever know. Is this understood, Bryco?"

"Yes, sir. Only, I do not understand why you are telling me this." Indeed, Bryco was feeling a tremendous amount of fear at the moment. Maksimilian was usually not so trusting, and something seemed to be amiss if he was confiding in his third-in-command.

Maksimilian smiled with one side of his mouth, and a couple of sharp teeth stuck out and curled over his bottom lip. "Bryco, I am telling you this, because I do trust you. I will be the first to admit that Tilgé is strong. I have never met a fighter quite like him, and he has the spirit, too. What he lacks, however, is discipline. He is like a lapdog for me, yes, but a poorly trained one, goes off barking when I tell him to heel. The chain of command is a complete mystery to him. Sometimes, I wonder if his interest is even that of the Light." His eyes stayed focused on the green blade. "But you, Bryco, are skilled in *mysteria* and the sword. You know who is in charge, and you never question those above you. I have hardly ever had a problem with you, and you never make the same mistake twice." Though he was speaking the truth, he was not mentioning the fact that he was simply trusting Tilgé less and less. The man was too unpredictable. "Bryco, when I first saw you fight on the field, I knew that you had what it takes to be a member of the Enigma Brigade, and I still see that potential even now." Maksimilian paused. "I want you to kill Tilgé."

Viso began looking around frantically for Captain Maksimilian and Bryco, but he could not find them anywhere.

The entrance hall of the fortress was relatively small, and white pillars lined both sides of the hall. "Captain?" he called as softly as he could. "Where are you?" He opened his heart to *mysteria* but could sense nothing. Cautiously, he went left into the next room, some trophy storage.

As soon as he did, a sound came from the entrance hall. He was sure it was Maksimilian. Perhaps, Viso had been early after all.

With a smile, he returned to the room but was rapidly astonished to find it was the robed woman with a large soldier beside her.

Before Viso could do or say anything, the woman whipped out a rifle and loosed fire on him. The barrage of bullets hit him squarely in the chest, bloodying his golden robe. Instantly, he collapsed. "How? Wha-?"

The woman did not allow Viso to finish his questions as she fired upon him once again until he was a fleshy, bleeding mass on white marble floor of the entrance hall.

The large man asked her carefully, "He was one o' da people ya were searchin' fer?"

The woman nodded. "Yes, he was one of the Brigade, but I do not think that he is the only one here. I do not even think that he was the one to kill those guards at the front. The others must have got here just before he did. He was just unlucky."

Bryco was bewildered by what Maksimilian was telling him. "You want me…to kill Tilgé, sir?" He knew at least to not ask "why" directly.

"Yes, Bryco. If you do that, you shall be the second-in-command, and the future Captain of the Enigma Brigade." Though he was talking to Bryco, his attention was more focused on the glimmer of his Sword. That Spirit Sword was trying to tell him something, but he was not sure what that was yet. He knew that he was getting closer to some unseen force that the Spirit Sword could notice, but Bryco's Light was not revealing it yet. It had to be somewhere in this disgusting place.

Suddenly, he felt something even more powerful than the hum of his Sword. "Bryco…Viso was just killed. Someone killed him two levels above us."

Bryco looked up at the ceiling in wonder. Killing a member of the Enigma Brigade was nearly impossible to do, yet four of their group had died five years ago, and now, a fifth had been killed. "Are you sure, Captain?"

Maksimilian gave Bryco an icy glare. "Yes, I am sure. However, I cannot sense whoever has done it, but I am confident it happened above us. We must hurry, Bryco. Can you make your Light larger?"

At Maksimilian's command, the Light grew to illuminate even more of the filthy floor. It was astonishing to see the rusting walls and mud-laced stone ground that held no items on it whatsoever. There were only a couple of doors in the long hallway. It seemed completely empty.

As they continued through the floor, Maksimilian's Steel of Life began to glow brighter and brighter, but the hall remained entirely empty.

Suddenly, Bryco whispered, "I think the Emperor Regin is nearby. There is a strange sickness that is seeping into the water, and if the rumors around the streets bear some truth, then it is likely that the Emperor Regin is the possessor of that sickness. He is nearby." In actuality, the whereabouts of the Emperor Regin were the last things on Bryco's mind. He had scarcely a few minutes ago learned that his Captain was over a thousand years old and that he had a mission to kill one of his comrades.

Maksimilian tried to maintain a calm composure. He was finding that ever since meeting that annoying Prince of Light, he had been quite shaken. "The Emperor Regin walks in the path of the Light, Bryco. He has sworn his allegiance to the Emperor of Light, and, therefore, he is trustworthy. For now, let us worry about the matter at hand. The Sword is reacting to something inside this hall, and I intend to find out what it is."

Though he did not ask, Bryco had a feeling that their reason for being here had nothing to do with finding the Y'mordi or Captain Terrell. For the first time in his career, he was doubting more than Maksimilian's methods. "Sir, what will happen to the Enigma Brigade if I kill Tilgé? We will have only three members: you, me, and Sume."

"Who said anything about 'if you kill Tilgé?' Bryco, it is an order, not a simple request. If you defy me, you are defying the will of the Light. You are clever, and I am sure that it is not that difficult of a concept to grasp." He did not mention that he did not like the way Tilgé had been eyeing the Steel of Life recently. The thing with dogs was that, even if they knew they were not supposed to, they often liked taking their master's things. "As for such a small Brigade, I am confident that once the Prince of Light steps up to the Throne, more members shall be recruited. Have faith in the Light, Bryco."

Bryco knew that he had a profound faith in the Light, yet he was beginning to doubt Maksimilian's interpretation of it. "Yes, Captain," he replied simply.

Maksimilian, however, could sense Bryco's hesitation.

Before he could think further on the matter, the Steel of Life stopped shining. Then, both Maksimilian and Bryco saw an object leaned against the wall. Cautiously, they approached it and beheld an ivory suit of armor.

"Your Sword was reacting to this?" inquired Bryco in disbelief.

"It is simply a suit of armor…" muttered Maksimilian. The statue held a massive shield in its hands, and the helmet was well constructed. However, the whole suit looked far too heavy for any person to be able to equip. With a rapid slash of his katana, the stone armor crumbled, and the shield fell to the ground. Maksimilian finally recognized the helmet. It had been the suit of armor that Lord Victor Ferro had used a thousand years ago, or at least, that was before he had become the Y'mordi known as Y'ran. Had the Sword merely reacted to a memory of that armor? If it was not for the Sword's ability to grant him eternal life, he would have thrown the Steel of Life into the ruins of the stone armor right then.

"Bryco…let us leave this place now." He did not know what happened to Viso up above, but he was not eager to go against an unknown enemy without preparation. Besides, Viso was dead. Nothing else was to be done for it. "Perhaps, we shall go and seek out the Prince of Light. Then, you may have your chance to fight Tilgé. I want you to bring his head back to me. He is a traitor to the Light, and he needs to be made an example for any others who enter the Enigma Brigade without the will of the Light in their hearts."

"Yes, Captain," replied Bryco acquiescingly as he summoned a Gate comprised of Light.

The two of them entered the Gate, and Bryco's brilliant ball of Light vanished, returning the room into darkness.

"What was dat?" asked the large man in utter surprise. They had both seen a light coming from the room, but suddenly, it had disappeared. "It's all dark now."

The woman beside him muttered, "That is no problem." She stuck a hand into her robe and pulled out an electric torch, some of the Capital's finest technology.

The dim torch created a circle of light that surrounded the two for a few yards in front of them. The area was chilling, and mud seemed to coat the floor of the hallway. "What is this place?" she asked, her voice echoing along the rusting walls eerily.

"Nuttin's here, Miss Stehl."

"That can't be right. There has to be something here, or else the Enigma Brigade would not have just been down here. They are elusive enough as it is." She truly did not want to believe that she had come this far only to have found one of the Brigadiers.

"Miss Stehl, if ya don' mind me askin', why is revenge da main t'ing on yer mind? Da Emp'ror Regin has gone an' locked 'imself up, an' yer only worryin' 'bout revenge?"

Stehl regarded Mirah with a sorrowful expression. "When you've lived your whole life in the military, there is not too much to hold on to in life. When the Brigade attacked the fortress, I thought that there was some punishing that needed to be done, and I knew that no one else would step up."

"Ya wanted to be a 'ero," muttered Mirah knowingly.

"Yeah. Women have hardly any rights here in the Eastern Continent, and I thought that maybe…maybe I could change that by doing something for the sake of the country. Then…I met someone here before I left…He was actually the one who saved me from the Enigma Brigade. At first, I thought I wanted to just kill him, but then, I realized he was tall and strong and powerful, everything a woman could ask for in a man. I started to see that both of us had something in common."

"Oh? An' what's dat?"

Stehl replied with a subtle smile, "We both wanted something greater than what we had. He wanted freedom, and I wanted a purpose. Somehow, being with him gave me that sense of purpose. Do you understand, Mister Mirah?"

"I t'ink I do, Miss Stehl," replied the large man.

Before they could continue their conversation, Stehl noticed something in the glow of her torch. To the side, there was a great pile of rubble. When she raised the light, the ceiling had not crumbled or anything, so it made her wonder what could have caused such a pile of rocks to come into existence. "What is that?" she asked with curiosity.

As they approached the white stone, Mirah responded, "I t'ink it was a statue."

"A statue?" As soon as she examined the pile of stones, she noticed that she could indeed pick out what appeared to be the helmet of a suit of ivory armor. Though the rubble was made of stone, it was hollow. The whole thing had once been a suit of armor, though she marveled at how any one person could have possibly worn such an extremely heavy suit of armor.

She bent down to examine it further and was surprised to notice that the light of her torch was revealing a lot of the debris in the water around it: This suit of armor had only been destroyed a few minutes ago. "They were here..." she muttered. "The Enigma Brigade was here just a little while ago." In fury, she kicked at the pile of rubble and ended up stubbing her toe on the armor's shield. "Ouch!" she cried.

Mirah commented softly, "Dat is a nice shield, wouldn't ya say, Miss Stehl?"

With a doubtful glance, she regarded the enormous shield, but something caught her eye then. It was the tiniest sparkle of light, but it felt as if it was something more than that. She knelt before the pile of rubble once again and proceeded to flip the shield over. She was entirely baffled by what she was seeing.

Fragments of a Spirit

"How has Matthew been doing? It has been several weeks since I have heard from him, you know," said the elderly man with the black streak in his grizzling hair, his face full of concern.

Drage replied casually, "Matt is fine, the last time I checked. I left him on the Northern Continent. He was with one of the other Guardians of Light, and they are trying to end the civil war there. I assure you that he is alright, sir."

"That is good." The old man sighed. "So, you are his brother, right?"

"Half-brother actually," muttered Drage awkwardly. "John was my dad, and Elizabeth is my mom."

"Ah, I see."

The two of them were presently inside Derek's tiny cottage in the middle of the forest. He had left Aria and Tilgé in charge in his absence. The tea kettle that rested on the stove was brewing tea on its own, much to Drage's amazement. He had remembered Matthew telling him the story of how he had met his real father and had mentioned this exact same tea kettle. Derek was the Prophet of Wind and a master of the abilities of Time. Though he had gone slightly insane after his wife

Elizabeth had left him, seeing Matthew again and spending the past five years with him had lessened the worst of the mental problem.

Derek continued, "Your Majesty, what are you and your troops doing here exactly? I do not mean to be a bother or anything, but I have protected this area for a long time. I just…don't want anything to happen to it."

Drage sighed, "Sir, the last thing I want is for your home to be affected by this, but I might not have a choice in the matter. Even now, the troops are becoming more and more accustomed to these woods. They are learning every rock, pit, and tree. With that knowledge comes an advantage, an advantage that is hard to find in a battle of such a grand scale as this one is going to be."

"Are you trying to use my home as—?"

"No, sir," interrupted Drage. "Look, I am going to do everything within my power to protect your home, but I just want you to know that it is not my highest priority right now. I have troops to keep alive and a great decision to make. Because you loved my mom and cared for Matt, I am even more willing to help you, but I can only do so much. I want you to understand that." Though Derek at first had trouble believing Drage's sincerity in his words, as soon as Derek looked into those blue, diamond eyes, he found that he did believe Drage after all.

"Your Majesty, I am curious about a rumor I heard in your camp…"

"Go on," encouraged Drage, eager to hear the old man's words.

The Prophet hesitated in consideration before saying, "They said that your sword is what won the battle, that it came alive at your command."

Drage shook his head. It seemed that rumors had a way of both escalating and altering the truth. "Master Janus, what you have heard is only partially true. You see, I bear one of the Spirit Swords." To illustrate his point, he summoned his Sword into his hand. Derek's eyes were mesmerized by the clear reflection that the blade made as if it were made of only glass. "This one is known as the Sword of Destiny, and it does indeed possess a fragment of the Great Spirit. However, lately, that fragment has been livelier and livelier. Today, the fragment spoke to me. It asked me to open my heart to it, and as soon as I did, it did something to me. It was as if it was casting a spell through me, and the Sword emitted this phenomenal blue light. When it was gone, all of the Shadows had been killed, and I obtained these blue eyes."

"Those blue eyes?" Derek said disbelievingly as he pointed at Drage's eyes.

"Yes, these eyes. They were brown when I was born, but Maris placed a curse on me five years ago that turned my eyes black. Today, the Spirit turned them blue. Believe me, not as confusing as it sounds."

Derek chuckled at Drage's almost humorous nature. "I know a thing or two about the Spirit Swords as it happens, and I think I can explain what happened to you today, if you are interested in learning that."

Drage smiled anxiously, "Sir, I would be more than happy to hear what you have to say about the Spirit Swords."

"I thought you might be." Then, Derek began, "A thousand years ago, the Great Spirit divided itself into five pieces, and these pieces found blades of metal in which they could live eternally. Though each piece was a different segment of the Great Spirit, they each wanted to be at the heart of the battles of the world. They wanted to be of most use in protecting this world. One went to the Southern Continent. One went to the Eastern Continent. One went to the Western Continent. One went to the Northern Continent, and as for the last one, nobody ever knew what became of it. Nevertheless, there were five of these fragments, as you called them, and each one corresponded to the five core Elements."

"They correspond to the Elements?" Drage had never heard this part of the legend and was quite baffled by the idea.

"Yes," explained the Prophet. "Supposedly, the color of the blade's glow can reveal the Element. I am assuming based on the new color of your eyes that the Element of your Sword is Water, a fitting blade for one of the future leaders of Gevás."

"What about the others? Like the Behemoth?"

"The Behemoth? Which one is that?" inquired Derek, trying to remember the Sword.

"It is the considerably heavy one that brings its wielder luck."

"Ah, yes," said Derek, finally remembering it. "The Behemoth is the blade of Earth. Somewhere out there, there are the Swords of Fire, Wind, and Nature, too. Regardless of the connection to the Elements, the Swords have greater abilities. The Great Spirit admired and despised many qualities of humanity, but those particular qualities were divided evenly amongst the Swords. They are rather picky over their owners and have in the past been known to strike those who tried to wield them without respecting the choices of the Great Spirit.

"However, the legend also shows that the fragments found themselves trapped inside the Swords. They want to be freed and, if possible, reunited. They long for a way to truly connect with the world again, and so, at times, they have used their abilities to communicate with their wielders."

"The glow…" muttered Drage in understanding.

"Yes, that glow is their way of letting you know that they can sense something of interest, such as other Spirit Swords, ancient artifacts of power, things like that. The glow usually brightens as you get closer and closer to that object. Also, in some battles, men have reported to the Swords speaking to them and acting through them. According to those stories, the fragments of the Great Spirit ask for the wielder to open his heart to them, and then the fragments manipulate the person's heart so that they can do as they want. The warrior Tatsu once came to the realization that the Spirit Swords were a form of directing one's *mysteria*. You can cast spells through the blade itself, and certain powers will be magnified by it. What happened to you today was nothing more than the Great Spirit's fragment using your heart to release its own power. It wanted you to utilize the Sword's full capabilities."

Suddenly, the tea was done, and the Prophet of Wind cast a rapid spell that sent the tea kettle floating over to where they were seated. Carefully, the spell began to pour their tea.

Drage stared intently at the Prophet, amazed by his explanation. "So, the Swords are even more alive than I thought…So, how did my eyes change colors exactly?"

Derek struggled mentally as he said, "Well, I think that it happened because you opened your heart…too much, perhaps. I have often heard that the eyes are windows to one's soul, and if that is true, then it stands to reason that if the color of your heart changes, then so will the color of your eyes. The Great Spirit had to have affected something inside of you. Do you have any idea what that could be?"

"Yeah, my Darkness. Maris's curse subsided after the Great Spirit entered my heart."

"That could be it. Still, it is only a theory of mine. I am not quite confident of the idea as of yet." Derek sipped his warm tea thoughtfully.

After Drage did the same, he asked, "Master Janus, would you mind if I asked you a question of advice?"

"Feel free. Though I was by no means a fan of your father, I find that you have more of your mother in you than you do of him, physically and mentally. I would take you as my own kid if that was allowed."

Because he had not truly known his father long enough to really be insulted by Derek's remark, Drage smiled at the old man before replying, "Thanks…Anyway, one of the Y'mordi offered me a very difficult choice today. I would explain the technicalities of it, but I think I will just tell you what the choice is."

"Very well."

"I can either fight alongside my troops in the morning and challenge Gaspard one on one. I would then have to worry about finishing the conquest of the Western Continent and the Northern Continent. Then, I would need to find a way to get rid of this curse before I took the Throne, assuming that that is what I choose to do."

"Alright, what is your other option?"

Drage hesitated. Based on Tilgé's reaction to the choice, he felt as if it was almost cowardly even considering the other option. "Or I can finally locate Maris's spirit tomorrow and get rid of this curse once and for all. Aria would probably lead the troops into battle against Gaspard, and then, I could finish this War without the pressures of the Darkness, and I could ascend the Throne easily."

Derek folded his arms as he commented, "Hm, that is quite the most difficult dilemma, is it not? Hm…It seems that the Y'mordi do not give out very easy choices." Both Drage and the Prophet of Wind were silent for several minutes as Derek began to puzzle out what he thought the best action was. Between these minutes, Drage drank much of his tea thirstily and nervously anticipated Derek's response. He was partially glad that Derek had not instantly argued that the second option was out of the question. It meant that he was not an idiot, though Tilgé seemed to find that particular option to be a reckless move.

Finally, Derek replied, "I think that it is fair to say that you can do both things: You can fight Gaspard and go against Maris's spirit."

Drage shook his head in utter perplexity. "Sir, I don't think you understand. I can't do both. Even if I was to hurry, the way to Maris's spirit will only be open for a short while. If I choose one, then that means that I cannot do the other."

"Perhaps, you do not understand what my specialty is," rebutted the Prophet.

"Huh?"

"As I am the Prophet of Wind, I happen to have a knack for one of the forms of Wind. That form is Time, and it sounds like you do not have much of that, your Majesty."

All of a sudden, Drage understood to what Derek was referring. "You could do that? I thought there were some Time laws or rules or something that prohibited you from just allowing me to essentially be in two places at once."

"There are rules, but they do not affect such a situation as this. Most of the rules are about traveling between different times, and that is not what you are trying to do. I can freeze the entire battlefield in time, so that you can enter that Gate and get rid of your curse. Once you are finished there, all you have to do is return here with a Gate of your own, and I will be waiting and will unfreeze time for you. Then, you can fight Gaspard and beat him to a bloody pulp for all I care."

"Master Janus, you are brilliant!" Without warning, Drage went over and hugged the old man. "Thank you so much! You have just solved so many problems at once here. Thank you, thank you!" repeated Drage, a grin widening.

Derek chuckled with joy at Drage's enthusiasm, "As I said, in many ways, you are a son that I never had. You remind me so much of your mother. How is she doing?" He looked down. "Despite what happened with her and your father, I never quit caring about her."

"Oh, she is well. She—" Then, he remembered it had been a while since he had talked to her. She did not even know that he was back in Gevás. He sighed as he decided that that dilemma would have to wait until after this War was over or at least until the next morning's battle was finished. "You know, maybe you can see her again. I know that she never mentioned you, but that does not mean that she did not want to. There were several things that she had never told me, Master Janus, and I think that maybe you were part of the reason. Maybe, she still cares about you. Whatever the reason, she might want to see you again. Right now, though, I have a War to worry about."

Derek smiled. "You are Liz's kid, that is for sure. You have that same spirit and will that she had. You're not like Matthew. He always had my...how shall I put it...my contentment with the way things are. He does not dream big as you or Liz do. We seek to live life comfortably while you both reach for the stars. I am proud of what I am. However, it does mean that Matthew or I could never find the place called Paradise."

"Excuse me?" inquired Drage curiously.

"Oh, it is nothing, just an old man's legend. Forget I even said it. As you said, you have a War to worry about."

Drage nodded, reminding himself to ask Derek about this later. He remembered Paradise being something related to that mysterious figure Ace. "Thank you for your help. Shall I see you at the camp in the morning?" He stood from the table.

"Yes, your Majesty."

Turning toward the curtain that took the place of a door, Drage responded, "Good, I shall expect you then."

After Drage told Aria and Tilgé about what the Prophet had told him, Drage sat down by the meeting table to hear their thoughts. "That is such good news!" exclaimed Aria, nearly leaping with excitement. "I had never even thought about using spells of Time."

Tilgé groaned as he leaned against one of the poles that held the tent erect, "Do you even know how to use any?"

Aria retaliated, "No, but I shall learn one day. What spells do you know, Tilgé?"

The Brigadier said something incoherent before asking Drage, "Do we know that we can trust the old man?"

"Yes, Tilgé, we can trust him. He is Matthew's dad after all, plus he served the Emperor of Light at one point, as well."

"Oh, yeah? Well, why did he quit?"

Aria responded to Tilgé heatedly, "Perhaps, the Prophet wanted to take care of a family. Maybe, the Emperor of Light was not treating him fairly."

Tilgé snapped back, "The Emperor of Light knows best in all cases!"

Aria grunted, "Will you be saying that same thing when Drage is crowned?"

Though Tilgé wanted to answer, he found himself stumbling for the right words. Even with Drage standing right there, Tilgé found it hard to submit his full devotion to the young Prince. Saving him from speaking, a Gate appeared near where they were standing, and Maksimilian and Bryco came out of it. Tilgé immediately saluted the Captain and said, "Captain Maks, you're back!"

Maksimilian replied softly, "Yes, Tilgé, we are back." Maksimilian had used the connection that all the Brigadiers had to their Captain. He had been able to sense Tilgé even from several miles away.

Bryco was almost hiding behind Maksimilian. His face was paler than usual, and he was staring emptily at the ground.

Drage roared at the red-haired man instantly, "Captain, where have you been?"

Maksimilian's lip quivered as he struggled not to snarl. "Your Majesty, several years ago, there was an assassin who had attacked the Brigade and was added to the 'Most Wanted' list in Apolis. I had just found a lead that hinted at the assassin being in the Capital at Immyx. I apologize for any lack of clear communication."

"Your apology is accepted, Maksimilian, as is your resignation."

"Sir? You cannot—"

Drage held up a demanding hand to silence Maksimilian. "Maksimilian, to me, you are a soldier. Whatever you did to prove yourself to those before me, you have not done for me. You have only shown me disrespect and a clear disregard for the way that things are to be handled. I will not force you to step down from the Enigma Brigade, but as far as I am concerned, you are no longer the Captain. You are to take Tilgé's place, and he is to take yours as he has been second-in-command. I may not be the Emperor of Light yet, but I am Prince, and unless you want me to make your punishment worse when I do become Emperor, I suggest you not complain."

Maksimilian's fists tightened, and his teeth clenched. Every instinct begged him to run a blade through the Prince's heart, but he simply responded, "Yes…your Majesty."

Tilgé could not help but feel a secret, overwhelming joy that he was finally going to be the Captain of the Enigma

Brigade. He had never had that much ambition in his life, but leading this military force had been his greatest goal.

Bryco, on the other hand, paled even further at what Drage was saying. He knew that later Maksimilian might explode with the anger he was feeling now. He thought back to being in the Emperor Regin's castle and realizing Viso had just been killed. Maksimilian was cold. He would want blood tonight.

Drage added, "Tilgé, stay with me. I might need your help. Maksimilian, Sume, and Bryco, I need you to go with Aria to rally the troops. We have a battle to fight in a few hours."

Everyone in the area could sense that Drage's anger was not an uncontrollable rage or a passionate hate. It was disciplining his soldiers.

Outside the campsite, the sky began to light up with the colors of the dawn, and Drage saw Derek approaching him. "Good morning, Master Janus."

"Good morning, your Majesty. It is indeed a fine morning for a battle, would you not say?"

"I can agree with that," replied Drage as he took in the early current and smelled the natural aroma of the trees. "Once my scouts return, then we will only have to wait for Xarden to open the Gate."

Even as he spoke, he saw his scouts running toward him. "They are back quite early then," commented Derek observantly. Drage squinted as he regarded the scouts in confusion. What could cause them to be back so quickly?

The first scout yelled once he knew Drage was within hearing distance, "Your Majesty, they have your brother! Gaspard has your brother!"

1,000 Years Ago - 3

Tatsu's short white hair swayed in the chilling current of the Southern Continent. With a wrinkled hand, he stroked his Dragon's white-scaled side. Kohana moved her massive white head to rub Tatsu in return. Scouting the area around Apolis as per their usual rounds, they looked each other in the eyes fondly, Kohana twisting her head around to perform the feat. They both knew that after today they would be free at last. As Tatsu had once promised, they would both wander the world aimlessly and never have to fight another battle again.

It had been several years since they had first met. Their bond had only developed and become stronger. No longer did they question the amazing abilities they had. They had found a mastery of their connection and become formidable foes on the battlefield, as Kohana manipulated Tatsu's Sword and Tatsu manipulated Kohana's massive form to decimate enemies. Even their allies knew to step back when Tatsu and Kohana were around to aid in a fight.

Even though it had been around ten years, the two both looked and felt older than they really were. They had decided that it was the negative effects of this Spirit Sword that had affected them in this way. Though it had the ability to physically slice through almost any spell and cripple sorcerers, it made its wielder age. The only reason that it affected Kohana as much as it affected Tatsu was their extremely close connection. What one heart felt, the other felt as well.

To the two of them, today's battle felt more like a new beginning rather than the end. It would mark the first time that the Great Lord of the Light Lux would actually fight Dagan.

Careful not to scratch Kohana's delicate and frail side, Tatsu began to strap her armor onto her body. The simplistic belt buckles kept the operation easy and comfortable for Kohana. That had been one of Tatsu's greatest concerns over the years. Though many soldiers and even the Great Lord of the Light himself had criticized him on his choice of unprofessional and unorthodox methods and equipment as a single fighting unit, Tatsu had only strived to utilize what Kohana herself had found comfortable.

As he adjusted the final strap, he asked her worriedly, "Is that too tight?"

"No, that is fine. It feels quite comfortable."

Tatsu did not have to look into her heart to know that she was telling the truth. Using a spell of Water through Kohana's heart, he manipulated the current so that it lifted himself up and onto her back. "It is almost over, Kohana. Can you believe it? It is our last battle, and after today, it will be clear blue skies for us."

Kohana nodded eagerly. "It will be beautiful, Tatsu. However, they say that today's battle is going to be our hardest yet. There are no more secret weapons. All cards are going to be revealed in this battle. Do you think we can do it? What will happen if we fail?"

"Of course, we can do it. There have only been a few battles we actually had trouble with, and it was not because we were weak. It was because we…hit a few kinks."

"A few kinks?" asked Kohana with a skeptical grin.

"Yeah, just a few kinks. There were a few times when we had to rely on luck and—"

"—and it did not work," she interjected. "There is so much room for something to go wrong today. I can almost feel it going wrong, but I cannot figure it out. It is the same feeling you get when you leave the city thinking you forgot something, but you cannot figure out what it is that you forgot. It feels like that."

"Then, you should have nothing to worry about. How many of those times had I actually forgotten something?" he asked proudly.

Kohana raised a claw and began counting off one talon after another, "Well, there was the time you forget to get your Sword. A few months ago, you left a few soldiers behind before an attack. Just the other day, you could not remember to pick up your armor from the blacksmith. Then, you—"

Tatsu interrupted with a grin on his face, "Alright, alright, I get the concept. Sorry!"

"Hm, well, I have a feeling that something quite unexpected is going to come from this battle, and it's making me anxious and scared at the same time."

As Tatsu began to adjust himself on the seat, his back cracked noisily. "Oh, how I hate being old," he commented, half grumbling. "I feel and look like a seventy-year-old."

Kohana snapped at him, "Do not even start that with me. It is one thing being an old human and another entirely to be an old Dragon. Once today's battle is done with, we are throwing out that stupid Sword. After today, it would have served its purpose, and it is only making us older. I am done with it." She refused to relent on this particular subject. Though the mystical blade had saved them on numerous occasions, she hated the Sword's side effects on them.

"Alright, alright," agreed Tatsu. "Once the battle is over, I am throwing it out. It can be someone else's problem. Trust me, I don't like getting older any more than you do."

"Good, are you ready to start our rounds for the last time?" she asked gently.

Tatsu looked around the walls of the beautiful city fondly. "Yes, I am ready. Let's fly."

Without needing any more encouragement, the White Dragon leaped into the sky, and her wings stretched out and billowed like sails in the strong current. As she flapped her wings, her body swam upward, and she began to go past the walls of the city. With watchful eyes, the two of them began scanning the frozen plains outside Apolis and started searching for any signs of something out of the ordinary.

As soon as they were out of the city, they saw a dark figure on the horizon. Using Kohana's heart, they could both sense that the figure was indeed a person, though they could not identify much more than that.

Kohana rapidly approached the figure, and they were both amazed to realize gradually that the figure was indeed one of the Y'mordi. Ready to fight, Tatsu drew his Sword and noticed its silver glow. He had begun to realize that the Sword responded in such a manner to other Spirit Swords, the Y'mordi, Dagan, and even the Great Lord of Light Lux.

Kohana landed smoothly on the frozen soil near the city walls, and Tatsu leaped nimbly off of her back. Immediately, Kohana assumed her aggressive stance, while Tatsu put his Sword in a ready position. "Y'mordi, what do you want? Why are you here?"

The black robed figure pulled back his hood to reveal a middle-aged man with red, short hair. The man began clapping with a grim smile on his face. "It has been a while, Tatsu and Kohana." His clapping ceased. "You have done well these past few years."

Kohana snarled fiercely as she remembered the man who was talking. She sent a thought to Tatsu, *Do you not remember this man? He was the one who attacked us when you first found me, the one who almost killed you with your Sword. That is him, Y'ran, the General of the Shadow Armies.*

"What do you want?" Tatsu asked threateningly.

Y'ran wiped the grin away instantly. "Tatsu, I want that Spirit Sword."

Tatsu clenched his teeth, "Why do you want it so badly? Are you all not strong enough as it is? Why in the world would I give you such a powerful Sword?"

Y'ran spread his hands to show that he was not trying to begin a fight. "I want it because of that power. No amount of *mysteria* can affect it, and it can prevent some mages from being able to cast a single spell. Why would I not want that is a better question. Besides, I am sure that you would rather me have it than Maks have it."

"Maks? Do you mean Maksimilian?"

Y'ran snarled in reply, "Yes, I mean Maksimilian. He has been seeking the Spirit Swords for a while now, though I think that he might already have one now. I can assure both of you of this: When this battle is over, regardless of who wins it, Maks will come looking for that Sword of yours. If you have dreams of your own freedom, then what freedom is there in being constantly hunted by someone as powerful as he is?"

I do not like him, stated Kohana. *But I think that he has a point. I, too, have noticed Maksimilian's odd behavior the few times that he was around you. Nevertheless, it cannot be in our best interests to give the Sword to one of the Y'mordi.*

Tatsu began, "Even if what you said is true, what makes you think that I want to give it up?"

Y'ran laughed deeply. "Look at you. You both are relics now, thanks to that Sword. You would be dead in a few months if you kept it for that long. I know you do not want to keep that cursed blade. You would be fools to do so."

"Perhaps, you are right," remarked Tatsu without lowering his long, silvery blade. "However, what makes us not just throw it away? Why would we give it up to our enemy on the day of a battle as great as this one?"

Y'ran hissed, "You know the power of that blade. You throw it away, and it could end up in anyone's hands. Power belongs with those who know how to use it."

Kohana snarled back, "Power belongs with those who will not abuse it, shadow scum."

Smiling, Y'ran said, "Of all the Y'mordi, I am the one least likely to even use this weapon against you all. There is someone looking for that Sword, and he will find it if you keep it. He will kill you if he finds you. If you throw it away or hide it, he will find it and still kill you. He is a traitor to the Light, and even your Lux could not protect you from the hands of this man." He folded his arms. "The Spirit Swords have powers in Oathkeeping. Use yours on me. It will prove I do not lie."

At the challenge, the Sword glowed with silver light of its own accord. Tatsu gripped it with both hands in surprise. In both his and Kohana's minds, they heard a voice whisper, "He speaks the truth, but his identity is a façade." The light shot out from the Sword and surrounded Y'ran.

When the light faded, Y'ran's black robe faded into black wisps, transforming into a red draping suit, and a crown appeared on his head. It did not take long for Tatsu and Kohana to recognize the person standing before them, though they knew that it was the very same person who had threatened their lives years ago.

"You are Lord Ferro?" asked Tatsu in wonder. "That's how you disappeared all those years ago. You became an Y'mordi...Why did you do this?"

Y'ran folded his arms as the red robes faded into black once more, and his crown vanished. "The Dark Lord Dagan promised immense power to those who joined him, and I wanted that power more than anything else. However, I want a backup plan in case this battle does not play out as I have planned, which is why I need that Sword."

Although Tatsu was tempted to ask what Y'ran's main plan was, he regarded the Sword in his hands hesitantly, "This is your *backup plan*? You do not plan on using it in today's battle?"

At first, Y'ran struggled mentally with the right answer, and finally, he said, "No, I will not use it during today's battle. As a matter of fact, as soon as you give it to me, I will place it somewhere safe, somewhere hidden, where only I will be able to find it." Y'ran stood relaxed on the hill overlooking the dragon and soldier, but he did not raise his hammer. For a dark-robed Y'mordi, he appeared as non-threatening as possible.

Tatsu sighed as he asked curiously, "Why do you not just kill me for it? Usually, the Y'mordi are a little more aggressive about their wants."

Y'ran grunted. "You will find that I am not like the other Y'mordi. I do not kill you solely for the reason of my respect for you both. Not even I would stand against the two of you in battle."

"Respect?" growled Kohana in surprise.

"Yes," replied Y'ran hesitantly. "You are both strong and independent of the rest of the world. You do not stick to many of the world's stereotypes and rules. Rather, you make your own rules and demand for your rules to be followed. Regardless of what you were told when your bond first formed, you stuck together. You went against Lux's strict military procedures and methods, and made your own. I respect that." Y'ran felt quite awkward talking so highly of someone beside himself.

Both Kohana and Y'ran were extremely stunned when Tatsu threw his Spirit Sword to the Y'mordi. "Take it," said Tatsu softly. "Since what you say about the traitor after us is true, I will not risk our lives over a blade. Just leave us alone." Then, he climbed up to his spot on Kohana's back.

*Tatsu…*she started.

However, he interrupted, *No, Kohana, he is right. We will not need that Sword anymore. Even for today's battle, we do not need that Sword to be great fighters. Plus, look at it this way: If Dagan wins today, then Y'ran will not need the Sword after all. If the Great Lord Lux wins, then Y'ran will be dead anyways. No matter what, the Sword is going to be pretty useless to him. He is offering to hide it for us. What is the worst that could happen to us?*

Kohana countered, *He could kill us with it later.*

Before she could take off, Y'ran spoke to Tatsu, "Listen, I want you to know something. There might be a way for you to go back to your real age."

Kohana's wings hesitated then. "What did you say?" she asked loudly.

Though he had not wanted to bring it up, he could not help but feel as if he owed the duo a debt. After all, he had tried to kill Tatsu years ago, and then he just took their Spirit Sword. "This is the strangest thing, but I believe that simply being in the air can reverse the effects. The Sword's Element is Wind. It makes sense."

"Being in the air?" repeated Tatsu doubtfully.

"Yes, I know that it is how the others had to get rid of your temporary *mysteria* barrier that you created when you cut them off with the Sword. Just a thought for you."

Then, he summoned a Gate that boiled the water around it.

Tatsu now had a standard steel sword and was quite content with it. It was roughly the same weight as the Spirit Sword, and it moved as freely. His eyes scanned the area below them in wonder. He had never in his entire life seen so many soldiers marching to battle. On the horizon, he could see the enemy troops approaching. The whole scene seemed surreal to him. "Kohana, if we do not make it out of here alive today, I just want you to know how much I love you."

Kohana replied simply, "I love you too."

They hovered for a while with the only sounds being the beating wings of Kohana. Steadily, they began to be able to see the Black Dragons that Dagan had acquired and had more than likely trained for battle quite well. The two of them knew that their responsibilities lay in defeating the enemy navy and Dragons first. Then, they would need to begin devastating the heavy artillery. However, such tasks were beginning to seem more and more impossible as they watched the enemy's armies multiply into thousands.

The White Dragon tilted her head up to the cloudy sky and released a spell of Ice, a white frozen ball of light, into the cosmos. As her head tilted back down, snow started to fall from the clouds. She said to Tatsu rather softly, "No matter what happens to us, this blizzard will remain for at least a few days. It will be a temporary legacy for us, I suppose."

Tatsu grinned, "Kohana, I am sure that after today, one snowstorm is not going to be our legacy."

Kohana retorted with a smile of her own, "Oh? You have something bigger in mind, then? What are you going to do? A cartwheel on the battlefield?"

The old man on her back chuckled humorously as he patted the back of her neck. "Maybe not this time, Kohana, but I think we can give them a battle to remember."

Then, the troops below them began to charge ferociously.

"It looks like it is time, love," said Tatsu with a sigh.

"So, it is time, then. Are you ready?"

"I am ready when you are."

As the snowstorm intensified to tremendous levels, claiming the sky as theirs, Kohana and Tatsu darted through the snow to engage the Black Dragons in battle.

Once they were close enough, Kohana began firing spells of Ice at her flying enemies. While a couple dropped to the ground, instantly frozen, many of them dodged the spells and came at Kohana with swords ready.

Tatsu switched bodies with Kohana, and he began using her claws to fend off the many deadly swords and began slashing at their exposed bellies when they raised their swords for another attack.

Meanwhile, Kohana used Tatsu's body and his new wand, and summoned icicles to throw at the Black Dragons. Several of these pierced through their thin armor.

The light snow continued to fall on the scattered bodies of the troops, both of Dagan's armies and of Lux's armies. Across the rotting field, there were several scorch marks that had been created when Lux and Dagan had begun fighting. The flash of light from the collision of the Sword of Destiny and the Behemoth had caused both of them to vanish along with many of the people who were close in proximity to them.

Everyone else had been killed by the blast.

A tall man with long, red, flowing hair stood there, though. Amidst the field of corpses, this man with green eyes stood mournfully. Step by step, his feet began to crunch through the two foot deep layer of snow and took him to the center of the battlefield. Here, the snow had melted and was just beginning to lace the wet soil again.

He could clearly see the imprint in the snow where the spectacular White Dragon had crashed onto the field and had begun fighting Shadows and many Y'mordi alongside her rider. He approached that imprint and began looking for any trace of where everyone could have gone. Along with that, he had the slightest piece of hope that one of the Spirit Swords was there. Thinking about those mystical Swords caused him to put a shaking hand on the hilt of his own Steel of Life, the blade that had constructed a barrier around him once the flash of light had appeared. However, there was not a single trace to be found. Tatsu's Sword was nowhere to be found. They had all died or disappeared.

A Servant in the Emperor's Council

In the throne room, the Y'mordi buzzed with emotion. "He killed Arnim!" roared Sarn at Pullatus.

Xarden smirked maliciously, "She will be fine. Wait a few minutes, and she will back here at the Palace perfectly healthy. Don't worry about it."

Sarn continued to yell at Xarden, "I don't think you understand: He killed Arnim! That stupid, filthy Golden Dragon killed Arnim! He needs to pay for this! We need to...we need to all go after him or something!" Despite knowing that her sister would be back shortly, she had never been in a situation where Arnim was killed in battle.

Pullatus responded, "You would like for us to have vengeance on the Guardian of Light?"

"Yes, yes!" exclaimed Sarn with a mischievous grin on her face.

Pullatus stood finally and remarked, "Do you want to lead the Y'mordi on your own then?"

At these words, everyone was silent. Though he had hardly changed his tone, the change in direction of his words alone was enough for them to realize that he was not in a pleasant mood. He continued just as softly, "Rexam Draconis will hopefully fail at the hands of the Great Servant of the Darkness. If he does not, then the Golden Dragon shall be a priority for another day. Remember that killing the Guardians of Light is by no means our highest priority. It is merely a means of making our control easier. I am still seeking the third Great Servant of the Darkness, and once I find this one, we shall use him, as well. Our actions shall remain the same until we have obtained the blood of all seven of the Great Servants of the Darkness. We already have Maris's. Is this understood, Sarn?"

Sarn bowed politely as she replied, "Yes, Lord Y'tal. The Guardians of Light are not our highest priority."

Pullatus sat back down in the black throne of the Palace of Shadows. "Good, Sarn. Now, I need you to return to Sharl Vran and observe the Great Servant. Do not under any circumstances offer him aid. This battle is his alone, but I want you to be ready in case he falls."

"Yes, Lord Y'tal," repeated Sarn as she exited through a Gate, still shaken by both Arnim's temporary death and Pullatus's reaction to it. Her pride was shattered.

Ixion remarked cheerfully, "I have spread the rumors wide and far, Y'tal."

"That is good news, Ixion. I am assuming that you have succeeded in rigging the battle, Xarden?"

"Yeah, I got it rigged, alright," said Xarden confidently. "In a few minutes, I am going to have to summon the Gate for the Prince, and when he enters, he will fight Gaspard on his turf. He has no idea about the trap. Meanwhile, I am going to get rid of the Prophet's Time spell and lead Gaspard's troops into battle."

"That is even better news. Tell me, Xarden: do you think Gaspard can defeat the Prince of Light?"

Xarden shrugged, unsure, "Who knows? They are both phenomenal swordsmen. Gaspard has several advantages in that he knows the area well, and he has the stronger Sword. However, the Prince of Light can use *mysteria*, and he has someone he is trying to save. I suppose that the most reasonable thing to do is to hope that at least the Prince of Light becomes wounded, because surely, that much will happen."

Pullatus nodded in understanding. While he was sure that all of the Y'mordi together could easily overpower the Prince, he still wanted their identities to remain in the dark for now. "Very well. Xarden, go to the Prince of Light, and we shall see how well he fares. If luck truly is with Gaspard, then perhaps, he will indeed maim the Prince of Light in some fashion or another. You are dismissed."

Once Xarden had disappeared through a Gate, Ixion began, "Lord Y'tal, what would you like for me to do?"

However, Pullatus had already left his throne and went to one of the massive windows of the hall. "I sense that Randir and Mali have found nothing on Earth yet. Perhaps, it is a myth after all."

"Sir?" inquired Ixion in puzzlement.

Suddenly, Ixion felt waves of pain cripple his body, and he collapsed to the ground, writhing in that stinging force. He began screaming in pain, and finally, after several seconds, it subsided to a numbing throb.

Pullatus spoke harshly then, "None of these plans are beginning to work. The Dragon should not have made it as far as he has. Apolis has been without an Emperor of Light for five years, yet it has stood. The Prince of Light has returned unscathed, and even our attempts at finding the Black Joker on Earth have failed."

Then, Ixion was flung across the floor to the opposite wall by an unseen force. Pullatus had not even blinked beneath his hood. Ixion groaned in his pain.

"With every action we make, we come a step closer and closer to revealing ourselves to the world, and there are several who already know of our existence." Casually, he strode over to where Ixion was crumpled on the floor. As an invisible spell lifted the short Y'mordi into the water and pressed him against the wall, Pullatus continued, "Why am I met time and time again with these disappointments, Y'xon?"

Ixion stammered, "Sir, I-I-I-I don't—"

Under his hood, Pullatus's eyes moved to the left, and Ixion's screaming body was thrown into the back wall causing his body to explode. Along with releasing sprays of blood, the fleshy mass expelled several streams of black mist.

Pullatus's thin mouth curved into a wicked smile as the body deteriorated into black mist. "All things fade, Ixion. Someday, we, too, will fade. However, until we get to that point, we will do as we vowed to do when we made an oath to the Great Lord of the Darkness. That Darkness is what binds us even now."

Then, he became aware of Arnim's respawning presence. A hundred tendrils of black smoke appeared and gradually began to twine around themselves to create a humanoid shape. After several seconds, the shape began to breathe, and with that first breath, the mist vanished revealing Arnim in her black robe. She did not have to raise her head to know that Pullatus was standing there. "Lord Y'tal, forgive me for failing you at Sharl Vran." She did not feel a need to explain herself. She had learned from Sarn's previous mistakes that Pullatus was not fond of any excuses.

"You are forgiven, Arnim." Calmly, Pullatus approached his throne again. "If you had only arrived a few minutes earlier, you would have been here for our meeting. There is no harm done, however. Your sister filled me in on most of the goings-on at Sharl Vran. She has already returned there and is going to supervise the battle there."

As soon as she saw and recognized Ixion's fading body, she knew that now was a time to take Pullatus quite seriously. "Lord Y'tal, what would you like me to do for now?"

"Arnim," began Pullatus coolly. "I find myself in quite a pleasant mood at the moment. Though we have encountered several rough spots over the years, the Y'mordi remain close to the Guardians of Light. What I want you to do is to speak to our friend in the Emperor's Council and ensure that this War will continue, regardless of what happens to Gaspard today. I feel that I would truly appreciate his reassurance. He has been a Servant of the Darkness for a long time. I only wish that he was a Great Servant of the Darkness. He has been quite a valuable asset over the years, would you not agree, Arnim?"

To this question, Arnim eagerly nodded and simply summoned a Gate. "Shall I report back here when I am finished, Lord Y'tal?" She was trying her hardest to avoid looking at the almost fully evaporated body that had once been Ixion. She figured that it would not take him long to be reborn, because he had been killed here in the Palace of Shadows.

"Yes, that shall be fine, Arnim. I will be waiting for your return." With a slight bow from the waist, Arnim left.

In a pristine side street in Apolis, two figures convened. "Lord Y'tal wishes to know if the War will continue even if Gaspard is to be defeated today," explained Arnim softly to the spindly, old man in the white robe before her. He had always been free with his information, a true Servant of the Darkness.

"Even if Gaspard is killed today, there is no way that the War will end. The Prince might do something crazy, but I cannot see him being able to both satisfy the anger of the rebels and keep the Emperor Regin on his side. The Emperor Regin is not a man that one can compromise with."

Arnim grunted in acknowledgment and then replied, "Is the Council going to be stable if the Prince does take the Throne? The Guardians of Light are quite revolutionary, it seems."

The man growled at her, "You do not think that I know that already? Marqest is a Guardian of Light inside the Council in case you have not forgotten, and it is misery trying to get him to agree to anything. The relic is relentless, and he is hard to keep in line."

"You did not answer my question."

The man's eyes widened in surprise. "Well...I am confident that the boy will have little sway over the Council's affairs. He did not show any true potential in leadership when I met him five years ago, and I certainly do not think that he has gained that in his absence. I would be lying to you if I told you that I thought that John had been a great leader, but I am utterly confident that his son will not be even half of that."

"That is good, Servant," Arnim muttered quietly. "I suppose that Lord Y'tal will be rather pleased."

"I am more than just a Servant," the old man remarked.

"No," rebutted Arnim with a flat tone. "You are a Servant of the Darkness and nothing more. And if you ever choose to think otherwise, it will take little effort for Lord Y'tal to kill you as painfully as possible."

"Little effort?" the man smirked. "I am sure it would take your leader more than that to kill me. I am not so old and frail as you would think, Y'mir."

To demonstrate, he attempted to raise his own scepter, but as soon as he lowered his hand, Arnim's gun was pointed straight at his forehead. He swallowed nervously. "Your words will give Lord Y'tal relief. He probably will not need to check in again for who knows how long."

"So?"

Arnim put the gun closer to his head. "So, that means that you are really unnecessary. I could kill you right now, and my master would have no qualms with me. You are a tool, a dispensable, cheap, worn out tool. You are a Servant of the Darkness and nothing more. Do you understand me?"

The man nodded. "Yes."

"That is much better." Then, Arnim summoned a Gate to return to the Palace of Shadows with the information she had been sent to retrieve.

Though the man had seconds ago had his life threatened by one of the Y'mordi, a smile lit up his face. He felt infinitely superior to the fifth-in-command of the Y'mordi. While six of the Y'mordi saw him as merely a Servant of the Darkness, there was one of them that knew his true form. That one was Pullatus himself.

"One day, we shall meet again, Pullatus, and when we do, the world would have changed a lot. It will be the time for my Rebirth. One more piece is still missing, though."

Then, Master Valdridge began returning to the Palace of Light for a meeting with the rest of the Emperor's Council.

Floating in the swirling cloud of darkness that was his own mind and spirit, Ixion struggled to be reborn into the Palace of Shadows. He could still feel the pain of death everywhere, but worse than that, he felt fear. Never before had Pullatus lashed out at him like that. He knew it was not a billionth of the Y'mordi leader's capabilities, but it still worried him that Pullatus thought of him as little more than a living punching bag.

Throughout his whole life, people had picked on him and despised him for what he was. He had been born in the capital of Rulia, Pureau, as a rat anima and an orphan named Ixion Medora. For years, he had had to steal for a living. He had not killed a single soul, until he had met the expert thief, Master Buay. The somewhat fatherly, yet too often drunk, man had taught Ixion everything he knew: how to steal, how to walk without anyone hearing his footsteps, how to hide, and most importantly, how to kill properly.

As soon as ten-year-old Ixion Medora had learned enough to be able to survive on his own, he had slit his master's throat in the night, the smell of the man's blood and alcohol filling the small hideout.

When the Dark Lord Dagan had been looking for those strong enough to serve him as his immortal soldiers, Ixion had leaped with glee at the opportunity that had presented itself to him and volunteered. Simplest to him had been the Trial of Will. Unlike the other Y'mordi, he truly had not had any traumatizing memories. Ixion's only fear was of death itself, and even that was not a paralyzing fear. He had never had any real commitments, so it was hard for him to be broken. The hardest Trial had been the Trial of Heart, the test of *mysteria*. Though he was rather skilled in the Element of Nature, it was a rather useless Element in battle most of the time. Thick trees could block most spells, but most attack spells in Nature were poison-based. Lord Dagan's *mysteria*-manipulating Shadows were immune to poison. Still, he had passed the test and had become the lowest-ranked Y'mordi.

Gradually, he began to feel his torso come into being.

He opened his heart steadily to the flow of *mysteria* and was surprised to find that Arnim was nowhere to be found in the Darkness. That could only mean that she had already respawned in the Palace. He was, however, glad that he had been killed in the Palace of Shadows rather than in another place. It meant that he would have less time in this excruciatingly painful state. He had to relive his fear of death over and over again as he had been the Lord of the Shadows to die the most frequently, usually due to Pullatus sending him on missions he simply did not have the skill to complete or due to his own ineptitude.

Then, he felt his arms and legs grow back. The pain subsided slightly as he felt life enter him once again, water filling his gasping lungs, instantly aware of coolness and heat.

It was rather appalling to him that Pullatus had thrown him into a wall as if he were nothing more than a rag doll or an unwanted tool. It definitely put his life into a new perspective. Over the years, he had served Pullatus as a spy, a thief, an assassin, and a scout. His abilities to sneak and steal had been his most prized possessions, yet no one else seemed to find his abilities as useful as he thought they were.

In the midst of the Darkness, his heart sighed heavily. He was becoming more and more tired of being treated like a pile of dirt, by Randir, Xarden, Pullatus, everyone. However, there was not much he could do to truly redeem himself in the eyes of his peers.

Suddenly, an idea came to him. He knew what he had to do to earn more respect. However, it would take quite a bit of time in preparation, potentially several years. He had to be strong.

Finally, his head appeared, and he could see the dark wisps that were surrounding his body. He waited uncomfortably as the Darkness filled his insides, providing him with organs and flesh. As the itching and squirming feelings passed, he was able to take a breath. Once he inhaled the intoxicating Darkness, it began to fade, and he could make out the throne room of the Palace of Shadows.

Arnim and Pullatus were already standing there and talking amongst themselves. Ixion immediately knelt before Pullatus, "Forgive me, Lord Y'tal. I did not mean to insult you so."

The leader of the Y'mordi responded softly, "Your errors are forgiven now, Ixion. Arnim has just returned from talking to our friend in the Emperor's Council and has revealed that our position there is rather secure."

"That is rather good news, my Lord," replied Ixion brightly.

"Yes," said Pullatus. "Yes, it is. However, I have a mission for the two of you to accomplish now."

Arnim muttered, "What would that be, Lord Y'tal?"

He explained, "I need for the two of you to go to Macela. I have found reason to believe that one of the Great Lord of the Darkness's five Demons can be found on that island. I do not know which one it is, but I am sure that it could be of some use to us, nevertheless."

"Lord Y'tal, is it not a little early to be calling upon the Demons?" asked Ixion nervously, aware of the high, powerful nature of the mindless beasts that had been Dagan's favorite pets.

"Actually, I would agree with you if it was not for one of the Demons being found and exterminated already."

Arnim was stunned by this revelation, "One of the Demons was killed? How is this possible? They were blessed with the Great Lord of the Darkness's own power."

Pullatus continued, "One of the Guardians of Light, the anima from the Northern Continent, had killed the Spider in one of the caves there five years ago, destroyed it with several spells. Something had likely caused it to awaken, but the coming of the Guardians of Light at that exact same time must be more than a coincidence. Perhaps, the Demons are sensing their approach and are trying to fight against their Light. Regardless of the reason, I would rather that we have complete control over these Demons now, instead of them waking up prematurely and then getting themselves killed. Now, I need the two of you to go and investigate that mountain island. Go, now."

Ixion followed Arnim into her Gate.

Behind them, Pullatus smiled beneath his hood. Even if his plans were not working now, he was going to prepare for the next time that he had one of the Great Servants of the Darkness in his grasp. He would be much more prepared next time.

Morgana's Seal

A s soon as Randir and Mali entered the circle of stacked stones, their shoes flattening the dew-wet grass, the entire Ring of Elders appeared around them. Instantly, the Elders drew their wands, and spells erupted from every wand to attack the two Y'mordi. Randir and Mali stood back to back, using their individual weapons to shield off the constant barrage of spells that trapped them inside the stone circle.

Mali commented, "Well, I think we found where the Black Joker is concealed, would you not agree?"

"It appears we have certainly found something, Hector," replied Randir with a soft nod. "I am wondering where the head is, though, and her young apprentice."

"Heh, I do not think that they matter right now. I am going to try to sense any barriers." Cautiously, Mali opened his heart to *mysteria* and began examining the area while his katanas were still fiercely fending off the spells of the Elders. Then, he sensed something extraordinary. "Victor, that stone in the middle. There is some kind of aura surrounding it."

Randir snarled, "Well, it is not like we can just stop blocking these shots and worry about that. These Elders are going to have to go."

"Fine, protect yourself for a little while," Mali remarked, and before Randir could protest, Mali was gone in a flash of Light. Instantly, Randir began to notice that the Elders started falling, their clothes stained red. Finally, the surviving Elders realized that Mali was attacking them too fast to see, manipulating a Light spell, and they changed targets from Randir to Mali. He blocked the blasts with his katanas, and Randir started his assault on the Elders by tossing several scorching fireballs at them.

However, green see-through barriers shimmered into existence around the Elders. In Mali's surprise, one of the Elders blasted him painfully against one of the large rocks with a Force spell. Then, Randir saw the caster of the barriers. It was the head: She had finally entered the battle, though her apprentice was still nowhere to be found. As soon as the other Elders realized that she was there, they stopped casting spells.

The head roared, though everything was quiet now, "Randir, this must end! I have told you that I do not know where the Black Joker is, and I told you the truth. However, I know without a doubt that he is not here."

"Then, why is there a barrier here?" he inquired.

Elizabeth sighed, "There was someone imprisoned here. This is true, Randir, but it is not the Black Joker. There was an evil witch several centuries ago named Morgana, and I will readily admit she is powerful, though not a tenth as powerful as the Black Joker was. She was imprisoned in that altar for a number of crimes, for punishment. You unleash her, and the Ring will imprison her again. She is not as powerful as your Black Joker."

Randir stammered with rage, "So, you are expecting me to believe that you imprisoned a weakling here?"

"Yes, Randir," Elizabeth replied. "I am expecting you to believe that. It is the truth. She was not too powerful for us unlike the Black Joker. It was a punishment for her crimes. There is no Black Joker here. Whatever made you think that he was here was a good guess, but it was wrong."

Randir said coldly, "It seems like I have a choice here." He noticed Mali start to get up then. "I can leave you alone and leave Earth empty-handed. I could release this Morgana, and if she is who you say she is, then she could kill several people before being captured again. If it is the Black Joker, I would be able to use him. It seems to be in my best interest to go on ahead and try to free whoever it is."

Mali rapidly brought down another Elder, and the spells began again to fly across the circle of stones. Randir and Elizabeth, however, ignored the other Elders. They were focused on each other.

A stream of Flame left Randir's outstretched hand and moved like a snake to strike Elizabeth. She swished her wand, and an equally powerful stream of Liquid circled around her and then destroyed Randir's spell as it tried to engulf him.

He rapidly constructed a shield of Heat that evaporated the water as it came near him. As soon as she dispelled her water, he shot a bolt of Lightning at her. She leaped forward at the same time that she divided his spell with her own spell of Force. The red Lightning began to encircle the area and stayed connected to the outer ring of Stonehenge. It created a wall of sorts that prevented anyone else from entering.

Cameron and Helen stepped through the Gate and appeared in the plains outside of Stonehenge. Instantly, they were surrounded by several spells that were going back and forth. Cameron immediately created a barrier around them. As they looked around, they became aware that many of the Elders were fighting one of the Lords of the Shadows. Once Cameron began to sense his master, he found that she was inside the now shielded Stonehenge. The formation of rocks had a wall of red Lightning surrounding it, so that no one could step into it. Though he felt a strong urge to help her, he saw how many of the Elders were falling to this other Y'mordi.

"Helen, do you see that guy in the white robe who keeps darting about really quickly?"

"Yeah, so what?"

"I am going to go after him first," replied Cameron.

"I? Don't you mean we?" inquired Helen with a brave smile.

"No, I mean I. This barrier is centered around you. That means that no spell can hit you, and you can't cast any spells either. They would just bounce around on the inside of this bubble. You would be putting yourself in even more danger if you tried." Then, before she could protest, he stepped outside the barrier and began heading toward the skirmish.

His wand pointed at Mali, and he cast a complicated Earth spell to alter Mali's katanas, weakening their physical makeup. The next time that the Y'mordi tried to block a spell with his swords, the katanas shattered due to their new weakness. The Elders' next spells blasted Mali several yards backward. Once Mali tried to get back up, Cameron shot a bullet of steel from his wand by using another Earth spell.

The bullet pierced through the Y'mordi's side, and his hands went to clench the wound. Without pausing, the remaining Elders simultaneously released spells of Force at Mali. The strength of the invisible blast was equivalent to the force of an eighteen-wheeler on the interstate. Mali did not stand a chance against the spell.

Helen ran up to Cameron with the barrier still surrounding her. "Cameron, where is my mom? She's not in there, is she?" she asked as she pointed to the electric formation of Stonehenge.

Cameron sighed, "I am afraid that she is. It would be better if you stayed here, Helen."

Before he could walk away from her, he felt an immense flare of *mysteria* in the area. He knew at once that it had come from Helen. He turned and could clearly see the furious glare in her eyes. "I want to come, too," she muttered.

He shook his head, "Helen, you don't know any spells. What in the world makes you think that I would let you go in there? You can't fight!"

"Yes, I can. I am sure that I could create some of those simple blasts anyways."

Then, Cameron put his wand inside her barrier. A purple cloud of Poison entered it and put her to sleep instantly. "It's for your own good," he murmured as he turned to face the stones with the Elders beside him.

It took two of the remaining six Elders to dispel the wall of Lightning. Instantly, the Elders began repeating Cameron's spell of Earth to create bullets to shoot at Randir.

The red-haired Y'mordi was standing over Elizabeth's collapsed body which was resting on the central stone of the formation. As soon as Cameron got close, one of the Elders cast a sidelong spell of Force at him that sent him flying outside the formation, seeing Cameron as not strong enough for this fight.

He looked up in a frustrated shock. Instantly, Randir swung his hammer, and a thick beam of Flame emanated from the metal head. It formed a thick ring of inferno that shot forward and wrapped around several of the Elders, and they fell back as they attempted to extinguish the fires.

Cameron watched as Randir held a knife high over Elizabeth's body. Quickly, he stood and shot a spell of Force at Randir. The spell knocked the knife out of the Y'mordi's hand.

The red-haired man regarded Cameron angrily. "Finally, the apprentice shows up. Now, however, your master is not in a state to save you. Would you challenge me alone, boy?" he asked. "I am ready to end this now if you are."

Cameron spat at the black-robed Y'mordi, "You ask me if I would challenge you alone? You are one to talk. You had to have your friend help you, even before my master arrived last time. I ask you now: Would you challenge me alone?"

Randir leaped at Cameron with his long hammer flailing and his voice roaring furiously.

Ducking to avoid the attack, Cameron followed up with a spell of Force to attempt to knock Randir backward. The Y'mordi was knocked into a large stone, but he quickly recuperated and shot a fireball toward Cameron.

After blocking the fireball, he asked Randir, "Why were you going to kill her in cold blood like that? You could have been destroying the barrier."

"Simple, the barrier cries out for the drink of blood."

Cameron gradually understood, "The barrier…needs a sacrifice?"

"Yes," replied Randir as the two began to circle the stone altar. "I figured the head of the Ring of Elders might like to be that sacrifice. Boy, you had better back down now. I was able to defeat her, so what makes you think that you can do any better? If you try, you will only get yourself killed."

"You're wrong," remarked Cameron stubbornly.

"What?"

"I may not be as strong as my master is," he said as he stepped closer to Randir, "but I can do some things that she can't."

Randir smirked, "Oh? And what abilities might you possess? Can you Teleport? Can you perform a Heartlock? A Heartbind? Can you even sustain your own life solely through the forces of *mysteria*? There are so many of the ancient powers. Do you possess a single one of those, boy?"

Cameron's lip trembled in fear for a moment, but he stood his ground, raising his wand at the Y'mordi. "No, I do not have any one of those."

"Just as I thought," muttered Randir. Then, Randir created a more focused spell of Heat that warmed up the base of Cameron's wand, and in pain, the young apprentice dropped the wand onto the grass.

Randir summoned a beam of liquid Lava, and suddenly, Cameron did something entirely unexpected by either of them. A thick stream of Water appeared in front of his chest and shot forward, without his using a wand. A wand was designed so that it could focus a person's *mysteria* and make the transition from the heart to the physical world easier. It took quite a gifted mage to be able to cast spells without the use of a wand, scepter, or other aid. Indeed, it was often just a talent a person could be born with, a talent that none of the Elders possessed.

The Y'mordi all possessed the ability, but they had been practicing for centuries.

The two streams of *mysteria* collided at a central point, and the spells seemed to push against one another. It took little effort for Randir to be able to force the spells to move closer to Cameron. The apprentice could feel the intense heat come closer and closer to his body. Already, he was beginning to sweat.

"Enough," said a voice.

Both Cameron and Randir ceased their spells and looked to see that Elizabeth had arisen.

Randir growled, "Break this barrier, Elder. You cannot win against me."

"Maybe not," remarked Elizabeth simply. "However, I have assured you that the Black Joker is not here. You can go back to your leader in Gevás and tell him that such a person does not exist. You have hurt enough people here, and no matter how hard you try, we will keep trying to stop you. The only thing you are doing here is wasting your time and making our lives just as hard."

"But the Black Joker-?"

"-is not here," repeated Elizabeth. "Open your heart, Randir. Do you sense the wealth of power that you imagine the Black Joker would have? Of course, you do not. I do not know how many times that I am going to have to say it to make you believe me. He is not here."

With a sigh, Randir began dejectedly, "You know that even if I tell my leader that the Black Joker is not here, he will not relent. He has his eyes set on this world, and when he has such a goal, he does everything in his power to achieve it. Even if you underestimated me, it would be a million times more foolish if you underestimated him."

Elizabeth continued sternly and confidently, "So what? If he comes to fight, the Ring of Elders will meet him in battle. No amount of convincing will stop that."

"I just hope you know what you are getting yourselves into," explained Randir.

"We are aware of the consequences."

Randir chuckled then. "I am sure that you are. Very well, head of the Ring of Elders. I have fought, I have looked, I have killed, and I have exhausted all methods to find such a person as the Black Joker. It is going down in my book that the Black Joker does not exist."

This statement brought a slight grin on Elizabeth's face. "Thank you, Randir."

He wagged a finger threateningly at her. "Do not think that I am going to stay the nice guy the next time I come. My loyalty is to the will of the Darkness, not to the Y'mordi, not to you, not to anyone. Got it?"

Elizabeth nodded in a quiet understanding. "Thank you again for helping my son."

"I am not so sure that I will be able to do that again when I return to Gevás. I believe that he might take the Throne."

"What?" asked Elizabeth in puzzlement. "Dragenopn is here on Earth, not Gevás."

Randir shook his head. "No, he has been in Gevás for a couple of weeks now. Think about when the last time he called you was."

As she paled, he summoned a fiery Gate and left the air-filled, dusty world of Earth and returned to the watery world of Gevás.

Cameron approached Elizabeth hesitantly. "Master…what shall we do now?"

Her eyes regarded him coldly, "Cameron, was Helen with you?" Now, she had reason to be concerned for both her children.

He winced under her glare, "Yes, master. She kind of…bullied me into it, but I had her protected by a barrier, and when she tried to fight, I…put her under some sleeping gas. Forgive me for disobeying you…"

"The only thing that you have done wrong was not informing me of your ability to cast battle spells without a wand or any other aid. That was quite an impressive duel, my apprentice."

"You're not…mad?"

Elizabeth assessed her emotions carefully as she replied, "Well, I am not pleased that you disobeyed my orders, but I know how Helen can be, and it does not surprise me that she was able to bully you in the slightest. To be honest, I should have expected as much. You handled yourself today in a way that demonstrated how much I have taught you. I am proud that you did as well as you did."

"Thank you, master," said Cameron with a respectful bow. It was not often that the head of the Ring of Elders complimented him, and he made sure to show his gratitude when she did. It was a partnership that he wanted to develop for years yet.

"As for your question, I suppose that the first thing we need to do is to make sure that we can heal the Elders that survived and to wake up Helen. Then, we need to begin fixing the damage that was made to this place. It is an ancient structure, and I do not want for the seal that imprisoned Morgana to appear as if someone has tried to break it recently. Such a sign of weakness might encourage others to try their hand at it. The next thing will be to figure out where my son has gone. If Randir speaks the truth, then Dragenopn went to Gevás without telling me." She was not sure what that meant. Drage had left during the water world's time of war. She hoped Matthew and Aria were taking good care of him.

"Yes, master," responded Cameron as he began scanning the bodies of the remaining Elders to see if there were a few left that could be healed. As soon as he saw the rising chest of one of them, he ran to the older man's side and began weaving spells of Nature to heal the struggling body.

Tilgé's Hand

Across the grassy plain, Drage could see a Gate appear. It was his sign. At the same time, a scout roared, "The enemy is approaching!"

With a quick nod, Drage signaled to Derek, the Prophet of Wind. The old man rapidly created a spell of Time that froze the entire battlefield except for Drage, himself, and the Gate. The grass stopped waving in the current, the soldiers were immobile, and even the fish above were hung still in the water. After Derek gave the Prince of Light an encouraging smile, Drage ran toward the Gate with the Sword of Destiny in hand.

As long as time remained frozen, he would be able to come back and still save Matthew and the others. Though he was concerned about Matthew's being captured, he knew Matthew would come out of this ordeal safely.

Derek watched as Drage entered the Gate and was somewhat proud of himself for having offered this ability. Because of his abilities of Time, he had been able to help the Prince of Light. The boy seemed almost like a second son.

Then, Derek saw something in the corner of his eye. He turned to see that a black-robed figure was approaching him.

His eyes widened in horror. Someone had found a way to bypass the Time spell.

The figure raised a long, silver scepter and tapped it forcefully on the ground. Suddenly, his Time spell shattered, and both sides charged at one another, Shadows and rebels merging with Drage's soldiers with the ringing sounds of swords clashing filling the water.

In frustration, he reset the spell. When the Y'mordi realized that he was not going to give up, he came closer and shot Ice spells at Derek, the white frozen balls of light threatening to freeze Derek solid. Pushing up his sleeves, the Prophet of Wind started the duel with the Y'mordi Xarden.

Drage found himself in an ancient building. Stained glass windows towered above him, and vines and cracks lined the walls. The pale morning light crept in through many of the shattered windows and revealed the clouds of dust that filled the water.

Cautiously, Drage stepped forward. His feet crunched the loose rubble noisily with each hesitant step. The blue glow of the Sword of Destiny shimmered brightly, illuminating most of the narrow hallway. He could almost hear its voice inside his heart, compelling him to move forward into the next room. He could not sense Maris's spirit anywhere, but he knew it had to be around here somewhere. Surely, this was not a trap.

The warm temperature of the water revealed to him that this place was probably still somewhere in the Western Continent. Then, the current shifted inside the ancient building.

"Welcome to the Temple of the Spirits, your Majesty..." whispered a voice on the current.

Drage whirled around with his Sword ready, but there was no one to be found. His eyes darted around the hallway, but he could not see anyone.

The voice continued, "You have caused me great pains, your Majesty. Today, the wrongs you have committed will become repaid. Your death shall hardly be justification, but it will be a glorious start."

Drage's eyes squinted in confusion. "That doesn't sound like Maris…" he muttered. Then, he called out to the voice, "Who are you?"

Then, a figure appeared from the shadows of the hallway. "I am called Gaspard." The man wore a white, loose shirt and heavy armor for his waist and legs. In both hands, he held the extraordinarily large Behemoth which was shining with a golden glow. "I am here to kill you, your Majesty. Only then will this suffering end. Once you are gone, this War will come to a halt."

Drage gaped, horrified at what was happening. He could not believe that Gaspard was here. That meant that this whole deal *had* been a trap. Maris's spirit was likely not even here. Xarden had known that Drage would try to come here, and so he had placed Gaspard here.

Finally, he managed, "The Temple of the Spirits, you said? Where is this at? I can tell that we are in the Western Continent, but I can't figure out any more than that."

Gaspard replied calmly, "This is Saldir, my homeland. The people of Saldir have for centuries prayed to the Great Spirit and have anxiously awaited its return. Though your people find reason to believe that the anima are unholy and unclean, the people of Saldir have prayed to the spirits of the anima, the descendants of the Great Spirit."

Drage interrupted Gaspard's explanation, "Where is Matthew?"

Gaspard looked puzzled then. "Matthew? Who is Matthew? I have never heard of the person in my life."

As much as Drage wanted to attack him for the sole reason of lying about the fact, he could sense only truth in Gaspard's heart. "Gaspard, I don't know what's going on here, but something is not right. I think we were both tricked by the Y'mordi."

"The Y'mordi?" inquired Gaspard with the same confused expression. "What are you talking about? The Y'mordi have been dead for about a thousand years. I think you are the one who is trying to trick me." Without saying another word, he swung the Behemoth. Once gold met blue, brilliant sparks flared.

The two forces met on the battlefield with Aria and Tilgé leading Drage's troops and Xarden leading an army of Shadows. What seemed to be a thousand spells shot amongst the soldiers, a storm of shooting lights, and they decimated Shadows and armored soldiers left and right. Blood spurted through the water, and fireballs exploded like cannons across the armies.

Among the panicked melee, Bryco rushed to find Tilgé. His face was pale as he knew what he had to do. Maksimilian had only repeated his previous order as the battle had begun, though Bryco remained hesitant.

As soon as he found the lightly armored Brigadier fighting the Shadows in a flurry of attacks, he approached and called out to him, "Tilgé!"

The Brigadier looked at him with that fierce look of battle upon his face. "What is it?"

Bryco came closer and continued to fight with his back facing Tilgé's own back. "I have to tell you something, and I need you to listen to the whole thing before you say anything, alright?"

Tilgé responded with a compliant grunt.

"Tilgé…" Bryco started hesitantly. "I know we have been far from good friends. If anything, we have been slight rivals, and I am not trying to change that at all."

"What's your point, Bryco?" interrupted Tilgé.

Bryco snapped back, "Be quiet and listen." Tilgé winced in surprise at Bryco's sudden aggression. "Maksimilian wants me to kill you." Then, Tilgé's eyes widened considerably. "He thinks you don't have the necessary discipline to lead the Brigade, so he wants me to kill you and take your place."

Tilgé hesitated before speaking softly, his tone betraying his hurt, "Are you going to?"

"No," responded Bryco with a look of pain in his eyes. "I could not do it, no matter how much I can't stand you. Even if you are not the most disciplined of us, you don't deserve to die for it."

"So, what are you going to do?"

"I don't know. I suppose after this battle, he will probably kill me."

Tilgé killed one of the Shadows and whirled around to face Bryco. "I can't allow that to happen. Look, you could say that you killed me, and I will just disappear. If he is wanting me dead, he will make sure that it happens. I have to get out of here regardless."

Bryco shook his head, "It's not that simple." He blocked another attack from the Shadows before blasting it with a spell of Light. "He told me that he wants your head."

"Fine, say that you disintegrated me with one of those funny spells of yours. I've seen you do it. Then, you can give him this." Without allowing Bryco even a moment to protest, he took his own sword and cut off his hand.

Matthew, Lilian, and Senagul were trapped in a cage at the rear of Gaspard's forces. Senagul was the first to awaken, and as he looked around him, his excitement rose. "Wow, a real battle!"

Lilian groaned as she woke up steadily. "Sena? What's going on?" She rose onto her four hooves shakily, "Where are we?" Gradually, she realized that they were in the middle of a raging battlefield, and they were prisoners. "Matthew, wake up."

The dark-haired young man got up and muttered, "Lilian, what is happening?"

Senagul responded, "We are in a battle! It's awesome!"

Matthew snapped awake fully and stood in the cage. "I am assuming that this metal is resisting any spells?" he asked Lilian. She nodded sadly.

"I can get us out of here!" exclaimed Senagul gleefully. He managed to squeeze his furry body through one of the narrow gaps between the bars.

Lilian and Matthew were quite astonished to find that he could indeed fit through the tight gaps. Matthew asked, "Sena, can you go and find Drage? Or even Aria? We can't get out of here by ourselves."

"Be careful, though," added Lilian with worry.

Then, the squirrel anima scrambled amid the battling soldiers to try to find Aria or Drage.

In the Temple of the Spirits, Drage blocked another slash of the blade of the Behemoth. It took all his strength to do even that much, but he was able to attempt several strikes in retaliation at Gaspard. Once Drage could start a powerful combo of attacks, it took a lot of effort for Gaspard to be able to stop it and put in his own attack. The way of the Dragon allowed Drage multiple moves before Gaspard could even attack, but Gaspard's way of the Shark constantly surprised Drage, with strong attacks forcing Drage gradually back toward the wall.

As Drage learned from his mistakes and tired, he pressed himself forward until Gaspard found himself being pressed backward toward the room where the altar of the Great Spirit was held.

The Sword of Destiny reached to take off Gaspard's arm, but it met only the blade of the Behemoth, causing sparks to explode from the collision. Gaspard took a step backward at the same time he swung the massive Sword around to try to hit Drage, but the younger man ducked and was able to aim a kick upward at Gaspard's hands.

In pain, Gaspard dropped the Sword and found the Sword of Destiny pointed at his throat.

"*Lies, Gaspard. Do not believe the lies…*" repeated the mysterious voice that had never left his head since he had received the Behemoth.

Drage heard it, too. "What was that?"

Taking the opportunity, Gaspard turned and ran toward the room with the altar.

Drage followed him in pursuit, filled with a strange pull on his heart toward the altar. As soon as they both entered the room, he understood what the force was. He could sense the essence of the Great Spirit all around him, a tremendous force that rippled and sparked in the water around them. Suddenly, he felt his heart being forced open, and the Sword of Destiny exploded in blue light once again.

He began to hear voices then, but Gaspard could not hear anything. The swordsman had no idea what was going on around him. Only the blue light flooded his vision.

"Dragenopn Helius, Prince of Light, you have been deceived," began the voice. *"I now possess the spirit of Maris. When he died five years ago, his spirit moved on to a higher place. He no longer holds the curse on you."*

"What?" inquired Drage. "That's not right. I can still feel his Darkness inside me." His heart pounded, refusing to believe what he was hearing. "It still eats at me. If he does not hold it, then who does?"

The voice responded, *"No one holds it, Prince Helius. The Darkness that is inside of your heart is yours alone. Everyone has some Darkness in their hearts. You only became aware of it when you had learned what Darkness felt like. When Maris faded, you noticed that there was Darkness left behind, but it was never his Darkness. You feel as much evil and temptation as the rest of the world. You have been deceived."*

He looked distantly into the core of the blue light. "The Darkness...has been me all along?" He considered the idea before saying, "Are you the Great Spirit?"

"No, I am merely a remnant of that entity. I have resided in the Sword of Destiny since the time of the Obsidian Wars. Perhaps, one day, I would like to reunite with the other four remnants, but that day shall not be today. Prince Helius, it is not that you should hate your Darkness. It is that you should love your Light."

Then, as quickly as it had come, the light vanished, and Drage was alone with Gaspard in the room.

"What just happened?" Gaspard exclaimed. He had been standing there the whole time, watching Drage as he conversed with the spirit in the room. "Why is the Great Spirit not answering my prayers?"

Drage sighed as he glanced at his Sword in fascination. "Because he does not exist anymore. Gaspard, you were deceived just like me. You were lied to."

At the mention of lies, Gaspard was taken aback. "What?"

With a step forward, Drage began to explain, "The Y'mordi are real, Gaspard. The person who gave you that Sword was an Y'mordi. Was he dressed in a black robe?"

"Yes," stammered Gaspard in disbelief.

"Did he promise you something great if you killed me?"

"Yes," Gaspard muttered even more quietly. "But he was a messenger of the Great Spirit."

"No, he wasn't, Gaspard. He was one of the Y'mordi, a Lord of the Shadows. He has been trying to kill me for a while now, and they were just planning on using you. They convinced me that I had a choice of coming here and getting rid of a curse that I had thought I had been suffering from or to fight you in Rulia. They tricked me, too."

"You can't be…that's not true."

Drage threw Gaspard the Sword of Destiny. "Open your heart, Gaspard. In both of our Swords, what is left of the Great Spirit resides there." Gaspard considered what Drage was saying doubtfully, but he complied nevertheless and was amazed to sense the wealth of power that was emanating from the blue-shimmering blade.

After hearing the voice of the Sword, he realized. "You are telling the truth…" he murmured. "Now, you are going to kill me?"

Though Drage could feel the pull of the Darkness in his heart, urging him to decapitate the man before him, he ignored it and found his Light instead, the light of forgiveness, of mercy. "No, Gaspard, I am not going to kill you. Rather, if you are willing to devote yourself to the Light, I am willing to make you a member of my highest guard, the Enigma Brigade, if that pleases you?"

Aria was casting spells as fast as she could to eliminate the army of Shadows, her wand waving in front of her and rehearsing all the motions she had learned at the Academy, and her Phoenix Regiment had stood beside her, casting spells to add to hers. Where was Drage? What had happened to him? Something was not right. He was supposed to be here.

She was even more stunned when a small squirrel began clambering its way up her phoenix-decorated robe and sat on her shoulder. "Are you Miss Aria?" it asked her.

After casting a devastating spell of Fire, she turned to look at the squirrel anima. "Yes, I am."

"Lilian and Matthew need your help. They're trapped in a cage near the back."

Aria instantly turned to one of her Phoenixes. "Do you have a spare wand?"

"Yes, madame," replied the Phoenix as she handed Aria a wand.

She quickly cast a spell that destroys such barriers and then handed the wand to the squirrel. "Listen, little squirrel, give this to Matthew and tell him to rewind it a minute or two. He will know what I mean. Go quickly," she ordered.

With a rapid salute, the squirrel anima was gone.

From behind the rebel troops, Sena communicated Aria's words to Lilian and Matthew, handing Matthew the wand. "Rewind it?" repeated Lilian without a clue as to the phrase's meaning.

Matthew took the wand eagerly and pointed it at the bars. He focused on a simple Time spell, and the wand repeated its previous spell. The barrier around the cage disappeared. "It's all yours, Lilian," he said gladly.

Trying not to reveal her surprise, Lilian held a hand up, and a blast of Force knocked front of the cage to the ground. "Good job, Sena," she said encouragingly.

"So, can I help fight this time?"

Matthew grinned at Lilian as he said, "I don't know. What do you think, Lilian?"

She smiled back at him as she reached out to grab his hand. "I think that that will be fine. Let us get rid of these Shadows now." Another white aura surrounded her as she transformed back into a horse. "Hop on!" she said as Matthew and Senagul quickly complied.

As soon as Drage and Gaspard entered the battlefield, Drage was stunned by what was happening. Lifeless bodies were trampled amid the clashing of the two massive forces, their cries and spells roaring out over the sounds of swords meeting. He cringed when he saw Derek's lifeless body.

"Gaspard! You were supposed to kill him!" roared the Y'mordi.

The two turned to see Xarden facing them angrily.

Gaspard replied with a snarl, "You lied to me! You all lied to me!"

Xarden twirled his scepter boastfully. "Fine, I will kill both of you myself." However, he did not expect for the two of them to rush at him at once. While he was able to block the Sword of Destiny, the Behemoth came at him with such force that his scepter went flying. He dodged Drage's next attack and then pushed him into Gaspard. As he turned to see that his army was failing, he created a Gate and left Rulia to enter the Palace of Shadows.

Drage looked at his army coming closer and closer to victory. He raised his Sword high and focused his own Light on the blade. In wonder, he felt his *mysteria* enter the Sword of Destiny and come out as a blinding, blue light. The remaining Shadows faded instantly. Victory was his.

Together

"Cairon…" Draconis muttered.

The Black Dragon responded coldly, "So you two are behind this rebellion? I know that you are the Dragon Elani, but I do not know who you are, Golden Dragon." His voice was deep and rumbled throughout the massive, dark throne room of Cairon's castle. A black mist curled around their feet, running up the walls, barely allowing light to come in through the stained glass windows, and rolling along the high ceiling even.

"My name is Rexam Draconis, and you have seen me before, Cairon."

Cairon raised a brow at Draconis's words. "Oh? And where have I met you previously? I do not recall ever having met you."

"That is because it has been a century and a half since you last saw me. Whenever you raided the Imperial cities, there was one particular house that you destroyed. Though you did not hesitate to kill almost everyone in the village, there was a dragonet in that house that you did not kill. You merely pushed him to the ground and moved on. That dragonet…was me,

Cairon," explained Draconis as he took a step forward, putting himself a few feet in front of Elani.

The Black Dragon's eyes widened in horror. "That was you? You survived the raids?"

"Yes, Cairon, and I have returned now." He could sense how tense Elani was becoming. She wanted to start fighting immediately. "As the present laws stand," he started, realizing the flaws in those laws perpetuated by the lies regarding the Divine Dragon of the Heavens, "I am the true heir to the throne here. Because you took the Crown dishonestly, I am going to give you the chance to step down and redeem yourself now. You could be free of all guilt, and your people would be given the rights you have sought for ages."

Gradually, Cairon remembered which Dragon this was. With a calm tone, Cairon replied, "You have no idea how long your sapphire eyes have haunted my dreams, Rexam Draconis. I do not know why I saved your life that day. Perhaps, I felt sorry for you. Maybe, I felt that it would not be right to kill one so innocent, as you seemed to be. The mercy I gave you that day…I have wondered for so long if it was a sign of weakness on my part or if my entire cause was unjust. Now, my greatest enemy is that dragonet I could have and, perhaps, should have killed years ago."

Draconis repeated, "I am giving you a choice."

Slowly, Kusvor Cairon drew his weapon. It was an elongated form of the twofold, reaching almost eight feet in length. As soon as he did, Elani drew her twofold, and Draconis drew his goldfoil. The larger Black Dragon called, "Now, behold the threefold." He pressed a switch on the side of the sword's hilt, and a third blade came between the two blades. The weapon now looked like a three-pronged, straight eagle claw. To make matters worse, he drew a second threefold.

Elani gasped. Then, she yelled confidently, "You think that you can defeat us just because you have a more complex weapon? The way I see it is that this is a battle of two against one."

Cairon smirked, "The way I see it is that I have six blades, and you, together, have three."

Then, Cairon leaped at the two in a momentum-building spin. Draconis leaped to meet him, and his sword was able to block Cairon's first attack, but the second threefold came at him from the side. Elani rushed to block it, and immediately, both Elani and Draconis found themselves hard pressed to fend off Cairon's formidable attacks.

Deciding to divide Cairon's attention more effectively, Elani soared over his head and landed behind him. As soon as she spun to attack him, one of the threefolds blocked her attack. Draconis was paying close attention to how uncanny Cairon's movements were. Without even looking, he was able to both block off Elani's attacks and try to land his own strikes on her while he was completely focused on Draconis. He knew at once that Cairon had to be relying heavily on *mysteria*.

Gradually, Draconis began implementing a spell or two into his fighting so that he could sense everything just as Cairon could. He knew that even if he was an inferior fighter, he was far more adept at using *mysteria* than Cairon could possibly be.

Elani, however, was finding her stamina weakening. She had never met a person who could both match her speed with a sword and surpass her strength at the same time. Each time she guarded herself, she had to take a step backward from the shaking force. Immediately afterward, she would find the threefold ready for another attack. Cairon's arms extended so each one handled each of the Dragons separately.

The threefold's claws raked the air in an attempt to slash her legs, but she leaped nimbly over the threatening blades. Once she landed, she charged at Cairon and tried to slash him. He flicked his wrist, and his weapon came again between them, forcing her back once more.

Draconis pressed just as hard as Elani did. Though the goldfoil was thin, he was able to match Cairon's attacks and attempt a few of his own. The blade was certainly light enough to allow for rapid attacks.

Cairon teased with a toothy grin, "What is the matter with the two of you? I am hardly even trying here. Can you not give me a real challenge?"

Enraged by the taunt, Elani fought with more determination. Though her muscles were already weakening, she found the strength to continue. Each block became a means of pushing his blade away so she could try a different strike, but he only knocked her away with a kick and regained his space.

Draconis was trying his hardest not to begin casting spells. It was not that he had developed a dependence on *mysteria*. It was merely that he was used to the idea that if he needed to use it, then it would be at his disposal. However, in this battle, it was a test of honor as much as it was a test of strength. Draconis could not win this battle dishonorably. It would go against the moral code of the Dragons, and he would more than likely not be considered worthy of taking the throne. They all were using it to some extent, anticipating the next attacks, but full-out offensive spells were out of the question. Draconis wanted to defeat Cairon through superior swordsmanship.

As he was struggling to match Cairon, the massive Black Dragon suddenly cast a spell of Darkness. The black clouds pushed Elani and Draconis backward, placing them on opposite ends of the room.

Then, he spread his wings and soared straight upward. Though the thin layer of black mist covered the ceiling, walls, and floor, Cairon knew that there was a glass dome above him. He flew straight through it, and the glass shards fell to the floor along with the torrents of rain from outside the fortress.

Elani and Draconis leaped into the air, and their wings spread out behind them as they ascended to reach Cairon. Once they exited the castle, several other Dragons shot past them, still fighting. Both Draconis and Elani were amazed that the aerial battle had extended to reach even the top of the castle, winged forms crashing into each other with deafening roars. Then, they saw Cairon and rocketed toward him.

Lightning flashed and boomed around them, and the wind howled deafeningly, causing the three Dragons to be completely unable to hear anything else, not even each other or the clashing of their swords.

Draconis and Elani quickly dropped their previous strategy of trying to surround him. In the skies, that advantage was minimized. There was plenty of room to maneuver, and there were even more weak spots for all three of them. Even if they flanked him now, he could still move up or down to escape.

As their blades crashed together against the roar of the rolling thunder, Cairon finally decided to push his spellcasting a little further.

The dark clouds began to whirl around them, hiding the castle and ground below them. Then, the clouds started to enclose the remaining space, enveloping the three in darkness. Draconis immediately repelled the clouds with a spell of Wind, feeling the spell justifiable as Cairon had been the one to summon the clouds. He had cast the spell just in time as Elani barely blocked another strike from Cairon's dual threefolds.

Understanding it was now acceptable to cast spells since Cairon had no problem doing it, Draconis directed the nearby lightning to attack Cairon, and a bolt hit one of his threefolds, sending jolts up his black-scaled body, but instead of frying him where he hovered, the practically glowing sword was cast out of his claws.

Inspired by Cairon's small defeat, Draconis rushed the Black Dragon as fiercely as he had inside the castle. Elani did the same, and Cairon found himself transforming from the aggressive stance to the defensive one.

Elani gradually realized that Cairon was losing his strength, too. In reaction to this knowledge, she persisted even more strongly in her attacks.

While they now flanked Cairon, Draconis paused a moment to cast a powerful Wind spell, but as soon as he did, he felt Cairon's threefold pierce his side in a deep slash. The blood that leaked from his wound was washed from his scales by the freezing downpour, but the deep wound stung painfully nevertheless.

"Rexam!" called Elani as she tried to divert Cairon's attention. "Are you alright?"

The Golden Dragon could not hear a word she had said over the thunder, but he responded with a weak thumbs up, hoping that she understood the signal. Earthans and Gevátians knew the meaning of the simple sign. He was not quite sure if most Dragons did as well. He shakily raised the goldfoil and rushed at Cairon, though his side was now excruciating.

In one rapid motion of his wrist, Cairon blasted Elani away with a sphere of Darkness and then parried Draconis's attack. As the Golden Dragon's momentum kept him going forward, Cairon stuck one claw with its five razor-sharp talons into Draconis's fresh wound. The Golden Dragon roared in blinding pain as Cairon pulled him to the Black Dragon's side. "I am going to kill you now," yelled Cairon maniacally as he brought his weapon around to finish Draconis.

Before he could do anything, however, Elani was at him again with her twofold attacking in an unstoppable flurry of slashes. Cairon was forced to release Draconis and begin blocking the attacks.

It took all of Draconis's effort to perform the simple task of hovering then. He clenched his blood-red side agonizingly and tried to refocus himself so that he could aid Elani. Holding out one shaking, bloodstained claw, he cast a fireball spell at Cairon, and the Black Dragon dodged it as he soared back to the fortress.

Cairon was the first to enter through the shattered dome with Elani and Draconis close behind him. The dark mist that had obscured the walls of the castle had exited through the hole in the glass dome, leaving the walls, ceiling, and floor with their old glimmer of gold.

As soon as Elani landed on the floor, Cairon lunged at her. She had not expected such a sudden attack, and her blade was pushed away from her, giving Cairon the necessary time to rake his claws across her snout, sending Elani flying.

Before he could rush to deliver the final blow, Draconis stepped in between them. "You and I both know that this battle is between you and me, Cairon. I have been in your dreams as much as you have been in mine. I am tired of hiding. This shall end now."

Though his side was still dripping large amounts of blood, he held his goldfoil in a ready position, his body shaking.

Cairon said softly, "There is no honor in killing those who are weak and injured."

Draconis retorted angrily, "There would be no honor if I was to surrender, and since when has honor played a part in your decisions? You murdered my family years ago, and you have murdered countless others since then. What do you know of honor, Kusvor Cairon?"

The Black Dragon winced sharply at Draconis's words. Beyond the Darkness that was possessing his heart, he could feel the bite of regret and the memory of how dutiful a Dragon he had been when he had planned his raids against King Vran. He had followed the code. He had pursued honor. Well…he had pursued justice, even at the risk of personal honor.

Then, the Darkness compelled him, and the threefold reached out for Draconis. The Golden Dragon dodged the attack, and the two traded blade attacks in the large room with the rain still coming in from the shattered ceiling.

Draconis strived to keep up with Cairon, but he felt his strength slipping as the blood continued to pour from him. He found he was stuck on the defense for the moment, struggling to block Cairon's pushing attacks. His blue eyes glanced at the unconscious Elani hopefully, but her only movement was her chest moving up and down rhythmically. He was alone in this battle. His vision began to blur, and he took several steps backward.

"That blade…you poisoned it?"

Cairon replied simply, "Yes, with a lethal poison, in fact. Shall I give you the honor of making your death as quick and painless as possible, Rexam?"

Suddenly, Draconis realized that if he died, the rebellion would have been for nothing. Elani would die. All of the rebel Dragons would die. More importantly, Lly would have died for nothing. With Cairon's heightened powers in *mysteria*, Draconis was the closest person to an equal in power in all of Sharl Vran. Honor was not the highest priority here.

Reaching into the depths of his heart, he summoned as much *mysteria* as he could and focused a spell of Nature on his wound. An added spell of Water helped to clear out the poison that was filling his body and then heal the wound.

Cairon watched in shock as the scales around the claw marks began stitching themselves back together. "That is not possible..." he muttered in disbelief.

"It is real, alright," remarked Draconis confidently. "What is more is that you could have wielded such power too, but you gave in to the Darkness." In a rushing sweep, Draconis found his strength renewed. He attacked with such speed that Cairon was struggling harder than ever to keep up with the younger Dragon's frenzy.

As he tried to land a strike at Draconis, the goldfoil went in between two of the blades, and Cairon tried to wrench the golden weapon out of Draconis's claws but was surprised to find that it did not work. The golden sword kept going through the gap. Draconis allowed the goldfoil to keep going at its current momentum while he dodged Cairon's attack. The thin sword entered Cairon's shoulder painfully, and before the Black Dragon could do a single thing, Draconis leaped toward Cairon and kicked him forcefully in the chest.

The Black Dragon was sprawled out across the ground, and Draconis pulled the goldfoil out of the Dragon's bleeding shoulder. He held it at Cairon's heart.

"So," began Cairon weakly. "Is this how I am going to end?"

Draconis responded with a blasting ball of Light. The spell was directed straight into Kusvor Cairon's heart, and he felt the Darkness melt away instantly.

Cairon's face softened as he fell to his knees. His words changed dramatically in that instant, "Rexam, I am so sorry." He breathed heavily, realizing the nature of his actions more fully than he had in months. "I do not know what came over me." He could hear Dragons dying outside the castle. He could smell their blood, and it sickened him. "I don't…" he started, faltering, "I do not deserve to live, Rexam."

"No," replied Draconis, struggling to put his own feelings of vengeance aside. "I am not going to kill you. Doing that will not solve any problems. There has been enough killing already."

The Black Dragon's eyes widened. "You are not…you are not going to kill me?"

"No," Draconis repeated. Instead, he offered Cairon a claw. As soon as the Black Dragon took his claw and started to get up, a watery Gate appeared between the two Dragons, and Sarn threw a disc of Force at Cairon. The disc decapitated him cleanly, and, as the body fell, Sarn lifted it with a spell of Air. The two rapidly disappeared into another Gate.

Draconis was dumbfounded by what had just happened.

Elani stirred then, several feet away, "Rexam? What happened?"

He shook his head, equally puzzled. "I have no idea, but Cairon is dead. The Golden Dragons are free at last."

"And are the Black Dragons to be banished once again?" she asked hesitantly.

"No, Elani, not this time. I shall not do this as Cairon did it, or Vran did it, or how any of the Kings did it. Today begins a new chapter for Sharl Vran."

"You mean Sharl Drake," argued Elani.

Draconis turned his golden head to her in wonder. "What do you mean, Elani?"

She explained, "The name of the world is based on the name of its King. King Vran was the last one to take the Crown, and so the world was called Sharl Vran. Cairon did not inherit the crown, so it kept its previous name. With you leading, it shall be called Sharl Drake."

Draconis smiled at her, nodding. "We are in this all together, are we not?"

"Yes, Rexam. We are." She could not believe that it was over. The battle had shaken her considerably, and she was even more bewildered as to how Draconis had defeated the monstrous Black Dragon, but that matter was not of great concern now. The issue at hand was what to do with the future.

As the two flew to exit the room and enter the storm, Draconis released a spell of Light that dispelled the entire sky of black clouds. The lightning faded, and the light of the sun began to illuminate the capital.

Draconis used a spell of Air to make his voice louder as he roared above the din of the persisting battle around and below him. "Listen to me, everyone! Cairon is gone!"

Gradually, the battle stopped, and the Dragons hovered to listen and react. The proclamation generated many cheers among the Golden Dragons and the rebels, though the Black Dragons immediately appeared downcast.

Draconis continued, "However, my rule shall be different from those who have led before me. Neither the Golden Dragons nor the Black Dragons shall be banished. We are all Dragons in the eyes of your new King. Each Dragon is different, and it is illogical for one to try to say that any one tribe should be treated as a group different from other Dragons. The old hierarchy was based on a myth of the Divine Dragon of the Heavens, but that myth told many lies. It does not matter what the legends say about which Dragon should be on top. There is no superior tribe. There is no inferior tribe." Elani confidently took his claw in hers and beamed up at him. He clenched it tightly as he grinned back at her. He whispered to her, "This world has been in darkness for too long."

His short speech caused every Dragon in the area to roar with cheers and joy.

The hundreds of attending Dragons were all seated uncomfortably in the throne room of the castle. Beside the throne, a second throne had been placed. In the first, Draconis sat, while in the other, Elani sat.

Master Volwyth the Red Dragon approached the two with the Crown in his claws. His deep voice rumbled throughout the room, "Rexam Draconis, do you promise to your people that you will do everything within your power to guide them with a system of order and fairness?"

The Golden Dragon in the throne replied just as loudly, "Yes, I promise this."

"Do you promise to your people that you will watch over their actions and reward their good deeds while punishing their bad deeds?"

"Yes, I promise this."

Master Volwyth continued with a final question, "Do you promise to your people that you will lead them with a code of trust, honor, dignity, and pride?"

Draconis responded, "Yes, I promise this."

"As the leader of the Red Dragon tribe, I, Volwyth, on behalf of the Dragons of Sharl Vran, bestow this Crown to you." After saying such, he placed the immense Crown on Draconis's head and finished, "All praise King Rexam and Queen Elani, the King and Queen of Sharl Drake!"

The hundreds of Dragons in the assembly stood and cheered in celebration. The era of fighting and suffering was finally over. Amid the jubilant chaos, Draconis turned to face his new wife, and the two smiled at each other. Together, as Golden and Black, the two had brought the world even closer together. Draconis said softly, yet loudly enough so that she could hear, "You know, Elani, Lly would be very proud of you. You did what both of you sought to do a century and a half ago."

A tear rolled down Elani's black cheek as she smiled. "The three of us will always be together, will we not?"

"Yes," replied Draconis. "Together, for always."

The New Laws

Drage stormed into the council room of the Palace of Light with Aria, Matthew, Lilian, and the Enigma Brigade, including Gaspard, behind him. The Emperor's Council was instantly stunned by the intrusion of their meeting.

Valdridge asked, flustered, "What is the meaning of this, Prince Helius?"

He countered rapidly, "I am no longer the Prince, Master Valdridge. I am taking my place as the Emperor of Light now. And, the first thing I am going to do as the Emperor is to end this pathetic War. It has been going on for long enough."

"But-but-but your Majesty, you cannot just become the Emperor once you decide to do so. There is a ceremony and a process."

Drage turned to Marqest, "Master Marqest, as soon as the Emperor of Light dies, who steps up to take his place?"

"The Prince of Light, your Majesty," Marqest responded with a knowing smile.

"Y'see, Master Valdridge? It depends on when I am ready to take the Throne, and by that understanding, I am now the Emperor of Light. Mistress Leona, can you see about returning our troops on the terms of surrender? Master Valdridge, I need you to talk to those who are still leading the exiles. The laws of outcast are going to be done away with, so I need you to carry that message over to them."

As he continued to bark out similar orders, the Emperor's Council began rushing to do the Emperor of Light's bidding. Once the Council was gone, Aria pecked Drage warmly on the cheek. "Thank you," she said.

"For what?" Drage asked in bewilderment.

"For not leaving me for Earth this time."

Matthew came up to the two of them and hugged both of them. "I am so glad that we are back together again." He seemed to ignore the fact that his father had just been killed by one of the Y'mordi.

"I don't think I could leave you guys again. As much as I'm going to miss my friends and family back on Earth, I think I've realized that my real home is here. Besides," began Drage jokingly. "What would this world do without me?" He did not feel regret or sorrow, not even hesitation for this new role. He felt ready and hopeful, prepared to help make a difference in this world. He had seen the Light, and he knew it was possible now.

Aria nudged him painfully in the ribs. "Oh, shut up, you big goof." At this comment, all three of them started laughing.

Lilian came up to the three and asked softly, "The War is over, then?"

Now in the throne room, Matthew turned to her and grabbed her hands enthusiastically, "Lilian, the War is over. Drage is getting rid of the exile laws. It's not just about the War anymore. The whole exile will be lifted. You are all going to be free now."

Then, Senagul scampered up to Matthew's shoulder. "You mean, we can go anywhere now?"

Approvingly, Matthew nodded.

With a bright smile, Lilian gave Matthew a tremendous hug.

Drage commented to Aria with an overwhelming glee filling his heart, "Y'know, I never thought I would see the day when Matt got a girlfriend."

"Oh, stop picking on him," replied Aria as she shook her head in mock disappointment.

Drage put his hands against the back of his neck and made as if to relax. "Hey, it's been five years. I have a lot of catching up to do. If I don't start picking on him now, I will have that debt for a while, y'know?" He eyed the throne at the end of the hall with a suspicious glance. That would be his seat of office for years to come. Yet, now when he looked at it, he did not think of his father sitting there. It finally felt like it was his throne now.

Aria suddenly pulled Drage close to her and planted a soft kiss on his lips. "Sometimes, I like it better when you don't talk. When you try to think, bad things start happening. Leave that job to me."

"Got it!" responded Drage as he looked fondly into Aria's eyes. It was then that she noticed his eyes were no longer blue. They were not black either. They were as brown as they had been five years ago before the curse had ever affected him.

"Drage…your eyes…"

He shook his head. "I don't even want to know what color they are now. Right now, I feel like me again. Not possessed by a spirit…or a curse. I'm just me."

Her grin widened, but she said, "You know, if you are ending the nonhumans' exile, then the leaders of the Eastern Continent are going to wage war against us, and that includes the Emperor Regin."

He sighed, "I know, but I think that war is more than just a physical thing. It is also mental and emotional. That means that when you are fighting, you are fighting for something that you believe in. It is not the way of the Light to outcast those who have done nothing wrong. I will not fight for that."

Aria glanced at him as if she was looking at an entirely new person. "You have changed, Drage. It's like I'm staring at the old you again."

"Maybe not the old me. Maybe, I'm just what I would have been, had a lot of stuff not happened. You are right though," he sighed again. "The Emperor Regin is going to want a fight. Though the Third Obsidian War is ending, a new war is about to begin. I'm a little worried that is going to be a much harder and much longer war, though. Regin has trained soldiers and plenty of them, too. From what I have heard from others, the people from the Eastern Continent are particularly stubborn."

Then, Matthew approached him. "Hey, Drage, I think that Lilian, Sena, and I are going to spread the news around the Northern Continent. I guess we will be back soon, hopefully a day or two."

"Matt, thanks for everything," Drage said simply. "I will see you in a day or two then."

Matthew waved a silent farewell as he followed Lilian and Senagul into the Gate.

Matthew, Lilian, and Sena stood sorrowfully in front of the makeshift grave marker that stood at Derek's grave in the forest near the still blood-stained battlefield. It was a simple pile of stones, but it had been the best that Matthew had been able to make at the time before he had left the battlefield.

He commented, "The death of a loved one is a hard thing."

Lilian wrapped a soft arm around his rough, hairy one. "This is true. However, think of what his body will give to the earth itself."

Matthew's first reaction was one of shock and slight terror. Then, his features softened. "You are right. With death, there is life." He held his staff out in front of him. Several ravens were etched onto its surface. His father had once told him that the ravens were the symbols of the legendary organization called the Keepers, those who specialized in the powers of Time.

Focusing on a Nature spell for the first time, he caused grass to grow from the recently dug soil. Then, a small sapling appeared from the ground there. "He always loved this forest. I think it is alright for it to be forever close to his heart."

"Come, Matthew. There may be others we can still save from death. There are those still injured." Her tone was so soft and gentle. Perhaps, that was one of the things that Matthew loved so much about her. She never became angry, and she was always calm and logical.

"Yeah, let's go, Matthew!" exclaimed Senagul as he jumped onto Matthew's dark-haired head.

"Hey, cut it out!" he said as he tried to get the squirrel anima off of him. With a giggling squeal, the squirrel escaped Matthew's reaching fingers and went to Lilian instead.

Matthew and Lilian shared a fond look while Senagul was breaking into nearly uncontrollable laughter. Lilian waved a hand, and another Gate appeared. This time, they had some real work to do.

In the throne room of the Palace of Shadows, Randir stood trial in front of Pullatus. "Y'tal, I am not saying that Earth is entirely useless to us. I am merely informing you that the Black Joker is not there. There is no such thing. I am convinced that it is nothing more than a legend. If he was real, then he was killed back then."

Pullatus remained doubtful. "Mali, does Randir speak the truth?"

"Yes, Lord Y'tal," lied Mali.

Pullatus nodded in understanding. He knew that he could trust Mali. Ever since joining the Y'mordi, Mali had done his best to serve Pullatus's will. "Very well, Randir, I suppose your past sins *may* be forgiven. Nevertheless, I do wish you had come up with something. You seem rather empty-handed."

Randir winced at Pullatus's words. He could remember how Pullatus had referred to him as nothing more than a tool before his venture on Earth. He realized that Pullatus's opinion of him had not changed, not that it mattered to him one way or the other. He needed to still try to find a way to break the connection between him and the Darkness. Randir needed a way out of this mess. If the Black Joker was not the answer, then perhaps, there was another ancient power in some world or other that could break his connection. "Y'tal, I did manage to find something here however."

Silent anticipation was Pullatus's answer.

"There is a computer, a database, hidden on Heaven's Isle. It seems that it was owned by the Prophet of Water, but since he is no longer there, it is fully accessible, even to us. It has gathered information for centuries. It knows things about many of the worlds, and I think that we could use it to our advantage."

Pullatus considered the idea before saying, "I suppose that this information is something useful. You are both dismissed until I have found the next Great Servant of the Darkness. I suppose that it shall not take me too long."

Once Mali and Randir left the Palace, Randir muttered, "Thank you, Hector. Thank you for not telling him the truth…about me trying to find a way to sever this connection."

"I told you," explained Mali with a bright smile. "I am not sworn to Pullatus. I am sworn to the Darkness, and I shall choose to serve it. I agree with you. Perhaps, we should be seeking the Great Servants as well. If we find one before he does, we can kill it, and we will be one step closer."

As they stepped outside the Emperor Regin's fortress with only the mysterious silver blade in Stehl's hand, Mirah commented in exclamation, "I t'ink I 'ave seen dat blade before. It was said dat da Lord Ferro left it behin' when he disappeared. A mystic weapon, dey say."

"A mystic weapon?" repeated Stehl in fascination. "How so, Mister Mirah?"

"Eh," began Mirah hesitantly. "Dey say dat da blade ken resist any o' dat *mysteria* stuff. No spell ken touch ya. I t'ink dere was some weird side effec' or somethin', but I don' remember."

Stehl grinned as she became entranced by the silvery blade. "A weapon that can ward off spells, huh? This could be useful in fighting the Enigma Brigade. They are almost gone now. I can feel it. I shall call this weapon the Lightslayer. It will kill those who claim to serve the Light but commit wrong nevertheless."

Mirah winced at the wholly unattractive name. "Eh, forgive me if I say somethin' offensive, Miss Stehl, but dat is a rather ugly name fer a weapon. Ya should use its real name."

Despite herself, she felt quite offended by Mirah's insult. She glared at him as she said, "Well, what name would that be?"

He could sense her anger in her voice but replied, "Bein' from Pert City, ya learn a lot about legen's an' such. Well, someone named da Sword to honor a soldier back den. Da blade was called Kohana's Fang."

The castle was alive with servants, the castle's walls golden and shining again. His attendants spanned every tribe, and after the first few days, Dragons had quickly gotten over the fact that it was an intertribal marriage, especially when the political lines dividing tribes gone. Everyone knew how Queen Elani had begun the rebellion, and everyone was just as proud of King Rexam. Their marriage had successfully ended most of the problems and stereotypes of other Dragon races. Even the status of the Silver Dragon had become quite elevated once the truth of the myth of the Divine Dragon of the Heavens had been revealed to the general public. Of course, there were some who still rebelled and held on to their purist beliefs about the Divine Dragon, but they were few and not welcome in the Imperial cities.

Master Volwyth, King Rexam's personal advisor, approached the throne with a great smile across his muzzle. "My Lord, a message just came for you from one of the legendary humans."

"A human? Please, what are the contents of this message?" requested King Rexam eagerly.

The Red Dragon cleared as his throat as he began, "'Hey, Draconis, or should I say King Rexam? Ha, this is your old friend Drage, or should I say Emperor of Light Dragenopn Helius? Hey, I have a longer title than you do! Anyways, I know how seriously you held your debt to me and my family, so I just wanted you to know that I hereby free you of your services to me. Your duty to Gevás is finished. Also, I thought you might like to know that the War is over here. I have gotten rid of that pesky exile law, and so freedom and merriness is abound. Congratulations on your crowning and marriage, and I hope to see you soon. Drage.'" Master Volwyth was considerably shaken by the message he was repeating. It felt far too informal to be saying it to the Dragon King, but the King had requested for the message to be repeated nevertheless.

King Rexam could not help but smile. "The boy finally did it. He became the Emperor of Light. I wish I could see him, now, though. It has been a little over five years, so I suppose he looks quite a bit older."

"Who would that be, Rexam?" called Queen Elani as she entered the room.

"Dragenopn is an old friend of mine from Gevás. It seems that everything is going well, though I suppose with his latest political move, he will find himself in another war soon."

Queen Elani looked at him questioningly, "You are not thinking of going back now, are you?"

He shook his head instantly. "No, he has his duties, and I have mine." He felt relief at Drage's dismissal of his duties to the water world. It removed a huge burden that had weighed on his heart. "Nevertheless, I see no harm in sending him a reply. Volwyth, do you think you could manage that?"

"Why, certainly, my Lord," replied Master Volwyth promptly.

King Rexam began, "Alright, here is the message I would like for you to send: 'Your Majesty, thank you very much for your kind message. I am glad to know that you remembered me and removed my debt to you and your family. It eases a lot of guilt that was on my mind. I hope that, if you have the free time, you will come and visit me in my castle in the air. I would love to show you around sometime. My name may not be as great as yours, your Majesty, but my castle could beat yours any day. Draconis.'"

Both Master Volwyth and Queen Elani looked at each other in dumbfounded surprise. They had never seen King Rexam sound so joking. Usually, the Golden Dragon was rather serious, but now he was boasting and joking with a human. Nevertheless, Master Volwyth replied simply, "It shall be done, my Lord."

Maksimilian exhaled in satisfaction as he equipped the golden robe with the phoenix on it once again. Though Drage had reinstated him as the Captain again, he still felt an overwhelming hatred for the Emperor of Light Dragenopn Helius, but, now that the boy was the Emperor, he was not sure he could truly act on that hatred yet. He had been both surprised and impressed when Bryco had killed Tilgé in that fateful battle. According to Bryco, he had blasted the temporary Captain with a powerful Light spell, and all that had been left was Tilgé's hand.

Though he had been disgusted by the bloodstained thing, Maksimilian had accepted it and declared that Bryco was to be the second-in-command. Emperor Helius had relented and had allowed for Maksimilian to finally resume his position as Captain.

One interesting thing that had come out of this whole ordeal was that a new member had been added to the Brigade: their previous enemy Gaspard. Neither Maksimilian nor Bryco trusted the man, but they did not have much of a choice. Maksimilian had wanted to kill the man, but, to his pleasure, he had realized relatively quickly that Gaspard was the wielder of one of the five Spirit Swords, the Behemoth. That Sword was one that Maksimilian had been wanting for quite a while now.

Bryco cautiously stepped up to his Captain and said, "Sir, the Emperor of Light wishes to see you. He has a scouting mission for us."

"A scouting mission?" repeated Maksimilian calmly.

"Yes, sir. The Emperor of Light is seeking someone who is particularly skilled at digital technology for some reason. He thinks that the Enigma Brigade can start looking for this person."

Maksimilian sighed and replied with a dejected tone, "So, we are going back to what we used to be. No longer are we the Emperor of Light's best soldiers but his spies. Bryco, inform Sume and Gaspard that we shall have a meeting shortly. I shall go and speak with the Emperor, and I shall learn the details of this mission."

As Bryco left, Maksimilian put a nervous hand on the hilt of the Steel of Life. The Behemoth would be his once Gaspard was killed. The only problem was that Maksimilian could not be the one that killed him. That would look too suspicious. He had to come up with a different strategy.

It was almost a full year later when Drage finally decided to go and visit his friend Draconis. He had received a rather friendly message from the Golden Dragon via his advisor who happened to be a Red Dragon.

Though many of the leaders in the Eastern Continent had already begun fighting the Southern Continent on the grounds that Drage was a horrid tyrant and an animal lover, Drage had scoffed at the remarks and inspired a new hope in the people of Helio. The world was nowhere near as divided as it had once been. People began seeing the anima as more than just primitive savages, and the Northern, Western, and Southern Continents were joined in a sort of alliance. The Eastern Continent definitely had its work cut out for it, but Drage remained optimistic. He did not hear or notice anything out of the ordinary, but he knew the Y'mordi were still out there, planning their next attack.

"Drage, are you almost ready?" Aria called as she created a Gate that boiled the water around it. She was in her nicest clothes. She did not wear her phoenix-decorated robe. Instead, she wore a robe colored bright gold, similar to the uniform of an Enigma Brigadier. Drage was wearing fancy clothes as well. He was wearing golden pants with a white shirt and a black coat over it. It was the Gevátian equivalent of a tuxedo.

"Yes, I'm ready," he said as he followed her into the next world. They were both immediately captivated by the gorgeous, blue skies and thick white clouds that filled their vision. Dragons soared through those skies in groups of three or four as they chatted amongst themselves. They were amazed at the diversity of the groups. Red Dragons were with Brown Dragons, and Green Dragons were with Silver Dragons. Whatever segregation had been going on in Sharl Drake was no longer occurring.

When they turned to see the enormous golden castle, they both gaped at the phenomenal size, much larger even than the Palace of Light. As they approached the front doors, the two guards, a White Dragon and a Black Dragon, bowed to them before opening the doors.

Aria and Drage were stunned by the beautiful, golden walls, ceiling, and floor of the entrance hall. "Drage, this place is amazing!"

He responded with a laugh, "Yeah, Draconis wasn't kidding. This place beats my Palace hands down."

Another set of guards bowed before them at the doors to the throne room and opened the doors for them. The throne room was even more spectacular. There was an immense glass dome above them, and the traffic of Dragons in the sky above was perfectly visible through it.

In the room, there were several rows of seats that held large amounts of Dragons. Aria was surprised to notice that there were several robed humans in the seats among the Dragons. This meeting of the rulers Lord Helius and Lord Drake seemed to be a rather grand occasion. She was eternally glad that Drage had recommended that she wear such fancy clothes.

Before she could ask Drage who the humans attending this event were, they saw Draconis. He looked happy on a whole new level, they both decided. His wife looked equally content.

Though Aria stopped where she was, Drage kept going and gave Draconis a warm hug. "How've you been, you big lizard?"

King Rexam replied with a grin, "I am well, your Majesty. It is good to see you again."

Drage nodded, "It's great to see you, too. Well, do you want me to start this, or are you going to?"

Draconis shook his head humorously, "I think you are supposed to start it, your Majesty."

"Fine," responded Drage as he stepped away from the Dragon King and approached Aria. Then, to Aria's surprise alone, he knelt before her and took her hand. "Aria Newman," he began, and immediately, Aria was dumfounded. She could not believe what he was doing in the middle of the Draconian throne room. "Will you marry me?"

She smiled so widely that she felt as if her mouth would be sore for weeks. Her heart soared with both the embarrassment of the eyes on her as well as the love she was feeling for Drage. "I-I...*yes*, Drage." The crowd of Dragons and humans went wild with cheers, and even Draconis and his wife were clapping. Aria whispered into his ear as he held her hands gleefully, "Did you have to have a room full of random strangers to propose to me?"

"Oh, they're not here for the proposal." He turned to face Draconis. "Now, it's your turn, right?"

"Right," said Draconis with a chuckle. "Would the two of you please step forward?" Once Drage pulled Aria forward, she was even more astonished: Drage was planning to have her married right here.

"Drage, this is—" she began, but then, he gestured behind her. She turned her head acquiescingly, and her amazement only grew. The hoods that hid the humans' faces were lowered, and she watched as Drage's mom, Drage's sister, Matthew, Lilian, Senagul, Marqest, Mistress Leona, and Master Valdridge revealed themselves in the crowd. Mistress Leona mouthed the word, "Surprise!"

Aria put a hand to her mouth. "You didn't!" she exclaimed.

Draconis continued with his own grin and a sheet of paper with Drage's messy handwriting on it. "Do you, Dragenopn Helius, Emperor of Light, take Aria Newman as your awful, wedded wife?"

This time, Drage tried his hardest not to laugh. He leaned forward and whispered, "It's 'lawful', not 'awful.'"

Draconis squinted at the tiny metallic sheet. "Oh, I see. Do you, Dragenopn Helius, Emperor of Light, take Aria Newman as your lawful, wedded wife?"

"I do," Drage responded.

"And do you, Aria Newman, commander of the Phoenix Regiment, take Dragenopn Helius as your lawful, wedded husband?"

"I do," she replied with a shaky voice, still entirely stunned by what was occurring as her sweaty hand grasped Drage's.

"By the powers vested in me, I pronounce you husband and wife. You may now kiss the bride."

Drage held his wife's hands tightly and dipped her backward. He leaned forward and planted a wet kiss on her lips.

The whole crowd stood and began clapping once again. A tear ran down Elizabeth's cheek as she clapped. She could not believe her twenty-one-year old son was now married. So much had happened in the past year, but, somehow, everything had worked out. Somehow, he was all grown up.

Draconis called out, "Let the celebration begin!"

Epilogue

"Do not be angry with him."

The wind swept around them coolly, and the sky was filled with clouds that turned pink from the brightness of the warm sun. That orange glow surrounded them as they flew.

Out here, where no one could tell them what to do, where there was no fighting, the two of them of felt so free. Not a worry or a care haunted their thoughts, and the past was completely behind them. The world they had left behind was no longer a concern to the two of them.

Several rocky islands floated past them as they soared. They noticed the mountains and lakes that lined the edges of the islands, but these held little interest with them. Their interests were elsewhere.

Her wings had to do little work to carry them through the cloudy sky. Occasionally, their bodies would go straight through one of the puffy clouds, and they would exit the other side feeling cool, the clouds' mist clinging to their bodies and glimmering in the sun.

While she loved the exercise of the flapping of her long, slender wings and the wind in her face, he enjoyed relaxing comfortably on her back and looking up at the clouds that surrounded them. Every once in a while, he would stroke her neck fondly, and she would hum lovingly in appreciation.

With each passing second, rather than feeling more and more tired, they found that their energy was gradually rejuvenating itself.

"Do not grieve me until then either."

They could remember how the battle had gone. At one point, they had crashed into the ground, and each had fought valiantly against their enemies, but it was she who realized it. It had to have been some foreign instinct or sensing, but regardless of how it happened, she had felt the imminent light from the two Swords coming, the one that would end the War in a blast of power. Though he had first protested the retreat, it took only seconds for him to realize how she felt and to believe her.

The Gate she had summoned had brought them to this world, this world of sky, and air, and wind, and clouds. The place was a dream come true for the both of them, and neither had said a word to each other since they had left the watery world behind them.

"There is a time to grieve…"

Gradually, Tatsu's hair began to turn from white to its original dark color. The wrinkles on his face and hands began to straighten, and his body began reddening with warm life. At the same time, her dull and missing scales began growing and shimmering. From their almost gray shade, the scales started to gleam with that fresh white color. Her eyes regained their former color, and waves of energy washed through her body.

It seemed to be that Y'ran had spoken the truth. Exposed to the world of Wind, the Element that corresponded to Kohana's Fang, their ages rewound themselves, and the ill effects of that cursed weapon were starting to reverse. The years rolled back for them until they found that they were in the same condition as when they had first met several years ago. Though they continued not to say anything, they could feel each other's renewed vigor and life and joy.

Neither of them could tell if the sun in the distance was rising or setting, but that question was not pressing. The feeling of the wind in their faces was enough for the time being. Anything beyond that was irrelevant to the two of them.

It was not long before her wings' speed increased naturally as her energy flowed through her muscles in excitement. He turned around from his laying position and sat upright on her back. His smile widened as he began to truly take in his surroundings with a rekindled interest.

Then, they became aware of birds flying a little bit above them. The two of them turned their heads uncomfortably to watch the small silhouettes as they traversed the skies, and for the first time in their lives, neither of them envied those birds. They were free at last, and they felt no connection to what had happened to them hours ago, or days ago, or even years ago. Their life existed only in this solitary moment of freedom and contentment.

He stroked her neck again, and she plunged straight downward with a rush of excitement overwhelming her. He struggled to hold on, but as he did so, he laughed along with her. He whooped and cheered as if it was the most fun he had ever had in his whole life, and it probably was.

"…and a time to celebrate…"

Once Kohana straightened herself, Tatsu said, "We did it. We don't have any more duties, or responsibilities, or problems, or anything. It's just the two of us."

She replied softly, "Oh, I think we will still have a lot of those soon. It is only a natural part of life. Problems are abundant, and we will have to have duties if we are to ever interact with another being. Responsibilities come even in survival." When she saw his downcast expression of disappointment, she added with a comforting smile, "But it is still just the two of us. It is you and me in this humongous world of wind and sky."

He did indeed brighten at her words, a smile spreading, and he asked in fascination, "So, where are we exactly? This must be another world, but it does not look like Earth, I don't think."

"You are right," she agreed. "I do not recall anyone saying Earth had these floating islands. I believe we are in the world of Dragons. I have heard legends of this place from other Dragons, though I did not think that it was real. I suppose that when I tried to summon a Gate, I had this legendary place in my mind. The laws here are supposedly ridiculous and separate all Dragons based on their race." The clouds continued to rush past them, and below, they could see the floating islands, the Dragon lands.

"Sounds rough. Are we going to have any problems with that?" he inquired with slight worry.

She shook her white head. "No, we will not have a problem with that. Our home shall be in the skies, not those islands, and who knows? Maybe, I will teach you how to fly." A sly wink from her made him laugh again.

"...and even a time to fight."

"And what will I have to teach you exactly, love?" he asked jokingly. "How to use a sword? Or how to shoot an arrow from a bow? My skills are quite limited, you know."

She grinned and replied, "Perhaps, they are limited. Surely, you have learned something of use over the years."

Then, he thought of a brilliant idea. He offered, "Well, I know how to juggle."

"Juggle? What is that?" she inquired, entirely puzzled by such a foreign concept.

"Well, I would need several small balls to explain." Without even the slightest of hesitation, she created three balls of Earth in his hands. He was stunned by her quick thinking. Carefully, he stood, and her head swiveled around in mid-flight to watch him. Staring straight ahead, he threw the three balls into the air and managed to continuously toss each ball to the opposite hand in a fascinating display. Intrigued, she created another of the balls in his hands, and he struggled to keep the four balls from falling below them.

After she added a fifth one, however, they all escaped his grasp. They both laughed in unison as she darted forward with all of her might. The wind felt like a wall of force to both of them.

"But no matter what happens to me, you, or the rest of the world…"

"That was amazing!" she exclaimed, inspired by his mediocre performance. "You will have to show me how to do that! I am sure I could manage two and probably even three, but it will take a lot of work to master four or more!"

He patted her neck with a laugh. "It is not too hard, I suppose. With someone as bright as you learning, I am sure it will be easy for you. However, I don't think it would be too easy for me to teach you how to do it in the sky like this. We will have to land eventually."

She nodded approvingly, "Yes, I agree. We will need food and water anyways. If you become either hungry or thirsty, let me know, and we shall stop for a while."

"I am not hungry or thirsty now. Are you?" He could sense through his heart that she was, though she was trying her hardest to hide it. She was enjoying this experience of flight so much, and she did not want it to end.

"Maybe a little…" she said hesitantly.

"Alright, well, let's stop at the next island, then, alright? Then, we can get back up here and fly until we get hungry again. Sound good to you?"

She nodded eagerly. "Love, that sounds amazing."

"…you have to keep going."

The two of them, man and Dragon, Tatsu and Kohana, continued to fly into the dawning of a new day and looked forward to whatever lay ahead of them. The pink of the sky slowly faded into a bright blue, and the sun began to warm the air around them, so that the chilling force of flight was diminished slightly.

Tatsu was the same young man that he was years ago, and Kohana was the same White Dragon that she was at that same time. The only difference from their present selves and their past selves was the strength of the connection they now felt.

They had gone through so much together, and friends had died around them. Over the decades, enemies had been defeated, and nations had both risen and fallen. In the time that they had known each other, change had affected every day of their lives, but the one thing they always had in common was each other.

Every morning, even this particularly beautiful one, the two had been more than optimistic. They had looked forward to the day with open hearts and had lived each day as if it was their last. This constant philosophy kept them young at heart no matter how old their bodies had become, and that philosophy had been an inspiration for others. Their greatest lesson to their fellow soldiers had been to never just accept things. The best thing to do was to enrich the world, leave it a little better than they had entered it. They wanted to live for the next day.

Tatsu and Kohana gradually faded into the light of the sun as they soared to seek new places and meet new friends. For them, it was a new beginning.

"Live for the future."

www.ingramcontent.com/pod-product-compliance
Lightning Source LLC
Chambersburg PA
CBHW060143260626
47160CB00001B/104